THE
SURVIVOR

THE SURVIVOR

TOM HYWEL

authorHOUSE®

AuthorHouse™
1663 Liberty Drive
Bloomington, IN 47403
www.authorhouse.com
Phone: 1-800-839-8640

Published by AuthorHouse   14/01/2013

ISBN: 978-1-4772-5023-5 (sc)
ISBN: 978-1-4772-5024-2 (e)

CONTENTS

To those who, finding themselves swept
up in the unceasing power-struggle that corrupts
all who engage in it, resist the pressures of the
compliant majority, even at the cost of their lives:
God give them strength.

*

"You will recall a remarkable discovery we made when we conquered
Germany—that there were actually no Nazis there at all, just millions
of 'decent Germans' suffering . . . because of the awful things they'd
been made to do by other people . . . Why the western world should be
avid to swallow this . . . eyewash, no man can say."

Nicholas Monsarrat
Foreword to Heinz Schaeffer's *U-Boat 977*
(London. William Kimber, 1952)

1

PREFATORY NOTE

THIS is a work of fiction. It owes to reality only its historical setting in time and place, the inclusion of certain historical figures, none of whose actual words have been reproduced bar those clearly represented as quotations, and loose references to some aspects of a German naval officer's wartime career.

He was *Kapitän-zur-See* Wolfgang Lüth, a u-boat commander and, latterly, commandant of the German naval officers' training college (*Kriegsmarineschule*) at Flensburg. He was also the U-Boat Arm's (*U-Bootwaffe*'s) highest-scoring commander of WW2 and the service's only holder of the Knight's Cross of the Iron Cross with oak-leaves, swords and brilliants. These distinctions together with his untimely death in puzzling circumstances, his support but not membership of the Nazi Party and his command of two u-boats of the types commanded by this story's main protagonist, Gunnar Altmann, are the only personal factual likenesses between the two. Unlike Altmann's, Lüth's story is entirely free of any suggestion of misconduct under his country's rules of war, and his death was conclusively explained notwithstanding sensational speculation in the press. None of it, however, suggested or indicated suspicion of a fate similar to Altmann's. Nor does this story; and if there was a Gunnar Altmann in the officer corps of the Third *Reich*'s *U-Bootwaffe* he shares only his name with the man the story is about: bar the above, any resemblance he or his fictional contemporaries bear to anyone living or dead is coincidental.

T.H.

27th November. 2012.

PROLOGUE
THE SCHOONER

AS he hauls himself through the hatch ónto the bridge the breeze strikes cold and clean. Spray sweeps the group of men standing in the inadequate shelter of the bulwarks, darker shadows in a night of shadows beneath lowering overcast. The boat rolls as she quarters the swell and carves her way through the moderate head sea. He takes deep breaths, relishing the air as an intoxicant after the clinging fug of the boat's interior, relieved only by the draught of the diesels' inhalations.

"*Kaleu*—?" Close at his side, oilskins gleaming with moisture, the first watch officer, who called him to the bridge. A ship in sight.

"Yes—where is she?" He has to raise his voice against the crash and hiss of the wash and the seas breaking along and over the low-lying hull. The Atlantic in restless mood, and a lull between rages. He glances round, his vision slowly adjusting to the darkness.

A hand on his shoulder, the other dimly pointing, ahead and to port. "Red three-oh, *kaleu*. Crossing to starboard. Close-hauled—" pause as a dollop of spray whips their faces "—close-hauled, port tack—"

"A sailing-ship!"

"Schooner, *Kaleu*—tops'l schooner."

A ghost. There she is, a group of pale shapes against the overcast. Perhaps a kilometre, no more. No lights. A ship from the past. The *Flying Dutchman* comes to mind, and he smiles; a thin, unamused twitch of the bearded lips. *We'll see.* He takes the proffered binoculars and studies the enlarged shapes for a moment. No trace of a light, only an occasional flash of luminescence where the seas break away from her side. *No wonder the lookouts haven't spotted her sooner. Another few hundred metres and she'd have dropped past unseen.*

5

"Be a pretty sight in daylight."

Ignoring the other's remark he exults silently. Here's the chance he needs to redeem himself—and the boat—after that shaming affair at base, the cause of his being here far to the south and east of where he should have been two months ago instead of enduring the consequences of an embarrassing failure on the part of several of the boat's crew, officers included. Himself included. The contents of the signal received from C-in-C U-Boats have been wounding beyond imagining; and there's no escaping them. The flimsy is in the safe under his bunk, but its words are impressed on his mind like a carbon copy, readable at will. Or against it. As now, and as the fuzzy geometry of the schooner's sails dances in the salt-smeared lenses phrases and passages from the signal pass before his mind's eye—

. . . commanding officer . . . entrusted with the boat's safety . . . occupied port . . . . duty towards the Fatherland and your Führer *. . . betrayed my trust . . . Germany's prospects . . . cannot afford to be without battle-ready units . . . negligence . . . the most rigorous correction . . . failure to properly attend to their harbour duties . . . officers and petty officers directly responsible . . . disciplined in accordance with the Navy's Articles of War . . . you will be separately advised . . . mitigating circumstances . . . no further action . . . attend classes . . . Operational Training Programme . . . such time as your command is again ready for active service . . .*

—concluding with the mark he will bear for the remainder of his career in the *Kreigsmarine*:

You are hereby severely reprimanded and your Service Record endorsed accordingly.

   (Signed)Dönitz.

   Rear-Admiral.

It arrived soon after Dönitz's inspection of the crew on the quayside, an acutely shaming public spectacle with the rim of the boat's flooded bridge standing no more than a few centimetres above the oil-slicked surface at her berth a few paces away. The only redeeming feature, if that's what it was, of the situation was that no-one had drowned. In the small hours, roused from a waking trance by the distinctive sound of water rushing into the open torpedo-hatch of the motor-room, accompanied by the reports of parting moorings, the sentry had the presence of mind to shout a warning to the harbour watch on board before rushing off to summon help. Rudely woken, the watchkeepers scrambled to safety as the boat slid from under their feet, full of the muddy water that had been trickling in via a partly-open sea-valve for hours until its weight immersed the open torpedo-hatch. A *Maschinistensmaat* in charge of the shore maintenance party concerned came forward to confess his fault in forgetting to check the hatch before going off shift, leaving it open in direct disobedience of the base commandant's standing orders. They were clear enough, but that apart it was evidence of negligence on the part of the watch aboard, in particular of its officer, the second watch-officer, a *Leutnant-zur-See*, newly-promoted: returned, reprimand attached, to his former obscurity.

The open valve drew attention to a continuing problem and further questions about base security including the wisdom of employing French technicians on maintenance work. Sabotage is a constant threat and its prevention a major headache. And although it has served as one of the "mitigating circumstances" in Dönitz's deliberations on suitable punishment, it could equally have added to the magnitude of negligence in its not being anticipated. Nevertheless, it reflects on himself, the boat's commanding officer, and the fact still smarts, a personal disgrace. The knowledge that Uncle Karl had chosen to be lenient is, in a way, greater reproof: he didn't merit it, and the words of the admiral's reprimand awoke echoes of a moment long ago, as it seems in the light of events, when he was younger, handled his responsibilities with a lighter, and perhaps surer, touch. He remembers the chilly scrutiny of the naval college's commandant outlining the likely consequences of failure in the final examination's mathematics paper, at which he had allowed the midshipman a second attempt as an exception to the rule: *If you fail you will be letting me, this college and Germany's navy down. And you will be out on the streets as far as the service is concerned.* He had passed. Just. And by that margin was accepted for training in the u-boat arm, the branch of the navy on which he'd set his heart from the start. To his perhaps greater relief was the knowledge that he had justified the commandant's apparent confidence, or at least hope, in him. Its forfeiture would have been worse than the friendless streets.

It might have been something similar in the case of the open hatch, but he was saved, as he sees it, by the fact that the u-boat arm needs men, especially qualified—and experienced—men, who, on balance, are more expensive and time-consuming to produce than the craft they operate. Negation of the service's trust as expressed in the training it gives, implied in stupid errors and omissions—in failure—is as much deserving of retribution as the crimes themselves. The element of shame is cogent and painful. Perhaps Dönitz knows as much, and gave it a place in his considerations. It's small comfort to know that he would have done so only because he credits his commanders with a conscientiousness and pride in their calling by which shame can come only from a sense of their own blameworthiness, and of the dismay it causes among those who count on their proficiency. Even now, a couple of months later, his lips draw taut as he relives the scene on the quayside, the boat's crew assembled in parade order facing their commander-in-chief and his aides, listening to the bitter words of recrimination and regret. To even the least perceptive of them it was clear that, apart from anger, Dönitz felt, for the service he loved, shame at least as deep as their own for themselves. The commander's subsequent impression has been that every man would give his fortune to undo the blunders that brought disgrace—even, and worse because it evaded tragedy, ridicule—on everyone. He can only guess at what has passed between Dönitz, Raeder and the *Führer*, knowing that Uncle Karl has been unflagging in his promotion of the *U-Bootwaffe* as Germany's pre-eminent war weapon, meriting priority in the contest for expansion. Three hundred boats on active operations is the goal, and he, one of the commanders concerned, has featured in an episode that will undoubtedly have been used against the admiral by his rivals, particularly the discredited Göring. *Damn!* And again, *damn!* His sheer impotence in the face of unalterable history, local and minor as it is, recent as it is, makes him tighten his grip on the binoculars.

And there are the meetings with his wife, whose regard for him, her love apart, is above all else in his life the thing that makes it worth living. Part of that regard, he feels, is for his professional accomplishment in the service of the *Reich* and as head of his family. In her eyes, he knows, he stands tall among men, a husband for whom other women can, and do, envy her. Except, perhaps, in the means by which he attains to that standing. The anxiety that is her constant companion when he's on operations is beginning to show in her face, in the cornflower-blue eyes, in her touch; even in her step, which shows a faltering of confidence at every succeeding reunion; an uncertainty of his continued existence she is unable fully to conceal from a man attentive to her every mood and expression, discreet in his responses and sensitive to her deepest fears and hopes without overt reaction. He supports by collaboration her efforts to give nothing away in her talk or demonstrations of affection; expresses in various ways his gratitude for her cheerfulness, even to restraint in his references to the boat, though she never fails to express an interest, painful though the association must be to her. He is humbled at thought of his good fortune in being the beneficiary of her lifelong favour, which, in addition to everything else, has given him two children about whom he prefers, when at sea, to avoid thinking, avoid acknowledgement of a fundamental fear. They are his future—his and hers both, but while their protection is paramount, it cannot be a matter of removal from the play of events that is everyone's birthright and burden. In their vulnerable state of dependence on the care of others—of their parents—they represented a possession of which he knows he could be deprived without warning. As they could of him. The war heightens the risk from all quarters, and only his skill and diligence stand between it and its fatal realisation . . .

Into the voice-pipe he calls for slow speed, hears the order repeated, and feels the changed vibration of the deck underfoot. Now the schooner will draw ahead and run across the bows. A sitting duck. To the voice-pipe again: "Tell the *Funkmaat* to report any signals on the distress frequency." His tone is hard, accents clipped. To the watch officer: "We'll use the gun, with the searchlight. Alternate h.e. and incendiary. Get the crew up. Quietly! Don't sound alarms. If she's under sail only they might hear us." *Not likely, of course, for she's to windward; but why take needless chances?*

The night conceals the watch officer's hesitation. But at his order men tumble up from below and make their way to the foredeck, gathering round the gun, snatches of excited comment reaching the bridge on the breeze.

"*Silence on deck!*" The watch officer leans over the forward dodger, furious. "Report readiness!"

A figure, one of those who has just emerged from below, reports itself: second watch officer. The gun-captain.

"Very well. Take charge."

"*Kaleu.*" The officer moves over to the first officer, they exchange a few words, the first officer reports the gun-captain in charge. Spray bursts over them as a wave thumps against the conning-tower, falls back and away, hissing.

That's the gun-crew soaked through, he thinks; then, tight-lipped, that it will wake them up, wash away the accumulated drowsiness of suffocating confinement. He orders the first officer to have the stern tube ready, and to start the plot. The schooner is too small a target for the expenditure of a torpedo, but in an emergency they should be prepared.

"*Kaleu.*" To the voice-pipe, the first watch-officer requests the rangefinder binoculars.

Minutes pass. The searchlight is fitted to its mounting and the first watch-officer mounts and adjusts the rangefinder glasses. Slings of 88mm shells are handed up from below and down to the gun-crew. The attention of everyone but the lookouts is on the schooner. She sails on, inching across from left to right, still barely visible.

"Stern-tube ready, *Kaleu.* Plot engaged."

"Very well."

Whoever she is, he reflects, the night favours her. Whoever, but with no lights, and no signal about a sailing-ship from headquarters, she's the enemy. Alone, vulnerable, and—unarmed? What's she doing here a quarter the way across the Atlantic to America—making for a safe haven; maybe something less innocent? A decoy, perhaps. Or even a hunter, a killer waiting for the prey to disclose its presence . . . He knows about Q-ships, used in the last war. But in this one? They were never very successful in their day; in this war of advanced technology they'd be a joke. Or a tragedy: if she kills one incautious victim before she's herself killed it'll be a profitable feat. It could happen tonight, by whim of a perverse fate. Attacking on the surface at such close range risks a gun action that places the u-boat in its weakest position, the unarmoured high-tensile-steel hull vulnerable to a single hit. All he can do is to be ready for instant retaliation with the eels. One strike will do it. If the torpedo isn't a dud.

Of course she might be innocent—neutral; but without lights she's inviting attack. His thoughts touch on the orders to commanders, amended a couple of times since the opening of hostilities and the arming of merchant ships by the British. They call it defensive, but a gun is a gun, and in the hands of some crews stretches the meaning of the term far beyond its limits. Orders, but open to interpretation. In the original they were as archaic as this ship in the night—

Commanders will adhere strictly to international prize law in relation to merchant shipping.

All merchant ships are to be stopped and searched.

Only ships of hostile flag/s or carrying war materiél to hostile ports are to be sunk, after allowing abandonment by crew.

Warships and armed merchant ships, or merchant ships in convoy escorted by warships, may be sunk without warning.

Passenger ships are not to be attacked.

And after experience of action exposing the flaws, amendments were made—

Any vessel using radio to signal attack or confrontation to be sunk forthwith.

Neutral merchant shipping is to
    avoid behaving in a suspect manner
    steer a steady course
    refrain from using radio
    stop when requested
    show navigation lights
    travel alone, unescorted.
Regulated zone extends westward to longitude 20°W.

Well, the prize-law rule has long been discredited and dropped. As for passenger ships, Lemp's sinking of the *Athenia* effectively nullified the ruling on the first day of the war, without adverse consequences: he's still on operations despite the Allies' protests. And what u-boat commander would hazard his craft by approaching an unknown vessel on the surface with a "request" for papers? Ridiculous! The boat is built for stealth, not hellfire glory in the open or some quaint notion of chivalry on the high seas, as various sentimentalists, journalists and pulp fictionalists portray it. And by this time every nation with a merchant fleet knows that sailing without lights in a war zone is tantamount to a hostile act. The longitude by dead reckoning at the change of watch was just short of nineteen degrees west: war zone, even granted the normal extent of navigational error.

"Gun ready, *Kaleu!*"

He'll have to take a chance on the searchlight's working. The schooner is almost dead ahead now. Range about seven hundred and fifty metres. Hardly even good practice, apart from the difficulties created by the boat's motion. "Very well. Target is the stern; deck or hull, but deckhouse if there is one, for the wireless if she has one. Fire as you bear."

"Searchlight on!"

To his relief it works. The beam lances through the darkness, conjuring the schooner into startling substance against the pitch-black background. Three masts, two square sails on the fore topmast. The patched off-white sails dazzle night-blind eyes where the searchlight-beam strikes them, partly cut off in their own shadows like the dark of the moon. The leech of the mainsail, a graceful curve, trembles like the muscles of a nervous deer. Above it the gaff-topsail strains taut, sculpted from marble. His eyes narrow, taking in the details, selecting the essential, disposing of the superfluous. No time to waste. The vitals must be located, struck, destroyed. Gunnery is like a surgical operation, but the object is to quiet, not quicken. His scrutiny takes in the visual play of wind on canvas—ethereal, improbable, ephemeral—and moves downwards. White dots of faces turned to stare, hands held up against the glare. A low deckhouse beneath the mizen boom, painted white. Very convenient. Crossing her stern now, the bearing opening to starboard. No sign of armament. Maybe they're waiting. If she is a Q-ship they'll go all the way to abandonment, leaving gun-crews in concealment, luring the attacker to point-blank range. If so, they're in for a hot time of it.

The second officer cries "On the deckhouse!" and from the foredeck the acknowledgment; then: "Fire!"

Studying the target through smeared lenses he flinches at the gun's bark. The flash splits the night and acrid smoke gusts back over the bridge, clawing at the throat. Now the schooner's watch knows everything. And if she's armed, so will he, sooner or later.

The gun-layer's cry, thin on the breeze. "Check, check, check! Up ten!" The round has fallen short. Damn!

"Her name, *Kaleu*—" The second watch-officer's eyes are pressed to his glasses' padded lenses.

"Yes—?"

"I think—a bit rusty—*Anne-Marie de . . .* something. Port of registry . . . looks like—Brest. Hard to be sure."

He swears. French! What the hell is she doing out here? But wait—French by name doesn't necessarily mean French ownership, business or manning. It needn't even be her real identity—and without lights! It doesn't make sense—

"Fire!" Another crack and a flash, and a sudden blossom of crimson and gold, and a following report. Hit! Right aft, on the counter below the poop. That'll upset the steering. *Watch for her taking a sheer.* A third round and another brief glow from the target, and an accompanying thump, higher up this time. The second watch officer: "She's luffing, *Kaleu*! Coming round to port!"

He puts his mouth to the voice-pipe "Port easy. Steer two-five-oh" and listens for the repeated words. The boat begins to respond and the gun falls silent. From the pipe the helmsman's hollow tones: steady on two-five-oh.

The schooner has luffed, now lies well out to starboard barely half a mile off, opening her port side to view, fore-and-aft sails flapping, losing way in the head sea as the square sails on the foremast come aback. From the boat's bridge they see a pinpoint of light moving about on deck. Someone's flashlight. Unnecessary, even comic, in the searchlight's beam. An order from the gun-layer, and another crack and flash answered by a thump and glow, just abaft amidships on the deck line. It throws a rosy tint into the sails for an instant, and picks out the figures on deck. For a moment, watching intently, he feels a pang, but suppresses it. *War's no place for sentimentality. All that's in the past, part of the weakness of peacetime, and a flaw in human nature that leads to—war, which comes of an excess of sentimentality, a rooted conviction of right. As now. A paradox.* Another bang and flash, another explosion on the schooner, this time a flicker of something more than a flashlight. *Fire. She's on fire.* Another round strikes, this time at the fore end of the deckhouse, which bursts apart in a puff-ball of flame and flying planking, ripping the mizen into a flurry of burning tatters and strips, splintering the boom, and the fire begins to take hold, moving forward into the main rigging and canvas. It flares upwards, drawn out in banners of red and orange by the wind. Through the glasses he watches the figures rushing about and feels—what? Elation? No, not that much. Satisfaction, perhaps. Not at the shooting and the target's inevitable end, but at the moral of the tale. Foolishness brings its due reward. Some fool has taken the war for a game, and will pay accordingly. If there were fewer fools in the world, there would be fewer wars, and fewer wasteful actions like this. Damn the fools! They deserve their fate. He will not shrink from his duty. Yes, that's it: he feels anger, justifiable anger, at the stupidity of these people, who thought they could evade the known danger by behaviour that's nothing better than an impudent challenge to fate! He clenches his teeth as another round strikes home. Now they're swinging out the boats, scrambling about like lunatics in the glare of the searchlight and the leaping flames. Two boats, one each side of the poop, where the deckhouse's wreckage is burning fitfully, obscured by belching smoke.

He bends to the voice-pipe. "Dead slow both engines. Let me know if she won't steer." Another report from the gun blanks out the reply. "Did you hear?" The voice in the pipe repeats the order a second time.

"Shift your target—aim forward."

"Shift target forward, aye *Kaleu*!"

"Fire!"

The schooner is beginning to pay off before the breeze, swinging sluggishly to port towards her attacker, but with the foretopsails aback making no forward way. Still showing her port bow and side, she takes the round on the deck-edge forward, and splinters and shards of steel bulwark burst upwards like so much straw and cardboard. The next is incendiary, hitting another deckhouse just abaft the foremast, which disintegrates like its partner. Flames lick up through a puff of smoke, catch at the torn foresail and suddenly sweep aloft, opening up in a ragged fan of gold as the topsails catch, shedding burning debris on deck and into the leeward seas. The jib and fore staysail fly free of their sheets to flutter like broken wings above the bowsprit until their halyards part and they collapse in ballooning bags. The schooner's incipient turn becomes a bodily sagging-away before the wind, which, having given life, is now feeding death: she's burning fiercely almost from end to end, her top-hamper a tangled mass of streamers and rags of flame breaking away on the breeze. The sea is a heaving plain of breaking and merging reflections in molten copper and brass, on which he sees the boat moving away from the schooner's side, oars waving, dipping, splashing.

"Boat away, port side aft!"

He glances at the lookout and nods. In the glare the man's face is thrown into highlight and shadow, the beard round the jaw-line adding a satanic touch, incongruously framed by the black sou'wester and oilskin collar. A look round at the faces about him, two pressed to binoculars, four turned outwards towards the invisible horizon, their night vision destroyed by the conflagration. Seven men on a u-boat's bridge are a tight fit. If he has to dive it will be minutes before they, and the gun's crew, are clear. Anxiously now, he studies the schooner and the boat. If she's armed the situation is approaching the point at which it will have to show or be silenced for good. As he watches, the mizen-mast leans over to port, hesitates, then falls in parabolas of sparks and streamers of flame, striking the water a few yards from the boat in a flurry of spray, and he hears—no, impossible!—he hears screams. He trains his glasses on the boat. It's crowded, an indefinable massy bundle silhouetted against the blaze beyond. Shouts can be high-pitched, especially heard over distance, he tells himself. There are men in the water, too, waving. His lips tighten. They'll have to take their chances. This isn't a rescue-ship. And he will have to bring the business to an end. The schooner's hull is steel, or iron. Burnt-out it will float, advertise his presence, or recent passing . . .

Impatiently, he snaps, "That's enough pyrotechnics, *Zweiter*! I want her sunk!"

"Aye, *Kaleu*." The second watch officer leans over the forward dodger. "Shift your target—h.e. only, on the waterline!"

Bang! A plume of orange-tinted dirty foam alongside, and the burning mainmast totters, hangs undecided for a moment, then falls to leeward like the mizen. Another shell strikes farther aft. A third doesn't register. He hears the second officer chastise the gun-crew. "Over! *Wait* for it, or fire on the downward roll!"

Ten strikes are enough. One over, one short. Good shooting, he muses; the gun-crew has earned its treat. The hull, seat of a pyre in the night, glowing red-hot in patches along the sheerline, settles lower and lies over towards the u-boat exposing what was the deck but is now a white-hot crucible in which nothing could be living. No concealed guns there now, he thinks with satisfaction. If there ever were. The foremast goes the way of its companions, and after hesitating momentarily, the dismasted hull rolls its sheer-strake under in a furious billow and roar of steam, pauses again, then slips away in a maelstrom of spray and steam and boiling, debris-strewn seas, and night sweeps back to reclaim its own, pressing in on the searchlight's beam, finally extinguishing, in alliance with the sea, several isolated clumps of flame. The end is complete and total, unlike the usual death-throes of a ship amidst spreading pools of burning oil, flotsam, overturned boats and rafts and groups of lifejacketed survivors; and the escorts cutting through the lines of blundering merchantmen in the acetylene glare of star-shell. Of course there's no oil in this case, and no escorts; but there are boats; and survivors.

Lighting a cigarette, he is surprised at the abruptness of the finale; at the precipitate moment of transition to calm from chaos, from violence that erupted into the profound dignity of the ocean's unquiet slumber with the blare and bluster of a street riot, departing as swiftly as it came, its effect the loss of another increment of the innocence in which all things have their beginnings. The ocean has become party to the violent act by its mere presence; accomplice to it by its concealment of incriminating evidence. By the tiny measure of a ship's fabric and the lives it has borne the ocean's innocence is diminished. And, he thinks, will be further diminished by an immensity of increments by the time this war is over; diminished to the point of villainy. The sea will become willing accessory to unimaginable scenes of carnage before the business is done, its sublime power subverted to serve the basest aspirations of mankind as it has been challenged and harnessed to serve the greatest. The question is, which is it serving in this theatre of conflict—and is he, the commander of a tin-can u-boat, a transient speck on the stream of time, ever likely to be able to answer? Perhaps better not to try. He has his orders, which, for the present at least, is enough.

He peers at his wrist-watch, holding it up to catch the searchlight's diffuse glow. The action has lasted barely thirty minutes. It seemed an age. In one sense it has been an age, in which irreversible changes have occurred on the face of the world. To the extent of what has taken place, even such a miniscule event in a remote location, the world has aged. Shaking himself, he looks up. "Keep the light on that boat!" His voice is harsh. He is afraid of its betrayal, so snaps the words off like pistol-shots, blinking in the sudden cessation of glare from the dying schooner. "Stand down gun's crew—"

"Gun's crew stand down, aye *Kaleu!*"

"Disengage the plot, *Einswo!*"

"Plot disengaged, *Kaleu.*"

He is aware of their glances, the curiosity, and puzzlement maybe. The same lookout calls, "Second boat, same bearing, about a hundred metres farther out!"

Throwing his cigarette-end away he raises his binoculars. The searchlight picks it out: another overcrowded cockleshell dipping and rolling in the tumbling seas, a cluster of white faces against the black backdrop. *God in heaven—how many of them are there?* A trading schooner of her tonnage wouldn't have had more than a dozen men on board. Those boats are carrying at least thirty between them, with others in the water. He bites off an exclamation, bends to the voice-pipe, orders half-speed ahead and hard a-port.

"Hard a-port, aye."

16

He brings the boat round in a tight circle away from, then back towards, the boats and the people in the water, reducing speed again as he approaches the first boat. Swamped, he notes, floating on its buoyancy tanks or provision-lockers or something, and the seas breaking in among the huddled occupants, sitting in water to their waists. They show no interest in the approaching u-boat, their heads sunk between hunched shoulders. He counts seventeen when the boat is still fifty metres away, and as he feels the anger rising the first watch-officer cries, "A baby, *Kaleu*! A baby—here in the water—!" His voice breaks on a note of disbelief.

Shouldering the lookout aside he peers down at the broken water surging along the bulge of the ballast-tank. Drifting aft, already almost lost to sight in the darkness: a doll, a rag doll, rolling over loose-limbed in the surge; tiny, unreal; gone. A doll. A child's doll. A baby would not be floating like that. But even a *doll*—? He looks up, his mouth dry, shakes his head at the first officer, and sees the boat closing on the starboard side. He orders stop, then slow astern, and the boat drifts slowly past the gun-platform. Its people have their backs to the searchlight's dazzle, except for a man in the sternsheets, wearing a dark jersey, bareheaded, bearded, holding up a hand against the light.

In English he calls down, "What ship?"

The man cups his hands at his mouth. "*Anne-Marie de Bretagne. Français! Et vous—?*"

He ignores the question. "Captain—where is your captain?"

The man shakes his head, shouts back, "*Le capitaine—il est mort!* Dead! You 'ear? You 'ave killed 'im!"

He rubs his chin, feeling the stubble rasp. Four days out. He won't get a shave now until they return to base. A month, maybe; maybe longer. The first watch-officer is staring at him, eyes glittering in the searchlight's reflections. His words take some moments to register. Women in the boat.

And two children. "*—Kaleu?*"

He holds the officer's gaze for several seconds, his mind a blank, then, feeling the anger rise again, hot in his throat, he swings back, shouts down to the man, "Come on board! I want to talk to you!" To the first officer: "Two men—down on the casing. Get him aboard. Quickly!"

But the man refuses to move. Surveying the huddled humanity in the boat he sees that the first officer was right: five women, it looks like. The children are forward, where a thwart keeps them above most of the water. Wearing coats. Nothing on their heads. About eight or ten. Two boys. He feels frustration mix with his anger, then, abruptly, despair. What in the name of God have these people been doing in a darkened ship? What blind fool—what criminal maniac—has sent them to sea under such conditions? On whose orders? For what reason? Furious at the unknown, he gazes impotently at the swamped boat as the implications of the situation whirl round the pivot of his mind, eluding his attempts to arrest and examine them.

The lookout on the other side of the bridge announces, "Two bodies, port side amidships, close-to."

Dimly visible in the reflected light they drift past, limbs spread, flexing uselessly, supported face-up by their lifejackets, which give them an imploring look, but they are beyond hope, beyond help. He watches for a second or two then turns back to the first officer. "I want that man up here—train the flak gun on them!"

The second officer hesitates fractionally, then moves. The gun isn't loaded. He steps out onto the after platform and unlocks it, swings it round to aim into the boat. The barrel catches the reflections of the searchlight-beam, gleaming menacingly.

He leans over the dodger again, shouts at the bearded one. "If you do not come aboard I will fire on your boat! Two men on deck—let them help you over! Don't waste my time like this!" He avoids French. It might be useful for the man to think he can't speak it. He might even be fooled into thinking the u-boat is British. Might, but not if he's familiar with matters at home. Still . . .

The man arrives, breathless, soaked, dishevelled, glaring. Youngish, well-built, dark, shoeless. Blood is running over one bare foot.

"You are?"

The man looks his interlocutor up and down, showing no distress, no particular excitement; running a large hand through his hair, he sucks in his cheeks and spits over the dodger. "Lebrun. *Maître d'équipage . . . Vous êtes le capitaine?*"

"Answer my questions—bosun?"

"*Oui*—yes." The man staggers as the boat takes a sharp roll, grabs for the dodger, and a shadow crosses his features. He is exhausted. At the offer of a cigarette he shakes his head, squares his shoulders.

"What port are you from—where are you bound?" He watches the man, lights a cigarette and finds his hands trembling. Damn this business—a charade! What good would it do? There's only one way out of this, and knowing anything about these people will make no difference. Not now. He can't resurrect their ship.

Not concealing his contempt, the man says, *"De* St Malo . . ."

"For?"

The man keeps his eyes on his questioner's intently, as if taking mental note. He is not afraid; nor insolent; but defiant, and self-confident in spite of his obvious exhaustion. With a downturn to his mouth he says, *"Pour*—Boston."

"Are any officers with you?"

"Non! Le second, le second aide—" He shrugs again. *"Ne sais pas—mort, sans doute."*

"Crew?"

"In my boat—four . . . *Dans l'autre, je pense deux*—two men."

"How many crew—how many sailors signed on?"

"Matelots? Huit—eight. Myself, *charpentier, voilier* also. Altogether *onze*—eleven."

"Officers?"

"Le maître—et deux aides, et le mécanicien . . . Trois—three, and *le capitaine."*

He grunts. "Who are these people—passengers?"

"Qui d'autre? We do not man the ship with old men and women and children, *capitaine!"*

"Why were you without lights?"

The man glances over the bulwark, down at the boat, held alongside by its painter and clear of the ballast-tank by boathooks in the hands of the men on deck. Some of the men in it are bailing, to no effect. It will not stay afloat for more than a few hours, if that. He returns his dark gaze to the officer in the crumpled white cap and shrugs.

"C'est la guerre, capitaine. War. We 'ave no escort—better to sail unseen—"

"And risk attack?"

"With lights also!" The man laughs scornfully. *"Milleure chance sans q'avec!"*

He grunts again, draws on the cigarette and throws it half-smoked to leeward. Turning back to the man with a hard stare he asks, "Who are your passengers—what are they?"

The man's eyes shift to one side; his discomfort is evident. After a pause he says, *"Emigrés*—emigrants. They go to families in America . . . There are no regular liners, *capitaine."*

"And they pay well, eh?"

A shrug. *"Mais oui*—of course!"

"French?"

"Quelques-uns, je pense . . . But I do not ask. It is not for me to ask, *n'est ce pas?"*

His eyes narrow as a suspicion dawns. "Jewish?"

The man shrugs again. *"Ne sais pas.* I say—I do not know."

"They are Jewish refugees—fugitives—yes?"

"I cannot say, *capitaine."*

"You've said enough. They are Jewish refugees. You are carrying illicit cargo—"

"They are not—*cargo, capitaine!"* The man spits, on the deck this time. "They are *passagers.* Old men, women, little children. You 'ave killed some of them, wounded some—"

They stare at each other. At the flak gun the second officer looks on; leaning back against the forward bulwark, one hand on the searchlight, the first faces the little tableau, sensing the tension. The lookouts keep their vigil. Spray flies over and amongst them all with increasing frequency. The wind is rising, and the seas with it. Someone down on the casing shouts something to the boat.

"How many?—how many altogether?" *What the hell does it matter? They're Jews, a handful among millions. The national blight. The Fatherland's well rid of them.* Better had he allowed the schooner to sail on. Better for them, for him, for Germany. If the schooner had been showing lights he would have stopped her, checked her papers, let her go . . . Wouldn't he? As it is . . . *Damn them! Damn the fool of a skipper! Well, he'd got his deserts, at least—*

"Trente-et-un—thirty-one, *capitaine; et un petit*—one baby. Altogether thirty-two."

The tiny body in the water. A doll, certainly. Not a baby. So small—a doll for sure. But if the baby, it's in a better place . . . Thirty-two of them! In that schooner! No state-rooms for them. They'd have been crowded below, probably, like cattle, and paying through the nose for the privilege. Damn that skipper, that damned Frenchman, whoever he was. Damn him to hell! He lights another cigarette, and is struck by a whim, a sudden, irrational stroke of curiosity, purposeless, futile. He says, "Where is the baby?"

Another shrug. "I do not know. 'e is not in this boat."

"A boy?"

"Mais oui!"

"His parents?"

"I think—*le père*—*mort. La mere*—" He shrugs again.

Not much chance for a baby—and what's the point in inquiring? To satisfy the first officer? To offer it and its mother some kind of special treatment—like a passage back to France after a month or so on patrol? The whole thing is a waste of time. What's been done has been done; he can't put things to rights even if the situation were to demand it. The whole point of the exercise was to sink the schooner, not to mount a rescue operation. He's not responsible. But the doll—

"Other children? I see two boys in your boat."

"Three young girls, *capitaine*—"

"In the other boat?"

"*Ne sais pas*—'ow can I know? There was no time—"

He gestures impatiently. It's enough to explain the doll, to remove doubt. Otherwise this line of inquiry is a nonsense—sentimentality, establishing nothing of value. If fault lies with anyone it's the schooner's owner—her master.

"What was your captain's name?"

"*Le maître?*" The man sounds surprised. "Calibourdin . . . *Le Capitaine* Jules Calibourdin."

"Was he the owner?"

"*Oui*—'e and 'is wife—"

"His wife was on board?"

"*Non.* She remained. *La directrice de compagnie.*"

The man grimaces, wipes runnels of salt spray from his face, and adds with an edge of mockery in his tone, "*Peut-être*—per'aps—you know of 'im?"

"Enough to know he was a damned fool—he and his wife!"

Lebrun stares, then laughs, and shrugs, moves to the dodger again to peer down into the boat, its burden still huddled in the swirling water, and turns to say, "I must go back to my boat, *capitaine*."

"In a moment . . . What was the ship's tonnage?"

"*Tonnage registré? Sept cents*—seven 'undred."

"Did you have wireless?"

"*Oui, mais*—but—receiver only. We could not get the parts needed for the transmitter—by order of the authorities, you understand."

"And your occupation—your trade?"

"*Pendant la guerre*—" The man gives a low snort. "Survival, *capitaine*! Stores for the occupation forces, between ports on the coast, sometimes to Spain . . . But much of the time—*amarré bord à quai.*"

"What's that?"

"Alongside—*au repos*—*inutile.*" The man spat again. "*Le navire—l'équipage*—no work, eh? No money, no food—and with families!"

"And in peacetime?" He doesn't want a tirade on the trials of life under occupation, which in any case is on generous terms taking account of the Franco-German armistice.

"In peacetime . . ." Another shrug. "In peacetime, for six months in the year we fish for cod, *sur les Grands Bancs*—"

"Fishing!"

"*Oui—aux de lignes longues*—long-lines, you understand? From *les canots*—dories."

He's heard of the Grand Bankers, the dory-fishermen and the fleets that left Spain, Portugal and France every year for the season, returning with the salt cod for which there had been a thriving market. A hard life, but one that provided a fair living; a reason for pride on the part of the men whose lives depended on it. Like this one. He studies what he can see of the man's features, feels, with a chill, something of a shared outlook, though this man has most likely been the sea's possession from boyhood. From generations back. Is it a valid comparison—a submariner's life with a fisherman's? Only in the fact of their common adversary, he supposes; otherwise, it's idle to suggest parallels between a man who wrests a living from the sea as a harvester and one who does something similar by destroying the other's claim; idle, and sentimental. He draws on the last of his cigarette and throws the stub to leeward. And in the other six months, he asks the man—what did the ship do? She couldn't afford to lie up, surely?

"*Non*—cargoes for anywhere between the Baltic and the Mediterranean. Bricks, cement, salt, fertiliser . . ."

"Under sail—or did you have an engine?"

"Yes—a diesel."

"Was it running?"

"When you fired on us?—*non. À la voile* from the time of leaving St Malo. We could not get enough fuel for use except *au besoin . . . Capitaine* Calibourdin was keeping it for use when approaching the American coast."

"How much?"

"Per'aps two 'undred litres, no more."

"In a tank, or drums?"

"*La citerne*—the tank—*au dessous de la machine à l'arriére du mât d'artimon* . . . Beneath the engine, you understand?"

Beneath the engine abaft the mizen-mast . . . That would explain the absence of oil, burning or otherwise, he reflected. Protected against shell-fire below the water-line.

The man is watching him intently, perhaps sardonically. In his wet clothes he must be cold, but there's no heavy-weather clothing to spare in the u-boat's outfit. These people will have to take their chances. They aren't favourable. There's nothing else he can do for them. It's time to quit this place.

"I must go back to my boat, *capitaine. Si vous me permis—*"

"Yes—" He gestures impatiently. "Get back!"

He calls for first-aid dressing-packs, a twenty-litre jerry-can of water, a case of condensed milk, some sausage, has them passed across to the boat, turns his back on it, orders slow ahead, and shuts out the sight as it drifts astern, swept by the seas. Not an hour from now, if that, he thinks. The supplies are wasted, especially the sausage . . . They're only Jews. A handful among millions. Cargo. Flotsam, on sea or land, damn them. Damn them for the trouble they cause the world, which would be a better place for their absence, or their return to some country of their own, such as the British seem to be attempting to establish in Palestine. And which, with the war won, will become Germany's problem . . .

The second boat is intact, low in the water with its load, but not swamped. Bringing it alongside he has more dressings, water, milk, sausage passed down. The sailors—just two, as Lebrun guessed—speak only French, or pretend to, in a dialect he finds difficult to follow, Breton perhaps. No officers, they say; but a man among the passengers stands up and cries, in German, "God will bless you, captain!"

What for? Angrily: *Sinking your ship? Killing your friends? Wounding them? Damned half-wit! Better had he called on God to strike down the man who has shelled the schooner into an inferno with no provocation. No provocation except the war, that is, and the order*

23

about showing lights, of which Captain Jules Calibourdin or whatever his name was would—or should—have known; their absence would have to be provocation enough. He has done his duty, will add the schooner's tonnage to his record. He could get the exact figure from the register back at Lorient. *Anne-Marie de Bretagne.* Beautiful name. Yes, she'd have been a pretty sight by day. Even with her cargo of Jews.

As he bends to the voice-pipe a thought occurs; he hesitates, curses himself for his weakness and straightens, calls to the man who has claimed acquaintance with God, "Boat ahoy!—is there a baby with you?"

The man rises again, calls back. No, no baby. No baby on board, only young children. The boat drifts away in the night. After a glance out into the blackness, towards the other boat, now lost to sight, he shrugs and bends to the voice-pipe again, gives his orders, and in the return of darkness as the searchlight is switched off the u-boat turns away, into the seas, tossing sheets of spray back over the bridge, her casing swept end to end, the waves parting in thundering cascades to either side as they advance, strike the gun-platform, the gun, the tower, in fountains glittering with luminescence, and sweep on. He feels relief. It was a doll. Only a doll. Damn the thing.

"*Einswo!*"

"*Kaleu?*"

"It was a doll—your baby. A damned doll!"

"I'm glad to know it, *Kaleu.*"

He stares at the first officer, detecting a tone, an inflection, a shade of meaning other than that of the chosen words. The officer's expression is invisible, his face a paler patch beneath the drooping brim of his sou'wester. About to speak, he pauses, then turns away to look forward as the boat starts cutting through the swell, now taking the seas on the starboard shoulder in a corkscrewing motion that will have them cursing below. Running on the surface in this kind of weather is always a trial, necessary to log a reasonable speed and to keep the batteries charged, more frequently than normal since the sinking: the base maintenance people didn't replace them, which they should have done. Just drained and refilled them, and they aren't accepting a full charge now. A damned nuisance; could be more than that. He keeps the surfaced periods in heavy weather as short as possible, concerned for his men, who, after all, are the boat's brains and nerves, not a single one of whom is superfluous to its smooth operation. They must be cared for like a family, with love and fair discipline, and always with concern for their wellbeing in conditions under which no dog would willingly live. They have to give of their best, at all times, and will do so only as long as they're confident that he puts their interests, man for man, as members of a fighting unit, at the top of his priorities. If they fail—if one fails—the whole operation fails. And it goes further than the boat's physical limits. They stay with her even at a distance, returning to her, sometimes by instinct, the sailor's instinct for his ship that seems to transcend the worst abuses of awareness, from jaunts ashore in an occupied country that in some respects harbours greater risks than the patrol. Hostile elements—local organisations, individuals—are untiring in their vigilance, quick to take the opportunity to strike a blow for their differing causes, as one in their common resistance to the conqueror. It's wise to keep to the bright lights and gay crowds, avoid the alleys and back-streets and little *bistros* where *la belle france* can turn out to be something less than *belle*. His concern includes their choices of local recreation, and the tenor of their domestic affairs. Family ties are important; family harmony crucial. If they encounter problems he will be ready with advice, with more practical help. He emphasises the benefits of civilised, considerate conduct on board as at home, and makes no secret of his support for family life as a crucial element in a nation's vitality and morale. Every man aboard knows of his wife and two young children: talk of them apart, the framed photographs screwed to the bulkhead over his bunk are on public display as are similar items throughout the boat: wives, girls, children, parents; and in their absence—nothing. He forbids the usual tokens of illusion and fantasy—the superficial comforts of even modest examples of the photographer's art and the more ambitious flights of some authors' erotic fancies—that underline, rather than assuage, the loneliness of the sailor's life; of any life in which war claims an active part. And in war it's all too easy to slip into barbarism, into coarseness of manner and outlook.

So, as well as rigorous enforcement of domestic morality, he sets the example, and because he so obviously lives by his declared creed and is, moreover, an efficient naval officer, they acquiesce without more than the stock grumbles that are their professional entitlement. They know about his own circumstances, observe his actions, hear his views and sentiments, and speak of him among themselves and with others, approvingly even when they gently mock his obvious sentiments, from his promotion of the National Socialist ideal, extended to the creation and nurture of the family unit as the bedrock of racial distinction and continuity, to his loyalty towards and care for his own family. They approve of her, too—his wife—in what they see of her from the photograph as well as his talk in unguarded moments: the blonde, handsome young woman whose unobtrusive, almost spiritual, part in the boat's affairs is symbolised in the motif painted on the conning-tower: a pair of hands clasped round the hilt of a short sword, point-down, poised for the plunge. As several knowledgeable personalities have explained, the hands are Siegfried's, the sword Nothung, Fafner's imminent doom and the boat's unofficial name. From the chess-school in the Lords he has overheard a snatch of the conversation:

"'Who was Fafner?' Not *who*, Kölm, you damned squarehead!—*what!*"

"All right—what, then?"

"Listen closely . . . Are you listening?"

"I'm listening."

"Close your mouth and stop dribbling . . . . That's better. Now—as everyone who doesn't look back on a schooling in the outer reaches of Saxony knows, Fafner was the dragon that guarded the Ring."

"What ring?"

"What ring d'you think, muttonhead?—the Nurburg-Ring!"

"You're having me on again, Falke. You think I'm stupid?"

"Don't ask, *Putsi*! If you don't get past the fourth move—check, and mate!—in the next game I'll know it!"

He guesses his obvious nickname without particular effort. And because he is also a skilled hunter, they respect the whole man. He's aware of his privilege, and he takes pains to preserve it. And so far his method has repaid the outlay, which is gratifying and encouraging. He feels he is doing a fair job of serving the Fatherland; would be worthy of whatever recognition might come his way, as promotion has done so far, and embellishment to the standard decoration of the Iron Cross, First Class: he wears the ribbon as his due, with pride but without ostentation, seeing it as recognition of not merely his own merit but also that of his men, and he knows they can withdraw it from him at will. It all depends on his integrity, his perception, his judgment: one mistake . . . His thoughts shy from the quayside scene.

Nearly a mile from the place where the schooner has gone down and where the boats drift unseen, he makes up his mind. No ships pass this way, not since the convoy system has settled down as the only chance of a safe passage for shipping between the Americas and beleaguered Britain. Now their routes pass farther to the north, and to the south and east coming across from the Argentine and Brazil, and South and West Africa. This area of the North Atlantic is all but deserted, crossed only by the solitary u-boats on their way to and from their Biscay coast bases and the patrol areas straddling the convoy route that carries the heaviest traffic, the great-circle lifeline stretched between Halifax and the Western Approaches, through the worst weather of which the Atlantic is capable. In winter it outweighs the firepower of attacker and victim alike, whose first battle has to be with the elemental forces that threaten indiscriminate annihilation; now, in late spring, comparatively benign, but a benign North Atlantic is nevertheless no place for a couple of overloaded, damaged ship's boats. This far out of the convoys' normal paths the survivors stand no chance of being picked up by a ship able to accommodate them, whether friend or foe: their fate is already sealed in the unavoidable finality of their predicament.

In its finality, yes; but need it be so in its form? Are they irretrievably locked into a sequence of piecemeal death by every agonising means at the disposal of nature in one of her rawest, most primitive and untrammelled states? He hasn't come across the thing himself—yet—but he has heard about it from other u-boat men: the boat first seen at a distance, a speck on the desolation of white-flecked grey, taking shape as it approaches under the uncertain press of a tattered sail, holding steadily to its course, its helmsman hunched over the tiller gazing ahead, ignoring the hails from the u-boat's bridge, its occupants in a huddle together, equally heedless. And it sails on, leaving a wondering bridge-watch, whose cries die when the officer with binoculars roughly silences their clamour. *All dead. Those are just the shells of men, steering to Kingdom Come or hell. The coxswain doesn't see us, only the place he's steering for. Let them go . . .* And the open boat, resting on its own reflection in a rare mirror-calm, no sails, no oars, just three remaining of however many had started out. Three whole, that is, blackened cadavers clad in the bleached remnants of clothing that fail, on the fourth, to conceal the gouged flesh and dried cords of tendons still holding the bones of one arm together: a wound, of a kind. In this case the u-boat's doctor, a young fellow barely out of medical school, is got back on board in a dead faint after depositing the bulk of his breakfast in the boat's bilge. As a subject for polite conversation, cannibalism is avoided.

He thinks of the children. The two boys sitting together in the first boat, others sheltering among the adults in the second, and the enigmatic baby. Perhaps, after all, the doll . . . And he thinks of the accounts he's heard, and of the rumours, at base and at home, about the Jews. Once, he remembers, he'd seen a train in a siding, cattle-trucks taking labourers to work somewhere—the Ruhr, it might have been. That was what he'd been told. He hadn't inquired further. War meant people on the move—workers, refugees, servicemen . . . What would be the outcome for that handful of *emigrés* if, by some miracle, they returned to their starting-point? He suspects something similar to that of the cattle-trucks' occupants without dwelling on specific possibilities—no, impossibilities, surely? Labour camps, yes; unquestionably. Unpleasant, but the Fatherland stands in need, and would pay. Subsistence, probably, but it is war . . .

As for the likelihood of a British ship stumbling on the scene—their navy is stretched to the last patrol-boat keeping the shipping-lanes—the convoy routes—open, and no regular merchant ship would take the chance taken by the schooner's master. No—there isn't the smallest chance of rescue for those boats. Not the smallest.

But if he were to signal—? He could transmit a short message; to all ships, and give the survivors whatever chance there might be. Yes, and perhaps exchange it for the only chance he has of passing undetected *en route* to his patrol sector: there's no certainty of there being no warship just below the horizon, whatever the reasoning against such a mischance. It's the unexpected that poses the greatest danger. So he would expect it, and avoid making signals not essential to his own survival. Besides, there's no guarantee that the schooner's master hasn't made a signal: there are other frequencies than the standard distress one, and the enemy might be using a special frequency unknown as yet to headquarters. That bosun fellow—Lebrun—need not have been telling the truth, after all; and in the short space of time between opening fire and hitting the schooner's after deckhouse a signal could have been transmitted by someone prepared for the possibility of attack—even assuming the radio had been in the deckhouse and not in a safer place below deck. In the master's accommodation for instance . . .

As it is, he won't report the sinking to headquarters until safely clear of the area—though what difference it would make isn't clear.

Wherever he is, a radio signal is an indicator of his presence, a possible pointer to his own destruction. So, then—why not at least a gesture that might save them without endangering himself more than otherwise?

Because, he concludes, if it would save them it would mean a ship close enough to present him with a problem, and if it happened to be a warship—and a merchantman is hardly likely to go out of her way to approach the vicinity of an operational u-boat—it's more likely to seek him first than to present him with another target while picking up survivors. And there's another thing, a threat that's been growing alarmingly in recent months: aircraft. It would take a couple of hours or so for a Sunderland to cover the distance from a land-base, but increasing numbers of bomb- and depth-charge-equipped planes are being kept in the air, within much closer reach of a suitably-placed target. Surface or air, the balance of risk isn't great, but in war it's enough. And—a clinching thought—after that business back at base the loss of his boat, with or without himself aboard, before it has even arrived at its patrol area is a prospective ignominy he can't risk at any price. Unbearable, even after death! He could not place such a burden of shame on his wife and children to add to the pain of their loss. No—in reality he has no choice, except in acting for the best in the circumstances—for making the best of a messy business, as it's turned out. Deliberately risking his command in exchange for a seven-hundred-ton museum-piece and the lives of a handful of Jews would be justly condemned as wilful negligence—unnecessary recklessness at best.

Which, with a now noticeable deterioration in the weather, is the deciding argument. He orders the two MG34's to the bridge. Obsolete, but obsolescence doesn't mean harmless: with a rate of eight to nine hundred rounds per minute of 7.92mm solid, explosive or tracer ammunition they are lethal in what's called anti-personnel applications. As now. It will all be over in a matter of seconds. There will be no pain, hardly awareness. And no drawn-out agonies of exposure in open boats. A surgical operation. A mercy, in its way.

He brings the boat round in a wide turn and she rolls heavily as she crosses the swell, making it difficult for the sailors to get the machine-guns fitted in their bulwark mountings, one on each side of the bridge. He puts the two senior petty officers in charge of them—chief quartermaster and chief bosun: steady, experienced men both. They will need to be. Everyone else he clears off the bridge bar the first watch officer, whose silence is eloquent. But he's a good officer, of proven, if uninspired, loyalty. None of the men on the bridge would willingly disobey orders, himself included. And he is perfectly clear about his. He will make theirs equally so as they approach the place.

He takes out his cigarettes and hands the packet round.

"Not smoking, *Einswo*? Steadies the nerves."

"My nerves are quite steady, thank you, *Kaleu*—"

"They do you credit."

PART 1
ARMING

I

ON the night of May 13th, 1945, the commandant of the *Kriegsmarineschule* at Flensburg, *Kapitan zur See* Gunnar Altmann, was shot dead by one of his own sentries, apparently because he had failed to respond to the challenge. In his standing orders he had underlined the passage *Ask only once for the password before shooting.* The sentry had disobeyed it only in repeating his challenge. The commandant was well-known to have followed, as he had urged and imposed upon others, the maxim of strict obedience to orders: to be shot through the head in such a clear implementation of his own instructions savoured of heavy irony outweighed only by the tragedy.

His identity confirmed by a number of fellow-officers and the college doctor, Altmann was buried in a full-dress Nazi ceremony three days later, his passing mourned by colleagues, friends and others including Hitler's successor, *Grossadmiral* Karl Dönitz. Making a temporary exception to their intention of erasing all traces of the fallen regime, the Allied authorities had given special permission for the funeral at Dönitz's request, but only after satisfying themselves, with more than a hint of the perfunctory, that Altmann's death had been an accident and not suicide. Yet some doubt remained. There had been nothing wrong with Altmann's sight or hearing, and according to the sentry, one Gottlieb, he had stopped at the first challenge, an indistinct figure in the gloom beneath the trees lining the path from the college's *Sporthalle*. His silence thereafter was inexplicable, for he must have known the password. At worst, he could have identified himself verbally, with supporting documentation. He had also remained in shadow, an anonymous figure to a sentry who, like his fellows, knew him by sight.

In different circumstances there would have been a more searching inquiry than that carried out by a board hastily-convened by Dönitz himself, under pressure to reach a conclusion, which was that it had been an accident. Despite it, rumours got abroad in voice and print, initially one that reports of the death were untrue, followed by a plethora of fanciful causes or reasons: it had not been an accident; it had been murder by persons unknown, or a planned killing by political or naval factions, or the British, or the Americans, or some Jewish revenge squad. Or—inevitably—suicide, an honourable response of an officer of the *Kriegsmarine* to his country's defeat, which had included the deaths of his wife and children in a bombing raid.

The *Flensburger Nachrichten* ran a leader headed *Commandant Altmann—Accident or Murder?* With no supporting evidence or reason it suggested foul play, and the rumours took second wind.

Hasty as it was, the inquiry had to consider every likelihood, and its only eye-witness was Gottlieb, whose answers, both before the board and to earlier questioning by Dönitz, were consistent and credible. As far as it went, incidental evidence by others corroborated them.

All that evening Altmann had been in consultation with the members of Dönitz's *Reich* administration in the hall, by this date its headquarters, from which the German surrender had been issued on 8th May. The return to his own quarters along the Black Path had taken Altmann for a short distance outside the college grounds, which, in the prevailing conditions of civil unrest, had been fenced and buttressed with guard posts manned by details from Dönitz's Guard Battalion—men drafted from u-boat crews. They were loyal to their service and to Dönitz personally, but were to some extent less militaristic, or more sailorly, than other naval personnel, certainly than soldiers. Thus the hesitation on the part of Gottlieb, who was barely eighteen.

As for Altmann himself, he had been under severe strain as the German collapse had spread inwards from the converging fronts to dissolve into civil and military breakdown while the Allies concentrated on consolidation after their thrust to the Baltic to cut off the Russian advance. Their success had been only a minor relief. He had been under strain for weeks, noticed, in the testimony of one of the college instructors, in his drawn features and changed manner. For example, three Type VII u-boats had turned up in Flensburg harbour under the command of a young *Oberleutnant* who, finding Altmann the senior officer in the port, had placed himself and his boats at the commandant's disposal, prepared to fight to the death, preferably with maximum glory. Altmann had exploded, calling the cigar-smoking adventurer a "damned pirate" and ordering him to "get the hell out". In normal times he had seldom been heard to swear, perhaps the lingering effect of his Lutheran church-going boyhood.

On top of his difficulties in keeping the college on an operational footing he had been burdened with responsibility for the security of the *Sporthalle* in its headquarters rôle and, *ad interim*, as welfare officer for his staff, finding accommodation for those who, resident outside the college with families, found themselves dispossessed, their homes either ransacked by roaming deserters or taken over by the British as billets.

And there had been something else, its effect open to conjecture but, to give Altmann the benefit of the doubt, possibly devastating and probably grossly demoralising. In his association with the senior officers and political figures surrounding, and paying calls on, Dönitz, he would have encountered incontrovertible evidence of the darker side of the National Socialism to which he had pledged allegiance and given his personal endorsement: talk among men now facing a near future in which they would be called to account for the events of the past decade and the parts they had either played in them or been witness to, at first- or second-hand. Some part of the summary harshness of the British military towards college staff had been a result of the revelations that had burst upon the preconceptions of a stunned Europe like a putrefying carcase as the Allies had stumbled upon, and liberated, the death camps in which millions had been subjected to the torments of the damned before wholesale extermination. To have called it murder, or even massacre, would have been a ludicrously palliative misnomer, and Altmann was said to have been shocked, depressed and saddened following an initial reaction of incredulous anger. It was thought by one or two to have broken his spirit; the loss of his family had already broken his heart. His loyalty to the *Führer* had been to a sham: he had suffered a vile betrayal of his most exalted notions of duty, honour and integrity. But his sentiments might also have nurtured a delusion of which he had been not wholly unaware, by deduction if nothing more substantial; an awareness, however, never allowed to establish itself sufficiently to prompt self-examination.

Yet he was no psychopath: the stark horror of the concentration camps would have had a profound effect on a man whose humanity, albeit flawed, had never been in question, even at his most professionally ruthless, and to balance the accumulation of reversals marking the situation in which he found himself at war's end, it appeared that he still had much to live for. He was young, well-qualified and experienced in his calling, and far from being listed as a war criminal was an acknowledged national hero for all the right reasons; and he could count on being needed in the Germany that would surely rise from the ashes of a purifying conflagration. The great majority were in a far less promising position from which to build a new life.

So the inquiry settled on accident as the regrettable end to an honourable career. It satisfied all parties, at least to the extent that any other conclusion would have been embarrassingly reflective of circumstances to which no-one felt inclined to draw attention. As the sole possessor of certainty, Gottlieb was exonerated from blame. He had done his duty, beyond which nothing had been expected of him, and he was cleared of all possible suspicion. He was also dismissed the service, to return to the anonymity from which he had briefly and so calamitously emerged.

In his eulogy Dönitz said, "Gunnar Altmann, we, your comrades, now take leave of you, a great warrior, a true and noble friend and a beloved member of the old guard of my *U-Bootwaffe*, to which my heart still belongs. Your unfailing devotion to duty and your Service will set Germany's coming generations a fine example. You will live forever in our hearts, the true hearts of your brothers-in-arms."

Emotive stuff. But who, and what, *was* Gunnar Altmann, and was "accident" a true assessment of his end?—indeed, was affirmation of the body's identity by only a handful of officers including the doctor who examined it the truth, or an agreed lie; and if a lie, for what reason?

At the time of his death he was thirty-three, the youngest, and lowest-ever ranking, of the naval college's commandants—he had relieved a retiring *Vizeadmiral* after a mere four months in the post of instructor and divisional officer. During that period he had been twice promoted, first to *Fregattenkapitan*, then to *Kapitan zur See*, the youngest post captain in the *Kriegsmarine*. Some were of the opinion that the promotion had been less for ability than for his being a favourite of Dönitz, who had long had him in mind for the commandant's post, hitherto reserved for flag rank: Altmann's untested rank was the lowest acceptable and, as others averred, a reflection of his outstanding ability as a naval officer. For there was no doubt of that, and if Dönitz had favoured him it had been with good reason. His wartime record as a u-boat commander, in terms of tonnage sunk, had exceeded even the quarter-million tons of the legendary Kretschmer, who had not lasted out the war, being—luckily for him—taken prisoner after an attack on a convoy. Altmann's recorded total had come to two hundred and seventy-three thousand tons—just fifty-two ships, accounted for over a span of sixteen patrols in only two boats. His last patrol had kept him at sea for two hundred and nineteen days, just topping *Korvettenkapitan* Kentrat's record two hundred and seventeen in U-196. It had been an achievement in itself, on the part of the entire crew but in particular on that of its commanding officer, whose force of personality rather than mere rank had been the stabilising influence in circumstances that in the hands of a lesser man would have skimmed the ragged edge of moral breakdown. Conditions in u-boats were at best trying, at worst terminal, and in war the tendency was towards the worst. Altmann would have confirmed that with room to spare.

Not much is known about his early years apart from his upbringing as a native of Lübeck, where his father ran a printing business and he attended a *gymnasium* before beginning a career in law as a student at Hamburg University, breaking it off before the end of the first semester to join the *Reichsmarine*. Moved, perhaps, by an affinity for ships and the sea, which in a native of Lübeck would have passed unremarked, he was at least equally driven by a well-developed sense of national pride and a firm belief in the cause of National Socialism, but stopping short of party membership and the kind of fanaticism exhibited by numbers of his contemporaries, which he found distasteful. His view of Nazism tended towards the honourably Teutonic, even the romantic, rather than the despotic; but either way he believed in the divine mission of the German race to pacify and order the world according to a natural ascendancy. In his outlook he became aware of an element of the medieval knight, epitomised in the decoration open to him—the Knight's Cross; but taking its place beside a certain sense of chivalry, and in a superior position, was a considered ruthlessness.

35

His induction into the navy followed the usual route starting with the entrance examination at the Kiel naval base—fourteen days of practical and academic tests and exercises of bewildering rigour and arcane significance, geared towards assessment of aptitude, from reflex action in the notorious light-switching game—pull the right lever to extinguish the coloured light before it goes out and loses you a mark—to endurance with the electric-shock machine and etiquette at dinner in the company of senior officers with their wives and untouchable daughters, encumbered with an armoury of cutlery to be correctly selected and used. As, for example, the uselessly blunt knife that accompanied the three-pronged fork at the dessert course, neither of which could penetrate the fresh orange indicated as a wise choice by the equine-featured wife of a *Kapitän zur See* left over from the Kaiser's destroyer fleet. The orange's refusal to be pierced finally diverted the attention of the surrounding diners from the warrior's exploits in mid-salvo, to Altmann's furious embarrassment and the old mare's dentated amusement. In the staring silence he was rescued by a young *Fregattenkapitän* two places to his right, who drawled, "Stick the damn thing in your pocket and eat it later—and now, tell us how you're finding this strange organisation of dispossessed Hippers—"

Which, Altmann later reflected, had delivered him from purgatory only to suffer proscription in the reaction to his enthusiasm for the u-boat, from which the young *Fregattenkapitän* rescued him again with a languid "Ah!—the warship of the future, eh? Dirty way of fighting, but it wins wars—or could, if certain armour-plated dinosaurs could be brought to see the obvious . . . So you plan to follow in the wake of the piratical Weddigen?" He glanced round, to a ripple of malicious amusement, "Gentlemen—and ladies—we have a modern Blackbeard among us!"

"But without a ship, *Herr Kapitan!* Where is he to find his u-boat after that infamous treaty?"

"My dear *Frau* Schrechter—he's clearly a man of iron will, and where there's a will the *Reichsmarine* will find a way—eh, *Herr* What's-your-name?"

"Altmann, *Herr Kapitan*—yes, I am certain of it!"

"Excellent! There's hope for the navy yet . . . Now, my friend—some of this *schnapps*-like cognac to toast the future u-boat, your iron will—and the torpedoing of Versailles!"

Any candidate dim enough to emulate the offhand manner displayed, with intent, by some officers was ploughed. Altmann survived.

And was taken to the navy's unyielding bosom, beginning with three months' square-bashing and associated exercises at the camp on Dänholm, an islet of bleakly utilitarian distinction immediately offshore at Stralsund. The recruits were treated—and kitted out—like infantry in a process designed to filter out the runts, which it did, painfully, with Prussian rigour and thoroughness. Altmann discovered that he thrived on it, pleased with the effective simplicity of the disciplinary system and able to ride the excesses of the NCOs' methods with an absence of self-pity that earned their respect, grudgingly enough. Most of them were failed officer trainees, each with a well-polished hardwood chip on his shoulder. As Altmann later remarked, the aim of the training was less to teach than to test and note strength of character and to get rid of the reactionaries. The defining theory was that only those who know how to obey are fit to command; prophetic, in its trite way.

The most climactic of the outdoor attractions—the ultimate destructive ordeal—was the Valley of Death, less of a metaphor than a literal truth. With twenty-four-kilogramme packs on their backs, gas-masks slung and rifles at the high port, clad in heavy grey serge under the pot-like steel helmets, the trainees marched to a gap between two small hills, where they assembled in readiness for the order—*Double!* Up one hill to halt on the order, turn and run down, across the valley and up the opposite slope to halt on the order, turn and repeat the run in the opposite direction, halt on the order, turn . . . Then with gas-masks on. Casualties—those who actually lived—were given their cards while the remnant lurched, grimly singing, on to further diversions, Altmann among them feeling, if anything, that he was gaining strength—mental and physical—rather than wilting. He passed the course but at what level is unknown: all records were lost or destroyed in the war that was on its way. On an informal note, however, his friend Otto Greischen, who rose to the rank of *Korvettenkapitän* only to die in the *Scharnhorst* when she was bombed and severely damaged off La Pallice in 1941, before her epic channel dash in company with *Gneisenau* and *Prinz Eugen*, remarked on Altmann's conduct as one of a small group of kindred spirits on the course. In the diary left to his family he wrote: *Altmann never complains, though he curses these swinehound POs as we all do and has twice been punished for helping poor bastards who can't stand the pace. It earns him no friends, and already he's had a formal warning from the commandant. The bad POs hate him, especially that pig Stahl, but they can't break him—not yet. The good ones look on, and treat him fairly, without favour. He says he has to do things the hard way to prepare himself for u-boat work, though we have no boats. He's determined to get into that filthy trade, if it ever revives, God help him.*

Similarly, but with some approbation, in the next stage of the training and first taste of the sea on a three-month cruise in the square-rigger operated by the *Reichsmarine*, the smart little steel-built jackass barque *Niobe*. She accommodated up to fifty officer-cadets and fifteen trainee petty officers besides her standing complement of six officer-instructors and twenty-five ratings, and took certain records—and twenty-seven cadets, among others—down with her when she was struck by a white squall on a Baltic cruise in 1932. Her loss, coinciding with Hitler's rise towards total power in the elections of that year, possessed a certain symbolism: as she had gone down with a body of men trained and training in an honourable, if bellicose, order, so the old imperial Germany finally sank from sight with its residue of autocrats in the imperialist tradition, superseded by an entity of a wholly different political and social character. The only evidence of Altmann's time aboard that illusory evocation of grace and beauty lay in his own mention of it in conversation and his naval college lectures, in which it was his custom to remind his audience of the value of the experience not only in practical terms but also in the way a sailing-ship has of bringing a young man face to face with himself in conditions that exact answers; answers that remain with him as a gauge for the rest of his life, for better or worse. Altmann was no sentimentalist except, perhaps, in his broader view.

Which fitted him to withstand the shock of change in the next stage of indoctrination, an extended voyage in the light cruiser *Köln* as a *Seekadett*, in practice an ordinary seaman, still learning—to obey, but also something of the men to whom he would soon be giving—or relaying—orders by carrying out their duties as the ship's crew, which included dirty, and wearying, work, such as watch-about before the furnaces in the boiler-rooms, shovel in blistered hand and a stoker PO within arm's-reach. In *Köln* Altmann circled the world, and saw in the ports of call a very small part of it, helping to show the flag—of the ill-starred Weimar Republic, already cracking under the political pressures that would shortly sweep it away. The cruise lasted eight months, and brought him into contact with his future enemies—and, in a national sense, victims; and perhaps, by a quirk of fate, in a particular sense in some cases. Who could tell, and who would ever know?

How was this experience meant to benefit the future naval officer? According to an unpublished manual on training in the *Kriegsmarine*, the navy's official style following the Anglo-German Naval Agreement of 1935, he would

... stand as a representative of his people. He knows that his country is judged as he is judged, and he therefore recognises early on the importance of strict self-discipline and an increased sense of personal responsibility. The impression he gets of other lands and other peoples, their circumstances, their opinions and peculiarities, teach him to look upon his own country with so much the greater love.

Whether or not Altmann registered the element of disdain for foreigners in this fragment, if it had appeared in this or similar form during his training, his subsequent career certainly demonstrated self-discipline and a sense of personal responsibility. As for his regard for his own country, the nature of events took inevitable effect. By this time he could not have been in ignorance of the activities of Röhm's SA, for copies of the National Socialist Party's mouthpiece *Der Angriff* and the Hitlerite *Volkischer Beobachter* were circulating among ratings, petty officers and officers, cadets and midshipmen included. The *Reichsmarine's* official attitude towards them was ambivalent, but most senior officers could be relied on to confiscate copies on their own initiative: in their obvious appeal to the lower and lower-middle classes they were seen by the old guard as an echo of the troubles that had erupted on the lower deck in 1918. Chief among the new developments evident in their portrayal of German affairs was an overt anti-Semitism with which a few officers—mostly junior—and middle-ranking—were in agreement. Times were hard. Someone was to blame apart from the Allies, who, after all, had implemented a programme of industrial revival financed by generous subvention. Some senior officers indicated sympathy, if not approval. They were the forward thinkers, the populists who saw that the old order of an aloof executive had played a ruinous part in the chaos that had heralded the armistice. If it were to remain extant the navy would have to take the path evidently being followed by the new *Reich*, even if it found the figures apparently in the van distasteful. Hitler, after all, was no Junker. He brought qualities of a different odour to the podium.

Be that as it may, the cadets were faced with another examination shortly after the cruiser's return to Germany, a perisher that chopped the failures and promoted the successful to the rank of midshipman—*Fähnrich zur See*—to move on to the naval college and training for commissioned rank, Altmann among them. It was June, 1931.

The *Marineschule*, to give it its pre-Hitler title, a red-brick Gothic megalith overlooking the approaches to the harbour from the Flensburg district of Mürwik, was known as the Red Castle by the Sea or, by its progeny, the *Mutterhaus*, in the way some of Altmann's future victims knew their wooden-wall training ships as their "wooden mothers". As with the Spartans, their flesh-and-blood mothers had dropped out of their everyday occasions and perceptions, or were supposed to have done, and the same training manual referred to the school in the female pronoun, as a ship, and

. . . the place where every military virtue is found in its purest form; where every military concept is used as a tool of education. Her effect, her influence, in the German Navy is without bound, since she is the first and most important source of every officer's training and since every officer will pass on to those he will command that which she has taught him.

The training reflected the aims of the college's founder, the Kaiser, namely at a navy to rival the world's strongest at the time—1910—and a soundly-trained officer corps. The world's strongest was, of course, the Royal Navy, which received an unexpected, and disconcerting, bloody nose during the ensuing war but went on to show remarkable powers of recovery and retaliation after an initial drubbing by the u-boat in the war after that. The *Mutterhaus* produced a serious antagonist whose chief weakness lay in the schizophrenic national leadership that failed him in his time of need—fortunately for the civilised world.

II

IT was Sparta that came to mind when Altmann entered the main building on that June day: he halted to adjust to the effect of whitewashed walls, bare except in the halls, where ship-models in glass cases, plaster and bronze busts, portraits—of ships and men—in heavy gilt frames, flags, pennants and banners, evoked past glories in a silent conspiracy of rebuke, voiced instead by a creature in gilt braid, calf-boots and belt with side-arm, who inquired his business in a series of sharp barks. By now barks had become a *lingua bien connu* to him.

"Altmann, Gunnar." Click of heels, stiffening of spine, shoulders back, stomach in, eyes front. "*Fahnrich zur See*, reporting for training—*sir!*"

The buttons, belt and boots circled him slowly, each steel-heeled, measured step echoing among the busts and glass cases like the ticking of a great clock. A goateed admiral—Tirpitz? Scheer?—fastened an unwavering glare on him from the opposite wall. He returned it, wondering, then turned his head to follow the movement of the booted one. The ticking stopped and a warm tobacco-tainted breath at his right ear snapped, "Eyes *front*, maggot! D'you want to go on commander's report?"

"No—*sir!*"

"Don't sir me, midshipman! Sir the officer of the day—his office is at the end of that corridor. Tell him why you're late, and why your turn-out's a disgrace to the service! He'll have your lights for breakfast! Leave your gear here. When the officer's finished with you, come back for it if you can still walk. Clear?"

"Aye,—" Altmann swallowed, at a loss.

"Aye, officer-of-the-watch!"

"Aye, officer-of-the-watch!"

"Right—now, *march!*"

It was a send-up, of course. On his return from a disappointingly genial session with the officer of the day, an elderly *Kapitanleutnant* with a limp who assigned him to his division and wished him success, the officer of the watch—a mere midshipman, like himself—startled him with "How did I do?"

After a pause to marshal his thoughts, Altmann replied cautiously, "Overcooked, actually." He smiled faintly, a trace of grimness in it. "*Maggot*, even . . . And your lanyard's adrift."

Hans Liebeherr, from Mainz, introduced himself and they shook hands and shared the joke. Liebeherr's father farmed hops, but word was getting around that there would be changes soon, among them government policy favouring increased food production; his father feared some form of collectivisation and a change of crop. Taking all this in, his son had decided against the agricultural college in Mainz in favour of the navy, and Liebeherr senior had gracefully conceded the contest. He talked of retirement and a move, possibly out of a Germany in which making a living had become a confusing struggle. Liebeherr was in the same training class, had arrived before time, and landed the duty. "Should've known—too keen. Gets you nowhere."

Altmann liked him. They found they shared certain views, had been on successive cruises in *Köln*: Liebeherr on the cruise before Altmann's, but had picked up a bug and been at home under doctor's orders for five months, touch and go, and only stayed in the running by the skin of his teeth and the fact that a highly-selective *Reichsmarine* stood in need. So he'd slipped a class and joined with Altmann's. A friendship germinated, and flourished in the discovery of shared aspiration.

One day, strolling up from the jetty after an hour's dinghy sailing: "D'you know a u-boat school's started?"

"No—why should you be interested?"

"Because that's for me, if I can make it—to hell with surface ships and all their bull!"

"After your performance when I arrived I'd've thought they'd be just your pigeon—"

They halted, and turned to scan the prospect of the harbour, glinting in the summer sun. Liebeherr lit a cheroot. Altmann refused the proffered pack and took out his cigarettes. Through the drifting smoke Liebeherr said, "Don't rub it in, chum . . . Well—what about you—floating bullshit or grey wolf?"

The impenetrable orange intruded, and the amused, clean-shaven features of the young *Fregattenkapitan*. Altmann said, "The warship of the future. Dirty way of fighting but it'll win wars . . . I've never had anything else in mind—"

Puffing out a blue cloud Liebeherr punched his companion on the shoulder and grinned. "I knew it! From the moment you arrived looking like a damn hobo I told myself, he's one! Hasn't changed his shirt in weeks!"

Altmann sniffed. "Mother'd love you!" He drew on his cigarette, caught and held Liebeherr's eye. "What's this school use for boats? I thought we had none."

"Torpedo-boats. But the word is that it's using a Finnish boat. German design. Everyone travels to join it in civvies—"

"The treaty?"

"The damned treaty . . . But it won't stick. Mark my words, Maggot."

Otto Greischen continued his diary at the *Marineschule*, and his friendship with Altmann, content to occupy the third, lesser, corner of a triangle, firmly wedged into the conventions of surface warfare. He amused himself by observing the interplay between the two would-be sea-wolves, an amusement tempered with self-mockery in its consciousness of a trace of contempt for a weapon tainted with foul play from the start—and a certain lack of breeding. There was no history to it of much note; certainly no record of honourable glory in battle, as had the surface fleet. Well, glory perhaps; but honourable—when you sneak up and shoot the victim (it would hardly be an opponent in the accepted sense) in the back, as it were? Greischen preferred the open approach, a head-on clash of Titans and a fair trial of strength—of will, spirit and skill as much as of weaponry. In the u-boat he saw the slyness of the weakling, including its waste of qualities deserving more noble employment . . .

Altmann is the quieter. He thinks about things, weighs up the situation, and acts with a kind of implacable conviction, perhaps too slowly. There's a distinct inertia in his method, while Liebeherr is impulsive, quick to sum up and act, careless of the details in his certainty. If he makes a mistake he corrects it swiftly—if it's not too late. Altmann tends not to make mistakes. They form a couple, an attraction of opposites that stands them in good stead here among the crowd, but in confinement together—as in one of their nasty little canoes—would probably be the cause of disagreement and even serious dispute—fatal! They bounce off each other when there's room for it, but in a confined space there'd be trouble. Individualists. Is that what u-boats need?

Greischen was a team man. He cooperated well, thrived on consensus. The surface navy beckoned as a supreme realisation of destiny, recognised from afar. His vision was of battle-lines, foaming grey fortresses beneath unrolling banners of smoke catching the first golden rays of a certain, triumphant, Germanic dawn. His navy would be the harbinger of enlightenment to a mankind blinded by its own delusions, squalid in its materialistic immorality and impure aspirations. The *Kaiserreich* had got it wrong; allowed those same delusions to lead it to ignominy and destruction. The new order would profit from past mistakes, rise to heights of virtue and justice purged of the old, effete conceptions of autocratic hegemony—

"Not expecting much from a handful of rust-buckets, are you, Gretchen?" Altmann eyed him quizzically, and smiled. "They'd have trouble with a North Sea squall, never mind a triumphant dawn. Like that old wagon *Köln*. Anyway, you'd have to wait for the u-boat to clear the opposition—the Royal Navy's been enlightening the world for a couple of centuries—"

"Even off Jutland?"

"That was your old order, wasn't it?—in any case, you can't claim a victory. Scheer made a run for it. There was no British surrender, and most of them were still able to fight."

"Not according to old Müller—"

"His history's pure Grimm brothers! Read the leading light himself—there's a copy in the library—*High Seas Fleet in the Great War.* Scheer. Tirpitz's memoirs are there as well, if you can swallow two tomefuls of raw pomposity. Müller's an old gossip. Save his stories for the exams." Altmann slapped his companion's shoulder. "Never mind, Gretchen—it's not for us to worry. Come—I'll stand you a canteen coffee."

Dr Müller taught naval history, strictly by the book—the approved book, or approved pieces of it. In fact he hadn't taught his classes that the High Seas Fleet had won at Jutland; it was just that his method tended to produce varying conclusions among his students, whom he encouraged to think about events rather than merely register the facts. As a high-risk policy it occasionally brought frowning suspicion on his head from the commandant's direction, and from some of his own students, those of a pronounced patriotic turn of mind; but never anything more punitive. He was known, and tolerated, for his liberal outlook.

As for the rest of the curriculum, the field was wide, rigorous and generally exhilarating in its close interconnection with physical recreation. To the classroom's offerings of strategy and tactics, gunnery, navigation, mathematics, marine engineering, seamanship, naval architecture, oceanography, meteorology, English and French were added a choice of horsemanship, fencing, gymnastics, sailing, rowing, rifle-shooting, boxing and soccer—a minimum of three including a team game, which meant sailing, rowing or soccer, sailing also a single-handed option. The day began at six and ended at ten after evening quarters except Sunday, which began an hour later and ended an hour earlier. Music-making, drinking and smoking were banned within the school's boundary, and local leave limited, with amusement confined to inns, theatres and concert-halls approved for officers' patronage. The idea was to soak the embryo officer in his trade, and drain every last breath to that end. They were never as fit again in their lives, apart from the mental and physical aberrants, who fell out as the course progressed. While anticipating expansion, the navy was small enough and popular enough to be rigidly selective. Liebeherr had been lucky to keep his place through such a prolonged absence: his academic performance had saved him, and it kept him at the top of the class with no apparent exertion.

"Don't know why we bother, the rest of us," said Altmann. "Liebeherr's One-Man Navy, boneheads needn't apply; we might as well pack up and go home—"

Liebeherr gave his egg a liberal dusting of pepper and grinned. "Oh, I wouldn't take it that far, Maggot—the army's always glad of a bit more cannon-fodder." He picked up his knife. "Pass the axle-grease before you go."

"I'm watching you, Liebeherr—pride before a fall, you know . . . Here. I hope it makes you sick."

Altmann was less distinguished. He struggled with maths, hacked his way through the rest, was good at seamanship, especially the practical side of it. His sport was sailing, single-handed mostly but also as a crew-member when the mood took him. He liked the solitude of the small dinghy as a relief from the constant close company of the college. But taking the tiller or sheets in the larger boats—gigs and whalers—gave him a sense of shared excitement, which had an edge to it: you were being watched, and judged, on the spot, by your peers, who depended on you and each other. The brief comradeship in the face of a common antagonist—the wind's alliance with the sea—was gratifying without becoming oppressive. Just as he liked it. He thought horses, by contrast, the stupidest animals he'd come across. And Otto Greischen watched, and noted, and wondered.

Altmann also took up boxing, and was good. He had a quick foot and a sure eye, and a gift for ruthlessness without malice. It made him not just a good boxer but also a competent fighter who could be relied on to carry the contest through to its conclusion without compromise. He didn't win all his fights, but enough to earn him the respect of some hard men, and the hatred of others, baffled by the contrast between his habitual affability and his unbending, almost inhuman efficiency in the ring. Opponents who felt they could beat him knew it meant getting him down for the count or not at all. Points never added up to enough. And he possessed something noted with shrewd approval by his officers and admired by his brothers-in-stress—courage. A fight against an army man had to be stopped, with Altmann's cheek laid open to the bone by a slicing right cross. "Blood!" said Liebeherr to Greischen. "He must have borrowed some extra just for the effect—unless you meant to drown that bastard gorilla, Maggot . . . Still," he added, examining the healing cut, "it'd pass muster as a sabre-slash. Standard issue in the Uhlans but quite a distinction for a naval officer."

"Uhlans used lances," said Greischen. "They were lancers."

"Ah, but they settled disagreements like gentlemen."

"Yes? That means anything from cheque-books to lawsuits."

"Trouble with you, Gretchen, is cynicism. Old before your time."

"It has certain advantages, my dear Hans. Like the hindsight that comes with it."

"Don't argue, Hansel," interjected Altmann. "He takes notes. You'll eat your words sooner or later."

Greischen smiled. "If it's of any use to you, duelling was permitted in this place until a couple of years ago."

A silence fell, all eyes on the speaker.

"You mean—pistols at dawn, that sort of thing?" Liebeherr's genial scorn slipped. Greischen had upstaged him with elegant ease, and he tacitly admitted defeat. "Even—um—sabres?"

"I gather the choice of weapon was limited to cutlasses."

In vain, Altmann studied Greischen's expression for indications of devilment, and felt a twinge of envy for the man's urbane self-assurance. He gave away only what he chose to.

"Yes?" Liebeherr was impressed in spite of himself. "Presumably the navy, having so few ships, could afford to bury the occasional promising young officer . . ."

"Possibly. But the *Reichstag* thought otherwise and outlawed it—as I say, a couple of years ago."

"Ah." Liebeherr turned to Altmann. "So it'll have to be an illegal slash." He nodded significantly. "Your opponent was buried with full naval honours at midnight. Your secret is safe with us, Maggot; we can always say you got it defending the honour of the *Mutterhaus* in the ring . . ."

Altmann was not conspicuous by his physical stature. Of medium height and tending to slenderness, he was light on his feet but deliberate rather than deft of gesture, and he smiled only when something amused him. He had good teeth, minus a cuspid, left somewhere in the Valley of Death after collision with another rifle-toting cadet; and blue-green eyes under level brows as fair as his thinning hair—a sign, he said, if he felt it would stir up dissent, of early maturity. A short straight nose balanced a firm chin, and the thin line of his lips signalled something of his understated determination. Mentally, he exuded an impression of implacable decision. In certain circumstances it savoured of the stubborn. He had not decided to join the navy as a suitable occupation, or even his vocation: he had joined to find out about himself, a fact he was only at this stage beginning fully to realise, and it intrigued him. So he pursued it with unflagging zeal. Thus his choice of special service, which, in some of its prospective aspects, occasionally disturbed him. That, too, was part of the challenge, and it pointed towards the unknown. Nobody seemed to know much about the u-boat, or care; many expressed a form of unconcerned distaste. Liebeherr was the only one who positively enthused about it. Altmann's disturbance stemmed from an apparent lack of more popular interest in something he felt was going to be of vital importance to the navy as a potent fighting arm, his discomfort worsened by a feeling of helplessness. He couldn't talk people into going for it, nor did he feel any inclination to try, but it was a dispiriting situation. The navy's conception of war at sea had hardly got clear of the dreadnoughts now lying solidly on the bottom at Scapa Flow. The naval warfare lectures barely acknowledged the u-boat, had only reluctantly turned from the armour-plated behemoth on one hand and the turbine-driven vainglory of destroyers and torpedo-boats on the other to cast a rheumy eye over the pathetic travesty allowed by the Treaty of Versailles. No more than a hint was dropped in the direction of the open secret of the u-boat development programme and the diesel-powered heavy cruiser concept someone had called the pocket-battleship. And the u-boat was up against another problem, not technical but social: Weddigen had been a hero, but not quite the sort you'd invite to dinner in mixed company, a point of scornful amusement to anyone fancying himself a surface-ship man.

Then, to his delight and an unexpectedly heady upsurge of pride, an officer came to give the assembled midshipmen a talk.

"Some chap by the strange name of Gladisch," said Greischen, affecting uninterest. "Rear-Admiral. Apparently something to do with this u-boat business. In the *Sporthalle* on Wednesday. Frankly, I can't see what there is to talk about, since the whole thing's supposed to be a secret, as everyone knows, but it gets us off evening class. There's a notice on the board." He smiled. "Thought it would please you. Don't forget your autograph-book."

The talk was about motor torpedo-boats. A good speaker, the admiral entertained his audience with stories of embarrassing moments, but it was clear that in describing some of the tactics and manoeuvres he was referring to another type of craft, and it didn't need a Liebeherr to work out which one. Nor that the planned expansion of the fleet meant a new fleet altogether, a fleet standing in need of specialist crews, for which special training schools and courses would be developed. One was already in operation training serving officers, but would soon have to be expanded or another opened.

" . . . As I look about me, here in this famous hall, I see a select part of the flower of our proud nation, young men carefully chosen for the kind of training designed to furnish a great and developing navy with a corps of first-class officers confidently expected to prove themselves second to none in the world." The great man coughed and nodded at the college's officers ranged on either side of him. They nodded back in a little ripple of scalps *en brosse* of varying densities. The audience shifted nervously in its seats, sensing a climax perhaps not as welcome as it might be. They had learned, among other things, that the navy had a habit of softening up those trusting beings it had singled out for something uncomfortable by use of the simple but disingenuous expedient of generous, if not outrageous, praise. The idea was to lull its object into the belief that his modest achievements had brought their deserved reward; which they usually had, as he would discover. The members of the audience avoided one another's eyes as the admiral went on, "This is the first class in this college's illustrious history that will be given the chance to decide on either of two separate branches of the navy as a career, and, in the case of the new branch, to stand for selection for further training as a body of men of distinctive character and ability. I'm unable to give you more details, but in due course volunteers will be required, by which time you will be acquainted with all you need to know to enable you to make the right choice. For the present, gentlemen, I'll remind you that whichever branch of the service you make your career, it will be your honour and privilege to serve the Fatherland's most vital arm of defence, standing in a glorious tradition, playing a key part in the emergence of our nation from its time of difficulty into a new era of pride and prosperity. God bless you all in your onward journey."

"He made it sound as if he was looking for another suicide corps," said Greischen. "Hipper Mark Two . . . Training will consist of boozing, screwing, guzzling and singing the *Horst Wessel* before glorious immolation in the name of the Fatherland under the guns of—of—"

"Not Beatty again," said Altmann. "Surely some other comedian—?"

"How about the United States?" said Liebeherr.

"Joke," said Altmann, and Otto Greischen stared at him. "Not possible."

"That's right," said Liebeherr. "No-one's going to commit suicide in this man's navy. We stick to boozing, screwing and guzzling, and leave the glory to Horst Wessel."

There was a pause, then Altmann said, "Anyway, I'm going to try for it. I can just about handle the women and the booze."

"You're forgetting something, Maggot. It just might keep you amongst the floating bullshit."

"Yes? What?"

"You've got exams to pass. And even then bet your shirt the selection will be from the upper crust. How's your differentiation coming along?"

"It's the great unwashed who'll be selected," said Greischen, winking at Altmann. "For indifference to filth rather than differentiation."

"Filth, women and booze—unbeatable combination, Gretchen. You should try it. Puts hair on your chest," replied Altmann, but his eyes were on Liebeherr, who recognised the blue-green glint, and nodded, half-smiling a tacit acknowledgment. Maggot would will himself to pass. Otto Greischen grimaced and tugged at an ear.

The final exams were tougher than Altmann expected, and he sank into a mire of foreboding haunted by images of trudging infantry and flashbacks to scenes from the camp on Danhölm. Hans Liebeherr forbore from teasing him, but felt unable to offer anything effective by way of reassurance. Maggot's maths *was* deplorable, and he'd refused his friend's offer of tuition. Poor bastard, thought Liebeherr; failure would be as good as a death sentence . . . No, as bad as a death sentence. He imagined it happening to himself, and shuddered, wishing they'd get the results sooner than was customary. Two whole weeks was a kind of torture. Maybe it was deliberate; a last test: anyone who bayoneted the commandant's flatulent dog to break the tension would be chopped, pass or fail notwithstanding.

But instead of a bayoneted dog the end-of-course ball lifted the general air of oppression for an evening, though at the prospect Altmann's mood merely changed key rather than lightened. He was a poor dancer. The large woman—*Derfflinger*-class, observed Liebeherr—who taught ballroom dancing as part of the etiquette curriculum had cracked under the strain and denounced him as a barbarian with no sense of rhythm. He contented himself with the sketchy grip he'd gained on the waltz and fox-trot before running out of rhythm in the approaches to the quick-step. Which, as Liebeherr remarked, wasn't bad for a u-boat man, who needed to know only the Depth-Charge Dodge—"Pure improvisation, Maggot. Pick it up as you go along." Liebeherr, of course, danced like that American, Fred Astaire, earning the suspicious disfavour of certain officers as a result. Swing was frowned on by the establishment, a prime example of the decadence emanating from America since the war; its dance routines were effeminate, culturally debilitating. Not that he cared, noted Altmann. The man was incorrigible; he'd go far, damn him. And a farmer at that.

The ball was a big occasion. Senior officers were conspicuously numerous, their wives assaying the company from the safe elevation of their husbands' ranks, their daughters warily and variously demure and bold. The officer-instructors turned out in unaccustomed formality, rather more splendidly than the schoolmasters, and the midshipmen, slightly creased and self-conscious, smartly enough in their bum-freezers and daggers. The staff and fully-adult guests were regaled with champagne and various potions and the daughters, midshipmen and their guests with punch and a variety of soft drinks, and the buffet was a wondrous achievement.

"Sauerkraut and bratwurst's off, I see," observed Liebeherr. "Inevitable, I suppose, at the rate they've been dishing it up . . . Here, Maggot—try these *hors d'oeuvre* things. Never know how long it'll be before you see one again." He thrust a laden plate at Altmann and gestured at someone, excused himself and edged through the press of bodies.

Altmann munched ruminatively. Neither he nor Liebeherr had invited anyone, not having made any particular social effort among the district's eligible maidenhood, including the nurses at the naval hospital, who, he noticed, were here in numbers. Liebeherr was conducting a desultory correspondence with a girl in Mainz, while Altmann, whose liaisons had not stood the test of separation, had felt no particular urge to re-establish himself. He looked round at the throng, not ready to be absorbed, taking stock. The exam's shadow still robbed him of a clear view. He watched Greischen dancing with the wife of one of the divisional officers—was it Bauer? She looked more like his, Bauer's, mother—or he her son. Funny, the kind of women men married, compared to the ones they fooled around with, beforehand or after. Greischen was playing the correct naval officer; practising, probably—being old before his time. Altmann smiled. The way to the top—or rather, *a* way, and fraught with risk—was through the chain of wives. If *through* wasn't putting it too coarsely for such a delicate tactic. The navy—the surface navy, that is—was a social challenge in the absence of war, and Greischen well-equipped. He had what was called a courtly manner, Altmann supposed. And the bland good looks that distinguished the lowland German from the iron-faced Prussian—like old von Leumartz. Not actually old, but seemingly. Shooting, parade training, fencing, naval protocol, gunnery. He was fit, and not stupid; just rigid—and he had no wife. There he was now, talking to Müller. What a contrast, chiefly in the officer's total lack of humour. Altmann's mouth twitched at thought of the reproach attributed to the man by popular assertion: *You know, gentlemen, we Prussians have many faults, but a sense of humour is not one of them.* He had never heard it himself, and doubted its veracity, but taken as sufficient proof of the fact, Altmann detected something subtle at work, and as he watched, Müller suddenly guffawed at something von Leumartz had said. His face remained immobile. If he had actually uttered those words, they were a joke in themselves, too subtle for the Philistines at whom it was supposed to have been directed, who'd accepted face value, as they did most things. The apparent lack of humour might be a blind; a shield. Could von Leumartz actually be a shy man? The possibility struck Altmann as incongruous, but not unlikely, a new facet of life amidst a heady kaleidoscope thrust upon him from the day he'd begun the entrance examination. And, all unsuspecting, he was about to encounter another.

He caught sight of Liebeherr, standing back between a pair of potted palms. Liebeherr beckoned, and setting his plate down Altmann strolled over, evading the gyrating couples. "What's this, Hansel—skulking when you should be taking the floor by storm?"

Liebeherr put a finger to his lips. "Not skulking. Reconnoitring . . ." He inclined his head meaningly to his right, fractionally lifting an

51

eyebrow, and Altmann glanced across at a group of three girls, two standing, one seated on a *chaise-longue* in the bay of a curtained window. They cast covert glances at the two midshipmen, and smiled secretly among themselves. "Here, Maggot—rinse your tonsils in this. Special import." Altmann looked down at a silver flask in Liebeherr's hand, took it and raised it with a nod. "Rot-gut from that damned Jew—?" He referred to the college's supplier of dry goods and liquor, one Rosenbaum. Liebeherr had an arrangement with one of the firm's drivers.

"No. Sadly, he's just out of business, courtesy of the Röhmish hordes, so I hear. What you have there, little Maggot, has been procured at exorbitant cost from the depths of the good admiral's cellar—"

Altmann lowered the flask. "Idiot!—You'll come a cropper one day, Liebeherr, as sure as your arse points—"

"Silence, Maggot! Drink, but not all of it. Duty calls." He pocketed the flask as Altmann got his breath back. "I see that dog Gretchen steering for the Rhinemaidens. Come!"

The girl on the *chaise-longue* wore dark-blue silk; cool blue eyes held Altmann's gaze with calm inquiry, catching the chandeliers' sparkle with a suggestion of amusement. He was dimly aware, at the periphery of his vision, of blonde hair piled in heavy swirls above small neat ears bearing rather prim pearl teardrop earrings, matching a similar pearl on a fine gold chain at her throat; a complexion of pure cream with a bloom in it that made his throat tighten. Her face was an oval of perfectly symmetrical proportions—straight nose, high cheekbones, clear serene brow, chin sculpted by . . . Praxitiles, perhaps? A plaster copy of an Athena attributed to the Greek stood in the main foyer at the law school; some connection with an obscure point of jurisprudence. But she was also a goddess of war, he recalled. Absently, his eye followed the smooth curve of the throat, paused at the pearl, encountered taut blue silk and halted, alarmed, to return, resting momentarily on the dimple just to the left of the confluence of pink-brushed lips before regaining the blue depths, still amused, cool, appraising. And confusing. He was suddenly conscious of the scar on his cheek; still livid, or so it seemed as he manoeuvred the razor in its vicinity. Would it repel her? With an effort he regained control, clicking his heels as he gave a stiff bow made stiffer by the steely edge of his starched collar. "May I have the pleasure of this dance?" It sounded like an order. Liebeherr barking on that first morning. He cursed himself, but she nodded gravely, and rose

52

with an unfolding motion, as graceful as an opening lily, he thought, mildly surprised at his imagination; graceful, and with a faint smile that lay slightly to the dimpled side, devastatingly. Taking her gloved hand, aware of glances from right and left, he led her onto the floor past Liebeherr, who paused in whatever he was saying to the brunette and clicked his heels. "Mind the depth-charges," he murmured. Altmann ignored him, counting the beats of the music, trying to work out whether it was a waltz or a fox-trot. No—it was neither. A damned quick-step, probably. It would be . . .

"What did your friend mean?" she asked. Her voice was low-pitched, bell-like, and he shrugged. "Liebeherr? Oh, he just likes to be noticed. Talks for the sake of it." He laid a formal hand on the small of her back, which transmitted a current that made him shiver and lose the timing. "Other foot," she said, and the blue twinkled less coolly. He was just tall enough to look down into it, experiencing a desire to drown. A suggestion of perfume—warm, soft, like an embrace—made him giddy. He cleared his throat and changed step as if in column of threes. It had been easier in grey serge under a piss-pot hat.

She piloted him through three numbers, left him to his fate in a waltz with the commandant's wife, then abandoned him to black despair as she toured the floor with another damned twinkle-toes, that creep Fleischmann. Then, miraculously, she was beside him again, flushed, smiling at his obvious relief. She asked for a fruit punch and somehow they were leaning on the stone balustrade of the balcony with the dark pool of the bay spread beyond the cypress and fir lining the far side of the parade-ground. Overhead hung a quilting of overcast, reflecting in a soft glow the lights of the town. At his left shoulder her face was a pale glimmer, towards which he dared not turn. She laughed politely at his stories and jokes, which weren't at all funny, then they were back among the dancers. She lay back warmly in the crook of his arm, a gloved hand resting just detectably on his shoulder, a stunning novelty, and he dared not squeeze the hand he held for fear of destroying the fantasy.

By the end of the evening Altmann was desperately in love. Her name was Ursula. She agreed to write. The admiral was her uncle.

"You certainly have taste," said Liebeherr afterwards. "Or luck. Bordering on the voluptuous—and in one so young! It'll cost you, sailor . . . Ursula, of all the eleven thousand virgins—"

"What the hell are you talking about, Liebeherr?"

"Ancient legend, Maggot . . . The Old Man's niece to boot! Are you sticking with it?"

"She said she'd write."

"Ah." Liebeherr surveyed Altmann with a hooded eye. "It's that sabre-slash, you know. Makes you a man of unknown depths. She'll want to look into them."

"Let her," replied Altmann with a shrug. "She might find something I don't know about." And he remembered, gratefully, that she had affected not to notice the scar.

Altmann has fallen for a Brunnhilde. The exam has probably unsettled him, addled his judgment. Entanglement isn't a good thing at this stage of our careers, and my guess is that u-boats will test the arrangement to destruction. Rather that than the other way round, with the way things are going in the country. This Hitler—strange power over the masses—is a misshapen specimen, but he's getting things done and the navy's showing signs of new life. The word is that heavy surface units will soon be on the stocks regardless of the Treaty. Altmann says it's all hot air and the concentration will be on the u-boat. He thinks Hitler will follow Hindenburg, which seems likely after the results of the last election, and it's difficult to see anyone with a better chance. His party thugs—SA—are keeping any likely opposition out of the running, and they've got it in for the Jews, an ugly business. The Old Man gave us a lecture today, said the officer corps must stand above politics, but already most of the staff at Kiel and Wilhelmshaven are openly supporting the Nazis.

III

WHEN the exam results were posted Liebeherr appeared at the head of the list. Distinctions in all subjects. Prizes for navigation, mathematics, seamanship, best all-rounder. Altmann's name was absent. He stood before the notice-board feeling as he had when the fight with the army man had been stopped. The names blurred before his eyes and there was a singing sound in his ears, a sustained high C with a throbbing beat to it, through which he heard voices.

"Hey, Altmann—what's happened to you? Forgot to put your name on your papers?"

"Took the wrong exam," came another. "Better check with the army, Altmann!"

Ignoring them, he turned from the board and bumped into the commandant's messenger. He shouldered him aside but the fellow clutched his sleeve and tugged. "Altmann—wait! You're wanted, right away. Commandant's office—"

"What about?"

The messenger shrugged. "Must be the exam results."

"Is he in a good mood?"

"Breathing fire."

"Thanks, pal."

Striding along the corridor he sifted anxiously through the exam questions he could remember. That damned maths, it would be. Complete balls-up. Unless—no, not Ursula, surely? A warning shot: keep off the grass. No, no, couldn't be. It's got to be this damned exam . . . But wait! Liebeherr's flask—that cognac! Oh, God, this was it. Separately questioned so there'd be no collusion, then the sack. He was going to be cashiered, disgraced, humiliated. His step faltered, then picked up. He lifted his chin and pulled his shoulders back. His footfalls rang like a knell.

The singing in his ears had climbed the scale to inaudibility by the time he arrived at the commandant's outer office. He stood mutely watching the secretary, a passed-over *Oberleutnant* in a uniform that hung on him like a set of curtains. His neck emerged from his collar like a tortoise's from its shell and the pale-blue gaze settled on Altmann with supercilious detachment through rimless lenses. The expression on the skull-like face suggested that he'd just bitten into an unripe quince. After a brief exchange on the intercom, he said, "The Admiral will see you now," sweeping the figure before him with a look of sneering disapproval before turning his attention to his typewriter. He lived under sentence of universal homicidal intent among the midshipmen, spared only by virtue of the generous latitude of service and college discipline. Savouring the mental prospect of a satisfying end to a bloody encounter in the ring, Altmann braced himself.

Vice-Admiral Egbert Niethe-Grapow was a formidable figure; not in stature—a medium-height, medium-built, middle-aged man, his clean-shaven features were better-suited to the classroom than a battleship's bridge, which was where they'd been before their present location—but in sheer presence. His sea-grey close-cropped hair matched a piercing ice-blue scrutiny which never failed to render the rest of his person invisible to whomever it was directed at. Altmann avoided it by fixing his own gaze on a point directly in front of him, which extended through a tall window out across the bay towards the distant shore. Niethe-Grapow remained seated at his vast desk, his back to the view.

"All right, Altmann—at ease." The voice was light, its accents sharp and incisive, coolly-modulated; a voice used to command and instant response. Altmann clasped his hands at his back and shifted his feet apart a few inches, and allowed his gaze to drop. It encountered not the ice he expected but something marginally warmer, and a fractionally-lifted eyebrow. He was astonished. The Old Man was amused at something. Perhaps.

"You're wondering what all this is about—" A hand lifted to forestall an answer. "So I won't beat about the bush. The examination—you've failed your maths, which means you'd be washed out . . . Here, man—there's a seat behind you—"

The chill sweat suddenly on Altmann's brow accompanied a surge of nausea which ebbed as he turned and lowered himself carefully into the leather-bound chair. So this was it. Back to law school. After all that damned bullshit. All a waste of time, nearly three years—

The commandant was watching him, frowning. To his brusque inquiry Altmann asserted his wellbeing, just a passing discomfort; he'd skipped breakfast. Niethe-Grapow grunted. Meals were meant to be eaten. Proper diet was part of the training. Altmann nodded, said he'd just felt no appetite, and assumed a posture of close attention as Niethe-Grapow continued. "I've had a word with the headmaster, who tells me it's a borderline case, so I'm going to do something never done before, as far as I know . . . But first I want to know your intentions about your career in the navy."

Altmann focused on the pale-blue gaze. "Sir."

"Well—what type of ship do you hope for—which branch of the service?"

Altmann didn't see the point in this line of inquiry; in the circumstances it seemed superfluous. In which case it didn't matter what he said; one option would be as futile as the other. "U-boats, sir. From the start."

Niethe-Grapow actually smiled. Or at least, his thin lips twitched and the hard gaze seemed to take on an added shrewdness. "Yes," he said. "I hoped you'd say that. If you hadn't I wouldn't have been able to do what I propose to do."

"Sir?"

The commandant sat forward and steepled his fingers, elbows resting on the blotting-pad before him. Altmann's eye strayed momentarily to the strata of heavy gold braid. God, he thought—you'd end up dragging your knuckles in the dust given time. Almost with a start he returned his attention to the admiral's words. "—You're in the top third of the class; near top in practical subjects—sailing, rowing, seamanship. And I'm impressed with your boxing; not its science—you make too much use of your left hook, ineffectively—but what it tells me about you. You'll never make a Schmeling, but you've got pluck—and a good eye."

"Thank you, *Herr Kommandant*."

Niethe-Grapow inclined his head. "However, your maths . . ." He sighed, unsteepled his fingers and slid some papers about on the pad. Altmann waited, wondering. Finally Niethe-Grapow looked up again. "Failed by four percent." He drummed his fingers on the papers for a moment, then tightened his lips and levelled a hardened gaze at the pale young man before him. "You will take the mathematics examination again—different questions, of course—and if you pass I'll recommend you for the u-boat arm. If you fail . . ."

"Herr Kommandant?"

"If you fail, you'll be letting me, this college and Germany's navy down. And you'll be out on the streets as far as the service is concerned. Is that clear?"

"Yes, sir."

"Very well. You're to report to the headmaster on Saturday morning at ten o'clock. You will not tell anyone what you're doing. You'll be posted as a pass—*if* you do—and your application to join the u-boat arm attended to with the others . . . And Altmann—"

"Yes, *Herr Kommandant?*"

"If this piece of subterfuge gets beyond this and the headmaster's room both you and I will find ourselves before a court-martial. It will be your only distinction and my disgrace. Do I make myself clear?"

Altmann jerked to his feet, came to attention with a click of his heels. "Absolutely, *Herr Kommandant!*" He swallowed. All for four percent. Easier, if the Old Man was so keen to get him into u-boats, to have made a small adjustment to the marking. Perhaps it had already been done . . . But who, exactly, was so keen, and why? *Were* u-boats failing to attract enough men of the kind they needed? Or was it just that he was, in fact, ideal material—maths apart? An interesting thought . . . Unless—no, surely nothing to do with Ursula! Impossible—he had purposely avoided expatiating upon his hopes for fear of her possible reaction. There was the chance of her regarding u-boat men as heroes, if she regarded them at all; or equally the chance of such nether creatures being objects of odium. His steering the conversation, such as it had been, carefully around the whole matter should have ensured curtailment of any interest, certainly of any conclusions on her part that could have prompted an attempt to raise his standing in her uncle's steely eyes. He was letting his luck run away with him: volunteers were needed, and not enough were coming forward; if it were otherwise he'd have been chopped, and the chance of a second failure was real enough. *Then* what? But his spirits soared as he nodded curtly to the secretary on his way out. That damned differential calculus. He'd crack it this time. He had to, even if it meant crawling to that self-satisfied hayseed Liebeherr.

PART 2
PATROLLING

I

KRETSCHMER—"Silent Otto" for his disapproval, by example, of what he considered to be an excessive rate of signalling between boats and between boats and the C-in-C, handing the Allies intelligence on a plate—had lived through the sinking of his U-99 during a convoy action, but of the three leading commanders whose careers had been violently terminated in the same month in early 1941 he was the only survivor, to spend the remainder of the war as a prisoner. Prien, the "Bull of Scapa Flow", in U-47 and Schepke in U-100 had been killed with their commands. Hunted by escorts Prien's boat had exploded at depth, evidenced by the red glow seen by its attackers amid the depth-charge eruptions. Schepke had been forced to the surface, presenting a destroyer with an opportunity to ram. Some of the crew had succeeded in abandoning the boat before she'd gone down, but Schepke had died at his post on the bridge, where the destroyer's bows had struck, crushing him and opening up the pressure-hull to the sea.

Apart from the loss of three experienced commanders and their crews, Kretschmer having ratched up the record score of some 250,000 tons in the eighteen months of his active service, Gunnar Altmann was keenly aware of its parallel effect on the *U-Bootwaffe*: a sore blow to morale at a time when a reversal of the arm's fortunes was beginning to seep into the picture. Following the fall of France Britain was passing through a period of dire distress in the loss of merchant shipping vital to her survival as the stumbling-block to Nazi Germany's ambitions, but the running sea-battle had not been fought without profit: drawing every possible lesson from each attack, and forcing through the development of defence systems and technique to a point at which they were beginning to show calculable returns on outlay, the British were seeing not only a stemming, if yet far from a turning, of the tide but also increasing support from a USA waking up to the implications of a British defeat as well as admitting a grudging admiration for the unflinching determination of a free nation to overcome what had seemed insurmountable odds. Moral sustenance apart, Roosevelt was succeeding in his efforts to persuade Congress of the wisdom of material support, forthcoming in various ways including collaboration in the refinement of radar, which, it was becoming clear, represented a terminal threat to the u-boat's *modus operandi*. Located when submerged by the increasingly-deft use of asdic, the u-boat now began to risk moment-to-moment detection when surfaced, a tactic that had become the standard for torpedo attack at night. And of course it was necessary to run on the surface for a certain minimum period every so often in order to charge the batteries that powered the submerged boat. Radar itself was not new but its apparent development, approaching a state in which it could be fitted in ships and, more alarmingly, aircraft without occupying overmuch space and adding substantial weight, was sobering and potentially devastating. At the same time the escorting ships and aircraft increased in number as well as range of operation.

And on top of all this another event gave the British an advantage that dramatically increased their capacity for turning the tables on Dönitz's attempt to achieve what Göring's *Luftwaffe* and the *Heer* had not: Fritz-Julius Lemp, of *Athenia* fame, ran foul of three British escorts off Iceland. Like Schepke forced to surface, he was shot in the ensuing scuffle with the boarding-party which managed to recover several items of interest from the boat before she sank. They included an Enigma cipher machine and its code-keys, which opened to relatively effortless Allied scrutiny all wireless traffic between Dönitz's headquarters and the boats at sea. What was more important, the machine's capture was never seriously suspected, although Dönitz entertained a nagging doubt about the security of his communications until the end of the war. On balance, while the *U-Bootwaffe*'s morale developed a slight downward incline, that of the Allies rose, a see-saw that began to show a tendency to tilt in only one direction.

Reluctantly deferring to the twin dictats of low fuel and victuals, Altmann made the decision to end the patrol and return to base with only an embarrassing seven-hundred-ton French schooner and a full complement of torpedoes to show for it. Picked up against regulations from BBC and the British *Atlantiksender* broadcasts, the news was the build-up of German forces to the east, clearly if not officially in preparation for some kind of heavy operation. If for a possible if incredible invasion of Russia, it would open a second front of debatable merit which, if it achieved nothing else, as one Klaus Falke, *Maschinistensmaat* and the boat's chess-master and self-appointed oracle, averred, would give the *Wermacht* something to take its mind off its disappointment over the cancelled channel crossing.

"How can you say it's cancelled?"

"Because it is, whatever Goebbels says to hoodwink the Tommies and anyone else he thinks can't put two and two together—including square-headed Kölms from the depths of Saxony!"

"It's a postponement only—better to wait until the u-boats have made the Tommies think more about empty bellies and fuel tanks than fighting on the beaches—"

"Like we've done this trip, eh? One Froggie toy and a back-row seat at the latest production in the *Kriegsmarine*'s continuing battleship farce." Falke cupped his hands at his mouth. "Roll up, ladies and gentlemen, for the sequel to the priceless Gothic comedy *The* Graf Spee *Follies*: spectacle of the century, a stunning epic of naval mismanagement, *Bismarck!*, starring Günter Lütjens as the fumbling admiral—with full supporting cast of clapped-out British string-bags and exploding battle-cruisers."

"So the Tommies say—"

"And so does everybody else except Goebbels's Radio Fantasy Show! Oh, and not forgetting the entire North Atlantic operational fleet of u-boats with nothing better to do than hang about waiting for the Royal Navy to set itself up for total des—"

"Falke!"

"Yes, chief?"

From the watertight door to the control-room the chief *Bootsmansmaat* jerked a thumb over a shoulder. "Skipper wants to talk to you—jump to it!"

61

"He'll be wanting your advice about our next move, no doubt," murmured Kölm with ponderous sarcasm, and grinned at Falke's frowning glance as he got to his feet.

"Sit down, Falke."

"Thank you, *Herr Kaleu.*" Vaguely assuming its advisability in the circumstances Falke slipped into the formal alternative to the usual shorter appellation. He sensed some kind of crisis, and it made him nervous. Pulling out a folding seat he eased his backside gingerly onto it, in the way he would have squatted on a cold seat in the heads. Altmann favoured him with a disconcertingly steady gaze from eyes which seemed to Falke to have taken on a piggy look. He was, he supposed, in for a rocket, and the whole boat would hear it. Absently, he decided that there was no real need for a p.a. system. Not even for huckster acts. An ordinary conversational murmur would do, at least when running submerged. He arranged his features, mostly obscured by a thick reddish beard, in what he hoped was a properly attentive expression.

There was no privacy in a u-boat; not even for the commander, whose cupboard-like "cabin" was separated from the rest of the interior by nothing more solid than a green baize curtain. The only aspect of his existence that was private unless he chose to reveal it comprised the contents of his mind. Falke was treated to a selection from them in a moderate tone that emphasised rather than concealed the obvious implication: that talk of the kind the *Maschinistensmaat* considered witty would be differently interpreted by others, among whom it could and probably would increase the general feeling of despondency at the patrol's outcome. It was, Altmann reflected ruefully, the first of his patrols in command that had failed to produce a kill of any moment to the war effort, granted the schooner's minimal contribution to his tonnage score. However, in another way altogether it was proving significant, and the memory of the scene, stark in the searchlight's glare as the wreckage of the schooner's boats was scanned for signs of remaining life was becoming an almost daily recurrence, usually at times when he tried to snatch a few minutes' sleep. And on each successive occasion, he'd begun to notice, its transition from vivid factual memory to a grotesque phantasmagoria was measurable, as by marks on a scale of dread. Then, latterly, there had been the business of the *Bismarck*'s apparent sinking by a British task force, denied by German news broadcasts but all too graphically described by the British, the worst possible culmination of an operation ordered by headquarters with obvious reluctance as a last resort in the unwieldy battleship's apparently doomed sortie into the North Atlantic battle-arena. Between that and the schooner affair Altmann feared a faltering of morale in his crew, for which he could not blame them and which could yet occur. The whole patrol had been dogged with misadventure from the time the boat had sunk alongside at her berth. He would be glad when it ended, perhaps—hopefully—to allow a fresh start on a footing of proper preparedness, including a set of new batteries. Those damned batteries. On three occasions while attempting a convoy interception they had almost been the cause of his destruction, caught on the surface recharging, twice by aircraft coming out of low cloud—clearly guided by some location device, another threatening development in itself—and once by an escort in the wake of a convoy, either making a late rendezvous or catching up with it after some kind of delaying mission, perhaps a rescue. That had been too close for comfort, leading to a twenty-two-hour session in hell as the half-charged batteries ran low and the eerie tapping of the escort's asdic heralded successively closer patterns of depth-charges. Another four hours of it at most, if it hadn't done for him would have forced him to surface as the alternative to death by toxic asphyxiation. He put the escort's departure down to her running out of charges; possibly an act of God, though why God should concern Himself with the skin of a murderer Altmann could not determine, startling himself by his bringing God into his cogitations for the first time as a significant third party to events: startling himself, and acknowledging something he was already having difficulty in defining with any justification. He had never used the term "murderer" with respect to any war operation before, so why now? A slip of the mental tongue, he decided. But he was not convinced, aware of its having an effect on his thoughts and decisions that was subtle, corrosive and cumulative. He needed sleep, like all of them. That would put things back into normal perspective. Meanwhile, here was Falke.

"You know that conversation can be overheard at a distance in the boat?"

"Yes, *Herr Kaleu.*"

"Yes . . . And some is more—interesting—than the rest."

Falke waited expectantly. He had found that there were times when it was best to say nothing; to mark time rather than follow an apparent lead. This was obviously one of them. He maintained his attentive expression.

"Yours can be so, Falke. Sometimes a little too much so. Do you follow?"

"Yes, *Herr Kaleu.*"

"Mm." Altmann's gaze worked its way round the petty officer's features reflectively, finally halting at the eyes. Falke met it for a few seconds then examined his hands. He bit a piece of dead skin away from the edge of a fingernail and looked up. The commander's eyes were still there; cold, like the blue-green Atlantic silently enveloping the submerged boat. They seemed, thought Falke uncomfortably, to be reading something of which even he himself was unaware. He searched his conscience, and turned over the conversation with Kölm. What could have been interesting about it—to the *Kaleu*?

"War is a many-layered activity, you know, Falke . . ."

Falke nodded, vaguely relieved. So—this was to be a lecture rather than a carpeting. He relaxed a little, attuning himself to impending boredom.

"We—the u-boats—see front-line action—when we do!" Altmann smiled bleakly. "And this patrol has been particularly unfortunate, as we're all aware. At the same time, we're all aware of the fact that war switches between fortune and misfortune without warning—without rhyme or reason—and the next patrol is just as likely to be a success as this has been something less than that—"

Something less than a success? thought Falke. *A complete washout, more like! The* Kaleu *doesn't show concern, but it's obviously a black mark in his book, and he'll probably get a rocket. At this rate he'll find himself with a reputation for—*

"But there's more than one front line—apart from the military, I mean." Altmann regarded the petty officer dispassionately. It wasn't a matter of disciplinary correction as much as taking the opportunity to correct a few misconceptions—not only about the war as they were experiencing it but also about his views and intentions. He believed in keeping his crews informed, even to the extent of possible indiscretion, a risk he was prepared to take in the interests of the kind of discipline he believed worked more effectively in a small unit than the kind customarily exercised in surface ships. It was not typical of the u-boat service: some commanders were rigid disciplinarians, cordially hated by their officers and crews, though none the less respected. Prien had been one of them. So had Kretschmer, on a less inflexible note. It did not seem to have had any adverse effect on their fighting ability;

perhaps, indeed, it augmented it as its proponents had claimed, but who was to say that a different approach would not have produced even more success? Or perhaps, in Prien's case, have avoided the ending that had occurred? It was an imponderable, Altmann felt, and in the absence of any proven argument against his method he preferred to work on the basis of his own intuition and inclinations. One of the attractions of service in the u-boat arm was Uncle Karl's liberal approach to his commanders' independent turns of mind: briefly, the principle was that if it worked, in terms of measurable results, it was encouraged, a substantial element in the recognisably and uniquely high level of morale in the *U-Bootwaffe*: allow it to fall below some incalculable but finely-demarcated limit and you'd lose everything else—war included, if you accepted the "war-decisive" argument.

So, at its receipt, he had briefed the boat's company on the signal that had withdrawn them from their fruitless pursuit of convoys to form part of the u-boat reception committee, as he'd called it, for the Royal Navy's task-force harrying Admiral Lütjens's raiders after their emergence from the Denmark Strait. The frustration this had caused had been offset to some extent by the surprising destruction of *Hood*, reported with excessive enthusiasm by Berlin and admitted with subdued gravity by the British. But what at first had seemed to promise Lütjens's safe exit from the narrows turned to disaster when the battleship sustained shell-strikes that forced a change of plan. It rendered the u-boats assembled in a line from Cape Farewell in a south-easterly direction for a hundred miles or so impotent as the trap into which *Bismarck* was to have drawn her pursuers. Instead, incomprehensibly, she had turned away on a course parallel to the line and, it seemed, run foul of the British, first in the shape of an airborne attack and subsequently an engagement with the remaining units of the task-force that had sent her to the bottom. The bitterness felt in the boat at the news mingled with bewilderment at the apparent incompetence of the German surface navy. Only later were they to learn the facts, but meanwhile Altmann had a problem of morale on his hands. After two more abortive sorties against convoys escorted by, in one instance, a hunter-killer group, as the new freelance form of pre-emptive convoy defence was called, and in the other by what he identified as almost certainly American warships to augment the otherwise less impenetrable British screen, he decided to use Falke as a means of restoring at least part of it. His every word would be overheard and passed round the boat almost as soon as it was uttered. He would have to choose each with care.

"War is fought on several fronts which, perhaps, you haven't considered, or just allowed to slip your mind . . . As I say, there's the military; obvious enough. Then there's the technical, or scientific—work being done by eggheads in the background to develop weapons, from vehicles to warheads and control systems—clear so far?"

Falke nodded, frowning to indicate concentration, and dropping into less formal idiom. "Yes, *Kaleu*—perfectly."

"Good . . . And, still in the scientific field, the development of clothing, equipment, food production and preservation; that sort of thing." Altmann's scrutiny remained steadily on the now slightly strained features before him, and he continued, "I'm sure you could put together a complete inventory if you put your mind to it, hm?"

Falke shifted uncomfortably on his perch. So he was to be handed a task like a schoolboy given lines for some trivial misdemeanour: list all the "front-line" activities—other than the military—that supported a modern mechanised war. Marks out of a hundred and leave stopped for not making the pass-mark. Kölm was going to make a meal of this, damn it . . . He caught his expression as it started altering to gloom and nodded again. "A little rusty here and there, *Kaleu*, but if I had enough time—"

"Quite. We'll take your grasp of it as read . . . But in case you've allowed it to slip your mind, let me remind you about a most important front line. Communications."

Falke's grunt expressed mixed relief and recollection. Communications. Meaning—?

"Communications, and, necessarily dependent on it, or them, what we call propaganda. A most important front line, in which, as I gather from your conversation with the receptive Kölm, you've been taking a close interest."

Looking in vain for indications of humour in the *Kaleu*'s face Falke decided it safer to keep any similar indication of his own under cover. This particular conversation could go either way, and it seemed politic to avoid anticipating its trend. His attentive frown assumed a hint of ferocity. "Propaganda, *Kaleu*?"

"We've heard broadcasts from Berlin and London about the action—if that's what it was—between capital units of the British and German navies. We've heard of a possible outcome, one from the British side,

66

one from ours. They differ, as you've noticed. Here in our boat, seeing nothing of the action, we can't even venture a guess at the truth of the matter. All we can do is to accept the fact of the abandonment of the planned interception and, for whatever his reason, Admiral Lütjens's decision to adopt other tactics. The British say they've sunk his ship, our people maintain that the admiral decided on a change of plan, not yet for general disclosure. These are the pieces of the picture as we have it, with no means of knowing which are true apart from trusting our own side—not so?"

"Yes, *Kaleu*."

"Yes . . . So my advice to you, *Maschinistensmaat*, is to avoid taking up a position of your own in this front line, especially one likely to mislead your own side for lack of known facts, and await further information. You'll be doing us all a favour and yourself a good turn by avoiding declaring views which, proving to be wrong in due course, will give your detractors an opportunity to question your reputation for—um—illuminating comment."

"Aye, *Kaleu*."

"And another thing—in case *my* view is of any interest: having already sunk the *Hood*—which seems to be the case—it would be reasonable to assume that *Bismarck*'s gunnery was good enough to keep her other pursuers off her tail, if not do them some further injury, and so no longer require the services of the u-boat reception committee—wouldn't you agree?"

Falke nodded soberly. Maybe the skipper had a point . . .

"And a final thought: if the Royal Navy has lost yet another heavy unit to the *Bismarck*'s gunnery the British certainly aren't going to make it headline news copy! For all we know, that's what's happened, and we'll hear sooner or later. Meanwhile, we get on with our own affairs, which are quite enough to keep us all fully-occupied until we get home."

Falke nodded again. He was beginning to feel a little out of his depth, or at least without any tangible means of support for offering a different view. He wished the skipper would run out of ideas, which suggested his, Falke's, continued expression of agreement as his best course. He shrank from the prospect of an indefinitely-prolonged lecture prompted by his actively querying any of the skipper's theories; instead, act dumb and keep it as brief as possible.

But it seemed he had mistaken the *Kaleu*'s purpose, and found himself sitting through an extended homily on the *Reich*'s case for war as embodied in the tenets of National Socialism, a subject not only Falke but also most of his contemporaries regarded with circumspect approval: political rhetoric, even delivered in the *Führer*'s emotive manner, was apt to pall by comparison with the emotive effect of events in the field, meaning the North Atlantic. On balance, as a politically-malleable class inclined to swim with the stream, they accepted the way of life open to them as wage-earning craftsmen, taking its benefactions and meannesses in their collective stride, adopting the prevailing political stance as the line of least resistance and therefore personal wellbeing, most of them young enough to be unburdened with family responsibilities. Altmann held them in high esteem, admiring, for all their recklessness, their mostly unfailing courage in returning time and again to the conflict in which, despite its position of offensive initiative, their chosen weapon was almost as vulnerable to summary destruction as its target; in certain instances more so. The u-boat was an instrument of attack; in self-defence its capacity was deplorably inadequate, depending heavily on the wits of its commander—and the self-discipline of his officers and men, which in turn hinged about the service discipline to which they were all subject and characteristically responsive, personified in the commander and his way of exerting it as the C-in-C's proxy: Dönitz's presence, regardless of distance, was tacitly acknowledged by all and approved by most.

Altmann felt the moment was opportune to make one or two points, with Falke a convenient cover; almost a kind of medium. He smiled to himself.

The man could stand a few more minutes of concentrated expatiation; at worst he would dismiss it as bull; at best he might add it to his stock of patriotic—Altmann paused. He'd been about to put it as "sentiment", but just recently he'd been brought to think of sentiment, in its affective interpretation, as suspect. Sentimentality was essentially a fake representation of truth—a simulacrum of something that in its genuine form demanded effort, sacrifice, care, courage. Where sentimentality allowed casual assumption of a moral stance for as long as convenient, the real thing faced its aspirant with a challenge that, carelessly handled, would produce pain, and not only for its proponent. Love, for example—for a woman, a cause, a country—could be simulated, even to the extent of triumph or defeat; but the outcome either way would be valueless for the very reason of its originating force; if the love were genuine, though—emotional and intellectual as distinct from sentimental—the outcome would be similarly valued, and enduring, for better or worse. Men were ruined for love as they were exalted by it, in either case realising an essential element of nobility—consoling in the first instance, enriching in the second. For sentimentality—for a sentimental simulacrum of love—they were proof against cataclysmic consequences, subject only to a pale, impotent artifice as devoid of the emotional and moral exaltation of the genuine article as of its attendant risks.

And so to the Third *Reich*; to the *Führer*, to the exalted precepts of National Socialism—and the collective sentiments of his men as exemplified in the person of *Maschinistensmaat* Falke. Who, he noticed with a mental start, was studying him curiously. He cleared his throat.

"Are you a Party member, Falke?"

Falke's curiosity evaporated and he sat up, almost involuntarily coming to attention. For a moment he struggled to form his reply, and finally settled for a shake of the head and a denial in which he tried to convey regret and firm decision together. No; he was not a party member; was not active in party politics, though for a while before joining the *Kriegsmarine* he had been a member of the Hitler Youth, without particular distinction. He liked the orderliness and the sense of service to the state, which had rewarded it with cruises aboard the ships operated by the Strength Through Joy organisation. In this he enjoyed a kindred affinity. Soldiers—ashore, afloat, in the air—served the state, whatever its political ethos. Falke understood that, and felt it was as it should be. He would be in his present situation no matter what shade of national political philosophy had brought it about—wouldn't he? He did not ponder the question further; he was a practical man—a sailor, and somewhat more: a u-boat man, which meant a front-line fighter for a resurgent Germany. It was enough.

Did he not think that National Socialism as set forth and practised by the Hitler government had returned her self-respect to a Germany that had been shamefully exploited and mistreated after the armistice of 1918?

Falke's eyebrows rose and his mouth turned down. Exploited and mistreated? Well, his understanding of such matters was limited, built mainly on what he could remember from a schoolroom in which he had occupied a desk in the back row and a frame of mind more attuned to comics and schoolboy fiction centred upon sport, which meant rowing—he had captained his high-school rowing club in Hamelin, with the Weser at its door—and a keen interest in motor-racing, and the technical ritual and conventions of internal combustion engines and flight. His first hope had been to fly as a fighter-pilot, but he had neither the aptitude nor the school qualifications required; from which he had turned to the navy, thence to the *U-Bootwaffe*, where, on the whole, he had found a certain satisfaction, if sometimes too much excitement of a kind that tended to imbue a feeling of frustration. One could not strike at the enemy from a u-boat's motor-room as from the cockpit of a Messerschmitt . . . He supposed the Party's approach had, on the whole, been to Germany's betterment, always assuming . . . He coughed and subsided.

"Always assuming what, Falke?"

Falke coughed again, coloured up then paled, and said determinedly, "Well . . . That we win the war, *Herr Kaleu.*"

"Do you doubt it?"

After a pause the petty officer said, "No—no, not really . . . But I think it will take longer than we thought at first."

"Inevitably!" Pausing, Altmann felt he had sounded too hearty, so added on a more sober note, "All wars in history have taken longer than at first expected. But in the end the true qualities of a pure racial strain will prevail. It produces a character with the moral and spiritual integrity vital to the sort of effort war demands of great soldiers—our belief in ourselves alone ensures almost invincible ability in battle. History bears it out! A racially-degenerate people is at a conclusive disadvantage, having two enemies: one opposing it on the field of battle and the other rotting it from within—I mean the natural enmities and discords that no amount of sentimentalising can eliminate: the frictions between groups and individuals of a racially impure people that invariably create rifts in what should be a united front against a common foe. We Germans—the Aryan race—are free of such potentially calamitous impurities—"

The words slipped to one side as Falke divided his attention between their general meaning and the features of the man addressing him. *Kapitanleutnant* Gunnar Altmann, Iron Cross First Class, one of the *U-Bootwaffe's* more scintillating stars and something of a veteran—a professional, having entered the service a few years before the war, as he, Falke, understood it. Which accounted for his being a few years older than most, around thirty at a guess. Reliable man, cool in action, accurate in judgment, shrewd in tactics—safe, in other words; more likely than most to get his boat through a patrol in one piece, *Maschinistensmaat* Falke with it. Or, as things were turning out, this patrol excepted, simply through a patrol. And so, to the younger men—Kölm, for example—something of a hero: Siegfried, but getting on a bit—thinning, longish blond hair and patchy beard, steady eyes beneath a clear brow, thin-lipped mouth, straight, short nose with expressive nostrils—they moved as a graphic indicator of his mood; the only obvious one. Like a horse's, reflected Falke. And at the moment they were open, immobile: mood tractable. Maybe. They gave the lie to the eyes, which seldom showed anything other than steady appraisal; cool, detached, concealing more than they revealed. And that scar on the cheek: knife? bottle? some accident? Popular rumour asserted a duelling wound—but that had gone out of fashion with the horse, surely? And it was probably unlawful these days . . . On the whole it was easier to respect than like the *Kaleu*—

"—married, Falke?" Falke started guiltily and Altmann repeated his question. No, came the hasty answer. Not really thinking about it yet—what with the war and so on it seemed better to wait—

"Marriage, and the family, are the generator-room of the nation, Falke!"

"I believe it, *Kaleu.*"

"Mm . . . I myself have two children, and a third on the way. It implies confidence in the German nation, Falke. Confidence in its prosperous, happy and just future with a respected place in the world, setting an example of morality and patriotism by which lesser races and nations will be able to gauge their own standards—such as the degenerate British and their decayed empire. In my family I find not only the love and satisfaction every pure-bred German man—and woman—should expect, and get, from a well-regulated life, but also a yardstick by which I can evaluate other marks of fulfilment. In my case the Iron Cross First Class, my commission in the *Reich*'s finest fighting service, the honour of this command, my oath of loyalty to the *Führer*, my record of sinkings . . ." Altmann cleared a sudden roughness in his throat. "All these things are the fulfilment of ambition, but they're meaningless without marriage and family life, for the sake of which they are all sought—which, in turn, means for the sake of the resurgent German nation. These things are interrelated, dependent on one another, but at the heart of the system is marriage and the family . . . Yes?"

"Yes, *Kaleu.*" Bemused, Falke blinked, bracing himself for a long session. It had not occurred to him to connect things in such a complicated pattern of cause and effect: enough to know where to go to make the most of time at base, or at home, between patrols; enough to enjoy the company of girls and friends and to know where to find and how to make them, shutting out of his calculations the prospect of a tomorrow that might never come. It seemed too much like tempting fate to associate his private life with such earth-shaking considerations as the destiny of the German nation. That, as far as he was concerned, was the *Führer*'s job; it was why he had voted for him—at least, partly why. The other part was the absence of realistic choice, a state of affairs he accepted in the light of its apparent irrelevance to the advancement of its interests to which the *Führer* never tired of asserting the German nation was entitled. Let him get on with it, and if the u-boat found gainful employment as a result, it was fine by Klaus Falke, motorman petty officer third-class. Fine, that is, for as long as the boat was commanded by a capable officer, which, being the case, made his present position of, as he thought, verbal whipping-boy not merely bearable but also something of a duty, to be performed like any other. Falke refocused his attention with a lift of his bearded chin and a click of mental heels.

"Marriage, and the responsibilities of a family, are the nearest a man can get to a state of perfection," said Altmann, not without a note of inquiry, the object of which he quickly shifted by asking, "How old are you, Falke?"

"Twenty-three, *Kaleu*—"

"Twenty-three," mused Altmann. "Young . . ."

"Quite young, *Kaleu*."

"But old enough to start thinking seriously about your extended duty to the nation—"

"Perhaps you're right, *Kaleu*." Meaning marriage, thought Falke. Well, it was at least a new angle of approach, but in present circumstances he felt happy enough fulfilling no more than the mechanics of such a duty in a less permanent fashion—when he got the chance, as might come about in a few days' time . . .

Altmann sniffed and brushed at a drop of condensation that fell onto his right knee. The granulated-cork coating of the inner surfaces of the pressure-hull was running with moisture, and mould accompanying the stink of bilge, diesel-oil- and exhaust-fumes, chlorine and stale cooking, not to mention the animal odour of unwashed bodies accentuated, if anything, by the universal use of Colibri toilet water, formed the increasingly miasmic fug characteristic of the u-boat after several weeks of mostly submerged running. It was also cold; a damp, penetrating, bone-chilling cold that led, sooner or later, to the u-boat's trademark complaint of rheumatism. Half of us go around like old men before the age of twenty-five, mused Altmann, and not for the first time congratulated himself on his apparent immunity to date. The effects varied from man to man; as with alcohol. He himself did not drink. He had not done so since first assuming command, a decision sustained by clipping it onto his prospectus of duties to the nation, though the chief and more important reason, as he soberly acknowledged, was the matter of self-preservation. The difference between a depth-charge hit and a clear escape could be as little as a nip too many at the crucial moment. If he was fated to go to hell in an iron coffin it would not be because he hadn't been able to think straight through the rising fumes or after-effects of *schnapps*. And he was inflexibly strict about drink on board: no excuses would be accepted for its private possession. Instant dismissal and, wherever possible, court-martial on a charge of hazarding the boat was the clearly-stated penalty. Which, Altmann reflected with satisfaction, seemed to have been avoided by all. His occasional snap inspections had made the point at even the dimmest level of understanding: they were unpopular, but met their intended purpose, which was to save certain susceptible but valuable souls from themselves, in the process retaining them for the good of the *Reich*. What drink was consumed on board came from the official bottle, kept under close arrest and allowed general freedom only at the commander's discretion.

"I am," he said flatly. "And in my own marriage I've found the happiness that is every German's birthright—but not without making the necessary effort! My advice to you is to waste as little of your life as possible in the aimless pursuit of trivial, potentially lethal, pleasures. Believe me, Falke, the years pass quickly enough, and the best girls are soon taken—you know that?"

Falke did not miss the glance the commander threw at the framed photograph of the handsome blonde he had obviously taken young—two children and another in the oven before she'd passed her twenties, assuming her to be younger than her husband, suggested as much. And if they all looked like her—well . . . Yes, he nodded; the best girls certainly did seem to go early on.

"And one final point, Falke—"

"Kaleu?"

"Avoid Frenchwomen. They're not only dangerous, they represent a potential dilution of the Aryan blood-line to which, unless I'm mistaken by appearances, you have a legitimate claim."

"Thank you, *Herr Kaleu.*"

"Keep it in mind. Our relationship with the French has a bearing on the outcome of the war and Germany's distinction as a nation. Remember your self-respect, the reputation of the service, and that war-risk isn't confined to the Atlantic battle-front . . ."

"So he didn't take your advice after all," said Kölm, and sucked his teeth.

"What advice? He seems to be managing well enough as far as I can see." Falke drew a mug of black liquid from the coffee-urn on the galley bulkhead, sipped, and pulled a face. "We had a discussion about front-line tactics, and agreed to wait for further information."

"Ah," replied Kölm sagaciously. "Front-line tactics . . . As in the Coq d'Or's back bar. And a discussion! About the channel crossing—?"

Falke grimaced again at the second sip of coffee, threw the remainder into the galley sink, and turned to pull a suit of overalls from his locker. Kölm stood aside as his critic and mentor made his way to the motor-room. The discussion had, of course, become common knowledge, and Kölm felt obliged to admit that Falke had played his part with acceptable aplomb. Altogether an interesting interlude.

Later, the *Funkmaat* handed Altmann a coded signal, and Schreiber, the second watch officer, worked at the decoding machine for fifteen minutes or so. Altmann read out the result during the evening meal. All the officers were present. They watched the commander's face in silence, drawing no conclusions from its customary tight-lipped expression, beyond noting a certain pinched look about the nostrils.

"Well, gentlemen . . ." He took a breath and paused, glancing from one to another. "From the C-in-C, I need hardly tell you. It confirms the *Atlantiksender*'s news." He pushed his plate aside and smoothed the flimsy out before him, then read the pencilled message.

"To all boats from Commander-in-Chief . . . Reference last signal etc etc . . . Regret to advise that capital unit Bismarck *sunk in action against British naval units at approximately 1000Z hours 27 May, position approx. 48deg. 20min N, 21deg 05minW. Admiral Lütjens not among110 survivors recovered by British surface units. Boats in area*

*keep lookout for survivors/bodies but with caution in vicinity of enemy
surface units. Do not attack same in area BE until further notice . . .*
Signed Dönitz, Rear-Admiral." He looked up and raised his eyebrows.
"I'll read it over the p.a. after the meal."

"Took him long enough to let us in on the secret," said Schreiber.
"Must have known it at the time—three days! Or did he think she'd
gone into hiding or something?"

"Poor rate of exchange." Rogge, the first watch officer, unusually
loquacious. "One first-class battle-wagon with its paint still wet for a
Great War relic. We'll have to do better than that."

"You could make a living from epitaphs, *Einswo.*" Schreiber affected
admiration. "You have a gift."

"For the obvious." Regardless of circumstances *Oberleutnant*
Herbert Benedict, the engineer officer, exuded gloom like a persistent
oil-leak. "Better hope you don't have to think one up for us, with these
batteries the way they are."

"What interests me," said Altmann thoughtfully, "is what's become
of *Prinz Eugen* . . ."

No-one answered. Schreiber caught the engineer's eye and shrugged,
turning down the corners of his mouth.

Shortly afterwards, studying the chart and the pencilled cross
marking the battleship's last action, it struck Altmann with a cold
thrill of recognition that the position was barely eighty miles from
the *Anne-Marie de Bretagne*'s grave; and possibly closer, given
the navigational approximations involved. It was an unwelcome
reminder, and it lodged in his mind like a splinter, intruding on
what little sleep he was able to snatch as the boat's progress
brought it closer to base and deeper within the range of enemy
surveillance. It also took her past the scene of battle, some one
hundred and fifty miles to the north-east of it at the closest point.
On the bridge during the brief periods spent on the surface in the
extended daylight hours of summer, surveying the surrounding
scene, a panorama of countless herds of white horses pacing
each other at the gallop beneath rarely-broken overcast and a
spume-blotched horizon lurching in the binoculars' lenses, he had
to make a conscious effort to stop himself looking for wreckage,
broken bodies, a rag doll . . .

Whatever had remained of *Bismarck* had had more than enough
time to disperse beyond recovery.

II

ARRIVAL at Lorient was a chastening business. The sweeper led them through the minefield into the estuary and past its grey stone fort with a cursory air perhaps assumed on ascertaining that only one pennant flew from the boat's improvised signal-halyard; which, thought Altmann, was an unwarranted token of glory he would rather have omitted from the proceedings. A single pennant fluttering cockily in the sunshine of the summer morning was a poor showing for a five-week patrol, never mind the tonnage figure it represented; poorer in its flying over a boat with a record of bountiful harvests. He seemed to detect a note of irony in the tune struck up by the band on the quay, and in the waves of the assembled onlookers and well-wishers. The whole performance was a sham, he reflected, standing at the salute; a waste of time and effort, and he would have to go through the usual responses, accepting the flowers, the handshakes, the embraces, as a returning warrior bearing news of victory.

Below at last, the boat secure alongside, he faced the flotilla commandant—Straubhals, *Fregattenkapitan*—of a similar age and a pleasant, relaxed manner, with a leg-wound that had landed him firmly ashore after a convoy action in which his boat had been damaged in collision with a merchantman. He had got it back to St Nazaire in a sinking condition after an epic eight-day run rounded off with an attack by a Sunderland fought off on the surface. They had scored a lucky hit on one of the aircraft's engines, but the commander, on the bridge, had stopped a bullet as the plane turned for home. The story was well-documented, in doctored form open to scrutiny in the base library. Altmann had read it. He listened to Straubhals's answer to a question with mixed feelings, comparing their respective situations, the shades of fortune in war, the ways it exacted its price.

"*Prinz Eugen*? Oh, she broke off the action on Lütjens's orders and got clean away—made it to Brest without a scratch, now waiting for the next move."

"Which will be?"

The commandant smiled, stirring his coffee. "A moot point . . . She's in good company with *Scharnhorst* and *Gneisenau*—receiving rude visits from the RAF every so often and, as I say, awaiting orders."

"Another heroic showdown with the Royal Navy?"

"Word has it that Raeder wants them back in Kiel, but the *Führer*'s idea is to base them in Norway. Beyond that, I haven't the faintest

76

inkling, but I think you can count on the *U-Bootwaffe*'s keeping the North Atlantic to itself for a while yet—making special allowance for the enemy, of course!"

Altmann watched in silence as Straubhals sipped his coffee. Neglecting his own he caught the other's eye and said, "Something's happening out there . . . The escorts seem to be better organised, better prepared, as if they have some new way of spotting us. And there are more of them—with cooperating aircraft. The organisation's impressive, and getting dangerous!"

The commandant nodded. "There's talk of carriers sailing with the convoys—converted merchantmen. Perhaps that explains it. And of course there are airfields in Iceland, which closes the air gap with the extended range of air cover from Newfoundland . . ." He smiled and slapped his leg. "Thanks to this, I'll have no opportunity to find out for myself." Altmann didn't miss a hint of bitterness in his tone, and wondered which way the commandant would have chosen if he'd been able. "However, Altmann—" valiantly, Straubhals drained his cup "—I've work to do!" He rose awkwardly to his feet, and paused in pulling on his coat to throw Altmann a quizzical glance. "Times are changing, it seems . . . I'm sorry your patrol's been such a disappointment; I'll see to it personally that those batteries are replaced, apart from the other work—including improved anti-aircraft equipment, eh?" He patted Altmann's shoulder and added, "Uncle Karl sends his regrets at not meeting you on arrival. He's pressed for time lately . . ." Blue eyes set in the beginnings of tired folds of skin searched Altmann's features. "He'll see you as usual tomorrow with your report—"

"And excuses?"

"I don't think so . . . Just the usual chat." Shrugging his coat straight and pulling on his cap the commandant paused again to study Altmann's face in silence. Altmann returned the scrutiny expressionlessly, sensing something not touched on, and waited. But Straubhals said nothing, instead heaved a breath, nodded, and, in a strange gesture of regard, or perhaps mere civility, raised a hand to his cap-peak before swinging round to pass through to the control-room and the exit ladder. Altmann watched him negotiate it rung by rung, the wounded leg following the other's lead. A rather more glamorous disability than rheumatism, he decided, and sighed, looking round the cluttered space. If glamorous was the word for it.

And there was mail, of course. Four letters from Ursula, all about the children and her condition, barely touching on the far more worrying matter of air-raids. Frankfurt had become a major target; even its suburbs, but it was not in her nature to complain, even less when it would mean adding to her husband's fears; so he read between the lines and determined to move them to somewhere safer, some place in the country, before it was too late—at which his thoughts stalled. He would get a few days' leave . . .

With the others was a letter with a service post-mark, censored: from Greischen, now *Scharnhorst*'s gunnery officer. He could not be specific about recent events, nor did he shed light on the rumoured plan for a break-out from Brest, which he could not mention by name or hint; instead he remarked on the boredom of life confined to harbour routine enlivened with periodic air attacks which, he emphasised, were in the nature of flies pestering a horse; at best they offered opportunity for gunnery training, at worst disturbed his sleep. Again, Altmann read between the lines. Brest was on the RAF's doorstep. A battle-cruiser in port was the proverbial barn door whichever way you looked at it. Gretchen would be doing precious little in the wife-charming line; better to pin hope for promotion on the RAF, short of another sortie against the convoys, where at least there was room to manoeuvre. But a dash for Kiel—? Was Raeder planning to take them out of Atlantic service altogether? Surely the *Bismarck* fiasco hadn't given him and the *Kriegsmarine* cold feet? Altmann pondered the effect of withdrawing heavy warships, however inactive, from an arena in which they represented, if nothing more, a threat the enemy couldn't dismiss from his calculations. Skulking—that was a word for it—in Kiel they would be as good as sunk without the Tommies having to do more than keep an occasional eye on them, while the convoys would breathe that much more freely. But if they were sent to bases in Norway . . . That sounded a much more useful stratagem, but another point of issue between the *Führer* and his naval commander-in-chief. It would have its effect on morale. Perhaps Gretchen would be tempted to consider the u-boat as a better bet for promotion than a laid-up battle-wagon. He would suggest it in his reply. It was an amusing prospect—the dapper Gretchen among the great unwashed, cultivating indifference to filth, boozing, screwing, guzzling, maudlin renderings of the *Horst Wessel*. Or, more likely, *The U-Boat Song*, called by some *The England Song*. Altmann's smile wasn't wholly amused; you found promotion among the depth-charges, not in the uproarious, anaesthetic gatherings at the Majestic that tended to upset the locals. He took out a writing-pad and his fountain-pen, which had flooded again. He must remember to empty it before going on patrol.

The meeting with Dönitz in his citadel, Kerneval, added to a sense of impending cataclasm that until then he'd felt to be irrational. Facing the panel of senior officers in the forceful presence of Uncle Karl himself was always something of an ordeal that custom made no easier; if anything more nerve-racking on each successive occasion. His spoken statements were checked against his written report and patrol diary as he went along, charts laid out on the polished refectory table under the scrutiny of high-ranking eyes—and, on this occasion, eyes which lacked the warmth he'd enjoyed after previous patrols. Seven hundred tons was a ludicrously small figure; it lent the meeting an air of the ridiculous, a caricature of solemn ritual in which all present appeared overdressed, absurdly dignified, comic in grave discussion of such a trifle. And they were aware of the fact, thought Altmann; and not pleased.

As a result, after expressing, terse and unsmiling, their satisfaction with the report, if not the patrol's return on investment, they wound up the meeting in record time, leaving Altmann alone with a pensive Dönitz. Standing self-consciously a few paces from the rear-admiral, he surveyed the view through the windows of the grand salon: beyond the estuary the Atlantic, apparently innocent in its tranquillity, deceitful in what it concealed, a glittering expanse silver-edged against the pale sky; the buoyed channel leading into the river to pass beneath the fort and upstream to the harbour and the new concrete u-boat pens. They rose, an improbable massif, above the bank and the open jetties at which the boats lay exposed to attack, like anxious ducklings clustered about the mother. Beyond, Europe, as the physical entity of the Third *Reich*, stretched south, east and north to the borders with Spain and Italy through Greece to touch upon Turkey and the Black Sea, thence round in a sweep through Bessarabia and the Ukraine to the Gulf of Finland and across the Baltic to Denmark and Norway—Hitler's Thousand-Year *Reich*, still expanding. Expanding, thought Altmann, but confronted, impudently, by what Churchill had last summer bombastically called Great Britain's thousand-year Empire and Commonwealth. They couldn't resist it, these leading figures, as they puffed and postured: grandiose imagery snatched from the air for the purpose of the moment, which was to fuel the fires of mass enthusiasm—hysteria, in some eyes—toward the ends that justified the means. Like adding a seven-hundred-ton schooner to the juggernaut's mass. And killing all on board, as a calculated tactic. Well, it *had* been calculated, not an expression of hot-headed zeal; it had its justification, if it came to it. He hadn't touched on the matter in his report, and no-one had inquired. Why should they? It was enough to have given the pertinent details of the interview with the bosun, Lebrun. The assumption was that he had followed orders and left the survivors—the ship's crew—to their fate. It had not occurred to anyone to ask about passengers in connection with such a vessel.

Altmann's train of thought superimposed a sequence of images on the view through the windows but baulked at the point where he had turned back with the MG34s at readiness. He had no need to contend with it in his waking hours: it came unhindered in sleep, trapping him in its remorseless fascination through to the last flicker of reflection from the tumbling seas as the searchlight was cut and his ears rang on with the echoes of the machine-guns' racket. The first watch-officer—Rogge, the fastidious, reserved ex-destroyer man, flawed in some enigmatic respect impossible to discern except by intuition, but never enough to be a point of dissatisfaction, retching over the dodger into the wind, turning back, wiping his mouth with the back of a hand, to cast a glance at Altmann that glinted in the darkness with—what?—anger? fear? horror? But never a word. Like his commander, Rogge believed in the cause; he obeyed orders. It was the only way—

"A disappointing patrol for you, Altmann."

Dönitz had been standing with his back to the room, hands clasped behind him, a faintly Napoleonic figure but more upright, leaner, taut. Now, echoing Straubhals's words, he turned to face the younger officer, fixing a hard gaze on him that mingled shrewdness with sympathy. It was generally acknowledged that Uncle Karl looked upon his u-boat men with a protective concern that nevertheless avoided indulgence: he expected nothing but their best, would—and had—excised anything less. And he was known as a sound judge of that quality: excuses were worse than useless. Now he accompanied his words with a slight narrowing of the hard eyes and a deepening of the furrows at the sides of the mouth. Altmann nodded and agreed without enlarging, and Dönitz went on, "You know we must sink more ships . . . The u-boat is the war-decisive weapon, but only if used to maximum effect. We don't wish to waste our sword cutting cake, do we?" A flicker of a smile touched the tight lips. "It's not often that a boat returns with her full complement of torpedoes—especially a boat with such a record!"

He held up a hand as Altmann was about to answer, and continued, "But I appreciate the conditions—between that diversion at Admiral Lutjens's request, and your boat's batteries on top of the convoys' tactics . . . I wonder sometimes—" Dönitz sighed and shook his head, mouth turned down. "If I hadn't been assured of its impossibility by *B-Dienst* I'd suspect a breach of our codes." He shrugged. "My fear is that a boat might be captured, or boarded before sinking, and the code equipment—Enigma especially—fall into the enemy's hands. We wouldn't know of it, short of the near-impossibility of observation by someone nearby . . . It's the biggest problem we face, Altmann—knowing nothing of the circumstances of a boat's end. I mean, it's even possible that a boat taken in one piece would be used against us, and we'd never know it!" He sniffed, and smiled briefly at Altmann, who felt the admiral's sense of helplessness: he could see no way of guarding against such an eventuality, or of detecting it. But he felt that for all the enemy's seemingly improved evasive tactics—not by any means a consistent norm—it came of experience and the ability to act on it. The convoy escorts were simply getting better at their job: there was such a thing as a sixth sense, and it took time to develop. Some boat-commanders had it, but not, he felt, himself. Yet.

The admiral was continuing. "But I suppose . . . If that were to happen logic argues that you'd never find a convoy at all. I've no choice, you see—I must communicate with the operational boats, or you'd work blind. The war can't be won like that!"

Altmann nodded sober agreement, and with an impulsive gesture Dönitz indicated a chair as he himself crossed to another to sit back, turning his gaze up to the ornate bas-reliefs of the ceiling. After a short silence he said, "That schooner—" and switched it back to his subordinate.

"Yes, *Herr Admiral*—?" Altmann felt a tightening of his guts. He might have known there would be no avoiding the whole truth; perhaps the officers who had scrutinised his report had been briefed, had left the matter for the more effective elucidation of a private audience with the C-in-C.

"You were correct to avoid the use of a torpedo despite my instructions—on such a small target."

"Thank you, *Herr Admiral*."

"Yes . . . But your expenditure of ammunition was—ah—liberal, was it not?—especially the machine-gun supply."

Altmann cleared a dry throat. "I was afraid she was a decoy of some kind—perhaps armed. Sailing without lights . . ." He coughed again and Dönitz nodded towards the water carafe on the table. Altmann filled a glass, returning to his seat while the other man sat in silence, watching with an air of mild expectancy. There was no suggestion of censure. Altmann was aware of only professional, possibly usefully critical, concern, but he felt he would have to tread with care, allow the admiral to point to the expected conclusion—which was? He sipped the water cautiously. Dönitz looked on, fingers steepled, elbows on the arms of his chair, lips pursed speculatively.

Continuing, Altmann pointed to the possibility of concealed guns and the vulnerability of his boat, the need to keep the target's deck swept by machine-gun fire to protect his own gun-crew while in action. Such general fire used up ammunition faster than aimed, hence the figures. And he had succeeded with no loss of any kind to his command. Beyond that, he had provided the boats with a few supplies and cleared the area as quickly as possible—after questioning the schooner's bosun.

"The man Lebrun?"

"The man Lebrun, *Herr Admiral.*"

"I see. And you say nine of the crew survived—? "

"That's correct—seven hands, sailmaker and bosun."

"No officers—or the captain—the master?"

"Apparently not, *Herr Admiral.*"

As Altmann waited, Dönitz rose and crossed to the windows to stand again contemplating the scene, hands at his back. Then he turned, presenting only a silhouette. "When I received your signal, Altmann, I immediately ordered an investigation into the ship's movements at the port you say she'd sailed from—St Malo. The shipping office there supplied all details, including the crew list for a coastal voyage to Vigo, which was where she should have been bound when she crossed your path. Your figures match the ship's articles'—fifteen men altogether including the master, Captain Calibourdin, who was also the owner."

"Calibourdin—yes, *Herr Admiral.*"

"But, I regret to say, there was no-one by the name of Lebrun on the list."

Altmann grunted in spite of himself. "No, *Herr Admiral?*"

"No. The bosun's name was something like—ah—Bernot—"

Altmann saw again the bearded features creased in brief laughter in reply to his questions; surprise at first, then, perhaps, genuine amusement at the ease with which the deception had been carried off. And mockery: the expectation would have been a more ruthless approach, less readiness to accept an unforced statement. But Lebrun—plausible enough in the circumstances; a simple name, common and fitting . . .

"—but there was also another person. Supernumerary." Dönitz stepped back round the table and resumed his seat, smiling thinly. "Madame Calibourdin. Apparently her husband's business partner. In normal circumstances it seems she managed the schooner's affairs from a registered address in Brest. Closed shortly before the schooner's final departure."

"So who was Lebrun, I wonder?"

Dönitz sighed. "Possibly Calibourdin . . . But it's not important. The boats haven't been reported by any German vessel, and no word has been received from the Allies. In view of the weather at the time I imagine they were lost—all the survivors."

"That would be perfectly possible, *Herr Admiral*."

"However many there were, hm?"

Altmann looked sharply at the other, but met only a bland, rather wistful, smile and a gleam in the eye that could have meant anything. Yes, he said. However many.

The two men sat regarding each other in silence for some time. Altmann was aware of small sounds, near and distant—the sea breeze whispering at the windows, a vine-leaf tapping on a pane; somewhere a dog barking; a fussy tooting on a steam-whistle a long way off; the ticking of the clock on the mantelpiece above the elegant fireplace, cold at this time of year. It was an immensely peaceful room. War intruded like a mountebank, usurping the rights of civilised intercourse. They should be discussing—what?—the year's vintage, perhaps; share prices; travel to far-off lands; a funeral; recent literature; a Paris show; families. Instead they were—perhaps—sharing unspoken a piece of knowledge that, admitted, would blare and blunder round the room like a wild ass, laying waste all the apparatus of humanity, overturning the laboured structure of manners, in the space of a few words returning to its dark beginnings every token of advancement from the brute. Admission would be an outrage. To attempt its elicitation would be folly. And, Altmann felt, Dönitz knew it, and would not make the attempt. But he determined to guard his responses none the less, and sat on, awaiting the next move.

At length Dönitz said, "In war, Altmann, it's necessary to be ruthless—necessary to carry the fight to the enemy, deprive him of the room to manoeuvre, overwhelm him with every means at your disposal, give no ground, no quarter, and to keep on the attack until the objective has been gained . . . Would you agree?"

"Certainly, *Herr Admiral*!"

"Towards the enemy there's no place for peacetime values—compassion, love, mercy, charity. None for fair play, none for chivalry. You must always have in mind the truth, which is that he won't hesitate to take advantage of any sign or act of weakness, and that any kind of civil behaviour or sentiment will offer him that advantage—and be your undoing!"

Altmann nodded; there seemed no worthwhile response to such a concise summation, and as Dönitz spoke his tension eased. He felt the C-in-C's words were a tacit endorsement of his action. He was not to be called to account for it, even assuming he was correct in his suspicion that Dönitz's information had included far more than he had cited. They had been Jews, after all. There was no need to take things any further. As for the crew—well, it was unfortunate, but the ship had been sailing without lights, and her master knew the risk he was taking—

"Of course you're conversant with my orders about sinking unlit vessels without warning, and it seems you carried out your duty accordingly, Altmann. It's also quite certain that the schooner was making for somewhere other than the place she'd cleared port for, and Boston is as good as any. Why not a British port will ever remain a mystery, however . . . Perhaps she had contraband of some kind that would have meant trouble with the British authorities. You inquired into her cargo, of course?"

Nodding again, Altmann said, "She was in ballast, but I asked about her usual cargoes—in peacetime fish for half the year and such things as bricks and coal during the other half; in war, supplies as required. I took Lebrun—or Calibourdin—at his word, mainly to avoid wasting time. And there was no question of risking my boat by delaying for a search before attacking."

"Quite . . . You're familiar with my standing order number one five four, are you not?—Wait!" Dönitz got to his feet and crossed to the table and a case of papers his secretary had brought to the meeting. "I have a copy . . ."

Altmann watched expectantly. Number one five four. Well, he must have seen it, but with only a number his memory had a great wad to choose from. Some hint of contents would trigger the thing . . .

Dönitz turned with a buff manila folder and regarded Altmann reflectively for a moment. "Of course you should be able to quote it—and I! But let's not be pedantic—" he flipped through the folder's contents, settled on a page "—here we are. Allow me to refresh your memory—and mine, eh?" He cleared his throat. "Dated November nineteen-thirty-nine . . . It effectively displaces the Prize Law rules, which for u-boats are totally impracticable, as you know. Now—I'll read only the part relevant to our present interest . . . *Rescue no-one and take no-one with you. Have no care for the ships' boats. Weather conditions and the proximity of land are of no account. Care only for your own boat and strive to achieve the next success as soon as possible! We must be hard in this war. The enemy started the war in order to destroy us, therefore nothing else matters.*" He paused, cleared his throat again, and concluded, "And that, *Kapitanleutnant* Altmann, is about all you need to be able to carry out a successful attack—as you've proved!"

Watching the admiral Altmann smiled and thanked him, noting his change of mood as the conversation had shifted ground from the mechanics of the patrol through the attack on the schooner and into territory bordering on idealism—with which he agreed wholeheartedly, relieved that he appeared to have acted in a way that had at least allowed his superiors to retain a moral standpoint—if that's what concerned them, for the situation's morality was straightforward enough, defined by their actions within the tenets of National Socialism, embodied as they were in the person of the *Führer*. And it was well-known that Uncle Karl was among Hitler's most trusted advisers; even before Raeder, so word had it. Covertly, Altmann noted the admiral's altered mien: over the last hour or so it had progressed from a solemn reserve to a kind of grand exultation, signalled by the reading of standing order number one five four, as of a roll of drums, which avoided bathos by omitting the clash of cymbals at the climax. One thing about Dönitz as a commanding officer, thought Altmann—he was efficient, zealous, *au fait* with every detail of his department's affairs, demanding and autocratic; but, even at times when he exercised the other traits, he was essentially human: he loved his men, and would do all in his power including enthusing them with his own zeal to give the best parts of their characters every chance to contribute to the common aim. He felt certain, now, that Dönitz knew of the schooner's circumstances, but would never divulge his thoughts unless something obliged him to do so—like, for example, some kind of allied notification of discovery. And that, as far as he could see, was unlikely in the extreme: if any evidence of the action had come to light the entire world would have heard of it by now; that area of ocean had been fine-combed in the search for *Bismarck*'s survivors. But nothing. It was more of a relief than Altmann cared to admit.

For the rest of the interview Dönitz inquired about Altmann's family and gave him—in fact ordered him to take—a week's leave. "You must attend to their wellbeing, Altmann—and don't hesitate to get help from the Service if you need it. We aren't mere employees, after all! Germany needs her people, and values what they have to give, in return offering succour wherever possible. You can't command a u-boat at full efficiency if you're worried about your loved ones."

But there was something else, and after the geniality of informal matters, before bringing the proceedings to an end, Dönitz abruptly assumed a solemn air and seemed, for a moment, disconcerted, to Altmann's mild mystification—soon dispelled, and by a gesture that went further to show the C-in-C as a man of total commitment to his responsibilities and sensibilities. In a pause, he studied Altmann's features, while Altmann followed the gaze, wondering, before Dönitz turned abruptly to the case of papers to produce an envelope that Altmann instantly recognised, and a chill ran down his spine into his guts, where it hung, dreading.

"I learned of your friendship with another of my brave commanders, Altmann—through the flotilla commandant at St Nazaire, who sent me this a short while ago . . . As you see, you were the sender—" He extended the envelope, and Altmann took it with a glance at the name. The chill intensified, and he nodded, slipping the letter into a pocket. "He was a good one, Altmann—one of the best I had. I grieve for him and his brave men, as I do for Prien, Schepke . . . Men like them are scarce, and precious, and Germany cannot afford their loss in any respect. We've both lost a friend, and Germany a good and faithful servant." The admiral's eyes were bright, and fixed steadily on Altmann's. He nodded, tight-lipped, ending, "He'll be remembered."

"Where did it happen, *Herr Admiral?*"

"He was on his way to Genoa . . . We have an agent in Gibraltar. He notified Headquarters, giving full details. But we were also advised by the British. A destroyer support-group on its way out from Gibraltar to meet a Freetown convoy picked him up as he was entering the Straits from the Atlantic. Pure chance. There were five survivors. Three are now prisoners of war . . . Against such odds he died as a soldier should."

"Yes." Rising, Altmann turned to the view through the windows. A tug was passing below the fort at Port Louis, towing a barge. Edging towards the west, the sun was laying gold paving on the sea in a broad path touching the low shape of Île de Groix. A peaceful scene. But there were boats out there as he watched. Perhaps at this moment diving deep to escape the asdic or the depth-charges . . . *The Depth-Charge Dodge—Pure improvisation, Maggot! Pick it up as you go along* . . . Well. Hans had missed step, and that was it. The letter was addressed to *Korvettenkapitan* Liebeherr, mainly congratulating him on his promotion, and his recent Knight's Cross, down there with him. Medals weren't talismen, yet they led their aspirants into situations where more was needed than mere skill. And Hans's hadn't been enough.

"We must be hard, Altmann. Harder than the enemy. There'll be a great deal more of this sort of thing before the *Reich* prevails."

"I believe you're right, *Herr Admiral*. Thank you for telling me—and the letter . . . His family—"

"All in hand. They were properly informed. A memorial service was attended by his flotilla commandant—and myself."

"Thank you."

Leaving, Altmann shook hands with the admiral, whose parting words were to give his wife his respects and wishes for her happiness and safety. He caught a train that evening. While he was at home Germany invaded Russia. The goal was Moscow—before the winter. Altmann reflected on, among other things, the earlier such attempt, by another colossus risen from the ranks; and its outcome.

III

ALTMANN grunted his satisfaction, waved the periscope back into its housing and gave the order to surface, buttoning his leather coat as he waited. The conditions couldn't have been better, and this time the convoy hadn't vanished before he'd found it, called in by C-in-C on receipt of a sighting report from another of the seven boats—as Altmann had counted by their signals—now manoeuvring for position around the three ranks of merchantmen. It was a slow convoy—a painful six knots—so, weather permitting, could easily be shadowed for as long as necessary, though it was a mistake to allow time to pass for mere convenience. The escorts were vigilant, and the more time a boat spent on the surface—as when shadowing a convoy, even as slow as six knots—the greater the chance of discovery and all that came with it. Which, these days, meant a foretaste of annihilation. As developed by the enemy for use at sea, radar was exhibiting every sign of becoming decisive in what Dönitz called the "tonnage battle". If the boats couldn't sink merchant bottoms at a greater rate than the enemy was bringing them into service—most ominously from American yards, practically beyond reach of any means of disruption apart from sabotage, which lay in the realm of extreme hypothesis—then the war could not be won in the North Atlantic, which meant, quite simply, not won, since the North Atlantic represented the single most vital artery supplying the Allies' growing battle-worthiness against Hitler's Fortress Europe. And Dönitz was still short of the three hundred operational boats he had specified as the bare minimum to achieve supremacy.

But there was more to it than that, reflected Altmann. Mere numerical advantage wasn't of itself the key: much could be done with one efficient crew that might not be with two lacking the necessary qualities—which were more than mere skill in attack. Determination—stubbornness, as Uncle Karl repeatedly called it—was essential in the face of constant frustration, constant alarm, constant hazard, from an enemy that combined the developing adroitness of the escorts with the sea's practised vindictiveness. Between them they presented the u-boat with daunting odds that could all too easily convince a commander of his miscalculation as a reason to delay attack; to break it off altogether, even, in favour of some unforeseeable improvement in circumstances—as Dönitz had noted with emphasis in his standing orders. The argument depended on the premise that a determined commander lacking some element of skill could succeed where a skilled man lacking determination would fail. There were so many variables in this business that reducing it to a mere balancing of numbers struck Altmann as simplistic. The whole thing was a nebulous conception revolving about a matter of chance, and the u-boat as an attack weapon was beginning to suffer seriously from an imbalance of chance in its transposition of rôle from attack to defence at the instant of contact with a convoy: though a sinker of ships, in the face of revolutionary advances in the convoy's means of defence—as in its possession of short-wave radar—she carried out her attack herself in a state of defence, the most significant aspect of which was passive. Torpedoes apart, her inadequate armament left only the tactics available to her as a submerged fugitive. It was a nice paradox. And uncomfortable.

And there was another factor, by stretching a point falling into the category of luck as far as the boat was concerned but of sheer carelessness—incompetence—in its origins. This patrol had begun as a sortie against a major convoy mustering-point, the harbour at Halifax. The orders were reminiscent of Prien's at Scapa Flow: enter the harbour and take out as many of the assembled ships as possible, preferably also making good an escape and returning to base. The normal sensation of excited trepidation that would metamorphose into the nervous calm of imminent action was heightened by the prospect of an operation amounting to the deliberate springing of a trap that could close within seconds of discovery—which, at the latest, would be at the moment of the first torpedo strike, given a few moments of initial confusion. It was those few moments that would offer the only chance of escape. Earlier discovery would offer none.

Altmann had turned all this over in his mind from the time they had dived to cross the Bay undetected. But for only a few hours. On settling to the course terminating in the approaches to Halifax he had called for the chart of the harbour only to discover, incredulously, that the folio received from the flotilla navigator's office at Lorient lacked the small-scale chart covering the offshore waters of Nova Scotia and, more importantly, the large-scale chart and plans of the harbour itself and its approaches. Without them the operation was not merely more hazardous, but impossible. There was not even anyone on board with experience of the area. It had taken Altmann some time to regain his normal equanimity after an initial reaction of explosive frustration: in a mood of cold irritation he had castigated *Obersteuermann* Lothar Freigang, but with a sense of nugacity: no reprimand could conjure the missing charts out of thin air.

"Quite clearly, Freigang, you didn't check the folio on receipt—?"

The navigator stood stiffly before the commander in the control-room and swallowed on a dry throat. "That is correct, *Herr Kaleu*—"

"Why not?—you signed for it! Is it your habit to sign for things without making sure they're in order—or actually in existence?"

Freigang coughed for time. Altmann's cold stare didn't waver. "No, *Herr Kaleu*, but in this case it was for something from the flotilla navigator—I didn't expect a mistake like forgetting to put charts in a folio, especially charts for the actual—"

"Some advice for you, Freigang—"

"Yes, *Herr Kaleu*?"

"When it comes to your own skin, as is the case in anything and everything to do with this boat's activities, never—*never*—leave anything in the sphere of your responsibility to chance or, worse, to assumption, however justified you might feel in doing so. In other words, trust nothing and no-one but your own judgment based on personal inspection and confirmation. If you can't affirm it personally, you're obliged to accept it on the available evidence, however scanty; but to the extent of your personal, first-hand attendance to any matter for which you're responsible, that's what you owe it to your shipmates—and yourself—to do unless prevented. Is that clear?"

Well, thought Freigang—as clear as any of the *Kaleu*'s homilies; and at least this isn't the prelude to an official correction—by the *Kaleu*'s own definition he was himself open to criticism, and must know it. Mentally, he shrugged: it was part of the system for the senior man to relieve himself of some of the worry, if not the weight, of responsibility by dumping it on the other. There was no escaping the fact that the *Kaleu* had accepted his, Freigang's, word without following his own advice. Relieved by his line of reasoning, Freigang breathed more easily. "Yes, *Herr Kaleu*."

"At least we have charts of the North Atlantic and coasts of Greenland and Iceland apart from the European seaboard—or so I take it?"

"Yes, *Herr Kaleu*. All the others on the list."

"Which, of course, you've personally checked."

"I have, *Herr Kaleu*."

Altmann grunted. "And as far south as—?"

Freigang hesitated before answering. The *Kaleu* knew damn' well how far south the folio extended. Well, it was his privilege to test his subordinates for the hell of it; it was obviously his, Freigang's, duty to play along with the little charade. "To the Cape Verdes, *Kaleu*, and west to the Azores. The missing charts would have extended the westward coverage, of course."

Later, after an exchange of signals with the other boat on the operation with him, Georg Schewe's U-105, Altmann called a mystified Freigang back to tell him that Schewe's navigator had discovered the absence of the same charts. The fault clearly lay with flotilla command. "Even so, what I said stands, Freigang—apply it to everything you're responsible for. And think—if you'd checked the charts on receipt you'd have saved two boats plus flotilla command this embarrassment."

"Yes, *Kaleu*—I see that." And I see that the skippers concerned will have to explain their own failure to check: flotilla command will shit on them as C-in-C will by now have shat on it, thought Freigang. It was a small recompense for his unofficial telling-off, there being no lower-ranking colleague on whom he could drop the ordure in turn.

Waiting beneath the bridge-hatch Altmann reflected on the episode, irritated at his own failure in the matter, gratified at the chance outcome of a convoy within reach which, it seemed, offered the prospect of remission. If he weren't forced under before getting rid of all his eels here was an opportunity to turn failure into, perhaps, even greater success, in terms of tonnage, than would have been possible at Halifax. As for getting away with it, he could see little advantage in either case: the likelihood of being caught by the harbour defences was probably equal to that of being depth-charged to Valhalla by the convoy escorts, and on balance he preferred, as an escape-route, the unobstructed depth and breadth of mid-ocean to the coastal reefs and shoals of Nova Scotia. There would be something wretched about being trapped and pounded to scrap among the rocks like a nut on an anvil. Death on the high seas seemed a more worthy *exeunt* for the men who held the front line for the *Führer*. If they had to—

A cry from the control-room told him the boat was surfacing, confirmed by the sudden onset, the familiar discomfort, of its response to quartering seas, the heaving roll as each wave came in from astern and passed along the hull while crossing from side to side. He wrenched the lock-wheel round, welcomed to the open air by an icy deluge as he scrambled up the ladder followed by the watch-officer—Rogge—and the lookouts. Glancing round, dashing the water from his face, he took deliberate deep breaths of the tangy breeze. It fizzed in his lungs like champagne after the fetid stagnation of the boat's interior; seemed to lift him out of a swamp of mental and physical torpor onto a transforming height of sharpened vision, hearing, awareness: the very blood in his veins raced, invigorated, charged with a kind of effervescence. Breathing out in a grateful gasp that was part-sigh, he levelled his binoculars at a dark shape fine to starboard; fourth ship from the right in the rear line, it looked like. Tanker. He swung his field of view to the left. And another, two points to port. And farther left a less distinct shape. They usually stationed the tankers in mid-line, for the illusion of protection it offered. Farther to the right, next after the tanker, another shadow, low in the water like the tankers but, barely distinguishable, with massive bridged samson-posts where tankers had only token masts: bulker. Iron ore from somewhere on the St Lawrence, guessed Altmann. She'd go down like a stone, unlike the tankers, which usually died hard and slowly—and expensively, more often than not needing a quietus. But that had been in the Happy Time, when escorts were slow and insufficient and still working out the tactics of their trade. Now, one torpedo for each target was about as much as could be managed before having to hit the cellar with an escort barking like a hound at the door and others closing in.

Looking round, he saw no other shadows—no escorts just here, at just this moment, anyway. Only this rear rank of merchantmen, hapless as coconuts on stands in a fairground. The other two shapes beyond the bulker, though indistinct, resembled ordinary general dry-cargo carriers. Tonnages?—tankers around twelve thousand deadweight apiece, the bulker a little less, perhaps ten. The others?—hard to say, but likely to be anything between four and eight thousand gross. A worthwhile bag for a first salvo from the bow tubes—the bulker, two tankers and a fourth to the left, perhaps general cargo. After that—well, it would depend. Move up through the convoy if possible and see what the next line offered, if the escorts hadn't gate-crashed the party by then.

"Attack glasses and plot engaged, *Kaleu.*" Rogge at his side, his expression undiscernible in the gloom.

Altmann nodded and crossed to the big binoculars on their special mounting, ordering the engines to half-speed. And to Rogge: "We don't want to run them down when we've got a full bag of eels to play with, do we?"

"No, *Kaleu*. That would be wasteful."

Altmann glanced sharply at him. A joke? Perhaps not. Rogge took the war seriously, as was right and proper. Perhaps a little too seriously, though; setbacks could have a bad effect on such men, and setbacks were becoming more frequent on all fronts in recent months. The missing charts had thrown the officer into tooth-sucking despondency for hours after the discovery. Altmann wondered about his strength of nerve, his—*moral fibre*, as it was called; what it would take to crack him. He hoped he'd never find out. One way to make sure—in due time—would be to recommend him for command, but it would be a qualified recommendation: all right—dishonest. And he couldn't—didn't wish to—report adversely on the man, who was a conscientious officer, limitations notwithstanding. He'd have to give it some thought. Meanwhile . . .

Rogge stepped back to say, formally, "Permission to take up attack station?" His was in the conning-tower at the attack computer with its operator, the navigator, in contact with the second officer at the torpedo-control panel below. Altmann would take charge at the binoculars, selecting the targets, giving the executive firing order. He nodded at Rogge. "Carry on, *Einswo*. I'll start with one each for the tankers and the bulker, and whatever-she-is second to port there. Then through the gap and see what we've got in the next line as we reload."

Alone with the lookouts, Altmann trained the binoculars on the bulker. A small focus adjustment, pause to take in the significance of the moment, and give the order—calm, clear, decisive. A slight lurch of the deck underfoot, and that was it. No other indication of a lethal stroke reaching into the night. Altmann watched for a moment then bent to the binoculars again. Now the second ship to port. A few seconds to steady the image, count to five . . . "Fire two!" Again the slight lurch, and he stood erect, watching. From Rogge: "Torpedo running!" He had four eels in the bow tubes. Magnetic firing-pistols, which had given so much trouble at the start of the war, but were now, according to HQ, reliable. Well, at any moment he would know. Rogge would tell him when the moment of impact had arrived—and passed, if the eel was a dud.

Back now to the tanker to starboard; count to five, and another fish running. Any second now the first shot would register . . . Now the tanker to port. Like her companion she was deep-laden, sea-swept from end to end, easy to pick out of the darkness by the flame-like flicker of the breaking wash and the foaming water cascading from her tank-deck; more like a sea-girt rock than a ship.

"Fire four!"

"Torpedo running . . . First strike about now, *Kaleu*—"

As he straightened and turned his eyes back to starboard, towards the bulker, the first hit crowded hard upon Rogge's words, a muffled thud and a luminous disturbance in the water alongside. The torpedo had detonated under the keel. As Altmann noted the success with the usual flutter in the guts and involuntary clamping of the jaw a second explosion, more spectacular with a plume of orange-cored foam and debris alongside just forward of the bridge superstructure signalled a strike on the second ship to port. Two out of four so far. Excellent!

Then the third, hitting aft in a puff-ball of dirty flame and black smoke; but the fourth failed. Altmann cursed the offending torpedo and the system that sent boats to sea with gimcrack weaponry the effect of which on crew morale was clearly unappreciated by those responsible. For every torpedo that failed the element of corrosive cynicism among u-boat crews was further emboldened, further moved to open expression, and he was angered and dismayed by it. Uncle Karl's tonnage war apart, victory was not to the sceptic, the scoffer, the disheartened. And certainly not to the possessor of inert torpedoes. It struck him with a sense of the ironic, lately becoming uncomfortably prevalent, that the patient ingenuity behind the invention of the attack computer, by which the torpedo could be set to intercept the target on any bearing up to ninety degrees to either side, was totally negated by the defective design of a simple firing device. In some respects, he reflected, the early u-boats with their contact-detonating torpedoes that had to be aimed at the target had been a more effective—more "war-decisive"—weapon than the collection of inadequately-tested technological sophistication he had at his disposal. Even aiming these torpedoes with minimum deflection would be a wasted effort. The worst the enemy could expect from them was to laugh himself sick as they passed beneath his feet and whirred off towards the horizon or bounced off the target's hull to spiral to the bottom like so much scrap iron. Rumour had it that even some new-fangled acoustic torpedo had failed its testing stage after one had turned back and hit its own boat—without exploding, being a practice piece, though it would have been entirely in keeping if it had actually detonated. Altmann snorted bitterly. His boat played the sea-wolf, but a sea-wolf with rotten teeth, and he grinned at his simile, and at the contrast with the emblem painted on the conning-tower. His sense of its absurdity in the circumstances swept away the blackness in his mind, but the despondency remained. The war still had to be fought, and after all if three of every four torpedoes worked, it was just about a viable proposition. If.

A bloom of red and yellow far to the convoy's left. Another boat in action. That's better. It felt less lonely with hard evidence of another's presence. Of course actually sighting each other was almost unheard-of; they worked in loose cooperation, gathering at the signal from C-in-C or any boat that made first contact with a convoy, but to attack independently, continuing for as long as it took to expend their torpedoes or be forced to break off by the escorts. Or, of course, until they ran out of targets—so far not experienced by anyone, bar single-ship encounters. Like the schooner . . . *Damn!* Always it came back to that; Lebrun—or Calibourdin—on the bridge—just there—wiping the spray from his bearded face, accusing in his refusal to be intimidated by the situation. And the unseen baby; the doll drifting past. Rogge vomiting over the rail . . .

The corvette that had leaped on him out of the flickering confusion approached, passed overhead, hustled on. Still breathing heavily from the frantic action of the crash-dive, Altmann gave the order to turn hard to port and descend to one hundred metres. In the red glow of the attack lighting all eyes were turned upwards, ears wincing in anticipation. The first explosion was close, but not dangerous, a sound like an amplified hammer-blow on a part-filled steel oil-drum. Some lights went out, a gauge-glass blew out in a shower of ruby splinters, the hull shook like a tram-car crossing a bad junction; following immediately, the second explosion produced similar mild results and two more almost simultaneously a combined shock that killed a few more lights, greeted by shouts and curses from those affected; and nervous laughter. The fright was hard to conceal.

"Silence in the boat!" Rogge hissed the words in a fury. *"The next man I hear will do his next patrol in the army!"*

Altmann nodded to himself. Rogge displayed moments of surprising assertion for a quiet man. And was he being subtle, diverting thoughts from present woes to a next and happier patrol—even to the army and a worse fate in a punishment battalion? He rubbed his chin to conceal a smile.

Two more explosions, farther off, had the effect of a parting cuff, and calm returned. Altmann ordered the broken lights replaced. The corvette began another approach, this time signalled by the eerie tapping of detection.

"Damned asdic." Schreiber's face was running with sweat. "Like a damned lasso." Rogge gave him a warning glare.

"We'll see if we can shake it off." Altmann kept to a hoarse whisper. "*Steuermann*—bring her round to oh-eight-oh. Full ahead both motors."

The course he ordered lay towards the tanker that had been on the port bow, the one in the second line that should have received the sixth torpedo. Her propeller-noise was distinctive, with a coarse overlay caused, he guessed, by a damaged blade. It would provide a screen, if he could get under the ship.

To Benedict he said, "Twenty metres, *Ellee* . . ." and to the radio-man at the hydrophones: "She's about ahead now—that tanker with the chipped prop—call any change of bearing. You, *Steuermann*—steer on the bearing until I tell you otherwise."

"On the bearing—aye, *Kaleu.*"

The tapping had ceased. The next depth-charges burst, but at a distance. Perhaps the merchantmen were obstructing the corvette's freedom of action. But she was alone, or had been. The time to start worrying would come with her being joined by another escort, as she would be sooner or later. Two working together had been the making of reputations among Dönitz's heroes—those who survived the experience. A single attacker ran blind—or deaf—for a while after the depth-charges had disturbed the water and while turning for another approach; but with two working in synchronisation, one kept a finger on the target while the other did the donkey-work, and the results spoke for themselves. On top of that, escape from the asdic-beam on the surface, given the right weather conditions and time of day, or night, had become a path to suicide now that the enemy was evidently equipped with an efficient form of radar—and long-range aircraft, operating from bases as far into the Atlantic as the land-masses extended.

"Twenty metres."

The tanker's propeller-noise was plainly audible now, a rhythmic grinding, like a steel wheel on a stone surface, combined with a metronomic thumping. Altmann counted the beats—about sixty revolutions a minute. The boat was making a little over nine knots at her full submerged speed; she'd be coming up on the tanker at two or three knots, with about half a mile to go. Say fifteen minutes. The corvette would soon realise her mistake, and start another asdic search. Touch and go. But even if he could get under the tanker, what then? It was as much a trap as a refuge, with one possible opening—attacks by the other boats, drawing the escorts away. If that happened, he would be able to continue with his own attack. He leaned on the periscope standard and watched the depth-gauge. Steady on twenty metres. Benedict caught his eye and lifted an eyebrow, turning down his mouth and shrugging. He opened it to speak, but instead came the tapping, and he shut it, tightened his lips and shook his head, frowning. Altmann took a breath and nodded, lifting a hand to stay any move. Wait. She was a way off yet. In a loud whisper: "Can you get any more out of those coffee-grinders, *Ellee*?"

Benedict rolled his eyes. "Oh, yes . . . Maybe fifteen, twenty more revs. For about ten minutes before they throw their guts all over the motor-room, burst into flames and seize solid, but not necessarily in that order."

"Then what are we waiting for? Live dangerously for once!" Altmann grinned at the set features beneath the depth-gauge. The engineer had that effect on him: an urge to be flippant just to provoke his pessimism. But it also helped against the fear. They all felt that, and after a time knew how to tell it in each other; strangely, a kind of comfort rather than the destructive contagion common among less experienced crews. "Think of the story you'll tell your grandchildren!"

"Through a damned medium!" Benedict picked up the motor-room phone and spoke briefly before turning back to Altmann. "Fifteen minutes."

"Make it twenty and I'll take a magnum of Krug from you at the Majestic—break the habit of a wartime."

"Fifteen, and you've had your Krug, *Kaleu.* "

Men sat and stood at their stations, watching dials and gauges and indicators, gazing upwards at the dripping pipes and visible sections of hull-plating, studying innocuous parts of their surroundings with exaggerated concentration—anywhere and anything but each others' eyes. Altmann watched them absently, turning over his choice of moves if the depth-charging resumed before they reached the sanctuary of the tanker. Now the corvette's propeller, rapidly approaching, overlaying the tanker's grinding. A trickle of sweat drew an icy fingertip down his spine and he shrugged at it impatiently. He caught Schreiber's stare; the second watch-officer pursed his lips and nodded soberly, managing as always to look droll when others were skirting the outer edge of terror. He was young—this was his first posting after promotion from midshipman. Altmann had developed a regard for him as a focus of morale in the boat. His sense of discipline was nicely balanced by a humorous outlook at which he obviously worked as an affectation of scepticism; a man of the world whose mission in life was to turn pomposity and its accomplices on their heads with as much of the ridiculous as possible; and, Altmann had to admit, succeeding most of the time, occasionally too well. Schreiber was less of a stranger to hot water than most of his *U-bootwaffe* contemporaries. His reports from the naval college had been mixed—the views of a surface-navy system, reflected Altmann; the implication had been a washing of hands with respect to the man's selection for the u-boat arm. As it had turned out, a good officer, he had yet to spend time in the mould, a process greatly accelerated by present circumstances: among its other attributes war was a great force for early maturity. Holding Altmann's gaze, Schreiber made a dumb show with his hands, moving the left, stiff-fingered, edge-on across and above the right, held stiff-fingered and flat. Hunter and hunted. Schreiber smiled tautly and gave a slow nod. The corvette passed overhead.

"Down, *Ellee*—eighty metres!"

The first pair of charges exploded together just ahead of the boat, but at a shallower setting than her depth as Benedict increased it in a steep dive. Even so, the concussion was shattering, blowing fuses, smashing gauges and lights, dislodging fittings, throwing men to the footplates, upsetting the batteries. The motors faltered, slowed, resumed their speed, slowed again in response to Benedict's angry order on a still-intact phone-line. The emergency lighting came on, a dirty yellow effulgence which revealed a scene of disorder as men staggered about in dazed efforts to reinstate circuitry, reset controls, clear away debris, comply with orders. In the midst of it the second pair of charges detonated, this time astern and not as close, but close enough to kill the lights and throw everything back into uproar as men shouted and swore in the pitch blackness. From somewhere came the rushing sound of water.

Hanging onto the periscope standard, Altmann had stayed on his feet but struck his head on some hard projection. He felt the warm blood follow the line of cheekbone round his right eye and soak into his beard. *Damn!* He dragged out a handkerchief and dabbed at it in the darkness, blinking. His head buzzed.

"Eighty metres—I think!" Benedict's voice from the void. "Are you there, *Kaleu*?"

"Still with you, *Ellee* . . . Why've you slowed down?"

"Motor-room reports the starboard motor heating up. I'll have to look at it before I know for sure what's wrong . . . Bent shaft, maybe."

As he spoke the lights came on. Electrician's mate Hoffstadt stood at the auxiliary distribution-board, grinning wanly. "Secondary ring-main, *Herr Kaleu!*" he announced, as if introducing a mediocre stage act. "Seems in order. If the Tommy comes back and busts it I have a torch—"

"Cut the cackle and see to the emergency circuit, Hoffstadt," growled Benedict. "And where the fuck is that water coming in?" He glanced up at the depth-gauge. Eighty-six metres. He ordered an adjustment to the hydroplanes, watched as the needle moved back round the dial, ordered another adjustment stopping it at eighty, and turned again to Altmann. "Sorry about that—eighty metres now, *Kaleu.*"

Retrieving his cap from the plating, Altmann straightened to face Rogge. The first watch-officer looked shaken but in control of himself, and sternly dutiful. "Water coming in at the after heads, *Kaleu*. I have two men seeing to it. Forward torpedo-room reports a leaking tube-door. Number three. The outer door seems to be jammed, probably buckled. The leak is controllable, maybe it can be stopped. The emergency lighting circ—"

"All right, *Einswo*." Altmann blinked through a pink mist. Blood. He dabbed at it with the bloodstained handkerchief, and Rogge looked concerned. "Do what you can. The Tommy'll be back again shortly. Save the general report until we've got rid of him."

"*Herr Kaleu!*" Rogge saluted, and added dramatically, "You're wounded!"

"A scratch." Altmann shrugged elaborately. "I'll live . . . Keep me informed about leakages." He gave an uncertain Rogge a reassuring nod and inquired about the tanker's bearing, told the *Funkmaat* to keep a check on it. Then back to his station and Benedict, who turned from the motor-room phone to tell Altmann to forget the Krug: "—that motor's got to be shut down til I've looked at it!"

Altmann glanced at the pitot indicator. Seven knots and slowing. Bad. As he did so the *Funkmaat* reported the corvette approaching, and to corroborate his words the asdic's tapping resumed, a regular light hammer-blow on the plating, a man feeling for a weakness. Men paused in their tasks, eyes turned instinctively upwards again. Through all came the grind and thump of the tanker's single screw, taunting them. It was perceptibly fainter now. And other noises intruded. Two distant detonations, clanking sounds like strokes on a cracked bell, obviously of greater magnitude than depth-charges: other boats at work. And near at hand a new kind of sound altogether. It distracted attention from the asdic, overlaid the tanker's diminishing thumping. Everyone listened, partly-fascinated, partly-apprehensive, wondering. A metallic groaning and creaking interspersed with short shrieks and cracks and a sudden muffled booming followed by a chorus of louder shrieks and cracks, tailing off in an occasional groan to silence, punctuated by another distant explosion and the asdic's tapping.

"Sinking ship." Schreiber caught Altmann's eye, a sober expression on his face. "Down to Davy Jones." He glanced round meaningly. "An Englishman."

Taking a breath, Altmann nodded. Which one? The freighter? Perhaps the after section of the tanker—the forward part hadn't been damaged apart from whatever the fire would have inflicted. And that bulker had seemed buoyant enough, though it was always possible that she'd suffered more than had been apparent: if she'd broken in two the separate halves would almost certainly have been taken down with the weight of cargo in addition to flooded holds. Large holds were the type's weakness, where the tanker's strength lay in her multi-compartmented construction and the cargo itself, providing secondary buoyancy when it hadn't ignited. And the freighter's list could have increased to immerse her hatches, opened by the explosion and fire. All possible sinkings, all doubtful. They couldn't be claimed as anything better than strikes, short of his getting an opportunity to surface and check; of which, at the moment, there seemed next to no prospect. The corvette's propeller was clearly-audible again. Benedict caught his eye and shook his head, lips clamped.

This time the hunter dropped a pattern of six. Altmann gauged the moment and ordered a dive to a hundred and twenty metres, turning to starboard at the same time to run back along his track. The tanker had passed beyond reach. His only recourse now was to apply the evasive tactics of long practice and—as it was turning out in the face of the enemy's improving methods and equipment—diminishing effectiveness. His best hope lay in the fact that the corvette seemed to be still operating alone. A partner would reduce the chances of survival, let alone escape, to desperate proportions. There was a lot of bitterness among the convoy escorts after the years of struggle against a ruthless assailant; the tendency was to continue the attack against the u-boat when forced to surface, aiming at destruction with capture a poor second; which was, Altmann admitted to himself, no more than a return of their own medicine. No other war machine had generated, or deserved, in its opponent such implacable, almost personal, determination to bring about its total eradication. Those who had survived such onslaughts to become prisoners had been literally nothing more than the incidental debris of a duel to the death. The best the u-boat man could hope for as he trod water was a lifeline from a victor reluctant to offer himself as a gift to any lurking accomplice. There would be no special effort to take him alive; not even for whatever might be got from him by way of intelligence. The defenders of the convoys had become as ruthless as their attackers, as bent on unconditional victory, and the tide of war was showing signs of favouring them.

The charges shook the boat badly, but were wide of the mark owing to Altmann's turning away from his projected track, evidently catching the corvette's man on one foot. And in the turmoil of the explosions the asdic lost its target, giving Altmann a last chance to throw off his attacker before having to face him in the open astern of the convoy. The tanker missed by the fourth torpedo was still in the game, somewhere not far off and coming towards him, which obviated the need to hammer the motors. If he could slip under it as it came up with him and hang on for a while he had a good chance of final disengagement and—bitter enough prospect—probable retirement from the fray. He would be unable to catch up with the convoy again unless he could do so in a single night, on the surface; progress by day had become an open invitation to the enemy. Not that darkness was a safe cover. And with a damaged electric motor—if it was—there was no question of keeping up, let alone catching up, with the convoy submerged.

As he instructed the *Funkmaat* at the hydrophone to search for the supposedly oncoming tanker, the corvette picked them up again, and began another run. This time they were separated by a greater depth of water, and Altmann decided to bring the boat up rather than do what most did and take her down to the limit, and beyond, to lie low with everything shut down in the hope that the search would be abandoned. Whatever the other drawbacks of the tactic it failed on the single matter of the leaking torpedo-tube. A charge in the right place and a flooded torpedo-room would seal their fate. But he would keep his nerve and wait for the first charge to burst before giving the order. The hope was that when the disturbance had cleared sufficiently to allow the asdic's operation again it would draw a blank lasting long enough for him to locate and intercept the tanker. As he pondered this prognosis he realised, with a sense of frustration, that he had elected to try his only viable option. There was no other way through this *contretemps* short of risking being crushed like a bean-tin with the depth-pointer off the scale. He had always had an aversion to what he saw as meek submission to an undeserving enemy: if and when it came to a showdown he would follow Schepke rather than cower in the cellar—fight it out on the surface. That apart, the tanker offered the last chance he had of slipping away.

"I think I have the tanker, *Kaleu*—green three-five." *Funkmaat* Kuppisch's matter-of-fact tones. Already the corvette could be heard through the boat. Altmann jammed the extension phone against an ear and listened for a moment to the regular pounding of the approaching tanker. No damaged prop this time. If it was her. He didn't see how it could be any other on that bearing. But then, did it matter? Any ship would serve his purpose. The corvette was almost overhead.

At the first double explosion he ordered twenty metres, and watched as Benedict directed the ballast and hydroplane operation. A good man. Older, experienced, cynical, unflappable. Married, two children, worried. His pessimism was more than a front; it was also a crutch: fending off the sentimental it gave him something to play to, an act he was bound to keep up in the face of fear, and in doing so it became real. In acting the hardened campaigner—which in fact he was—he became the character in reality. But he still worried—about his wife, his home, his children; and about the boat. He was burdened with a finely-honed feel for his calling. He cared for the machinery under his charge. So now he was worried about the ailing motor, and as the charges burst he winced, not at the shocks of the detonations but at what he could feel going on in the motor-room.

They were close again. Again the lights blew out; the boat shuddered, and a valve sheared a number of flange-bolts to project a high-pressure

102

spray over the men at the controls, prompting angry exclamations but not, Altmann noted with a flush of pride, any overt signs of the alarm they must feel. Rogge's damage-control party worked through the ensuing explosions, in the pitch-darkness and, shortly following, the dirty yellowish emergency lighting, like gnomes in some fiendish subterranean quake-factory. The debris underfoot tripped and unbalanced them, and they kicked hams, lemons, hanks of sausages, sides of bacon aside as they manipulated wrenches and hammers, drenched through, desperate to arrest and reverse a sentence of death. Another jolt and its accompanying clanking concussion as a charge burst nearby and one of them dropped the bolt he was trying to force through the flange-gasket, dashed water from his face, turned at the touch of a man behind him with another, returned to the task and finally succeeded. Another of the party reached up under his outstretched arms and worked a heavy washer into place, then the nut. The water screamed as the spanners closed the gap between the flanges and another bolt was hammered into place.

Altmann counted the charges, noting with satisfaction their decreasing effect as the boat moved away and upwards. But he also noticed something else as the clamour subsided. The corvette's propeller-noise was not receding as before but seemed to have paused on a sustained note. She was either shadowing him, or circling, instead of moving off to come in on a run. As soon as the asdic picked him up again she'd close in giving him less time to take avoiding action. Kuppisch confirmed his suspicion, and the tanker's bearing. She was closing fast—her signature-tune was audible now. Good, for she not only offered cover but would also obstruct whatever movement the corvette's man was planning. Soon Altmann would have to turn back on his track to pace the tanker, slipping under the flat-bottomed hull a few metres below it. He would have to judge his moment by ear. There was no means of accurate range-measurement. The corvette's propeller-noise was increasing. He would make his turn towards it, perhaps catch her commander out again before dropping back beneath the tanker. He felt a smile tug at the corners of his mouth. If this wasn't an open invitation to collision and catastrophe he could think of no other description. What would the commandant of the u-boat training-school have said of it? Moot point—one brought either the wrath of Thor or the praise of cherubs and angels on one's head for action calculated to succeed only by a hair's-breadth, and it depended more on the mood of the day than on any intrinsic attributes. In the end the only gauge was the outcome, marginally less a matter of unquantifiable chance than that of the spin of a coin.

Six charges. The atmosphere in the boat was heavy, gritty, penetratingly damp, tinged now with the sharp bite of chlorine. The batteries. Some damage, perhaps. Eventually they would have to use breathing apparatus, depending on the duration of the corvette's patience. Or of the interval that separated her from ultimate success.

The asdic found them again as Altmann allowed the boat to fall back towards the approaching tanker, but as he took up a position he gauged to be directly beneath the plodding merchantman it wandered away. Perhaps the operator thought he'd picked up the tanker. Perfect! But not quite. The problem was the tanker's speed, that of the convoy, which, of course, was a knot or so faster than the boat's maximum on a single electric motor at full power—which itself could not be sustained indefinitely, partly because of the diminishing charge in the batteries, partly because of the stresses in the motor itself at speed. Benedict protested, then warned: Altmann's demanding whatever could be squeezed out of the ailing motor was asking for trouble. Real trouble. If it were run in its defective state at its maximum possible power it would fail altogether; probably cause a fire, or worse.

"Worse, *Ellee*? What could be worse than a fire?"

"A fire and a seized shaft. Then the diesel on that side would be useless as well."

The tanker drew gradually ahead. Its presence was like a steel-mill in full swing on the boat's casing, a gargantuan thumping combined with a background scream almost too high-pitched to be audible, almost physically cutting into its listeners' nerves. The racket was so abrasive and threatening that most of the boat's company decided it would be less nerve-racking to face the corvette.

"*Kaleu*'s being foxy," observed *Maschinistensmaat* Klaus Falke, laying a fifth card on each hand and setting the pack down on the folded blanket doing duty as a card-table. Cards took the place of chess while in action, filling in the gaps of tense inactivity between the periodic flurries of engagement. Chess was vulnerable to the violence of evasive manoeuvres and the shock of exploding charges as cards were not. Falke and Kölm were sitting on a bunk in the petty officers' flat. Kölm blinked at his cards and sniffed. Falke continued, "This cow of a tanker makes so much racket you could hold a festival of dance music here and not be heard by that pill-pusher." He laid a coin to one side of the pack. "Ten marks."

Kölm frowned at his cards, sucking his lower lip, finally laying down two coins. "Your ten and raise you ten." He looked up and lifted his eyebrows inquiringly.

Falke eyed him blandly. "What's this?—taking risks, *Putsi*?"

Kölm snorted. "Call or raise . . . Haven't you noticed?—we're all risking our stupid necks in this boat—"

"All right—your twenty and raise you twenty." Falke dropped the coins on the blanket. "It's all relative, you know. If you keep your nerve the risks of this game will finally outweigh any taken by the *Kaleu*. At least he knows what cards the Tommy's got."

"All wild," said Kölm, poking through a handful of coins and laying two on the little pile. "I call."

"Sure?"

"What d'you mean—*sure?* Why else would I say so? Come on—let's see what you've got, poker-face, before the music ends."

Falke sighed and turned up his cards one by one. Kölm looked on gloomily. Ten of hearts; queen of diamonds; nine of diamonds. Kölm's gloom lightened and he adopted a look of pitying scorn. Jack of spades. Falke laid a finger on the remaining card. "Want to raise it?"

Kölm's lip curled. "I'll let you off," he said. "You won't do much more with that than the *Kaleu* will do when the Tommy gets a clear run."

Falke shrugged and turned over his fifth card. Eight of hearts. "Straight."

Kölm gazed blankly for a moment then grunted. "Luck," he said, illogically.

"Of course . . . How's yours, *Putsi*?"

Kölm hesitated, wiped the back of a hand across his nose, then turned over the first card. Two of diamonds.

"That's a start," said Falke. "There's hope yet." He returned Kölm's sharp glance with a smile and a nod. "Continue."

King of clubs.

"Interesting," observed Falke. "Your options are lessening by the minute."

Gloom returned to Kölm's brow. He turned over the ace of diamonds and brightened, but only for a moment. Falke was nodding sagely, scratching his beard. He avoided Kölm's eye. Jack of spades. The clamorous silence was broken only by two distant detonations.

"Someone else taking Tommy's pills," murmured Falke. "Our turn again soon . . . Come on—the suspense is killing me."

Ace of hearts. Kölm heaved a deep breath and let it go with a blast that lifted the hair off his brow. "Pair."

"And quite a pair at that," agreed Falke. "A little more practice and you'll be in with a chance." He raked the coins into a palm. "Another round?"

"On the jetty at Lorient," said Kölm. "Too many distractions out here."

Falke laid a coin on the blanket. "Ten marks says we swim there or not at all."

Kölm stared at him. "Don't tempt fate," he said. "One's enough without your sort of luck in the pot. All it'll take is one of our own gallant aces to slip this damned tanker an eel and we're for the chop."

"Fancy ten marks on it?" Falke grinned at his companion. "Best way of making sure it doesn't happen—"

In the control-room the same thought crossed Schreiber's mind as he watched the navigator at work. "Sitting duck," he said soberly, "this fat tanker. And clever little us at her apron-strings. Suicide run."

Obersteuermann Freigang affected preoccupation with his calculations. *Zweiter* was apt to be flippant at the most untimely moments. It was difficult to know how to respond to some of his remarks, so he said nothing and jotted down some figures on a pad.

"Just our luck if our comrade-in-arms—*Kaleu* Schewe out there somewhere in one-oh-five—seizes his chance at glory and sends over a couple of eels from Uncle Karl. Even if they're duds they could probably knock a hole in us big enough for a fond farewell. That's the trouble with this wolf-pack act—" Schreiber fixed Freigang with a wide-eyed stare the navigator could feel "—how many boats have been sunk by their own side, d'you think, Lothar—to the nearest even number, say?"

Freigang ruled a pencil-line under a note on the chart, grunted, and turned a frown on the second watch officer, who smiled winningly through a villainous beard. "What's that—boats sinking other boats?" He shook his head reprovingly. "You should have been a war correspondent, *Zweiter*—just the kind of thing to jolly people along as they sweep up the broken glass on the home front."

"No—seriously, Lothar: eels zooming about among a crowd of ships and boats can easily hit something that shouldn't be there. All we ever

106

know is that u-unlucky number doesn't come home to Uncle. Just a loud silence. The assumption is that he's bought it in the glorious tradition of the service, courtesy of the Royal Navy or its transatlantic cousin, whereas all they've done is wonder what caused the bang . . . Just think—if Uncle Karl gets enough boats out here among the convoys the escorts won't have to do anything but stand back and let us get in each other's way." He paused, considering. "Taken to its logical conclusion, there'll be no need for escorts, and soon after that not even merchantmen. We'll be too busy trying to avoid hitting each other to worry about getting the enemy in our sights."

"Is this what you learn for your promotion examinations, *Zweiter*?"

"What—original thinking? Capital offence!"

"Ah."

"Not as crazy as it seems. Someone at HQ knows what he's doing, and it isn't Uncle Karl . . ."

On the hydrophone the corvette could be heard through the tanker's din. She seemed to have taken up station a short way off, slowing to keep pace with the tanker. It was clear to Altmann that her commander knew he was there and, of course, could not remain indefinitely—or at least not for as long as the escort could sit there, waiting. Eventually he would have to surface, even had he been able to keep up with the tanker. And—the thought caused a momentary chill—the tanker could always take an unheralded turn, under instructions or to avoid a casualty, or in following a zig-zag, leaving her parasitic consort exposed. In any event, a decision was becoming a matter of urgency. Altmann flipped through the options open to him, basing his judgment on a flat refusal to see the situation as the preamble to a fight in the open with only one tenable—or rather, untenable—conclusion. He was going to get out of this jam somehow. There had to be a way. The war was waiting. Uncle Karl was waiting. And Germany—the *Führer*—expected more of him than a craven acceptance of defeat—even a defeat redeemed by flying colours and last-gasp gun action—while a chance, however remote, of success remained, or at worst escape to resume the fight at a more favourable time. Considering the possibilities he reflected incidentally on the sequence of events that had led to this predicament, and wondered at his carelessness in letting himself be jumped by the corvette, like a first-tripper straight from school. If it hadn't been for the lookout's vigilance it would have been all over by now—either another shell or ramming would have put paid to the boat with the minimum of ceremony. A smart lookout and a cynical, wary, older man in the engineering officer had saved it and its commanding officer by a matter of split seconds. He had been given a chance. The sea—and war—wasn't normally as generous. Next time it would be different, and he knew he could not allow a next time. War, victory and the *Führer* apart, he had Ursula and the girls to think of. Or rather, to try not to think of at times like this. His week's leave had been an anguished business, exposing more raw spots than it had remedied, bringing him closer to a realisation of his own vulnerability to distressful forces that were clearly mounting as the war progressed, the kind of distressful forces that lay below the surface of conflict. They corroded, abraded, pressed, distorted and finally wrought the irretrievable, subtle destruction that rendered humanity gross, depraved and deprived, barely aware of its own spiritual, emotional and moral impoverishment.

Angrily, he shook his mind free of its entanglement, bitter in the knowledge that it had become a recurrent phenomenon and that, allowed to run, it invariably led him back to the encounter with the schooner as the locus of the several forms of distraction to which he was becoming prone and which had caused the lapse by which he blamed himself for the present dilemma. And here he was allowing it to intrude again. Biting off an exclamation he wrenched his thinking back to the matter in hand, and almost immediately hit upon the answer, controlling an impulse to smack a fist into a palm. Instead he called for the attention of Rogge, Schreiber and Benedict, but made no attempt to conceal his words from any others within hearing. They would have to know anyway. And there was no time to be lost. The pounding of the tanker's propeller was becoming a continuous clamour, now supplemented by the vibration felt throughout the boat. Time was not only running out but the boat's position relative to its involuntary guardian was also becoming dangerous.

"The range is the only difficulty." Altmann glanced about at his officers. "An estimate will have to do, and it might work . . . So we set three torpedoes for different ranges—a straddle, in effect—and hope. The bearing from the hydrophones isn't as accurate as we could wish, either, of course, but again the chances are better than even. We use our heads as much as the technology, for a change. Let's hope we haven't lost the knack . . . Any questions?"

"If this works, *Kaleu*, where to next?"

Altmann nodded. "Indeed! We won't be able to catch up with the convoy, and we've got six eels left—one unusable in the flooded tube. I'm not counting the two in external stowage. So five actually usable, including the two stern shots. We have unfinished business with this convoy, and we'll be in a position to intercept another if we have any eels left, so we aren't heading for home yet. Will that suit you, *Zweiter*?"

Schreiber nodded gravely. "Thank you, *Kaleu* . . . The sea-time will be useful."

"Towards promotion?"

"Towards my mess-bill at base. A small party—my twenty-first birthday."

"Change from nappies to pants?" inquired Benedict. "Or just weaned off the breast?"

Schreiber rolled his eyes at the engineer. "Nappies would have been useful . . . But who wants to be weaned off the breast? Getting onto it's the problem."

"Congratulations," interjected Altmann. "I wasn't on your guest-list?"

"You were on leave, *Kaleu*."

"Just as well, perhaps, hm?"

Schreiber smiled conspiratorially. "It was an expensive evening."

"We'll have to hope for another fortnight or so on patrol, then."

"At least, *Kaleu*!" Schreiber beamed round. "More days, more dollars."

"Let's hope not," said Benedict sourly. "With the dollar, the American way of life. I wouldn't wish that on a mad dog, war or no war . . . On the Tommies, yes; but not a mad dog."

"Yes, but *Reichsmark* hasn't the poetic resonance of 'dollar'."

Benedict snorted.

They dispersed to attack stations, Rogge joining Freigang at the computer and Schreiber attending to the computed torpedo-settings. The vibration from the tanker's propeller was becoming excessive as it closed up from astern, and Altmann voiced his concern to Benedict and his planesmen. As the torpedoes left the tubes they would have to act fast correcting the boat's normal tendency to rise. "In fact," added Altmann, "you can take the final firing order—number four will be the third and last—as the executive order to dive, and we'll turn to port at the same time. But keep the dive-angle shallow. We don't want our tail docked."

The corvette lay out to starboard. The turn to port would put the tanker between her and the boat, which, if the worst came to the worst, would allow at least a head start. And as soon as possible a return to the surface. The batteries weren't only running low, but also giving off chlorine now approaching toxic levels. Men were coughing, eyes smarting. There could be no question of continuing submerged for any longer than it would take for all this to pass. At the sky-periscope standard, Altmann acknowledged Schreiber's report: tubes one, two and four ready. "Computed settings correct!"

"Fire one and two!"

The familiar lurch, greeted with an impulse to cheer. Benedict watched the depth-gauge closely, the planesmen and ballast operator reacting instantly. The boat remained at depth. Good.

"Torpedoes running."

"Very good . . . Fire four!" Again the lurch. "Fifty metres, *Ellee*. Port fifteen the helm."

"Torpedo running."

"Very good."

"Fifteen port wheel on, *Herr Kaleu*."

"Very good." Surely, thought Altmann, there was a phrase other than "Very good"? It might be worth experimenting—when they were clear of this sticky mess. He added, "Steady her on two six five."

"Two six five—aye, *Kaleu*."

The boat sank away from the tanker like a pilot-fish forsaking its host, going into a moderate port turn as it did so, spiralling into the depths, away from a dangerous bolt-hole to—safety? Greater danger? Altmann resisted the temptation to cogitate. Instead he watched the depth-gauge and gyro-repeater and listened for the strikes. He caught Benedict's eye and gave a small nod. Benedict's expression was inscrutable. No-one spoke. The needle moved round the face of the depth-gauge. The vibration and din of the tanker receded and the atmosphere lightened, the tension almost palpably slackening.

The first strike was followed instantly by the second and then—nothing. Too much to expect a full house. But the double shock-wave jolted the boat, the most welcome jolt Altmann had ever felt. It was greeted with cheers and whoops and a grin from Benedict, which was an event. Returning it with a tight smile, Altmann turned at Rogge's voice. "Congratulations, *Kaleu*. That must be a record for guesswork." At the base of the ladder, the first officer looked pleased, in a rare moment of abandon. He even offered his hand, which Altmann took briefly, thanking him. "Let's call it calculation in the interests of self-respect . . . But it was your doing, *Einswo*. If you'd missed you'd have had some explaining to do."

The look of consternation on Rogge's face broke Altmann's reserve. He slapped him on the back. "Tommy's unlucky day, eh?"

With the bulkhead door open, Kuppisch turned with the hydrophone headset in his hand. "She's breaking up, *Herr Kaleu!*"

Everyone fell silent. Above the hum of the electric motor all could hear them, the familiar sounds of a ship going down. Luckily-placed, a single hit could have done it; two must have destroyed the warship's watertight integrity with catastrophic thoroughness. This was the game—kill or be killed, and on the other foot the *coup de grace* would have been continued to the elimination of the last shred of doubt. So with this outcome. And the boat was still in fighting order—just.

Later, after surfacing to discover an escort approaching the corvette's debris, forcing a return to depth, Benedict reported briefly on the situation. It was not as bad as he'd expected, but in some respects worse. The depth-charging did not seem to have damaged the motor itself, or the shaft; but a lubricating-oil pipe to the shaft-bearing at the pressure-hull gland had fractured and the bearing had run hot. In the process it had suffered a trace of wear and the resistance had caused the motor to overheat. The pipe was easily repaired—"No more than half an hour, *Kaleu*"—but in the long term the bearing was unserviceable, would ultimately cause wear in the gland and resultant leakage.

"It must be renewed. As it is, I can't give you better than half-speed on that shaft, down here or surfaced."

"A base job?"

Benedict's unblinking stare conveyed a mixture of wonder and pity for the unenlightened. "What else? I can't knock up a bearing from the scrap-box. I've tried to get bearing shells put on the list of standard spares but the desk-mechanics say it's not necessary for patrols of less than six weeks. As if time drops depth-charges!—this sort of damage could happen on the first day."

"All right, Herbert . . . Let's see what headquarters has to say. But first there's this damned escort. If she comes looking for us we might not have to trouble the flotilla engineer. And we have some unfinished business."

IV

IT was Altmann's last patrol in North Atlantic waters before the United States entered the war. Returning to periscope depth to make a final assessment of the situation in the convoy's wake, he discovered the approaching warship to be an American destroyer, a doubly-dangerous enemy in its immunity from attack by express order of the *Führer* but not itself prohibited from hunting the u-boat: the US government had placed a liberal interpretation on its official position of neutrality and in recent times one or two u-boat commanders had reported being hunted and depth-charged by American escorts, both in cooperation with the British and seemingly on their own initiative. Otherwise, Altmann reflected with some bitterness, he would have taken advantage of the situation and tried one at least of his remaining torpedoes—the two stern shots—on the destroyer as she lay stopped amidst the flotsam from the sunk Britisher picking up what survivors remained. As it was, however, he had an equally immobile target in the damaged bulker, which he could attack at periscope depth with a fair chance of escaping undetected. The escort could be expected to stick with the convoy rather than engage in a search. As it turned out, the first stern shot failed, but the second, fired after some twenty-five minutes of manhandling from its stowed position under the motor-room footplates, detonated fairly amidships to send the victim's two halves quietly to the bottom. The American carried out a half-hearted search without making sonar contact before breaking off to pick up more survivors, followed by a return to the convoy and legitimate business. Then, the decision made for him, Altmann limped home to Lorient to report the sinking of one six-thousand-ton freighter, one ten-thousand-ton ore-carrier and a corvette, and the destruction of a tanker of around ten thousand tons deadweight. As a war patrol it had not been an unqualified success, but had at least yielded a satisfactory return, granted its aborted original purpose. Meanwhile, at flotilla command there had been ructions and a purge of suspected spies in the wake of the missing charts: someone, rather than plain incompetence, had been responsible for the continued safety of the shipping in harbour at Halifax. And, thought Altmann with wry appreciation, perhaps for his own continued survival.

But not Greischen's. Of this time, looked back upon as one of mounting disorder both at sea and at the base as the war's brisk pace faltered on its several fronts, the return to Lorient remained clear on the horizon of Altmann's recollection. Following the usual, but markedly subdued, ceremonial including Uncle Karl's customary personal, grave, welcome, Altmann paid Straubhals a formal visit. The base commandant was his usual amiable self, but after bringing his visitor up to date with various items of news and comment upon naval and national affairs he paused to regard Altmann soberly before saying he was the bearer of regrettable news which, he felt, should be delivered in person and privately. In the sunlit calm of the office, over their cooling coffee, he told Altmann of an air-raid on the battleships at La Pallice which seemed to have moved headquarters to consideration of arrangements for their imminent departure.

"I can't give you details, of course—I've no idea myself beyond the fact that a move is definitely being planned for some date soon. The air-raids have been getting heavier and more accurate despite increasing the anti-aircraft defences, and the outcome is inevitable short of the ships' getting out of the trap they're in. As long as they can be kept in active condition, wherever they're laid up—or stationed in readiness—they tie down the enemy's resources to a greater or lesser extent. Bombed to a standstill where they are they'll free up a considerable weight of Allied naval power." Straubhals sighed. "Simple strategy." He eyed Altmann speculatively and, thought Altmann, with something like sympathy. Curious, he said nothing, but returned Straubhals's regard inquiringly. Straubhals sighed again and said he understood that he, Altmann, had been friendly with *Scharnhorst*'s gunnery officer—a *Korvettenkapitan* Otto Greischen.

"Gretchen? Yes. We've been friendly from the beginning, at the Danholm camp. Went on through the *Mutterhaus* together . . . He has a dim view of the u-boat arm—calls us the great unwashed." Altmann smiled. "Ladies' man. Immaculately turned out on all occasions, and quite intelligent with it. For a gunnery officer."

"Gretchen?"

"Nickname—particular about his turnout; in another man it might be effeminate, but not in his case—irony's the aim."

"I see . . . He wasn't married, I understand?"

"No. Not Gretchen! He specialises in charming other men's wives, especially if they're attached to rungs on the ladder . . . But he's no lounge-lizard. Navy comes first, with women the means to the end. In peacetime, anyway. In war—perhaps a little more ascetic: he has delusions of glory—looks forward to sea battles *a la* Heligoland, Coronel . . . He belongs to the Kaiser's navy, really. I suspect I haven't convinced him of the merits of the *Führer*'s cause. He's more likely to follow a man like Langsdorff than Dönitz—"

"A somewhat—necrophilic—tendency—"

Altmann grunted and studied Straubhals's good-natured features for a moment. "But you're speaking of him in the past—?"

Straubhals took a breath and produced an envelope from a drawer. "I've kept this for you—delivered a few days ago."

Altmann recognised Greischen's hand, thanked Straubhals and expressed surprise. "Why the personal delivery?"

"To answer your question, Altmann. Your friend died in an air-raid. The ship was quite seriously damaged, but not put out of action. Greischen was at his post directing the anti-aircraft batteries. It was a small bomb, fortunately, but it hit a vital spot. Altogether twenty-three of the ship's company were killed. I'm sorry."

Altmann looked at the envelope. That round, upright script—more like a woman's than a man's. Precise, accurate, just less than elegant, in light blue. Strange, he thought, that such a feminine touch could wield high-velocity explosives to distinctive effect, as Gretchen had done. Whether or not his rank had had anything to do with the influence of senior officers' wives, it had certainly been evidence of professional competence. But wasted: Germany's loss, a talent barely made use of while it had existed. Altmann's sadness mingled with anger.

"Thank you, *Herr Kommandant* . . . I'll read it later, since a reply won't be necessary."

Straubhals inclined his head and took a bundle of envelopes from the drawer. Altmann recognised his own handwriting and smiled his regret. "Do you want these?" asked Straubhals. "The ship's navigating officer thought you might."

"Thank you, yes . . ."

Altmann felt a sense of unreality. Would all his wartime correspondence return to him, in such circumstances? At this rate people would dread his letters. But who? Hans was gone; now the cultivated Greischen. There was no-one else other than official recipients . . . Apart from Ursula, and his parents. Abruptly he curtailed his train of thought. He must get Ursula and the children out of the city—to some place off the enemy's target schedule. Frankfurt was a prime objective, and night bombing far from accurate. He must request leave—

"I have rather more welcome news for you, Altmann." Straubhals was smiling, an eyebrow cocked. Altmann waited, wondering. "You're being relieved of your command—" he raised a hand to forestall the protest that rose to Altmann's lips "—but to proceed to greater things. You'll receive orders in writing, of course, but you might as well know beforehand, since you'll wish to make arrangements . . ."

"Yes, *Herr Kommandant?*"

"You're to commission a new boat. One of the long-range ones. Bigger, but I'm afraid rather less comfortable—or should I say more uncomfortable?—than your present vessel. A Type Nine."

"Oh." Altmann felt at a loss for comment, so waited. Long range. That would mean longer periods on patrol, more distant waters—the end of the North Atlantic, perhaps; something of a relief, at least in terms of weather. And perhaps better prospects of survival. Also, he thought suddenly, removal from the vicinity, however extended, of the fateful encounter with the schooner . . . That damned schooner and its phantoms—

Straubhals was speaking. "You'll take some leave first . . . At least two months, but part of it will be attending refresher and familiarisation courses. The boat is scheduled for completion in mid-December—" his mouth twitched "—the timing is, of course, carefully-gauged, but you can be almost certain of delays and Christmas with your family."

"Thank you."

"Don't thank me, Altmann. Mine is merely to deliver the message. But let me congratulate you. It will probably mean promotion—better pay if nothing else . . ."

Was there a hint of cynicism in the commandant's tone? His view of u-boat operations was naturally coloured by his situation, but it could hardly have been one of envy except for the fact that if he had still been in command—and not in any case withdrawn for staff duties as an experienced officer—it would have been in a state of bodily fitness. The wound evidently bothered him. It was, perhaps, an excessive price to pay for a safe job that would probably carry him through to the war's end—whatever its form. And that was becoming a matter for speculation, if not openly. The loss of *Bismarck* as a major way-point in its progress, and now the obvious state of naval impotence represented by the trapped battle-cruisers and *Prinz Eugen* with rumours of a hole-in-the-corner dash for a spread of destinations from the North Cape to the comparative safety of home waters rather than a sortie into the Atlantic and possible glory if not victory shed a sombre light upon a scenario developing other unwelcome distinctions. Altmann was aware of a sense of doubt about certain aspects of the war at sea not as evident in its progress on land, what with Rommel's advance in the desert and the eastern front's still hopeful outlook, with the Italian *faux pas* in Greece gratifyingly turned into a success for German land forces that seemed to have secured the eastern Mediterranean against Allied exploitation. If, that is, the news was to be taken at face value. In this Altmann cautioned himself, well aware of the element of fantasy to which official news bulletins and communiqués were subject; but even so . . . Morale was important, vital. It would not be for him to suggest that his prospective removal from the scene of his patrols to date was part of a greater strategy in face of diminishing returns. It would be better to see, and promote, it as evidence of an extension of German suzerainty over the high seas with the acknowledged war-decisive weapon. The Type IX boat was undoubtedly a great improvement on the Type VII, its range and hitting power alone making it the most advanced submarine design in the world—as far as he knew. With her twenty-four torpedoes, heavier deck armament and all-up complement of fifty-odd, let alone her impressive dimensions, he felt he was facing command of a ship rather than a boat, and he found the prospect both daunting and exhilarating. There would be more of a sense of aggressive ability than in the smaller Atlantic design, with which he had begun to feel a certain frustration. After this last patrol, with the missing charts and the aborted objective, convoy sinkings notwithstanding he had felt a depressing weight of disappointment, not only with the boat and its limitations but also with the way in which the patrol's preparations had been so carelessly handled at command level. He had tentatively considered the possibility of their being regarded, as individual boats, as expendable items in the greater scheme of affairs; begun to suspect that Uncle Karl's much-vaunted personal concern for his crews was in fact no more than a ploy, a subterfuge to maintain morale where the truth would render it a sham, a mere expedient, to be discarded at the moment of success or defeat. In some respects morale might take on the appearance of an expensive luxury, superfluous to requirements when the progress of battle seemed to be towards inevitable defeat . . .

Shocked at the trend of his thoughts, Altmann returned his attention to the commandant. He encountered the faintly whimsical gaze with a start, and coughed, saying he supposed he would be facing the usual post-patrol session with Uncle Karl.

Straubhals nodded. "This afternoon ... I imagine it will be a somewhat less chilly one than on the last occasion. All things considered you've turned an unfortunate episode to good account, Altmann—you'll find him a happier man this time, if not exactly a joyful one."

Rising to leave, Altmann asked about the missing charts. "I'd have thought you'd have mentioned the point first, *Herr Kommandant.*"

There was nothing much to be said, shrugged Straubhals—no question about the fault's lying with his own navigator, who had been dismissed together with his assistant. "The last I heard of it was that they were being taken for questioning on suspicion of espionage . . ." Again the smile, rather wistful. "A somewhat far-fetched assumption, in my view. But plain carelessness—negligence—is assuming a sinister aspect these days, Altmann. An indication of a state of mind, and not a healthy one." He came round his desk and laid a hand on Altmann's shoulder. "But it's beyond our power to influence, eh? Ours is but to do our duty—obey orders, and hope for the best. Uncle—and the *Führer*—know best."

Altmann returned his gaze. Were there doubts here, too? Or was this urbane, world-weary and casually perceptive officer merely showing himself to be more than just another cipher in the system? There was certainly more awareness in his views than was common among mid- and higher-ranking officers. It was dangerous territory. But Altmann's cogitation was interrupted by its subject's further remarking that an inquiry was scheduled for two days hence. "Dönitz will brief you. Nothing to be alarmed about. The idea is to formalise the facts as they're already known. You and your navigator will be required to testify as witnesses, nothing more. As I've said, Altmann, your subsequent action has more than compensated for the cock-up—from your standpoint, that is. It won't help my navigator's case. Frankly, I can't imagine what lay behind his oversight—which is all it amounts to. Unlucky for him that it's happened against the prevailing background of suspected sabotage among the base's local employees . . ." He sniffed. "In my view it's a mistake to bring in French tradesmen on such an obviously vulnerable and vital part of the war machine. But—" he shrugged again, and smiled without humour "—the decision is made by our betters. We must live with it, somehow."

And there was another matter. Almost as an afterthought Straubhals delayed Altmann's exit with an unexpected word of congratulation. An unexpected word, but not an unexpected reference: smiling, again with the hint of wistfulness, he told Altmann he had heard through the grapevine that Uncle Karl would be presenting the new boat's commander with a mark of appreciation. "Knight's Cross, Altmann—your total of tonnage sunk is short of the mark, of course, but that corvette escort's tipped the scales."

Altmann held Straubhals's gaze. "Seventy thousand tons, give or take a few kilos . . ." He blew out his cheeks. "Which makes a corvette equivalent to around five thousand . . . Stretching a point, *Herr Kommandant*, but who am I to complain? Very gratifying."

"No more than your due, in the circumstances—the least the Fatherland owes you! Dönitz will tell you all about it this afternoon . . ." He extended a hand and Altmann accepted a dry, firm grip, noting with renewed interest the Maltese cross at the other's throat. "Warmest congratulations, Altmann, and—" alluding to the oak leaves that would be the first embellishment, given sufficient opportunity and fortune "—good luck harvesting cabbages with your new boat!"

Altmann clicked his heels and gave a formal nod. "Thank you, *Herr Kommandant* . . . *Heil* Hitler!"

"That, too," returned Straubhals. The blue gaze was direct and guileless.

V

LEANING on the bulwark-capping of the bridge Altmann still found himself wondering at the boat's sheer size as he watched the broad hull—broad in comparison with the slim deck-casing of the Type VII—parting the swell, scattering schools of flying-fish to either side. She had come a long way since the commissioning earlier in the year.

He reflected on events since leaving the base at Lorient for home and the classroom preparatory to taking over the boat from the builders. As Straubhals had predicted, the inquiry had been a formality, from which he and Freigang had emerged without blame—to the navigator's relief despite his receiving an advisory reprimand. Moreover, Dönitz had been almost effusive in his satisfaction with Altmann's subsequent efforts, expressing his sympathy over the defective torpedoes and promising improvements. Which, in practice, had meant a return to contact detonators and a less effective weapon while trials of the *zaunkönig*—the homing, or acoustic, torpedo—were still exposing design faults that made it as dangerous to the boat firing it as to its intended target. The whole project savoured of tragicomedy, thought Altmann sourly; a ridiculous state of affairs that went some way towards negating the effectiveness of this new boat with her near-twenty-four thousand-mile range and double the torpedo capacity of the Atlantic boat. Contact detonators resulted in a messy explosion not as structurally lethal as that of the magnetically-detonated type: the victim was more often wounded than killed, and had to be stalked and despatched by further strikes or gunfire, adding to the risk of the operation.

Then there had been the ceremony of the medals, a dignified affair on the quayside beside the berthed boat, on a blustery sunny morning with the crew drawn up in unaccustomed smartness at his back as he faced the gaunt man who seemed to welcome the chance to express pleasure. Iron Crosses, and the Knight's Cross for Benedict as well as Altmann. Benedict's attempts to conceal his feelings—whatever they were—behind an inscrutable countenance were heroic in themselves, and Dönitz responded very properly with a solemn word of appreciation before ending up facing Altmann, at first with that direct gaze and tight lips then, as the boat's commander stepped forward, breaking the chill with a smile of obvious pleasure. Altmann faced a man under great strain, but determined, stoic, unwavering in his convictions, demanding of his subordinates. His "Well done, Altmann—I look forward to the next occasion!" was spoken with a genuine warmth that revealed, for an instant, the man behind the officer, and Altmann was touched.

"I too, *Herr Admiral*—and before we're much older."

A slight narrowing of the eyes accompanied a nod and the returned salute: the naval one, and Altmann wondered at its selective use, at its apparent—or perhaps unintended—point. If this process got as far as swords and brilliants it would be set aside. There could be no concealed, or mistaken, points in matters dealt with by the *Führer* in person.

And the war itself: developments had been startling while he had been standing aside, as it were: the Japanese attack on Pearl Harbor had come literally out of the blue, as staggering to Germany as to the Allies, but after the initial rush of elation signalled by the *Führer*'s prompt, if not precipitate, reaction in declaring war on the Americans the implications had settled like a cloud over the scene despite the resurgence of success in the shape of u-boat operations against unprotected shipping in US territorial waters. The second happy time—the opening stages of Operation Drumbeat—had lasted barely longer than the period it had taken for Altmann to work up his boat and crew to battle readiness; by the time of his departure from Kiel the easy pickings along the US eastern seaboard had all but gone. Coming late upon the scene, when the Americans had finally got round to imposing a blackout on their coastal illuminations from buoys and beacons to bedroom windows and road-traffic lights, Altmann had added eleven more sinkings to his record before the defences had rendered the area as hazardous as the rest of the North Atlantic's shipping lanes, and Dönitz's strategic withdrawal had been not merely to maintain the *U-Bootwaffe*'s claim to effectiveness but to retain the arm as a viable weapon: in response to further losses in the closing air-gap operations had shifted farther south and west into the Mexican Gulf and Caribbean, with gratifying results but, as before, for only a limited period before the defences forced withdrawal.

Seeking better, a group of long-range boats had been sent yet farther afield, and Altmann's cautious negotiation of the heavy swells and brawling seas off the Cape of Good Hope and the Allied naval base at Simonstown in the latter months of 1942 had marked not only a precedent in German u-boat operations but also, in some eyes, a degree of desperation in the overall strategy that gave the lie to the apparent improvement in Germany's fortunes at sea as Allied shipping losses mounted.

So far he had marked his presence in these waters with three sinkings off the coast between Cape Town and the Moçambique border: a five-thousand-ton Panamanian-flag freighter, a Norwegian freighter of similar tonnage, and an American, the lugubriously-named *Hiram K. Otis*, making eighteen knots on a course as steady as a train. She had driven herself down like a crash-diving u-boat, leaving two swimmers amidst a swirl of debris.

Altmann had given the attack to Schreiber. His request of flotilla command to bring his second watch-officer, promoted as a result, together with Benedict and a handful of others, to the new boat with him, had been granted after some prevarication, but Rogge's departure on a commanding officers' course had—to Altmann's secret relief—left open a post he'd argued was too important to be filled by someone unfamiliar with his ways. And Schreiber, he'd asserted, was a first-class officer. He hoped he'd been right. The man's only fault, if that was the word for it, was that at times he made Altmann feel his age. Benedict's presence was something of a compensation.

"Chester Ford." Standing barefoot and dripping on the deck abaft the conning-tower, one of the swimmers answered Altmann's question; about thirty, fit-looking, clean-shaven, dark hair cut *en brosse*. Grey eyes returned Altmann's scrutiny levelly. "Chief mate—I was on watch." Gesturing at the other hunched at his feet he added, "Red Kowalski. Ordinary seaman. Very ordinary. Lookout." The man sat hugging his knees, staring blankly at nothing, a mop of tight curls, reddish where not clogged with oil, oil-soaked singlet and dungarees, one shoe missing. "Reckon he's bushed. Teach the bastard to keep his eyes open. I told them enough times."

Altmann had regarded the pair with mixed feelings. Pathetic in their sudden change of circumstances, shock had not yet allowed the full impact of their misfortune to register. Or their fortune, he reflected: they'd survived. The officer gave the ship's name, said they'd been on passage from Bombay to Cape Town, cargo of bone meal, copra, steel castings, palm oil. But he couldn't remember the captain's name, or that of the owning company. Total blanks. He looked worried. Only the ship's name, which he repeated, adding "American" as if it hadn't been self-evident, and Schreiber avoided Altmann's glance.

There was no question of carrying prisoners and Schreiber's half-serious suggestion that they be offered the chance to volunteer to serve the Fatherland had met with a rebuke from Altmann that seemed to deflate the officer's normally robust spirits, and Altmann regretted his outburst, wondering at the cause: irritability had not featured to any significant extent in his management of the boat, either this one or the now-distant *Nothung*, until this patrol. He was conscious of physical weariness when having to stand-to at stations for hours on end, as during a hunt—of a target, or by an escort—but latterly also of a weariness of mind. One of the tolls of war, he'd concluded, avoiding the obvious connotation: the phantoms were his own private burden. No-one could share it with him. So he had snapped at Schreiber's witticism, a reproof he took in good part, shifting his demeanour to a more formal footing without any trace of resentment, and Altmann suspected him of more acuity than he usually demonstrated.

The Americans had reacted with seeming surprise and relief at Schreiber's explanation of Altmann's order to prepare an inflatable dinghy. "We will drop you close inshore," he said with a conspiratorial air. "You are lucky. This commander usually shoots survivors once they have told him what they say they know. Or sometimes he just dives without inviting them below."

Ford nodded a terse "Sure—we been told what to expect. Ask questions first and shoot afterwards, huh? Well, I told him all I can remember."

"My advice is to get away as quickly as you can, in case he changes his mind. He does that quite often." Schreiber touched his temple with a forefinger. "War. He has had some bad experiences at the hands of the British—and your own people!"

"Maybe he should take the hint," replied Ford dryly.

"I am sorry about your ship—but that, too, is war, not so?"

"Sure. Don't worry. We'll send you the check sometime soon."

Whatever else the Americans had had to cope with, a tossing among the breakers had been certain, and to Schreiber's circumspect observation that at least two men would remember the *U-Bootwaffe* for its humanity, Altmann demurred. "If they survive in that surf, *Einswo*, they deserve their lives—deserve to get through the war. But it will only be because we can't carry prisoners. Sailing in sight of this coast is asking for trouble, but it's not out of care for *their* hides!" and Schreiber had bitten off an impulse to suggest that the pair could have been set adrift from the position of the torpedoing if the boat's safety had been at issue. He sensed that it would have been an indiscretion, would have intruded on something Altmann had decided, if not to erase from his conscience, to at least attempt its suppression. It would explain much that the first officer felt was having its effect on his commander's handling of the job. It seemed to him that there was a certain lessening of conviction, but he was reluctant to affirm it to himself; it could have been merely an example of the warping effect to which one's perceptions were subject during prolonged periods of cramped isolation so ideally realised by the u-boat's demands. So he kept his peace, and dawn had found them far beyond sight of land again on the resumed course to the north-east.

Altmann swept the horizon with his glasses. The deep blue of the Moçambique Channel turned with distance into the silvered knife-edge of the untenanted horizon's meeting with the equally empty sky, bar the sun's unrelenting presence. The scene's peaceful immensity possessed an air of detachment from the u-boat's business that was almost reproachful, and, aware of it, Altmann allowed himself the luxury of critical contemplation. War—conflict—had this terrible capacity for reducing the most ineffable and profound aspects of nature to chaos in an instant; without warning, without preparation, without compromise. At one moment the soul and spirit would be sated—overwhelmed—with the depth and extent of peace and balance in the natural order of Creation, and the next devastated by their total destruction effected by the puniest of discordant forces: a shot from a pistol, a round from a deck-gun, a torpedo-strike. The colossal, unimaginable forces of nature everywhere about him, on the ocean's face and in its depths and in the overarching expanse of the heavens were impotent against the ability of even the least powerful of man's engines of destruction to wreak havoc, measurable in the slightest evidence of imbalance in a finely-balanced system. War's disproportionately destructive power shook the universe, Altmann reflected: its effects on the mankind that wrought it were lethal incidentals. But, given a just cause, it was necessary nevertheless, which in turn justified the determination required to wage it.

And for the thousandth time he leafed back through the intervals at home with his family while the boat had taken shape in the yard at Bremen, and later, while refitting at Bordeaux preparatory to the commencement of this patrol—the two parts of his contract with the Fatherland, by both of which he gauged his worth and debt of duty in the cause of National Socialism. And of love?—in the cause of love? He watched the boat's sharp bow dip as the swell lifted the stern and white water foamed up through the perforated deck-plates and the gaps between the deck-planking, washing aft in serial spouts of diamantine brilliance in the sun, cascading back to the swirl of bubbles passing along the side-tanks; the water was as clear as stained glass, the sunlight penetrating to unplumbed depths in a play of shaft-like beams in a pellucid, yielding, protean medium that could move one to something akin to love; even in periods of its elemental rage, as in most of his experience of the North Atlantic—and, more recently, in the turbulent seas off the Cape: but a love devoid of sentimentality; a love based more on respect than affection, though associated with feelings towards his officers and men, where affection could intrude and contaminate the requirement for strict impartiality. He felt he had come dangerously close to sentimental motives in bringing with him certain members of his old crew—Schreiber, a refreshing change from the lugubrious Rogge, whom he had recommended for command with misgivings

123

which he had allowed wartime necessity to surmount; Benedict, chief in a more substantial sense than hitherto, promoted to *Kapitanleutnant (I)* with a number two, *Oberleutnant (I)* Peter Henning, a serious young man apt to attach as much gravity to Schreiber's mock-mordant observations as to the intricacies of the technical manuals he seemed to spend most of his spare time studying; and, promoted to petty officer first-class, one Klaus Falke, at this moment with him on the bridge enjoying a cigarette. In the right conditions it was Altmann's custom to allow off-duty men up to the open air in twos or threes. There were others of his old crew.

Of the new, as he still regarded them, was Helmut Steinhoff, *Oberbootsman*, in murmured conversation with Falke. He had made strenuous efforts to select his company where the practice was to accept the choice of expedient, more so in face of the growing shortage of suitable people. And, barring certain exceptions, Schreiber most conspicuously, his choice had leant towards married men, which, in some respects, could be seen as unwise in a fighting service of such crucial value to the cause. But it was his firm belief that the married man was a more reliable craftsman: he had more to lose by carelessness, indiscipline, incompetence; and, on average, he was older and more experienced. The working-up trials had exposed weaknesses, and changes had been made. Now, after several months of active service, he felt he had the measure of them as a cohesive, effective group, and could afford to indulge at least a simulacrum of affection for them, and for this boat, so much sturdier, so much more of a dependable tool, than the obsolescent, all-too-frail Atlantic design. Even the class name—Monsoon—had a more expansive, confident ring to it. It embraced wider horizons, greater ambitions, broader influence. And reflected his higher rank—a signal from headquarters during the outward passage, shortly after Neptune's formal reception on crossing the line, had announced his promotion to *Korvettenkapitan*, with Uncle Karl's personal congratulations. Misgivings about the war's progress apart, he had had to admit a certain sense of vindication. His record of tonnage sunk, putting him among the *U-Bootwaffe*'s top scorers, had been recognised; and the higher pay was welcome. He had allowed a modest celebration: a tot of schnapps all round accompanied by grinning handshakes from the men and more sober congratulations from his officers; even Benedict had unbent as far as remarking that if the war went on long enough they'd have an admiral on their hands.

"Keep Uncle Karl company—he needs someone to talk to, what with one thing and another, but he's not the free agent he makes out he is."

Well, Herbert said these things; it was for effect more than in earnest; but there was something in it after all: the rank pointed the way to other, if not necessarily better, things. Like a staff job, if he kept his nose clean. Ursula would welcome that; she wouldn't concern herself about the fact of its being something of a reduction in function by comparison with action on the high seas. In this respect he felt no compunction about the question of love: now with three children, all utter charmers, and a wife whose Nordic beauty and serene nature was still a matter for general admiration and congratulation, to say nothing of his own ever-renewed sense of humble gratitude, Altmann had begun to see his family responsibilities in a light of considerably more warmth and humanity than that of duty to the cause. In fact he had come, with momentary alarm, to regard this part of his life as something that deserved a separate evaluation altogether. It was a novel idea that, to his irritation, intruded upon his views where they bore upon the domestic affairs of his crew. Some element of his argument in favour of duty to Fatherland and *Führer* seemed to have lost conviction, and that it might show was a matter for concern.

But Ursula stood firm as the guide, the beacon. The values she represented as a wife, a mother, friend and lover could be translated into advice, understanding, sympathy for his men that augmented the constant exhortation—expressed and implied—to loyal service as the key to ultimate victory. Ursula. Her power to calm his more extreme excursions into misgiving and morbid retrospection was, he realised, the most precious of his possessions in the circumstances, without which he suspected his present situation would never have come about. The *U-Bootwaffe* had more than its fair share of dead heroes. And, he thought, less than its fair share of victories, as a gauge of effort expended.

And there was another thing. His thoughts of home and family were now free of much of the anxiety that had clouded them ever more darkly as Allied attacks on Germany's heartlands had increased. By the time he had commissioned the new boat he had got them installed in a pleasant rented house in the village of Rauenthal, tucked away on the slopes north of the Rhine at a safe distance from Frankfurt and other likely bombing targets. Straubhals had a cousin there; Altmann had been grateful for his offer of help. But Ursula had been anxious for her parents, who refused to move from the city with her. A retired *Kapitan-zur-See*, her father was a leading member of the local defence volunteers: no *Engländer* was going to bomb him out of his place of duty. It had nagged at the back of Altmann's mind: she insisted on paying them frequent visits, which he could not forbid her. So, he reflected uneasily, his freedom was qualified. Just occasionally his thoughts betrayed him with possibilities, and at such times other dark alleys of cogitation; the clutch of floodlit images in the rising Atlantic gale had settled at the back of his mind like a flight of ravens, black feathers ruffled in the breeze of recollection, harsh cries echoing the machine-guns' hammering. He could suppress the scene in his waking moments, but in sleep was at its disposal, and the temptation to resort to the pill-box or, worse, the bottle, was another element of daily concern; it could be handled, he knew, for only as long as his sense of duty towards the boat, towards the cause, outweighed it. That, and the certainty of everyone's remarking any lapse on his part, especially a lapse from ground of which he made so much as part of his disciplinary method.

Abandoning his ruminations with an effort he swept the horizon with the glasses once more. Nothing. Not even a smudge of smoke. Peace lay heavy on the scene, oppressive, unwelcome. He craved action, of which there was less chance so far off the African coast, following courses well to seaward, a precaution against discovery by the frequent air patrols that protected coastwise shipping; better now, perhaps, to cruise within sight of it, closing to within touching distance of Portuguese territorial waters and the shipping concentrated about the port of Lourenço Marques. Time to add to his score, confirm Uncle Karl's faith in his elevated rank. He nodded to himself, then turned at the sound of puffing to see Schreiber emerging red-faced from the hatchway. The officer saluted.

"Lunchtime, *Kal-Kapitan*—" The hesitation at the rank appellation was ingenuous enough to be flattering "—You must have a raging appetite with all this fresh air. A bowl of cabbage soup and a slice of mouldy *Roggenbrot* will cure it—mention my name to the chef and who knows?—you might get an extra helping!"

Altmann glanced pointedly at the first officer's tanned midriff, tending to bulge above the belt supporting his shorts. Making an exception to his standing order on dress he allowed the watch

126

and others to strip to the waist in fine weather, believing the sun in moderation did them good. Their bodies had tanned, their beards and hair lost colour: a crew of Vikings, thought Altmann. Stripped-down Vikings. Or Siegfried's *Nibelungen*, a metaphor he had discarded more successfully than the more substantial phantoms associated with the boat he had left in the flotilla engineer's hands at Lorient, accumulated like a Chinese junk's devils. *Nothung* had established for him an identity that had become a curse. His decision to operate *incognito*, not showing even the flotilla emblem on the conning-tower, was a pathetically ineffective attempt to work on a clean slate. With every boat in service marked by some device—Schnee's snowman, Cremer's three fishes, Kretschmer's horseshoe, not as lucky as it might have been, von Bülow's Nordic dragon, the laughing swordfish of the 7th Flotilla, Barten's wedding-ringed dagger, Topp's red devil, the arms of a sponsoring city—his boat's lack of insignia rendered it almost more conspicuous than its sisters, and he had debated with himself the wisdom of his decision. Better had Uncle Karl enforced the official ban on all distinguishing marks; as it was, the personal insignia were for all practical purposes as revealing as the pennant numbers that had been painted out or omitted from the commencement of hostilities . . .

"*Kapitän?*" Schreiber, regarding him curiously. With a start he shook off the demons. "Dreaming," he said, smiling briefly.

"Your wife, *Kapitän?*" Schreiber nodded soberly. "And family, eh? So would I! But—" he shrugged, grinning self-deprecatingly "—as yet, no offers."

"Time enough to take on a married man's responsibilities, *Einswo*. First you need financial security; and you can't afford to make a bad choice: the right woman is vital—not only to the man but also to the Fatherland he serves, eh?"

"Right, *Kapitän*—the boat alone is enough to be getting on with." Schreiber nodded about at their surroundings. "I'll take her from you if you can bear to part—the soup's getting cold!"

"Where's he keeping it—in the fridge?" The temperature in the boat, which in the tropics on the outward passage and now in this improving sub-tropical weather of the southern summer, reached oven-like levels during the day when surfaced, resulted, when submerged, in heavy condensation and the almost visible propagation of mould; it also favoured the legions of cockroaches, weevils and lice sprung, it seemed, from the boat's very fabric. Among her crew it provoked Red

Dog—rashes and blisters like a more virulent form of the surface ship's dhobi itch, the term borrowed from the English who, it was gratifying to know, also suffered. The doctor—a luxury the potency of which was vitiated in certain respects by the customary nature of u-boat life—could do little more than to urge Altmann to allow as many men into the open air as possible, as frequently as possible. Where, as Schreiber had remarked, they exchanged Red Dog for sunstroke. He himself sported a disreputable straw hat obtained from the navigator of the milch-cow, the modified Type IX supply-boat, with which they had rendezvoused off the Cape Verdes to top up the fuel tanks and other necessities on their way south.

Altmann had brought the boat out into the Atlantic after crossing the Bay as quickly as possible—on the surface. Reliance on the Metox radar-detector had been a matter of caution rather than confidence, and on two occasions they had been jumped by an aircraft before the instrument had given warning. Altmann suspected the wilier pilots of switching off their radars, where fitted, at the moment of first detection to work on visual contact from then until final attack, which rendered the Metox impotent. Benedict's never-failing readiness and instant reaction had been almost psychic, and the boat had avoided damage, on one occasion diving so rapidly that the bridge had flooded while Altmann was still only waist-down in the hatch. Benedict's contrition had been comic, but Altmann had hastened to reassure him. "Make it as fast as you can, Herbert. Commanding officers are expendable items!"

"Some, anyway." Benedict had retorted. "I can think of one or two I'd dive twice as fast for."

"Yes? How do they qualify for such favours?"

"Bastards," grunted Benedict. "Motherless swine."

"So . . ."

But the fact remained that the Metox was not to be trusted, and as they had kept the Iberian coast below the eastern horizon, the tension in the boat had been electric, and played on the nerves. Alarm dives had become almost supernaturally fast, automatic reactions to the first indication of the presence of any other object—ship, aircraft or figment of an overtuned imagination. Only slowly, after dropping Gibraltar and the straits approaches astern, had the atmosphere in the boat lightened. It had been accompanied by gentler seas, sunnier days, calmer clearer nights, and fewer alarms. The last before passing the Canaries had been a destroyer, which appeared from the west at high speed making for them on an interception course with no warning from asdic or radar, picked out of the dusk by an alert lookout in time for an alarm dive to a hundred metres and a tense wait while the sound of high-speed screws increased, passed overhead, and receded.

"Two and a half minutes," announced a red-faced Schreiber when it was clear that the ship was bent on business other than u-boat hunting. He tapped his watch. "Held my breath for two and a half minutes. A record, I think."

"What for?" asked Benedict. "Plenty of air in the boat."

"Practice," explained Schreiber earnestly, winking at Henning. "Never know when it might come in handy. Dive too late—or too fast—and—" he swept a finger across his throat and beamed at Benedict "—I might be the only one to tell the story."

"Pity," said Benedict. "Facts are what's wanted, not stories."

"Trouble with engineers," said Schreiber sadly, "is they have no imagination. No sense of the romance of the sea."

Altmann's concern had been with their exchange of tension for boredom, the turning-point marked by the passing destroyer. Exacerbated by the effects of the increasing heat as the latitude decreased, it possessed the power to affect morale. From its sour ground sprouted the thorns and creepers of discontent and disagreement, normally of no significance, so that a man's way of eating a sausage, cleaning his teeth, holding a pen, could provoke an explosive remonstrance; a game of chess a sudden outburst of fury, even a fight. Boredom induced the blasé sins of carelessness, sloppiness; led to accidents, endangered the boat, and Altmann was all too well aware of the fact. He disapproved of idleness and unrelieved routine at sea as he disapproved of debauchery ashore, not only from a normally moral standpoint but also, and importantly to him, from the standpoint of the purity of the Fatherland's cause. It stood to suffer terminal effects from moral breakdown; the risk had to be eliminated at its first indications—indeed, in anticipation of them, and it was part of his duty as commanding officer to ensure as much.

The duty manifested itself in apparently tireless efforts in person—expressing a close interest in every man's job, every man's problems with it, every man's little triumphs and fancied or real failures, and it pleased them because it was clearly genuine; he fired off an endless round of questions to do with every possible circumstance affecting a man's work and leisure, and set up competitions, between the watches, between teams, between individuals—quizzes, board-game tournaments, song-writing and singing; even boxing matches, held on deck in the flat calms of the doldrums, when passing showers also provided gluts of fresh water, saved for drinking and cooking, profligately squandered in bathing. Soapsuds left an unlikely wake. He hung a clip-board in the heads for comments about the service, or about anything that came to mind including original witticisms, with choice items read out at the end of the week. Under the *nom-de-plume* of "Tommy", Falke emerged as a satirist of unsparing perspicacity who moved Altmann to discreet surveillance of a tendency to turn the beam of ridicule on figures all too easily exposed to it—national figures whose positions reflected Germany's stature. He would not permit open disparagement of the body politic, which would itself be a sign, or provocation, of demoralisation. His own authority depended in the first instance on a chain of deference, and at least an appearance of respect, towards leading figures of the *Reich*. The crew must never be allowed to think that doubt of the rightness of the Fatherland's cause and the competence of its overseers would be acceptable, even in jest, and his idea of a lying contest proved to be the perfect diversion, deflecting the thrust of cynicism into the formless matter of incredulity. It produced not mere lies in isolation but complete tales, the best of which the doctor noted with the aim of getting a collection printed and bound as a memento of the patrol, portrayed in one story as a pleasure cruise of grotesque proportions. They were complemented by an open-category poetry competition, which produced some—widely-approved—disgusting flights of imagination combined with surprising talent, again noted by the doctor. He himself gave a series of lectures on general shipboard hygiene and brought the house down with a dead-pan spoof on the perils of shoregoing. Rather bashfully, Altmann submitted a few verses on regular use of the heads, mistaken for lavatory humour by several over-enthusiastic individuals, duly chastised by Schreiber.

"A regular crap is no joking matter, Gerhard," he admonished. "Sign the book every time you go—I'll keep a check, and it's a visit to the medic if you miss a single day. Constipation clogs the mind as well as the rectum. In the end you can't tell which is which. Nasty."

In fact Altmann was in earnest about such matters, believing that from intestinal disorder came a plethora of shipboard complaints. Professionally as well as diplomatically, Lange expressed his agreement. He also agreed with Altmann's standing orders prohibiting strong coffee, and ice in drinks; they also forbade smoking on an empty stomach. A week after sailing Altmann had ordered a muster and short-arm inspection by the doctor, whose first talk on health, ostensibly directed at the single men, had concerned the risks of womanising in port.

"Bit late," observed Falke to anyone within earshot. "Or, on the other hand, a bit early. Time in harbour before we sign off back in Bordeaux or Kiel or wherever it'll be will amount to roughly nil. Absolutely no risk, apart from the heads seat. Remember to lift it when necessary."

Pleased to note that nobody exhibited symptoms of any serious social malaise, Altmann had felt justified in his severe castigation of one of the torpedomen, *Mechanikersmaat* Dieter Hille, who reported with an infestation of pubic lice.

"Crabs," said Hille's first confidant, Falke, with a shake of his head. He pursed his lips. "Not to be confused with the other seaside species of the same name, found in tins and on restaurant menus . . . I'm surprised at you, Hille my boy—men of the *U-bootwaffe* don't normally have to scrape the barrel for social diversion."

"Is it serious?"

Falke studied Hille's anxious features with the air of a bank manager interviewing an overdrafted client. He scratched his beard and raised an eyebrow. "Depends on the place of origin—?"

"She was a nurse—or is."

"Ah." With a sigh Falke looked regretful. "The worst kind. They come into daily contact with every kind of disease, as you should know. And that's only professionally . . ."

"Shit. I'll kill the bitch."

"It won't cure the problem," said Falke. "But diesel oil might—"

"*Diesel* oil—?"

"Shave off, rub it on—or in. Stings a bit. Chief'll be only too happy to oblige with a thimbleful. Alternatively, you could report to the *Herr Doktor*—"

"And get an official black mark and an educational lecture from the skipper?"

Falke shrugged. "Up to you, but there's always a chance you might have picked up something more—subtle, shall we say? Be a man, and see the sawbones. You can rely on learning the worst from him. I'm only an unqualified observer."

"For fuck's sake! I'll murder the cow if—"

"You've plenty of time. See the doc first."

At Lange's passing on the information in his daily report Altmann had treated the angry but shamefaced torpedoman to a lengthy homily. "—You know that any kind of ailment among the boat's crew can put us all in danger, Hille? And I don't mean from further infection—I mean from a less efficient operation! How can you do your job properly when your mind's on your damned reproductive organs?"

"I—"

"Be quiet! You're old enough to know better, and I don't want any half-baked excuses for something you knew carried a risk. I'd be guilty of not attending to my duty if I didn't have you transferred to the army, you know that? Luckily for you, it can't be done for some time, but this goes on the record, with a warning. You let us all down by bringing any sort of sickness on yourself, and in the end you betray the Fatherland. Your own hide is unimportant, except that its condition affects those who depend on you. Got the idea?"

"Yes, *Herr Kaleu*—but a nurse—"

"The worst kind, Hille—because no-one expects it of them, and the lowest swine under the sun take advantage of them. Think yourself lucky it's only crabs—and a conditional reprimand!"

"Yes, *Herr Kaleu.* Thank you."

"Don't *thank* me!—and take more care over your choice of friends—and what you do with them."

He also instituted news bulletins, appointing the second watch-officer, *Leutnant-zur-See* Markus Palmgren, honorary editor of a double-page daily.

"Why honorary, *Kaleu?* "

"You don't get paid."

"Yes—but—I mean—"

"What?"

"Oh—nothing. Nothing, *Kaleu.* I'll be happy to do the job."

"That's the spirit!"

There was an ingenuousness in Palmgren that invited gentle leg-pulling, but he earned general regard when he emerged, through the news-sheet, as a competent cartoonist and caricaturist. People paid him for their portraits, executed in ink and pencil-line, which revealed the subject's most risible characteristics to his pleased embarrassment and others' delighted mockery; but to the admiration of both.

The news was something of an incidental, until it revealed the business with which the passing destroyer had possibly been connected:

since the boat's arrival in South African waters British and American forces, after long Atlantic passages, had landed on the seaboard of north-west Africa to begin a pincer movement with the British advance from the spot, El Alamein, where Rommel's Afrika Korps had been brought to a halt by the limits of its supply-line and the appearance on the scene of a British commander named Montgomery. This was greeted with gloom amidst a scattering of irrational optimism, and argument that threatened to become more acrimonious than the normal vigorous interplay of different views.

But there were always the ocean and the weather to distract attention. Altmann had set up a regular weather observation routine and given lectures on meteorology that produced a couple of keen students, one—the boat's midshipman, Rudolf Hildegras, whose name combined with a wispy blond beard had earned him the cumbrous nickname of Seagrass—declaring an interest that might serve him after the war, in default of his prior aim at a career in architecture. He had no aspirations towards naval distinction beyond the war's demands. People were beginning to think about the fabled prospect of After The War, though in u-boats its likelihood, let alone imminence, was largely a matter of tacit fatalism. It seemed unlucky to assume survival beyond the current patrol, but it was perhaps a reflection of Altmann's competence as a commander that his crew felt the assumption to be even tentatively justified.

And he went further than the weather. He had begun writing a full-length work on matters of leadership, finding that his presentation of parts of the material in the form of lectures on history, touching on politics, helped him to order and clarify his subject-matter. It was his firm conviction—and a logical one—that the men should know what they were fighting for, beyond mere survival decorated with instances of triumph only barely removed from the personal. Not only that, but, knowing what they were fighting for, they had to be prepared to lay down their lives for it—for the cause. Naturally enough his politics were uncompromisingly slanted towards the National Socialist ideal, or his conception of it; his historical stance leant heavily on the presumption of ultimate German predominance on the world stage, pointing to events from the time of Charlemagne as indicators of an unequivocal racial and national destiny of which the *Dritte Reich* would prove to be the just culmination. Among other virtues it would be a nursery of the best human attributes—hard work, healthy living, the family unit, personal bravery and unswerving patriotism, and a moral responsibility that would avoid worldly hypocrisy by its partial abrogation to higher civil and military authority: matters of conscience could safely be entrusted to figures that personified the Fatherland's Godly surrogacy in the Party's hands. The concept of Jewry lay outside the pale of national virtue, which could be assumed and adopted with a clear conscience. He made no conscious attempt at humour, aware of what he felt were his limitations in that respect: neither in the abandoned legal sphere nor in his firm naval loyalties had he set out to amuse his compatriots. His goal and duty were to lead them with decision and conviction.

Schreiber enjoyed selective approbation of his handful of jazz and modern dance records, obtained variously from the milch-cow's navigator and black market sources in Bordeaux, succeeding in overcoming Altmann's initial disapproval of what he averred was subversive rubbish. Goodman and Gershwin had joined Beethoven, Bach and their contemporaries by a form of *force majeure.*

"What about German bands?"

Schreiber coughed and squared his shoulders. "Nowhere, *Herr Kaleu.*"

"Nowhere?"

"They play like marionettes."

"I see . . . Well, don't make a big thing of your Americans. We're supposed to be at war with them."

"They'll perform for the *Reich* when we've finished, *Kaleu.*"

"Mm. A doubtful blessing, *Einswo.*"

Not particularly bookish or musical, Altmann had nevertheless seen to it that a small library had been provided, together with a gramophone and a stock of records, all of improving compositions, as he saw them, by suitably national figures. There were plenty to choose from—Beethoven proved popular, Bach less so. Haydn's symphonies and string quartets produced spell-like silences among the listeners, most of whose experience and knowledge of classical music varied from sketchy to blank ignorance. Mozart's violin concertos had a similar effect, counterpoint to such rousing diversions as *Don Giovanni* and *The Marriage of Figaro.* Schubert's *Unfinished Symphony* moved one or two to momentary tears, surreptitiously controlled. Altmann favoured Wagner, whose popularity overreached the rest, and *The Flying Dutchman* and *Rienzi* were played to near-destruction. He reserved the four works of the *Ring* cycle for a use that went some way towards heightening his somewhat sanguinary reputation as a dedicated naval officer: as the patrol progressed he took to playing one or another of them as he followed and prepared to attack his targets, as long as the sea state allowed: the frequency of the performances emphasised the contrast between the Atlantic's moody restlessness and the Indian Ocean's normally benign composure. Those in the know referred the ignorant to the previous boat's name and the tonnage she had contributed to Uncle Karl's war balance, but it stopped short of full detail: the schooner's place on the record was taboo. For all practical purposes, including the personal safety of those in possession of the fact, she had never existed. Somehow, their presence at the scene, whether or not they had taken an active part—and in fact none of *Nothung*'s erstwhile crew could claim complete detachment from the action, since all had had a duty station—would imply complicity, with possible consequences of dire extent, such was the ambiguity of the political elements in the *Reich*'s legal affairs, both civil and military. Not only that, but also all were conscious of a certain element of shame in the episode, its Judaic connotations notwithstanding; and that it would not bear the kind of prideful reference to which any other successful action was entitled was a tacit acknowledgment of the fact that the war, at least as it affected *U-Bootwaffe* operations, did not seem to be progressing quite as had been planned, whatever was said or heard by way of positive assurance. Just conceivably there might come a time when evidence would be required by other than the *Reich*'s authorities, a possibility to which nobody dared refer while knowing it to be generally recognised . . .

And to drive his point home Altmann ended each day—each daylight day, formally at sunset—with the Berlin Philharmonic's recording of the National Socialist hymn: *Wenn Alle Untreu Werden* invariably secured the men's sober, even emotional, attention. And while Altmann was satisfied that it refocused their thoughts and beliefs it was, asserted Falke, *sotto voce*, somewhat less raffish than the *Horst Wessel* and less jingoistic than the *Beerkeller* rant of *Deutschland Über Alles*, which, as he pointed out, sounded less convincing in application to the *U-Bootwaffe* than to, say, the *Luftwaffe*—"At least," he ended with an affectation of critical regret, "until around September, nineteen-forty." To which his listeners had no ready answer.

In spite of himself Altmann approved of some of Schreiber's trendy offerings, which apart from American material included equally dubious home-grown items, distinctly inferior-quality *in situ* recordings from the mainstream cabaret of Berlin and Hamburg of which songs by Lale Anderson prompted applause from the cultural elements of the boat's company described by a sardonic Falke as low-brow. But low- or high-brow, inevitably, *Lili Marleen* became an almost constant feature of waking life in the boat, hummed and tersely whistled between the teeth at a decibel level just beneath the murmur of the electric motors and drowned by the rhythmic chatter of the diesels, like a breath of spring in late winter. But songs from Weill's *Die Dreigroschenoper* and *Aufstig und Fall der Stadt Mahagonny*, rendered in plangent tones by Lotte Lenya, prompted something akin to indignation among the party votaries on board, and Altmann felt obliged to suggest their withdrawal.

"No point in making your motives suspect, *Einswo*. American influence is one thing, but a Jewish composer and singer is asking a little too much of good German stock. You know, of course, that this stuff has been banned?"

"I've heard something of the kind, *Kaleu*."

"Yes...And personally I find it depressing. There's something—*black* about the melodies."

"It's the whole idea, *Kaleu*—dark satire."

"I think we have enough dark satire in our work, *Einswo*. No need to set it to music. Especially Jewish music."

At which Schreiber threw his commanding officer a covert glance of curiosity, confirming to himself yet again that there was more to the man than prosaic efficiency.

Apart from his own lectures on meteorology Altmann made use of the library and the music—the German music, classical, not the first officer's jingling—for discussion groups, which released some unsuspected enthusiasms; he also discovered and sounded, by shrewd encouragement, pools of knowledge deep and wide enough to be presented as lectures by their possessors—Benedict's dryly eccentric exposition of basic diesel engineering lubricated with judicious injections of its history, in which German innovation and invention had played a leading part, held the rapt attention of even the most unmechanical; Schreiber created a stir with not merely his grasp of mathematics but also a deft facility for lucid explanation—even of the differential calculus, Altmann ruefully noted; concentrated fare relieved by Lange's classes in first aid. The chief radio-man, *Oberfunkmaat* Joschen Schwebke, offered, diffidently, a series of lectures on philosophy, a subject with which he passed the time not taken up actually at the key or on the hydrophone, opening with a controversial discourse on Plato's *Republic* that interested Altmann, not least in Schwebke's speculative comparisons with modern systems of government, including, prominently, National Socialism, with obvious extensions to aspects of military service. They generated occasional additions to the boat's heated atmosphere that required Altmann's moderating intervention.

But, as Schreiber suspected, there was another purpose behind Altmann's vigorous methods of command. At a time when action was to be avoided, replaced by the daily monotony of passage navigation, he found himself in danger of succumbing to the *ennui* that pervades all such forms of isolation from the demands of normal life—and of the battle-zone; and with it the ever-present threat of involuntary recollection, prompted in his waking moments by anything among his surroundings bearing an exact or similar resemblance to elements of the fateful scene; and in sleep by the unavoidable recurrence of nightmare. He could suppress the waking intrusions, but his only way of controlling the sleeping descents into phantasmagoria was to fend off sleep itself. Which, he acknowledged with a sensation akin to fear, led inexorably to a decline in personal efficiency of the kind against which he had warned Hille. And occurring in the boat's commander as distinct from one of her torpedomen it represented a far greater potential for catastrophe. Moreover, being aware of it, he would be equally negligent of his duty in allowing it to continue.

So what was he to do? He could not renounce his command—hand it over to Schreiber, say, no matter how competent the first officer proved himself. The opportunity to apply for transfer to another branch of the navy, or for leave on grounds of physical or mental exhaustion, had passed; and in any case such a move would be terminally detrimental to his professional standing—would, in the circumstances, place him at risk of accusations of cowardice, notwithstanding the fact that the casualty rate owing, ostensibly, to nervous exhaustion among commanders in the *U-Bootwaffe* was a matter of common knowledge if not overt acknowledgment. Death at a hundred metres was a preferable option to death by tacit disgrace, except for its involving other, innocent, parties. And that, to Altmann, was unthinkable. He could not betray his men for want of moral integrity.

His only course was clear: he would simply have to brace himself to bear the ever-increasing weight of consequence, exerting an ever-tightening hold on his nervous resources and facing down the almost daily onslaught of—what? Guilt? No—that would be an unwarranted imputation of criminal culpability; it would be improperly assumed. Responsibility, then. Yes—he was merely undergoing the kind of extreme effect of a commander's responsibility for which no amount of theory could prepare him: the kind that would be encountered only in practice, and would be dealt with according to the individual's ingrained moral resources, albeit reinforced to some small extent by those elements of training and experience that had confronted him with tests of moral endurance. The official term had been "character", an absurdly inadequate expression typical of a system that took a certain kind of manliness for granted; a system the weakness of which lay in its avoidance of questions of human frailty. They lay in the realm of the unthinkable, embarrassing in their implications for a tradition of stern self-discipline, self-sacrifice and loyalty. The German officer did not admit to weakness, moral, physical or mental, except at the cost not merely of his professional, but of his actual, life. Which, in the final count, was a way of absolving himself from the disgrace.

Running along these lines, Altmann's thoughts invariably strayed to events that had marked the war's progress at sea to date, ultimately revolving about the *Graf Spee* incident, as some referred to it. Already Langsdorff's name was a matter for equivocation among naval officers; his suicide was variously seen as heroic, if ineffectual, a gesture of weakness in its apparent means of avoiding an action against the enemy that need not necessarily have ended in defeat; and even if it had, the defeat would have been in the glorious tradition of a proud service. An argument, Altmann reflected, that had been more than tarnished by the later encounter to which he had been, in a sense, witness. There had been overtones of ignominy in the outcome of the *Bismarck* affair and in the—albeit successful—channel dash of the battle-cruisers and *Prinz Eugen* that would find an echo in any attempt of his own to evade responsibility for what had passed in his own activities, unrecorded as it might have been. He must go on; must bear the weight; could not seek to avoid or share it. After all, Uncle Karl had been tacitly aware of the matter, and had not even hinted at a lack of confidence in his commander's competence. Which was another factor he had to take into account: weakness or failure on his part would not only put his men at hazard, but would also betray Uncle Karl's confidence, throw his judgment into question—above all cause him dismay, disappointment, regret. And there, mused Altmann, was his example: whatever he in his cockleshell had to bear by way of responsibility, Dönitz's equivalent was infinitely greater. And that the C-in-C's having to bear the consequences of mistakes and errors of judgment, fancied or real, quite alone, while maintaining an outward display of calm dignity at all times, was undeniable, meant that he, Altmann, could surely follow suit. He would have to mine ever deeper levels of moral resource, drawing on his reserves not until he felt he could go no farther but until he exhausted the supply, found himself beyond recovery, bereft of every last trace of self-justification. He had not yet even begun to approach that point, was prey merely to indications of possibilities, still possessed of the capacity to handle the mundane demands of duty to the boat, her crew, himself. It required effort, that was all; ever-increasing effort, certainly, but effort expected of him by the service he had chosen in favour of what he had correctly seen as less demanding options. Not for him Gretchen's immaculate progress to distinction—so rudely curtailed—via the wardroom's social intrigues, where the forms of disgrace were no less terminal but were also distasteful. Death in Gretchen's case—honourable as it had been—might have saved him from a different kind of untimely end.

So Altmann had braced himself, and discovered in his keenly-active interest in all aspects of his boat's affairs a means of recruiting the body of personal resource. But the phantoms persisted; and he had faltered, and sought other support.

"I prefer less—traumatic—methods, *Kaleu*. Among the common causes of lack of sleep are the things we eat and drink—coffee, for instance. We all drink too much. It's a form of poison. Try cocoa. The Royal Navy seems to thrive on it. And pills are—or can be—addictive. You come to rely on them." Lange tapped the bottle to eject half a dozen into a waxed-card pillbox and handed them to Altmann, holding his gaze with a steady stare. "These are killers, *Kaleu*. Secobarbital. Depresses the central nervous system. Principal action is on parts of the brain, but it also depresses the functions of body tissue. The effect is sedative. Larger doses are hypnotic. Still larger doses are fatal. Prolonged use creates chronic breakdown of muscular coordination, and the desired effect—sleep—becomes less potent, less recuperative. Don't take them unless you think you've got at least a couple of hours to yourself. One only, no more than once in twenty-four hours. There's no guarantee that you won't have nightmares. It's the best I can do for you. Or the worst." Lange's notion of the commander's nightmare was ludicrously innocent.

From time to time Altmann had opened the box and contemplated its contents, but nothing more. He couldn't count on an hour to himself, let alone two; as for the alternative to pills, it was too obvious; and in any case he was teetotal. The last drink he remembered with any pleasure had been that swig from Liebeherr's hip-flask on the night he'd met Ursula. So long ago. He wondered about Liebeherr, about the way he'd died, and why, apart from slipping up in the dance—missing his step in the Depth-Charge Dodge. Somehow he couldn't see Hansel resorting to barbiturates, nor—surely—succumbing to the bottle. But then, it was unlikely that he'd notched up a phantom kill.

On a lighter note, they had relieved the enervating effects of the doldrums' humid heat by preparations for Neptune's ceremonial visit, prompted, as Altmann had announced, by His Majesty's taking special note of the fact that only seven of the boat's company had previously crossed the Line and, per radio message in plain language, warned of his intentions. The proclamation was posted on the control-room notice-board. A joint work by Schreiber and Palmgren, it was elaborately-decorated with sea-serpents, dolphins, mermaids, sirens and nymphs and the seals of Neptune and the *Reich*.

BE IT KNOWN
that
I, NEPTUNE
Lord and Ruler of the Deep and all its Creatures, to whom all who venture upon my Domain owe Allegiance on pain of Perpetual Banishment,
HEREBY GIVE NOTICE
that, the undersea ship of war commanded by my True and Faithful Servant Kapitanleutnant Gunnar Altmann, having essayed to traverse my Domain from its Northern Reaches towards the Great Southern Sea manned by a Crew consisting in large part of Landsmen, will, on crossing the Great Equatorial Boundary, be subject to any or all of the Perils of the Deep including fire, wreck, stranding, mutiny, malaise, storm, calm, engine-failure, enemy attack and navigational error UNLESS duly granted safe passage by myself NEPTUNE, in person,

together with my Court and Officers, within one whole day's sailing of
the said Crossing,
TO WHICH END *the said Kapitanleutnant Gunnar Altmann is hereby*
requested and required to make all necessary arrangements to enable
his Command to be safely and expeditiously boarded, and to supply
my Chief Officer with all the usual facilities including a LIST of all
on board not able to produce duly signed and sealed Documentary
Evidence of previous such voyage or voyages.

Given by My Hand at Sea
on this Twenty-third Day of October, Nineteen Forty-two.

"I've crossed the Line ten times altogether, *Einswo.*"

"In what?"

"I was able seaman with the German East-Africa Line before joining
the *U-Bootwaffe* in 'thirty-nine."

"Then you're exempt from the ceremony, Pfeiffer."

"But I have no document."

"Ah. That's unfortunate."

"I'll have to go through it all again?"

"I'm afraid so."

"I see."

"Of course you could speak to the second officer—"

"What about?"

"I gather he's offering forged certificates, at a reasonable price."

"Oh . . . And will it be good enough?"

"Who knows? It's a gamble, Pfeiffer. If so—bravo!"

"And if not?"

Schreiber sucked sharply through his teeth and slowly shook his
head. "I don't know. I've never tried it myself."

"Have you crossed the Line, *Einswo?*"

"Oh, yes. In a square-rigger, *Kommodore Johnsen*, and later as a
cadet in the *Deutschland*. Her last cruise before the war . . . Twice in
each. We came back."

"And you have proof?"

"Of course."

"Maybe I'd better not try anything clever."

"Very wise, Pfeiffer. And this time keep the piece of paper safe, eh?
You never know when you'll need it again."

"Never, if I have anything to do with it, *Einswo*."

But there had been no question of a full ceremony, firstly because of the risk of surprise encounters with airborne or surface forces, secondly because of the dearth of *bona-fide* deep-water men eligible for positions in Neptune's court; they were outnumbered by the initiates, who could have proved to be more than the sea-dogs and police could handle if the usual ritual had been threatened. Instead, a more decorous affair saw Neptune and Amphitrite board from the foredeck on a day of oily calm and burning sunshine, actually Benedict and Schreiber suitably attired. Neptune, his crown fashioned from a catering-size tin originally containing *sauerkraut*, was stripped to the waist and a loin-cloth made up of strips of bed-sheet cut and dyed to resemble sea-wrack. He clutched a trident assembled from a deck-swab and a business-end produced in the motor-room. The mop-head end reposed in a bucket of motor-room bilge-water fortified with flour labelled *SHIT* in large capitals, placed at his side as he sat in near-naked state on a folding canvas chair just forward of the 37mm AA gun. Schreiber, his bust-line asymmetrically enhanced by two different-size pudding-bowls stitched into a cut-off undervest, and brush-like haircut enveloped by a green-dyed wig expertly coiffed by the cook from a length of unlaid hemp mooring-rope repeatedly boiled to soften it, and dyed green, moved Falke to inquire of anyone able to enlighten him where the first officer had obtained the lipstick, eyeshadow and rouge used to startlingly libidinous effect after shaving off a beard of precisely opposite effect. Just before he was made to swallow a moderately unpalatable pill composed of castor oil, flour, pepper and suspect egg, Henning remarked that even a Reeperbahn mermaid would have been challenged on her own ground. The pill had been prescribed by Lange in his capacity of court surgeon as the safer alternative to more traditional mixtures, safer less in the interests of the initiates' gastric processes than of the boat's potency and survival: it could not afford upset stomachs when every man's uninterrupted ability to do his job was so vital.

The court had consisted of the other five who claimed exoneration with proof of previous initiation, Pfeiffer's word verified only by his training record, nowhere endorsed by Neptune's seal, being accepted in view of the circumstances but on condition of his being made to swallow a soup-ladleful of a mixture of evaporated milk, sea-water and orange-juice labelled *Mermaid's Piss*, to revalidate his qualification as a sea-dog. The remainder—the landsmen whose presence had brought

Neptune aboard—were faced with a half-litre apiece to wash down the pill before being held head-down in a bucket of sea-water for a count of two and half minutes, chanted out by Amphitrite as the standard-setter. Then, dragged on their knees before Neptune, they received a mopful of the shit-bucket's contents full in the face and a sceptical word of welcome to the royal domains before being led away and given a small glass of schnapps to aid recovery, the only time, other than the marking of Altmann's promotion, they would get a taste of alcohol in the whole patrol.

The only casualty had been Hildegras. Admitting to an accusation of attempting to sail in blue water without permission, he had been made to swallow the pill and the mixture, then tipped backwards and his head immersed in the bucket while Amphitrite kept time with a watch that stopped in mid-count, unnoticed until a violent upheaval on Hildegras's part overturned the bucket, whereupon the police had hauled him back to Neptune's feet and a face-full of dripping mop, at which point he collapsed, deathly pale and spewing up sea-water. He recovered almost as soon as Lange administered artificial respiration, to be taken aside and given the ceremonial glass, from which he quaffed a mouthful before realising it was salt water.

"Swine," he gasped weakly, at which Amphitrite swung about with a look of horror on her face and commanded the police to repeat the proceeding. Gasping and retching, Hildegras crawled away from it to collapse in his bunk. He got a specially-endorsed certificate entitling him to roam the seas with immunity from seasickness.

"But I don't get seasick."

"It's the thought that counts, Seagrass."

"Piss off, *Zweiter*."

"Very apt."

Leaving Schreiber in charge on the bridge Altmann went below. Half-way through his soup, he was interrupted by a call in the clipped dispassionate tones of the first officer's official voice.

"Captain to the bridge—vessel in sight. Captain to the bridge!"

"I'll get Smut to keep it hot for you," said Benedict dryly, dabbing his mouth with a napkin.

Abaft the control-room, in the petty officers' mess, Falke looked up from his plate. "What's it to be this time?" he asked of no-one in particular. "We haven't heard the Valkyries for a while."

"How about *Begin the Beguine*?" Steinhoff was elaborately sardonic. "To suit the occasion—opening moves in the Battle of the Indian Ocean. *Jazzmeister Einswo* will be pleased to oblige."

"You're wrong there, *Bootsman*—the *Kreigsmarine*'s already opened it. *Graf Spee* sank the *Africa Shell* somewhere round here back in 'thirty-nine. The *Scheer* got three ships farther northward and the *Pinguin* got one somewhere off the southern end of Madagascar."

"And that's all?"

"All I know of without checking the records at High Command—what d'you expect—destruction of the British fleet?"

"That was the aim of the exercise, wasn't it?"

"Yeah. Was."

VI

TURNING to keep pace with her mean speed of around six knots, Altmann duplicated Schreiber's observations and finally ordered two shots to watch in disbelief as the tanker broke with the zig-zag—or perhaps followed its cunning complexity—at almost the same instant, swinging from one turn into another in a continuous movement. The torpedoes ran wide of the mark, apparently not even noticed by the ship's watchkeepers. Through the attack periscope he could see the officer of the watch, a white-clad figure in the shade of the bridge-awning, casually surveying the surroundings through binoculars but evidently missing the occasional feather of water betraying the boat's position. Embarrassed and coldly angry, Altmann ordered maximum speed and, slowly pulling ahead of the still zig-zagging tanker, made preparations to surface.

"Practice for your marksmen, *Zweiter*."

Palmgren nodded, solemnly tense, awaiting the moment as the depth-gauge pointer rotated smoothly towards zero. "They—we—need it, *Kapitän*."

"Take your time. I'm not looking for total obliteration. And she might go sky-high—her cargo's as likely to be spirit as crude or heavy fuel . . . In any case, wait for my order."

"Aye, *Kapitän*."

Yes, wait, thought Altmann in a snap reversion of sentiment on which he avoided dwelling. *Wait until I've given this one's people a chance. They deserve it after those misses. Surface, order them to*

144

stop, get the papers, give them directions, make sure they've got what they need, let them go. The ship must be killed, but not her people. Non-combatants . . . To his instruction to jam any wireless transmission Schwebke had replied, "Nothing yet, *Kapitän*—"

As the boat surfaced he scrambled into the sunshine noting the hiatus during which the boat was completely at the mercy of fate, the bridge a *mêlée* of shoving bodies assembling at their stations with painful slowness, emerging one by one from the depths, their movements strangely protracted, as if time itself had slowed, yet the clock raced ahead. *Move, damn it—!* He lit a cigarette to conceal his anxious impatience. Finally, the gun-crews stood ready, the lookouts had their glasses up and the bridge settled to its customary surfaced vigilance.

The tanker was so close he could count the plates along the sheer-strake, distinguish the Roman numerals of the draught-marks at her stem, the flying-fish breaking from the modest bow-wave tangling in confusion with others scrambling from the boat's turmoil. Absently, he noted the band of darker grey at the bow where the name had been painted out. At least it meant a belligerent's flag, whatever it was, probably British.

"All tubes ready, *Kapitän!*" Schreiber passed the range-finder glasses up. If anything the range was too short for his eels. Two of the gun-crew were passing shells down from the bridge locker, keeping their exclamations to a murmur. Discipline was good, noted Altmann, and nodded acknowledgment of Palmgren's carefully-modulated "Gun ready, *Kapitän!*"

Meanwhile, aboard the tanker were signs of alarm. The white-clad figure had vanished from the bridge-wing, others were running aft along the flying bridge, several were clustering about a spot on the tank-deck between the midship-house and the after accommodation at which the deck pipelines converged to form the shore-connection manifold. The scene was comic in its jerky, abrupt movement, and Altmann was half-smiling when the thought occurred to him like a douche of iced water—*What were they doing? God in heaven—is she a decoy—a Q-ship? If so he'd walked right into the trap, like a novice! Those pipelines clustered like that—they could easily conceal a gun; any one of them could be its barrel—*

"*Zweiter!*—one round, surface strike fifty metres ahead of her—when you bear!" On the voice-pipe to Schreiber: "Stand by tubes one and two!" He trained the ranging binoculars on the target.

A glance over his shoulder. The 20mm menaced the tanker: Bartels and another, the short, round-faced Knecht, a grocer's boy from Bavaria. Sweat glistened on his tanned cheeks, dribbled through his downy beard. He caught Altmann's eye and looked away, frowning at the target.

The deck-gun cracked, a split-second's pause as ears rang with the report, and with a muffled concussion a plume of white water sprang skywards ahead of the tanker. *"Reload!"* Palmgren's order came crisp and loud: no need for low tones; every need for clarity and authority. The spent shell-casing clanged, bell-like, on the deck-plating. *"Gun ready!"*

The groups of men on the tanker's deck had dispersed. Now three stood together on the bridge-wing, one with binoculars. Anxiously, Altmann returned their scrutiny. Just a tanker, unless they were going to wait until the u-boat lay closer-to. Altmann's mouth was dry, his throat sticky; he felt his stomach in a tight cold knot. His cigarette tasted bitter and he flung it away. After all the Atlantic's triumphs and disappointments, all its stark hazard and threatening calamity, it would be here in this ineffable expanse of sun-drenched blue, in a mirror-calm sea, that he would meet his Nemesis. Here, in this tranquil isolation, he would meet with the phantoms in a final reckoning, not in a display of heroics but in a brief flurry of humiliation before the concluding gesture. Which would be?—honourable suicide, perhaps, going down with his finger on the trigger, or trapped in the wreck of the bridge, like Schepke? Surrender and unyielding silence in the face of whatever happened to prisoners in the enemy's hands? In the opinion of some the Allies treated their captives with scant regard for rank or the Geneva Convention. The British in particular were known to be in an ugly mood; u-boat men were seen as outlaws, pariahs, in their ruthless disregard for humanitarian conduct let alone legal obligations. By their own actions they had forfeited whatever rights they might have claimed under the rules of war, and in such instances as this witnesses were for all practical purposes absent. As they'd been absent that night, he reflected: instead of witnesses all surviving participants had been just that—participants; accessories to the act, their silence assured, at least until the war's resolution. So it would be in this case, assuming, of course, that the situation turned out to be a mutually-armed action and not, as appeared so far, a potential commercial kill.

Altmann studied the tanker closely. By degrees, he felt the tension slacken. The crew's observable movements did not indicate or suggest the presence of a gun; no part of the hull or deck structures looked as if it concealed any kind of weapon: their function, including the pump-room housings, was obvious and normal; only imagination heightened by circumstances could have taken the pipeline manifold for a gun disguise. Men stood about now in full view, their initial alarm gone, gazing across the water at the u-boat in obvious inquiry. The officers on the bridge-wing stood openly, exposed to anything the enemy might decide to hurl at them. A party of men moved about the lifeboat on the lower bridge, evidently preparing it for launching, but not in any apparent haste. Altmann was conscious of an atmosphere of anti-climax savouring of the bizarre: the opening gunshot had been a melodramatic feint, a prod so timid that it had surely moved the tanker's people to blank incomprehension. Glancing to one side he saw that the ensign had been hoisted; now they'd know the u-boat for what it was: the play, the next move, was in his hands.

She was no decoy, he decided. Just what she appeared to be, nothing more—and nothing less: a worthwhile target. He grunted to himself and turned to Palmgren.

"Another round, *Zweiter*. Over the bridge this time. Don't hit it." He called down to the plot for the loudhailer microphone.

As the report of the gunshot lost itself in the blue expanse the figures about the tanker's decks ran for cover, ridiculously, like clowns in a circus act, but the men on the bridge-wing stood fast, one still scrutinising the u-boat through binoculars. Altmann nodded in acknowledgment of his cool-headedness. The captain, no doubt. Brave man, or a fool. He was not going to be stampeded into wasteful activity.

Altmann pressed the microphone button and spoke, careful of his pronunciation: "Stop your engines! Do not use your radio! Stop, or I will sink you! My next shot will be a hit!" He hoped the sound would carry; use of the signal lamp was a slow business when dealing with most merchantmen, though the meaning of the shot across the bows was unequivocal and—except in this case, it seemed—obvious.

"Gun ready!"

The man on the bridge-wing lowered his glasses and raised a hand, evidently in acknowledgment, before turning back into the wheelhouse. As everyone on the u-boat watched, the tanker's bow-wave began to subside and within fifteen minutes both vessels lay stopped, rolling gently in the swell, no more than three hundred yards apart. Further orders on the loudhailer brought the tanker's boat with her second officer alongside. He carried no papers, but confirmed the cargo: eleven thousand eight hundred tons of aviation spirit. High-octane stuff. The tanker was a floating bomb of cataclysmic potential. It occurred to Altmann that at this range her destruction by surface attack was likely to account for her attacker as well, and marvelled at the generally unruffled demeanour of her people. Used to their hazardous situation, the prospect of taking an unwary enemy with them must have been blackly amusing, not to say satisfying.

The second officer was tense, but clearly keenly interested in his surroundings, and stood looking about while he answered a few of Altmann's questions. The tanker was the *British Prowess* of the Anglo-Iranian Oil Company's fleet, on passage from Abadan to Cape Town to join a convoy for England. A motor-ship, seven years old. Captain Hugh Loftus. Thirteen officers, four apprentices, seven petty officers, two cooks, eighteen deck and engine-room hands and a couple of stewards. Including the master, forty-seven souls all told, mused Altmann. The petty officers and other ranks were Indian: Hindu and Muslim, and Goanese. A polyglot crowd, typical of the British with their empire's peoples to draw on. He wondered what the mood among the Indian crew-members was: were they willing participants in the war? Would they turn against their white officers in circumstances such as these? He glanced down at the boat and its crew of slightly-built brown men in blue denims, stained overalls, loose-fitting cotton shirts, baggy trousers, chattering among themselves in low tones, from time to time flashing glances at the boat's bridge, at the gun, at her men. They seemed neither particularly subdued, nor restive. Cheerful, if anything. Patient, like well-behaved dogs waiting for their master's return, trusting him. Their shy scrutiny was returned with interest by the u-boat's men.

Complacently, Knecht wiped the glistening metal of the 20mm flak-gun with an oily rag, scratched at a spot of rust with a thumbnail. The sea got to everything mechanical in the end, he mused; grease and oily rags were no better than a gesture in the face of the inevitable. Deftly, he worked the cocking-lever with a satisfying metallic *chunk!* It seemed to impress the brown men in the boat.

Altmann made an effort to sound neither friendly nor needlessly autocratic. The young officer remained stiffly formal, indifferent to the sweat gathering along the line of his jaw and soaking through his clean white shirt. He was almost a caricature of the correct Britisher, thought Altmann. His dress, his bearing. Whatever emotions might have been stirring in his breast, he was not going to hint at any of them except inadvertently. Squinting in the sunlight, Altmann studied the man as he lit another cigarette. The officer refused the proffered pack and waited, returning the u-boat man's gaze inquiringly. A pleasant young man. He might have been German with his fair hair, regular evenly-tanned features, blue eyes. Married, perhaps; or with a young woman somewhere, waiting and wondering. The war was hard on women; perhaps harder than on the men who fought it in direct confrontation with the enemy. Women hadn't the ability to detach their emotions from the impact—real and figurative—of action; had not the capacity for dispassionate execution of duty—barring exceptions, of course: there were a few; they tended to compensate by going too far towards the man's manner of dealing with the task—towards it and, inevitably, past it, into the realms of heartlessness, their perception of the man's *rôle*. Altmann regarded them with mixed puzzlement and distaste. War was a man's business; a rite of passage to which women were not entitled. Theirs was another function entirely, and the *Führer* had been emphatic on the point. In the development of a resurgent Germany the woman's function was clear, as important as the man's but wholly different: hers was the responsibility for a healthy-minded and -bodied rising generation; it was for the man to exercise discipline over it. War was above all else an exercise in impartial discipline, in detachment—indeed, sacrifice—of the personal element.

"You have not made any radio call," said Altmann finally. "I expected you to raise the alarm—call for help. Why not?"

As if bracing himself, the other took a breath. "I'm not allowed to give you any information apart from what I've told you, captain. I'm sorry."

"I see." Altmann lifted an eyebrow, half in amusement. *I'm sorry. So like the English—manners remembered in the teeth of calamity. Of course he's not sorry, but the conventions must be observed. The marmalade must be Oxford, even in the farthest corner of empire, as Greischen had observed. Well . . .* "So I'm not to learn why you're not in convoy or under escort, either?" The officer responded with a tight-lipped silence, and looked away, so Altmann continued, "And you are unarmed because of the nature of your cargo, not so? One round and you go up in smoke!"

Silence, uncomfortable; almost embarrassed, Altmann sensed. The man's shirt was soaked through now. Was he, under his outward calm, nervous? Quite possibly; after all, he was amongst his enemies, defenceless. Like the man Lebrun—no, seemingly the schooner's skipper, Calibourdin . . . *damn!* Altmann cursed his errant thoughts, but followed their lead in spite of himself. The Englishman was standing almost in the same spot on the bridge as had that damned Frenchman, and Altmann caught himself on the point of glancing down to see again the bare feet pale in the nether shadows, the blood draining away into the water slopping about, the soaked, clinging dungarees. He shook himself, drew deeply on his cigarette, held the officer's eye.

"Very well, my friend. You must carry out your orders. Your loyalty is commendable." He paused, studying the other narrowly in the sun's glare. "I take it you're carrying some quantity of diesel fuel—" This time a curt nod, and Altmann went on, "Tell your captain I wish to transfer it to my boat. I will come alongside. My chief engineer will supervise the operation."

At this the tanker's officer started, evidently surprised. Altmann felt everyone's eyes on him, and for a moment felt light-headed. The idea had popped up like a Jack-in-the-Box, ludicrous but frightening. What did he think he was doing, laying his command open to not just the possibility of attack by an escort, a patrol, which for all he knew was even now just below the horizon, but also a move on the part of the tanker's people in a spirit of defiance? The British were apt to take chances on the flimsiest pretext, and this situation was somewhat better than flimsy: even an unsuccessful attempt on the u-boat could result in serious consequences. A damaged hatch, for example, could prevent its diving, or at least delay it while repairs were effected, during which time anything could happen. The move he had in mind would have been questioned in company; on the commanding officers' course would have brought severe censure on his head, even reprimand. Might even have failed him—return to subordinate service for a period of reflection and contrition. On the other hand . . . U-boat men weren't chosen for their slavish adherence to convention, to prescription, to protocol. For their loyalty to the Fatherland and the navy and the *U-Bootwaffe*, yes; for their physical and mental resilience, yes; for their willing submission to authority in ordinary circumstances, yes. But they were also chosen for their capacity for individual resource; appointed to commissioned rank for their personal attributes as well as professional skill—physical and moral courage, intellect, enterprise; ruthlessness. Initiative. Uncle Karl allowed them considerable autonomy, expected them to act on their own deduction and judgment in the field of battle. The only thing that would decide between approval and condemnation was the success or failure of the operation—of the tactics adopted according to the turn of events, for which there could be no advance prescription beyond Dönitz's tersely melodramatic generality, "Go in and sink!"—a risibly ambiguous exhortation, Altmann had often felt. He preferred—in the right conditions—the Britishers' historical equivalent, "Engage the enemy more closely". No room for doubt there! You couldn't go wrong if you followed it: survival would guarantee approval, demise criticism at worst, but the dead were no more concerned about posthumous disgrace than about posthumous accolade. Dead incompetents—cowards for that matter—were as sublimely indifferent to—and proof against—opinion as were dead heroes. Not that death was an acceptable alternative . . .

The officer seemed to gather himself. He took a breath and said, "All right, captain. If there's nothing else I'll get back to my ship with the message—"

About to nod dismissal, Altmann caught himself as another thought occurred, and he chided his carelessness. It was obvious: effectively placing his trust in the tanker's master he would be guilty of the most reprehensible negligence. With nothing to stop someone aboard the Britisher making some sort of attempt on her, he would be wilfully hazarding his command and all her men. If he were to go through with this piece of recklessness, as it would be seen in the event of failure, he should at least take whatever precautions were open to him, and the obvious choice—the only choice, it seemed—stared him in the face: keep the tanker's second officer aboard the boat until the fuelling operation had been completed. Not just that, but keep him under threat of death in the event of any hostile move on the part of the tanker's people. A hostage, in other words. One of the elementary tactics of warfare, and he'd almost missed it in passing. Mentally he shook his head in self-reproof, only to stumble into a further glaringly obvious move: exchange the officer for the ship's master! Not only would it be a more potent precaution against any rash action on the part of the tanker's people but it might also yield information not to be got from a junior officer. Altmann bit his lip in irritation at his own slow-wittedness.

What was the matter with him? Perhaps he was beginning to register the effect of the lack of sleep—of proper, recuperative repose as distinct from a few restless, haunted minutes at a time—that had led him to speak to Lange. It was evidence of its debilitating effect that he now hesitated before acting on the decision; the tanker's officer was already turning towards the ladder to the casing—

"Wait!" Again, wait. Altmann raised a hand to stay the officer. "Better you don't go yet . . . You will remain aboard until we are alongside your ship, then I will exchange you for your captain until the oil has been transferred." He bent to the voice-pipe and summoned Schreiber.

The tanker's man paused, seemed about to speak, shook his head, and regarded Altmann with an expression conveying mixed anger and incredulity. Glancing at the grimly-smiling Schreiber and back at Altmann, he said tautly, "You're keeping me as a hostage, captain?"

"If you put it that way—yes. But you will come to no harm. At worst you will spend the rest of the patrol with us—"

"At best?"

Altmann shrugged, drew on his cigarette, threw the remains to leeward. "At best, as I say, you will be returned to your friends. Likewise your captain."

"And we go on our way?"

Sharply, Altmann refuted him. "Of course not! You will be given time to abandon your ship before I sink her. We are at war, after all! I will carry out my duty."

"I see . . ."

Altmann smiled, a bare twitch of cheek muscles. "Send your boat back to the ship. I will follow. You will speak to your captain to confirm my instructions. Now—" turning to Schreiber "—no torpedoes for the present, *Einswo.*" Then, on the control-room voice-tube, he requested Benedict's presence.

"Of course you're mad." The engineer arrived on the bridge growling. "But then, we're all mad. Sane men wouldn't be in this situation in the first place." The sweat was running into his eyes, dripping off his beard; he squinted, partly against the sun's glare, partly in an expression of resignation. He swept ineffectually at the sweat with the back of a hand. "I'll need to check the grade of oil. Can't risk gumming up the injectors with shit—or contaminating my bunkers with it, either! There's diesel and diesel, you know. If they use the stuff in their generators it'll probably be okay, but I won't take anything much heavier than gas-oil." He sniffed disparagingly. "Tell them I'll need a ten-centimetre quick-release connection—four-inch nominal. They should have it. If they haven't—"

"If they haven't?"

"Buckets and a funnel, if you must. Otherwise, we've enough for the scheduled patrol—"

"I'm thinking beyond the schedule, Herbert."

"Yes. Of course. I was afraid of that." The engineer laughed mirthlessly, tight-lipped. "We'd better clean them out of fresh vegetables while we're about it. Tinned sauerkraut loses its appeal after the sixth month . . . And fresh water. We can never have enough fresh water."

"It had occurred to me, Herbert . . . And don't worry—if his diesel's no good I'll look for another station. Even on the other side of the road."

Benedict's grin was fleeting and baleful.

In appearance Hugh Loftus first struck Altmann as an inadequate figure, but he quickly revised his opinion. Stepping clear of the ladder to the bridge after a descent from the tanker her master was red in the face and puffing, and he mopped his brow with a large damp handkerchief. Falstaffian in contrast to the lean youthfulness of the gathered u-boat men, he was short, stout, balding, clad in sweat-stained tropical whites that tended to detract from the dignity of his rank, while his obvious physical discomfort lent him a defensive air. There it ended, however: the small pale eyes glinted with a sharp intelligence that took in his surroundings at a glance to settle on the white-capped man regarding him quizzically, drawing tautly on a cigarette. "You'll be the skipper," he said in a high-pitched voice at odds with an assertive manner. "And a clever one at that . . . I'm Loftus." He jerked a thumb over a shoulder. "Master. That's all you'll get out of me, sir, so let's get done without wasting time!"

But inquiry disclosed Loftus's ignorance of German; indeed of any foreign language bar a smattering of Hindi, enough to facilitate exchanges with his crews. And his English—clipped, flat-accented, strangely-phrased—fell almost incomprehensibly on Altmann's ear: Whitley Bay, he explained dryly; even natives of Cullercoats had problems with it, and Altmann smiled thinly, sensing a joke at his expense. "Ah—as perhaps a Mürwiker hearing a Rauenthaler, eh?"

"Aye—like as not."

Altmann eyed him curiously. "Why did you not stop at the first shot from my gun?"

Loftus answered with a reproving glint in his eye that caused Altmann a moment's discomposure. "Can't just shut down without preparation—change from heavy oil to diesel or risk gumming up the works. Y'ought to know that, man!"

It was absurd, thought Altmann: did he expect to use his engines again? But of course it was an efficient procedure; the ship's people were clearly level-headed, competent . . . The little man's penetrating gaze did not waver. Whatever the effect of his physical stature Loftus's incisive manner, evidence of the self-confidence of a man in whom ultimate responsibility was balanced by the authority of rank—which, in a merchant service officer, depended on personal attributes as much as if not more than upon official sanction—commanded attention and respect. He made it clear that he was neither intimidated nor beguiled by the German officer's tactics, and Altmann was no more successful in obtaining information from him than from his second officer. A few personal details—no longer young but late married with a young son at school, come to sea as an apprentice with the company that owned his present command, held an extra master's certificate and was awaiting a shore posting as a Lloyd's surveyor—and a firm belief that Germany would lose the war—was all Altmann could extract by civil inquiry, and he had no taste for cruder methods, even as mild as threatening detention as a prisoner of war. The man would become an encumbrance in the absence of the supply vessels on which German naval strategy had been based at the beginning, and to which a man such as Loftus could have been transferred. The *Altmark* episode had signalled the failure of the scheme, since when the risks attached to the milch-cow's similar *rôle* had been underlined by events. Altmann was operating in remote waters; he had no brief to take prisoners of war when any information they might be persuaded to divulge would be uselessly out of date by the time it reached higher authority and probably irrelevant to the focus of the Axis war effort. Nor was he inclined to knock anyone about for the sake of whatever could be gleaned by way of localised intelligence, such as the reason for the tanker's sailing independently—beyond Loftus's single remark to the effect that the u-boat's presence had come as a shock, his diligent adherence to the zig-zag requirement notwithstanding. He refused to say whether or not he had had time to transmit a warning or distress signal, and expressed surprise at the near-miss.

"Two, you say! Third mate'n a bloody daydream again—" mopping ineffectually at a streaming brow "—well, this'll teach the young beggar, right enough. Should've 'ad 'im in miner's boots on watch so I'd've known 'e were awake!" But he exhibited no sign of humour. His words were terse, hinting at anger, and Altmann was aware of a flavour of farce in the scene. Instead, he invited Loftus below out of the sun and was gruffly refused. Doomed as she was, the captain preferred to keep an eye on his ship. So, shrugging, Altmann went on to order the destruction of the tanker's radio installation, and two armed men led by a belted and side-armed Hildegras returned to report it comprehensively junked. There had been no physical resistance, only enraged protest from the elderly man who identified himself as the ship's radio operator.

"I think he's been drinking," asserted a flushed Hildegras. "My English isn't up to much, but even so his words were almost impossible to recognise apart from *bastards* and similar compliments . . . No log-books."

Like the rest of the ship's official papers the radio log had surely gone over the side shortly after the u-boat's appearance. Ordered also to search the bridge and the master's and chief engineer's quarters Hildegras's party had discovered only empty drawers and a safe-door swung back on its hinges to expose the paperless interior. The ship could have been from and bound for ports other than those stated; only her name and various special but irrelevant details were revealed by several items of equipment and a few deck-plans and lists posted about the accommodation. Her call-sign was clearly marked on a plate screwed to the main radio transmitter. Benedict confirmed her cargo, reserving judgment on its specifics. Without a laboratory test, as Altmann would appreciate, it wasn't possible to say whether it was aviation spirit or for use in motor-cars. Its explosive properties would in any case be the same from their point of view.

War in the tropics, reflected Altmann, was a different proceeding from its North Atlantic equivalent; and looking round at the scene he felt an overwhelming sense of unreality. That anyone here should be at risk of death seemed ludicrously improbable. The flak-guns, the 105mm cannon attended by Palmgren and his men—all seemed no more lethal than stage props, mock-ups that would be scrapped when the bloodless performance was over. That the men in the two vessels lying at apparent peace with one another on a pond-like sea were under mutually-hostile orders was a trial of credulity that threatened to disperse in the surrounding stillness. The prospect of taking his departure of the tanker with a nod of thanks and a wave rather than by sinking her in fiery chaos contended for serious consideration, and he had to physically rid himself of it: the thump of his fist on the bulwark capping startled Schreiber out of his abstracted contemplation of a drifting jellyfish.

"We'll be out of it in another thirty minutes, *Kapitan*." Tapping his watch he mistakenly sympathised with Altmann's seeming impatience. "A couple of eels and we'll be twelve thousand tons closer to the all-time re—"

"Just make sure the damned things work, *Einswo!*" The glance accompanying the snapped words further startled the officer, and in some dismay he stiffened to attention, silently clicking his plimsolled heels, with an involuntary *"Herr Kapitan!"* The heat. That was it. The heat and the ominous stillness and the time all this was taking. The heat got to everyone in the end; the skipper would be better once they'd finished the business. Perhaps he was regretting his decision to turn a simple attack into a refuelling operation with complications. Perfectly understandable. Schreiber shifted his attention to the Englishman, perspiring, red-faced, no longer the undignified figure who had heaved himself breathlessly onto the bridge but a ship's captain killing time in the face of events beyond his control, displeased about the situation, and plainly worried. But whatever his sentiments, mused Schreiber, he gave them no expression beyond the set of his features, as grim as their clean-shaven chubbiness allowed. Abruptly, Schreiber sensed the man's tragedy, and shifted uncomfortably on his feet, as impatient as he thought Altmann to be, wishing they were done with this defiance—or temptation—of the gods. It would have been a relief if Benedict had found the diesel fuel unsuitable, but after examining a couple of samples from the tank and the supply line he had grudgingly pronounced it usable and the transfer had proceeded with painful slowness. Schreiber suspected the tanker's people of deliberate obstruction but refrained from comment. The tension was palpable; reference to the obvious was likely to touch off an explosion.

The Catalina appeared as Loftus was turning to leave the bridge for his own ship. Henning was supervising the securing of the fuelling hatch in the after-deck while the tanker's chief and third engineers looked on with interest from the rail above, their backs to the approaching aircraft.

If it hadn't been for the fact of the two vessels' mutual hostility the scene would have possessed all the excitement of a peacetime replenishment exercise, given the fact that, bar the one already afloat, the tanker's boats were swung out in readiness for lowering, their prospective occupants gathering at the davits, clumsy in their cork lifebelts.

Approaching from the blind side, the plane remained unseen and unheard by the u-boat's lookouts including the pair who had been posted on the tanker's deck: turning their backs they had moved to the head of the ladder with, evidently, a return to the boat in mind, as Loftus had stepped towards the exit from the boat's bridge. So nobody was aware of the plane's arrival until it roared overhead no more than fifty feet above masthead-height to go into a steeply-banked climb. Turning, it displayed the RAF roundels on the upper surfaces of its wings as they caught the sun in a momentary glint before a diving return run, able now to see the u-boat lying alongside the tanker, exposed to its fire. But, as Altmann reasoned, the pilot would not attack a target so closely in company with a ship of his own side; and a ship, moreover, liable to erupt like a volcano when struck by machine-gun fire, friendly or otherwise: the boat was safe as long as it remained alongside the tanker. Indeed, it might even be taken for a British one, unless and until signals had been exchanged with the aircraft's base. But even as the thought occurred to him, Altmann corrected it: the swastika at the ensign-staff was clearly not the white ensign even though it drooped in motionless folds. And the tanker's boats were ready for imminent use.

All eyes centred on the seaplane as it approached, its nose-mounted machine-gun trained on the boat, engines throttled back, a sitting duck if Altmann had chosen to open fire, sure to end its flight in a spectacular embrace with the ships if hit; so he motioned preventively to Bartels and Knecht, who tracked the plane with their weapon, blowing out their cheeks to ease the strain, Knecht's grip relaxed on the levers. The plane came on, retracing its original flightline to disappear beyond the tanker's bulk. They heard it droning away, then the sound began increasing and Altmann shouted at Knecht to ready his gun. As the man signalled acknowledgment the Catalina reappeared round the tanker's bows in a banked turn, its engines thundering on opened throttles, to line up on the u-boat from a direction and at a height at which none of the anti-aircraft weaponry could be brought to bear. Palmgren's gun-crew was at readiness, but the 105's rate of fire would allow no more than a single round before the aircraft passed overhead, flying closely parallel to the tanker's length to avoid hitting it as it fired on the u-boat. And they waited, as resolute as the steadfast tin soldier, for the order that came too late, shouted into the coarse buzz of the plane's gun and the hail of solid .303 that swept the foredeck and the forward face of the conning-tower and bridge.

"Clear the foredeck—get to hell out—!" was as far as Palmgren got before joining Altmann and the others sprawled on the deck-plating, flung off his feet by the force of a hit on his left shoulder. The plane's shadow flicked over them accompanied by a deafening clamour, giving Knecht the opportunity to add to the din, resulting in a break in the engines' roar. Lurching to his feet Altmann saw smoke trailing from the Catalina's starboard engine and a piece of something fall away from the tail to flutter down. As he watched the plane climb away it dropped a wing into a shallow diving turn that tightened into what would have become a spin but for the sea's intervention. It hit the water first with the wing-tip which barely sliced a silvery arc out of the surface before the aircraft tumbled over in a cartwheel to vanish in a towering parabolic gout of white foam and green water flecked with dark fragments, the whole sun-shot edifice, plumed and streamered and ragged-edged splitting into comet-trails of white water, seeming to hang motionless against the sky for minutes before beginning a slow collapse, absorbed fraction by fraction, fragment by fragment, back into the sea's ineffable calm, finally dissolving in a spreading swirl of ripples strewn with wreckage variously quiescent and, here and there, rising and turning as it settled or slipped beneath the surface. For a short interval the truncated arm of a rainbow stood faintly in the midst of the scene, fading as the misty residue of spray dispersed. The thump of contact that had terminated the engines' roar seemed to echo and re-echo in a retreating diminuendo until at length silence returned.

"Curiosity killed the cat." Schreiber broke it with a grimace, and Altmann, rubbing a bruised elbow, threw him a glance of grudging regard. The first officer displayed a deceptively-simple turn of wit he envied. "What the hell did he have to come back for? Me, I'd have kept well away from such an odd couple til I'd talked to someone somewhere . . ." He sighed. "New boy, for sure. Now he's a dead duck; no good to man or beast." He cocked an eyebrow. "Makes a change from tankers and bulkers and freighters, eh, *Herr Kapitan*? A first for us, anyway." He turned to the flak-gunners. "Well done, Bartels and Knecht. You have an eye for it . . . The proof of a craftsman is the way he makes it look easy—the dead duck wasn't the sitting duck it seemed, hm?"

The men grinned, though looking shaken, and turned to busy themselves with the gun as, snarling something through bared teeth, Palmgren shoved past Schreiber and half-fell down the ladder to the deck. Startled, with an exclamation Altmann switched his attention to the other weapon to look down on a scene of carnage no less shocking for its small scale. Palmgren was on his knees beside one of the gun-crew in a pool of blood that flashed the sun into Altmann's eyes. The others lay like broken dolls, torn and bloody, and the dull, rusty grey plating and sea-stained planking of the deck bore mute witness: for most of its length between conning-tower and bows it bore the splinterings and silvery scars of bullet-strikes. The men at the gun had been riddled with not only direct fire but also, it appeared, the misshapen ricochets that had done greater damage. Altmann stared down, numbed, and was caught by Palmgren's glare. "*Kapitan*—the doctor, quick! This one's still alive!" His shirt was soaked crimson, ripped at the shoulder.

Altmann swung about but already Schreiber was bawling down through the open hatch for Lange. He turned a flushed face up at Altmann, squinting into the sun. "Damned swine! If any are still alive over there—!" He broke off, his attention diverted by Knecht's exclamation. The *Matrose* was leaning over the railing of the gun-platform looking down at something on deck, and he beckoned urgently. Joining him, Schreiber swore before turning to the ladder with a glance at Altmann, calling back, "The captain!" as he swung down.

Resembling a dumped laundry-bag, blood spreading in patches over the white cotton of his uniform, Loftus was obviously dead. Turned to one side, his features were relaxed in an oddly peaceful expression, the mouth slightly open, as if he were regarding some sublime prospect, but the eyes stared at nothing. After a few moments kneeling with an ear to the little man's chest Schreiber looked up and shook his head at Altmann. Blood smeared the side of his face. Lange appeared, dropped down the ladder, paused with a nod at a glance from Schreiber, and hurried forward.

There were no survivors, of the aircraft crash or the gun's crew other than Palmgren and, for a brief interval, the man he had found still breathing. "A boy, no more." Altmann formed the impression that there was accusation in the doctor's words, but decided to affect nescience and ordered immediate preparations for burial. Of necessity and from courtesy they included the tanker's master, for whom a red ensign was passed down from the ship and her chief officer and chief engineer permitted to attend. The chief officer was an older man, Altmann guessed in his late forties, tight-lipped, sombre-faced and uncommunicative, who spoke a few gruff words over the body and nodded what Altmann took to be acknowledgment of the Germans' apparent consideration before accompanying the engineer back to the tanker as the boats were making ready to cast off. With four lookouts at high alert and both flak-guns manned Altmann stood off at some distance after ascertaining that the tanker's people were equipped and provisioned for the passage to the coast. The boats were in good condition. There were no sick or wounded to be cared for. Their chances were as good as they could be; better, in some respects, than his boat's, reflected Altmann: discovery in their case would mean succour; in his, further conflict, perhaps wounding, perhaps death.

Lange's examination of Palmgren revealed nothing worse than a flesh-wound to the upper arm and severe bruising, plus a sprained wrist sustained in his fall to the deck. "Lot of blood," Lange remarked blandly. "But the effect is probably beneficial if anything. Bit messy with that piece of shirt in it. All out now, but we'll have to keep an eye on it. The edges were a bit ragged for fine stitching, but it's not where anyone will see it, except—well—when it's not important."

"What d'you mean—keep an eye on it?" Palmgren's tone was shaky, his face drained of colour, beaded with sweat. Lange's touch was light but could not prevent the worst of the pain getting through the morphine injection.

"Tropical air, and the stuff we breathe in the boat. Tends to cause suppuration." Lange pushed a thermometer into Palmgren's mouth.

Palmgren spoke round it. "Which means?"

"Oh—blood-poisoning. Gangrene. Several possibilities."

"You suggesting I could lose the arm or something?"

"Not unless you're very unlucky."

"You rely on luck?"

Lange removed the thermometer and held it up to the light. "Slight temperature. Perfectly normal. Don't overdo things and it should drop back in a few hours . . . Luck?" He regarded Palmgren solemnly. "I thought they told you about that when you joined this firm. I wouldn't worry about the arm."

160

The burial proceedings had caused an unwelcome delay, and Altmann felt bound to give the boats time to get well clear before he administered the *coup de grace*. He decided to attack by torpedo on the surface, trimmed down at diving readiness, and briefed Schreiber accordingly.

"Two should be sufficient, *Einswo*. Palmgren can throw in some h.e. as well. Let's get it over with." As he spoke he was aware of a weight of weariness, half-wishing he hadn't decided to make such an elaborate show of the affair: it would have been more than fitting to have stopped the tanker and ordered her abandonment before simply destroying her and leaving her men to their fate in the boats. Or simply stopping her and getting the business done forthwith. Or, with better timing, expending another pair of eels without warning of any kind. He felt irritated with himself for having succumbed not only to sentimentality but also to—what?—conceit? Some kind of exhibitionism? Self-justification? Or had it been something to do with the nightmares—with the recurring, unabating abstractions that drained him of the vitality of which he felt in increasing need. The sheer inevitability of recurrence was sapping his powers of resilience; draining him of the nervous energy necessary to conduct the u-boat's business. This episode was a graphic example: he was forced to admit that had it not been for the phantoms' persistence he would probably not have gone through with such a plainly foolhardy stunt. No-one had made any remark—in his hearing—but he felt certain that they were giving his actions more than the customary critical appraisal. There was no danger of their making any trouble, but he felt an increasing conviction that the discipline of the service was playing a greater part in the boat's wellbeing than hitherto. Which meant, of course, that his own part was, however superficially, losing its potency. He would have to take a firmer grip on his reactions, on his thinking, on his powers of decision.

But there was yet another unplanned twist in the course of events. As Altmann looked on accompanied by Palmgren with his arm in a sling and a replacement crew, both torpedoes struck the target with eruptions alongside that burst instantly into towering flame, and the scene gained added drama from the mellowing light of the sun as it sank towards a meeting with the swathe of tarnished silver it had laid ahead of the burning ship. About to dismiss the gun's crew Altmann was interrupted by Hildegras's agitated accents on the control-room voice-pipe: the tanker was transmitting the u-boat attack signal. Impossibly, in the heart of the inferno someone was at the key letting the world know of the u-boat's presence. Some lunatic. Some suicidally brave man. Someone who gave sentimentality no place in his calculations.

"*Kapitän—?*" Palmgren was staring at him in disbelief. Speechless, he waited for an explanation.

Altmann's thoughts whirled, then locked. He snapped an order at Palmgren, noting the pause in the gun-crew's moves to secure the weapon, then their feverish reversal. The gun swung back to bear on the burning tanker, almost lost in the flames that fed a roiling mushroom of black smoke rising to heights at which it would be visible for scores of miles, a certain signal in the wilderness. The first round burst almost undiscernibly in the heart of the pyre; the next squarely on the dark patch amidst the flames, all that could be seen of the bridge. It was easy shooting, and once on target the gun pumped shell after shell into the flaming mass, bursting in momentary whitish blobs against the yellows and reds consuming the dark form of the bridge superstructure.

As he watched, Altmann's mind probed fiercely at the unbelievable fact of the radio transmission, marvelling at the prospect of the man at the key—the elderly man described by Hildegras, apparently the worse for drink, infuriated by the alien invasion, determined to exact revenge, even to the certain sacrifice of his life. He had remained behind, obviously; and obviously with the chief officer's knowledge and even blessing. At least, it would be reasonable to assume so: perhaps it had been in defiance of orders or simply without the knowledge of the officer in charge. Remained behind with the smashed radio equipment knowing his time was limited—and knowing, surely, that he had some chance of setting up the means of transmission, either by repairing the damage or, perhaps, by use of some piece of equipment Hildegras had not accounted for. Had there been an emergency or reserve radio hidden somewhere? No reason why not, whether as an official precaution or a private whim. The only other radio dealt with had been the lifeboat emergency distress transmitter: use of a hand-axe had preceded its dumping overside. And the power-supply: Hildegras had not mentioned batteries, and Altmann had not thought to inquire, but in all likelihood there was a bank of batteries somewhere at hand for emergency use, as in these very conditions. But too late now to worry, or castigate. The damage, if any, was done.

Drawing tensely on a cigarette, Altmann gripped the bulwark-capping tightly, feeling the blaze adding to the sun's waning heat on his face, cursing his carelessness in not taking rigorous enough measures—at allowing himself to be lulled by the outwardly docile behaviour of the tanker's people into an unforgivably lax frame of mind. And yet, that any of those men would have gone to the extreme of risking his life—sacrificing it—in a situation that could have only one outcome, struck him as incredible: not unforeseeable as much as unconscionable. The futility of it was pitifully evident. Even so . . . A last signal, a final tremor of the ether, might be just enough to turn the tables on the attacker; just enough to bring retribution, even if too late to prevent a successful action. The life of an elderly alcoholic weighed in the balance against the lives of the u-boat's crew—and the lives of all her prospective victims. That radio man was a hero, sober or not—assuming sobriety constituted part of the definition: surely more likely drunkenness, even if on adrenalin rather than alcohol, but there was no reason to reject alcohol's influence as a component of reckless bravery. And there was no guarantee that this man's bravery would be recognised—no Iron Cross, no Knight's Cross with cabbage leaves, knives and forks; no welcoming band, no congratulations. Not even an engraving somewhere. No return at all. Death—a horrific death—at the key, perhaps to no avail. And who would care—a mother? Wife? Children? Sister? Brother? Perhaps no-one, apart from his shipmates, and they might curse him, for there was nothing to stop the u-boat's commander taking further action against them in reprisal. Even as the idea occurred, Altmann's thoughts sheered off in alarm: not that road again. No more forays among the boats, even if there were no risk of a vengeful enemy arriving on the scene. No more phantoms to accompany those already proving themselves immune to the passage of time. And, while not expressly forbidden, fleet standing orders had avoided explicit condonement of reprisals. Such a crudely pointless measure lay outside the pale of prospective action on the high seas: the u-boat's *mode d'emploi* was stealth and anonymity. Hit and run. To entertain the idea of reprisal was to indulge conceit—sentimentality—to as great a degree as the extending of magnanimity towards one's victim—who was, after all, the enemy. Already, Altmann reflected, he had gone too far in that direction. He might yet regret his decision to allow abandonment of the tanker before sinking her, a decision the sentimental folly of which he had tried unsuccessfully to disguise by coercing Benedict's support in the matter of the diesel fuel, a contrivance the engineer had seen through from its opening suggestion. Uncomfortably, Altmann felt he had gone along with it more out of shame for his commanding officer than for his own self-respect.

And that man over there, now surely an indistinguishable crisp among the white-hot remains of the ship: what had he felt about the u-boat's actions—about the man in command? Angry, certainly; with the sentimental anger of a seaman over the destruction of his safe refuge, the enclosed, claustrophobic cocoon of the ship in which he had vested his hopes and aspirations; the ship as the vehicle of his disappointments, disillusionment; his obscure triumphs, his equally obscure defeats; the mould for his substance and spirit and thinking; his base for observing and assessing the world in which he had to justify his existence, or at least sustain it. His anger would have been at an unprovoked threat to his entire being, at a sacrilegious trampling upon his claim to human dignity and inviolability. Or perhaps merely with the disproportionate, hazily-focused indignation of the drunk, exaggerating his own reactions to events as a public assertion of his continued grip on rationality. The greater the depths of alcoholic immersion the more exaggerated the actions in an affectation of sobriety, a process in which dignity was transformed into pathos, and eventually wretchedness and its accompanying self-contempt. Perhaps—was it likely?—the man had chosen his fate as an escape of a kind that would absolve him from an unbearable burden of failure. It was a classically honourable way to go, in all conscience. Whatever was remembered of him thereafter, all would be vindicated—exculpated—by this final, supreme, act of self-denial. But it was also, Altmann reflected, in a certain tradition attaching to that newest of sea callings: the man at the key, last to leave the stricken ship, perhaps to go down with her. In the last resort, the call of duty prevailed, an unreckoned element of courage; even, in some cases, its substitute.

Mentally, Altmann shook himself. What ridiculously convoluted thinking, and with what purpose? Was he looking for vindication, seeking exoneration from liability for the life of a single man when there were so many more—men, women and children—on his hands? There were plenty like the tanker's radio officer among the sea's legion of followers, in thrall to the loneliness and obscurity of a way of life mostly out of sight and mind of ordinary men. Their war was a private affair, almost; and they conducted it without arms, which in certain circumstances cast them as heroes despite themselves. It was enough to know that where forty-odd men could have died as a result of his actions, only one had fallen—two, counting the tanker's master. Altmann was chasing a chimera by trying to read anything into it, especially anything that might affect his state of mind as an instrument of conscience. War was war. Its minutiae were in themselves of no significance to the outcome: they should have no bearing on his execution of duty to the Fatherland.

"He's stopped transmitting, *Kapitän!*" Schreiber clambered out of the conning-tower hatch.

"Cease fire!" Altmann leant over the forward bulwark as Palmgren relayed the order. "Secure the gun. Stand down your men, *Zweiter*—"

"Maybe no-one heard him." Schreiber took out a handkerchief and wiped his perspiring face, blowing out his cheeks. "He couldn't have been using the main transmitter. What a damned lunatic—!"

Throwing away the stub of his cigarette Altmann nodded. "Perhaps not, *Einswo*. I'm not waiting to find out. Secure the plot but remain at action stations for another hour. We'll stay surfaced for as long as necessary to get the batteries up to full charge . . ." He paused to acknowledge Palmgren's salute and report: gun secured, crew stood down. They lowered themselves one by one through the hatch to the u-boat's sweltering interior. Everyone below was grateful for the draught of fresh air when Altmann ordered the port diesel ahead at half-speed and turned back onto a southerly course. Presently they passed into the shadow cast by the smoke from the burning tanker; after nearly two hours' run, still within sight of the smoke and the sun an oblate crimson ball hovering low above the horizon, Altmann gave the order to secure action stations and handed over the watch to the navigator, leaving instructions to be called in an hour's time, or sooner: "If anything appears, afloat or in the air, make diving stations immediately, Eberle. Don't wait for my order. I'll take her in the control-room."

"Aye, *Kapitän*." *Obersteuermann* Eberle was a solemn young man. He took his duty seriously under the most concentrated provocation from certain of his compatriots. His attention to detail could be infuriatingly pedantic, but it came on the back of unshakable reliability. Altmann had determined to recommend his promotion to commissioned rank on their return, recognising the value of a competence that was reassuring rather than inspiring. Men who inspired others were prone to instability, never wholly predictable in the face of prolonged stress. And prolonged stress was becoming the pattern of u-boat operations as they dragged on past the point at which Dönitz had predicted their successful termination. Which, Altmann had concluded, amounted to an interpretation of failure that afforded little room for manoeuvre. The best that could be derived from it was the fact that a lost battle did not amount to a lost war: given the necessary respite and faith in one's cause one recovered from set-back.

Below, sleep evaded him and he took the pill-box from a drawer. He contemplated its contents for some time, glanced at the carafe of water in its rack, hesitated, and returned the box to the drawer. Only an hour—less—before his call; and the chance of a ship or aircraft putting in an appearance. The risk was too great. He lay back, throwing an arm across his eyes, and dozed. After a few minutes he slept, but did not find peace. Forty minutes later the alarm woke him. As he stumbled into the control-room the boat was already at twenty metres, and Palmgren had taken the watch. Altmann waved at him to continue as the navigator made his report: a trace of smoke to the south, fine on the port bow. It was barely visible in the last waning light of sunset. After a moment's consideration Altmann gave the order to surface.

A trace, no more. Thin, dispersing at no great height, standing at a small angle to the vertical. A response to the tanker's signal, perhaps; or perhaps another lone merchantman. Or possibly only one of several in company—a convoy, a hunting group. The light was fading: another twenty minutes and a darkened ship would be hard to spot even under the luminous canopy of stars, the great chandelier of the tropical night. A u-boat trimmed down, travelling at half-speed, would be almost impossible to see by eye except at point-blank range; even radar would be tested. And yet . . . For once, Altmann regretted the placid waters for which he had exchanged the Atlantic's furies. The risk of discovery was heightened; the enemy had the advantage in the hunt where the only cover was depth, and with it the unknown limit beyond which only death offered refuge.

It was likely that those in the approaching ship, or ships, had seen the tanker's funeral pyre even if no signal had been picked up. That much could be deduced with confidence; but the likely reaction was open to conjecture: a warship would investigate whether in receipt of a radio signal or not; a merchantman would be unlikely to divert unless to turn away. In either case the ship ahead of them would pass close by if both vessels kept their courses, so Altmann considered the obvious: attack, or turn away? A night's rest would be welcomed by all. Or would it? From his knowledge of the thinking of u-boat men Altmann knew such a comfortable notion was flawed: certainly some would welcome a chance to relax; but after the performance with the tanker at least as many again would be curious to see what he made of his subsequent opportunities as the commander of a fighting ship. Their regard for him was, as he was all too well aware, high; but at height was vulnerable: a fall was all too possible at the slightest pressure.

With him on the bridge, watching the distant smoke through binoculars held one-handed, Palmgren. He seemed to have shed some of his diffidence in the action; eyeing him, Altmann felt he had begun to accept the demands of duty in the interests of his birthright; had turned, as it were, to face the pursuing responsibilities of his service and his rank without either denying them or seeking to evade or diminish them. He had overseen the downing of an enemy, sought to succour the wounded, conducted a carefully-gauged assault on a redoubt, such as it had been, and sustained a wound himself. And all with a calm and self-possessed outward demeanour from which others had taken encouragement. Now, with the enemy (as it surely was) again on the scene, he would think poorly of a commander who chose the alternative that could only be seen as a weakness. The boat was at battle readiness. Battle offered, in all likelihood. There would be no question in Palmgren's mind.

Altmann touched the officer on the shoulder. "I'll take her now, *Zweiter*. Make action stations. We'll stay on the surface for the present." Turning to the control-room voice-tube as Palmgren nodded a terse acknowledgment and jammed a hand on the alarm button, he commanded, "Group up, both engines. Full ahead together. First officer to the bridge!"

Bending over the gyro repeater pelorus he noted the bearing. At the same time he noticed a further detail: the smoke had been joined by a tiny pin standing barely visible on the horizon. A mast—not a warship's signal-mast but a merchantman's topmast. Straightening, Altmann gazed narrowly at the nick in the skyline. If she was a merchantman, was she, too, alone? Or was she, as seemed more sensible, in company with others of her kind—other merchantmen; and if so, were they, as seemed equally sensible, under the protection of an escort?

He turned at the sound of Schreiber setting up the range-finder glasses. The first officer looked cheerful in the gathering dusk. "Another customer, *Kapitän*! Let's hope he steers straight for long enough to get an eel into him first time."

Yes, thought Altmann. Let's hope. Either that, or I could stop this one, too . . . But that would depend on a number of things.

VII

KONRAD Lange was the Metox's custodian. It had suffered rough handling during the patrol until, exasperated, Altmann had ordered its retirement as a piece of equipment the doubtful performance of which was far outweighed by its capacity for dangerous obstruction brought to a head by near-disaster at the hands of another Catalina.

"The damned thing's as good as an enemy weapon," he had fumed and Lange had felt, angrily, as if he were being held responsible for the equipment's failure. "The fact is we've dropped behind in the development of radar. I'll be saying so in my patrol report. Nothing else explains what's been happening—and not only to us! Sooner or later some plane will catch us out and we'll be just another statistic—"

"It'd be a relief to do away with it altogether," murmured Lange. "If we take its performance on balance since the boat's commissioning it's caused more trouble than it's worth—false sense of security for a start. Fatal."

Altmann had studied him moodily. "Right . . . I'll make it an order if it'll ease your mind. The Metox is officially discharged from duty aboard this boat pending formal inquiry. How does that suit you?"

"As long as its owner isn't included, *Kapitan* . . . I'll be happier with the lookouts' eyes and ears sharpened by the promise of a punishment battalion for failure."

Altmann's scrutiny hardened. "If I didn't know you better, Konrad, I'd have you down for a reject from the Uhlans—"

"A friend told me to try the *U-Bootwaffe* first, *Kapitän.*"

Altmann sat at his desk going back through his patrol diary; coming across the entry describing the Metox's inglorious performance his words to Lange stirred a memory . . . . . . *a sabre-slash. Standard issue in the Uhlans but quite a distinction for a naval officer . . . Uhlans had lances—they were lancers . . .*

Long ago. And long gone, with the early plans and hopes and the confidence of a resurgent Germany, an example of purity for the world, a new age of efficiency, purpose, morality. A sweeping away of the

168

accumulated detritus of a worn-out civilisation, a decadent world order led by a nation whose aspirations, realised, had reached and passed the apogee of their potential for order and justice, subsided into the stew of liberal policies that epitomised the moral ambiguity of social, economic and political degeneration, ripe for replacement by a new order led by the generation—and the race—that had passed through the refining process of defeat in war, a war that itself had swept away the dead matter of centuries, cleared the stage for the new players directed by the visionary who had set the example for his countrymen, the indomitable, charismatic *Führer* whose unfailing resolve stood as the guiding light that would bring his *Dritte Reich* the victory that was its right and proper destiny. Liebeherr and Greischen had died, along with others; but surely not in vain, not in the empty gesture of a rearguard action foredoomed to failure, as was the Allies'. This patrol, now nearing a successful end, was part of the proof of the pudding: the record of tonnage for which he had accounted had placed him near the top of the league. One more patrol would probably set him on the summit, a point of vantage from which he would be given the opportunity to play an even more significant part in the *Reich*'s inevitable triumph . . .

Lange lay on his bunk, to which he had retired with the aim of catching an hour of rest, if not sleep, with the boat at cruising depth, neither hunting nor hunted, but both evaded him as he lay staring up at the underside of the bunk above, listening to the sounds of the boat working all round him. He took out a water-stained paperback but read the same page three times without absorbing any of its contents, so laid it aside to free up his thoughts. They ranged back over the patrol. Successful, as normally gauged, but lengthy, and trying on all concerned, a test of individual resilience and group discipline and morale. It said much for the men and for the competence of the officers; but what it said for the German war effort was another matter: the action had been set in remote waters, where enemy shipping had been largely unprepared for submarine attack, and less directly crucial to the Allied cause than the convoy routes of the North Atlantic from which the u-boat had been—probably conclusively—swept into a central area beset by extended air cover and threatened by radar-assisted, increasingly numerous and heavy, not to say skilled, surface escorts. There was no other way of looking at it. The monthly total of enemy tonnage sunk overall might have increased—according to Dr Goebbels's loudly-bruited assertions—but spread more thinly over a wider battle-zone in figures that bore no direct comparison with the earlier, more concentrated, successes its effect was likely to be less definite; less *war-decisive*, as Uncle Karl—"The Lion"—had described it. No, thought Lange—there were aspects to this business that would not bear close scrutiny.

And at a more immediate, and intimate, level—like the commander's conduct? Lange's thoughts paused at a period that marked the patrol's defining action, the *British Prowess*'s part notwithstanding: the week of the guns, as Schreiber had termed it. The week in which *Korvettenkapitän* Altmann had seemed at odd moments unbalanced, his judgment sound enough in the timing and location and object of attack but erratic, if not eccentric, in its choice of method, which had arguably, in theory if not in the event, endangered the boat to an unnecessary extent. Lange pondered the effects of secobarbital—which, he reminded himself, Altmann had not referred to after its prescription. Without knowing whether or not the man had taken it a conclusion was impossible; nor would it be advisable to inquire. Perhaps after their return to Bordeaux. Which brought him to the still nagging question of the Metox. Perhaps its summary dismissal hadn't been as wise as it had seemed, especially with the planned passage through Spanish coastal waters before the final leg to the Gironde. The air patrols would be waiting.

The week of the guns. Seven ships had been sunk, in the process consuming all the 105mm and most of the machine-gun and 20mm ammunition, and destroying the 37mm flak-gun, which had exploded, probably owing to a faulty round but possibly to corrosion of the barrel, if not both. In doing so it had killed its layer and wounded its loader. The other deaths had been among the crews of their targets. Lange preferred the word target to its alternative: u-boat men were not criminals, but servicemen acting under the legitimate orders of their government.

The week began a few days after the *British Prowess*'s sinking and the appearance of the group of ships marked by the smoke, then the topmast, of its central unit, a merchantman of around eight thousand tons. She was under escort—two corvettes and a sloop, which aroused Altmann's suspicions, and decided him on his course of action. Concluding that a single vessel under heavy escort represented a target worth the risk to a u-boat and its crew, he attacked by periscope with a spread of four torpedoes, one at least of which hit home to result in a blinding explosion suggesting a cargo of munitions or something similarly important. It also resulted in immediate asdic contact and coordinated attack by the escorts causing electrical and other damage including a bent starboard propeller-shaft. Benedict's only option, he said, was to slacken the intermediate shaft-bearing and post a man over it with an oil-can until Henning, gratified at the opportunity to display his technical legerdemain, set up a drip-feed later refined with a recovery and recirculation system that remained in place until the return to Bordeaux.

The attack continued for some eighteen hours, slackening after about thirteen, Altmann supposed owing to the escorts' stock of charges running low. By then the air in the boat was heavy with chill humidity, bodily exhalations of both kinds and the inevitable efflux of chlorine from the batteries. All not actually employed were ordered to lie down, breathing sets to hand.

Towards the end Altmann ordered release of the *pillenwerfer*, the can of chemicals that reacted with sea-water to produce a mass of bubbles intended to decoy the asdic while the boat made its escape. It was a last-ditch unrepeatable trick that could be improved—as it was—by combining it with a discharge of oil to accompany miscellaneous debris stuffed into the ejector tube with the can. Reaching the surface following loss of contact as the bubbles dispersed it was meant to indicate a destroyed boat. It seemed to work, and four hours after the last depth-charge had shaken his boat—some twenty-two after diving to attack—Altmann surfaced, to be greeted by an empty ocean beneath a clear sky decorated with the first stars of the evening. No-one capped Benedict's cryptic "Lucky!" as the diesels took over from the electric motors. The escorts did not return.

Three days later, off the Mozambique coast, just outside territorial waters, the week of the guns commenced. Shipping to and from Lourenço Marques and the Cape supplied the targets, and Altmann attacked on the surface, at night or in the twilight of dusk or dawn, in choppy conditions, using torpedoes where success looked certain, and guns to settle all difficulties. But, economical with the torpedoes, his profligate gunnery moved many among the crew to look more circumspectly at their commanding officer, and wonder. One or two, of course, recalled a certain night in the North Atlantic with a storm breaking; but said nothing.

There followed a brief hiatus. Traffic was sighted but at too great a distance to be worth the effort of pursuit, while air surveillance began to interfere with Altmann's tactics. On one occasion a Catalina surprised him on the surface at dusk, when the Metox cable turned a crash-dive into a fiasco of near-terminal proportions. Only Benedict's cool reactions took them clear of catastrophe under the astonished gaze of the Catalina's crew: the re-surfaced boat dived again before the pilot repositioned his aircraft for another attack. Throughout, the Metox remained silent, moving Schreiber to call it the *Muet-ochse* in disparaging reference to its French genesis, and Altmann to end its further use. The episode seemed to effect a mood-change in him that echoed his manner after the boat's sinking at Lorient, and certain of his officers and men observed his approaches to further targets with mixed feelings.

Relief when their darkest fears went unrealised was tempered by a change of tactics marked by the attack on the British freighter *River Wye*. Stopping her with a single torpedo Altmann ordered her sinking with the deck gun, expending ninety-five rounds at a range of less than a thousand metres. Seventy-one hits were distributed between bridge and poop-deck housing, on which squatted a naval gun, never brought into use. Directed to cover it, the 37mm flak-gun crew had opened ranging fire; the first round had burst the barrel and set off several rounds at the breech, wounding both layer and loader, *Matrosen* Bühler and Klein; Klein was dead by the time the stretcher party got him below, Bühler following three days later. Altmann closed with one of the boats only to ascertain the ship's name and movements, offering no help of any kind.

On the same day the elderly Greek coal-burner *Attiki Trader* was halted by a single torpedo before Altmann's order produced a rain of high-explosive and incendiary rounds to hasten the crew's scramble into the boats.

"Once the bridge was demolished, with the radio, we hope, what was the point in the rest of it, *Einswo*? We might need some ammo one day. At this rate we'll be left with nothing but a few mouldy sausages to throw at the enemy!"

"Don't underestimate the effectiveness of the German sausage, *Zweiter*. Especially a mouldy one. Look at what it does to its own side!"

"For God's sake! Must everything be a damned joke?"

"Take away the joke, and what's left—apart from oak leaves and swords with a few sparklers for luck?"

"Shit!"

"Very delicately put . . ."

An overcast, blustery dawn revealed yet another Greek freighter, butting into the confused swell just off the one hundred and eighty-metre line roughly demarcating the south-setting Moçambique current and the opposing coastal eddy. A torpedo sent up a geyser of dirty water alongside before the ship took a sheer to lie rolling in the trough like a log and, surfacing, Altmann watched tight-lipped as Palmgren and his men, tethered by safety-harnesses to the gun, spent the next twenty-five minutes shelling the hapless steamer while her crew abandoned her to drift away among the white-caps. No wireless signal was intercepted, and the burning wreck had slipped beneath the seas by the time Palmgren reported his gun secured to a pale, expressionless commander.

The week of the guns culminated in an action shortly after rounding Madagascar's Cape Ste Marie on passage towards Réunion and Mauritius. They were in territorial waters, which, Altmann knew, were more than politically-ambivalent in view of the Allied invasion of the island at its northern end, a move aimed at pre-empting the likelihood of the Vichy French deciding to donate the territory to the Axis cause; but, he felt, the question was largely academic: they were unlikely to meet any naval patrols. Instead, they fell in with a south-bound freighter, the Bombay-registered *Ghodavari*, eight thousand tons. But size apart she presented no easy target: evidently on the alert—had she been warned of a u-boat's presence?—she was following a zig-zag while the conditions—light breeze, slight sea, long low swell, good visibility—favoured the gun. But the freighter was also well-armed; unusually so, with the common vintage 4.7-inch gun on the poop replaced by a more businesslike weapon Altmann guessed to be a Bofors, augmented by what looked like a heavy machine-gun mounted on either bridge-wing. They would threaten Palmgren's men as well as those on the boat's bridge, while the Bofors had only to score a single hit on the pressure-hull to seal Altmann's fate. Ordinary high-explosive would be enough; the boat's only armour was round the bridge, and light, providing no more than token protection.

A night action was obviously safer than one in broad daylight, and as it turned out Altmann took the action to greater lengths than any before, opening it with guns trained on the wireless installation but with an eye to the chance of a hit from the Bofors: he had to prevent its being brought into play, and he did so by arming two men with light machine-guns. In augmentation of the 20mm flak gun they would have less real effect on the target than on his own men, and Altmann felt vindicated at the atmosphere of heightened tension thus produced, contributing to overall morale by giving them a better sense of personal involvement than they got from merely attending to the boat's operation at a remove from direct action. He was pleased with the piratical effect of the combination of bearded countenances, untidily-trimmed hair, sweat-soaked unbuttoned shirts with rolled or scissored-off sleeves, grubby brown shorts and bare-ankled plimsolled feet. The most menacing feature of this alarming display was the emphasis it seemed to give to the eyes, which glittered less with the light of battle than with eager anticipation of novel diversion. For an uncertain moment it occurred to Altmann that they would kill, man to man, with less compunction than they'd have in firing a torpedo at a hapless merchant-ship; and that some part at least of this mood was a result of prolonged, claustrophobic confinement in a hermetically-isolated environment at constant risk of inescapable destruction. But—and this was the key—destruction by an enemy few of them at any one time were able to see; in some instances, such as the men who spent their entire time on duty and most of it off-duty in the intimate company of the diesels and electric motors, none at any time. Now they waited in the control-room, clutching their guns with the dangerous fierceness of amateurs. For a diesel- and electrically-powered ship, Altmann reflected, quite a substantial head of steam was waiting to be blown off. He hoped he wouldn't disappoint them.

He planned his approach well to one side of a near-full moon's line of bearing from the ship, and some way ahead of her, relying on its brilliance and that of the path it would lay on the sea to conceal his presence in the contrasting gloom to either side. It was a relief to realise that while he would be relatively invisible the moonlight might reflect sufficiently from the ship's light grey side and superstructure to give him a more visible target against the coastal background than he'd at first expected. On the whole, he decided, making the attack at this point rather than delaying it for the unforeseeable conditions at dawn had been the wiser option. And so it proved—in one sense, anyway.

At a range of some fifteen hundred metres, with the boat on an interception course at slow speed, Palmgren opened fire using the usual combination of alternate high explosive and incendiary ammunition, while the 20mm flak gun used tracer to concentrate on and around the Bofors, preventing its being brought into action while, hopefully, damaging it beyond use. To the extent that it did not fire a single round during the course of the attack the plan succeeded. And for good measure the light machine-guns in the hands of the desperadoes stationed on the after-deck like a pheasant-shoot maintained a merry chatter that probably kept heads down aboard the merchantman if nothing more bloody.

The din was overpowering, numbing the ears and transmitting itself also by the shuddering and vibration of the bridge and fittings all round Altmann as he watched, taking short puffs at a cigarette and glancing every so often at the moon and at the horizon by then hardening in its growing light. He made no move to stop the firing, mesmerised by the spectacle and sensation of the fury he had unleashed, and it was only at the cessation of Palmgren's gunfire that the others hesitated, then followed suit, the gunners' faces pale in the moonlight, turned towards the bridge in anticipation of a further order. Instead, as Altmann leant over the forward bulwark, Palmgren volunteered the information that he had only three rounds left, all h.e.

"Ready-use, you mean?"

"No, *Kapitän*—in total. Three rounds, and that's it. No more ammo for this gun."

What followed seemed, in retrospect, a manifestation of the irrationality that had characterised Altmann's actions all that week, evident to the more perceptive elements of the crew but, significantly, also to Altmann himself, and he ordered Palmgren to direct his last rounds at the water-line aft as the ship's turn exposed more of her stern to view. They struck home throwing up diffuse columns of foam and as the ship came to a dead stop in the water Altmann altered course to pass round her stern, opening the prospect of her starboard side, where the scene was of orderly abandonment in the three remaining boats. Through binoculars Altmann saw activity pause as men turned towards the approaching u-boat, clearly visible in the moon's wan light. At a range of about three hundred metres he stopped, by a conscious effort freeing himself of the thrall into which he had fallen, pausing on the point of ordering the 20mm to continue the attack accompanied by the gangsters' light, but at this range more effective, machine-gun fire. Instead, he ordered a ceasefire, turning to the watchful figure of Schreiber to add sharply, "Well—what are you waiting for, *Einswo*? If you miss at this range Russia won't be hell enough for you!"

"With the boats still alongside, *Kapitan*?"

"They take their chances . . . I'm not going to regulate my attacks to the target's convenience." More grimly, he snapped. "I've given you an order!"

Sensing his peril, Schreiber stiffened and saluted, biting his lip as it struck him that the gesture might appear to imply sarcasm—insubordination in the book. To correct any such misapprehension he turned hastily to the range-finding glasses and gave orders to the plot. It was a simple shot, but the first officer risked further reproof by going through the full procedure while watching the efforts of the boats' crews to clear the danger area. He could not bring himself to send certain death among an assembled company of defenceless men; at least, not without giving them a reasonable chance of saving themselves. He was conscious of his own nervousness at thus testing his commanding officer's tolerance: the breaking-point was never amenable to estimation, varying with the circumstances. At that moment he felt himself to be on extremely unstable ground, and silently cursed the apparent clumsiness of the boats' occupants. *For Christ's sake get on with it, damn you! I can't play the fool with the skipper just to suit your damned incompetence!*

The ship went down stern-first with an angry roar of high-pressure steam and quenching sea, leaving a wide upwelling pool of wreckage, oil, bursting bubbles, foam and wisps of steam and smoke like wraiths in the moonlight; and on the periphery the three laden boats. Altmann moved in among them, not to offer help but to confirm the name, ports of departure and destination, and cargo: eight thousand tons of sugar from Mauritius for Cape Town and beleaguered Britain; the lookouts called attention to a number of floating bodies, but Altmann returned no more than a grunt of acknowledgment. The remaining-ammunition count amounted to forty-two rounds of 20mm, eleven clips of light machine-gun and no 105mm.

"Which leaves us with sixteen eels, *Kapitan*." Schreiber's expression was bleak. The torpedoes added a further five sinkings to Altmann's record; two of his targets escaped damaged, one under heavy escort, the other limping into harbour among coral reefs that baulked the intended *coup-de-grace*. Three torpedoes proved to be duds. The last ship sunk was the Panamanian freighter *Star Mirzam*, carrying livestock which yielded two half-drowned sheep to supplement the by then seriously depleted diet; and Altmann left eight men adrift on a raft. Already past normal cruising range thanks to the top-up from the British tanker, his fuel had by this time run low, and he set off for home feeling satisfied with the boat, her crew and, with reservations, himself. His tonnage record was worthy of notice.

Approaching the Cape well to the south they sighted a large ship ablaze with lights. Altmann stalked her for a short distance out of curiosity, at first light discovering her to be the hospital-ship *Dorsetshire*. With no torpedoes remaining the obvious question did not arise, but he knew, by hearsay and well-publicised reports, of the British sinking of German hospital ships and saw no reason against returning the compliment.

"A hospital-ship, *Kapitan*?" For once Schreiber's flippancy had deserted him.

"Why not, *Einswo*? Her cargo's more dangerous to Germany than most of what we've sent down this patrol—and merchant seamen are non-combatants. The men in that ship are all trained soldiers, most of them probably repairable!"

"Yes, but—" Schreiber cast about for words, given pause by the expression in Altmann's eye. Its cold unblinking stare caused him a sense of impotence of which he felt ashamed, as if for weakness, and he shrugged, heaving a sigh.

Altmann watched him narrowly, then said, "War isn't for the squeamish, *Einswo*. The enemy will exploit any crack in your resolve—he's as determined to win as you are!" Pause. "Perhaps more so, eh?"

"*Kapitan*?" Schreiber looked pained. "If I haven't given—"

"No such thing, *Einswo*! But you must harden yourself. War isn't a natural state, and Germany was driven to it by the pig-headedness of ill-wishers. They seek to hobble us by rules—protocols, agreements, conventions, treaties—that work to their advantage and against German interests when there are greater enemies whose dearest wish is being fulfilled in seeing us at war with America and Britain! Our duty is to prosecute it to our utmost, win it, and in the greater strength gained from victory deal with the enemies who've used the cover of battle to pursue their malignant goals. Believe me, *Einswo*, a lot more depends on the u-boat's ultimate triumph than mere national supremacy in world affairs. The underlying threats are greater, more insidious, and we can't deal fully with them until we've settled the argument with the Allies. We'll never do it if we flinch at the darker aspects of war. Remember, we aren't on a pleasure cruise, or at a jazz performance—not even a celebration of Wagner! Our job is killing men. Everything else is incidental, hm?"

177

Schreiber stiffened, clicked silent heels, nodded grimly. "Of course, *Herr Kapitan!*"

"Of course, *Erst Offizier!*" But the companionable tap Altmann gave Schreiber's shoulder to soften the bite of his words did not soften the officer's set expression. He took the advice at face value. It was what he was duty-bound to do. Orders were to be obeyed, as his commanding officer obeyed those from higher up. Nothing could be clearer, nothing simpler; or more effective. After all, Altmann was the kind of man others would be glad to follow, and conditional upon satisfactory performance his first officer stood in a position of considerable official regard, well-placed for a bright future, granted certain occupational hazards.

So the *Dorsetshire* sailed on, oblivious of her moment of theoretical peril, leaving Schreiber, all too aware of it, to ponder the moral flexibility and ambiguity of war, and Altmann to review his convictions as so succinctly expressed in the knowledge that he had been powerless to suit action to the word. *Would* he have attacked the hospital-ship? In the mood of the time High Command might well have approved and the *Führer* hurled defiance at the Allies, but what of his own view, not as an officer of the *U-bootwaffe*, of the *Reich*, but as a man—and a human being?—which, he surprised himself by realising, implied a difference. Even so, whether he were held to account for his actions or merely left with their memory, there was more to the question than justification of the action, which could only be by the conventions of war—but conventions adopted as expedient rather than as ideals agreed by treaty. The real question was not about the means of justification but about whether or not justification could be assumed at all. To it the answer had to be a clear denial, but where would that leave the war—and his part in it to date? Gingerly, he turned the imponderable over in his mind and finally chose the solution he had found to be resistant to most arguments involving the ethics of conflict—the alternative to duty, loyalty and steadfast obedience to orders was the slough of sentimentality in which all questions of morality were inextricably mired. It could not be contemplated by a military man if he were to play his part with honour and valour. That was all there was to it. He was a soldier—in the broad sense—not a diplomat, a politician, a philosopher. It was not his duty to define and act on the ethics of warfare but to prosecute it to the full extent of his mental and physical powers.

And of his moral power—his moral integrity? Uncomfortably, as he had come to sense it, he left that to the Party, to the judgment of the men who had struggled against and finally triumphed over the inertia, hostility, treachery and spiteful opposition of the weaklings, perverts and racial underlings who had sought to keep Germany in thrall to her erstwhile conquerors and ever-present enemies. It was enough that he performed his duty to the furtherance and ultimate triumph of the cause, which would justify everything done in its name beyond question. In this it was his clear duty not to fail: it was not for him to consider what he might do as a man if there were any disparity between that and the necessary condition of a soldier of the *Reich*. He considered only the fortunate fact that he had been able to isolate and define sentimentality as the lure, the illusion, that led to failure and defeat. And having thus identified it he was confident of resisting it no matter the occasional discomfort it visited upon him in unwary moments.

Clearing the Cape he set a course northward well to the west of the convoy lane: with no torpedoes left his prime concern was to avoid shipping rather than seek it, and with only a few seconds'-worth of 20mm ammunition remaining his chances on the surface were for all practical purposes non-existent. If he were forced to surface under attack it would be either surrender or destruction—a sorry ending, he reflected, to a patrol that seemed, in some respects, to have set him on a path to distinction. Another in similar circumstances would see him top Schepke's and—significantly—Kretschmer's still unequalled totals, and vindicate all his actions including the occasional irregularities and gaffes; the memory of the sinking at the berth in Lorient still had the power to make him suck his teeth in renewed mortification. Whatever happened afterwards he could rest assured that he had done all that Uncle Karl, the *Reich* and the *Führer* expected of him. From then on it would all be garnish on the dish—and he smiled at the metaphor: his tonnage total had set before him cabbage leaves with knives and forks. The garnish of brilliants would, if he lasted that long, add the finishing touch with the flourish of a gourmet.

At that point he broke off the pleasurable indulgence, unwilling to let hypothesis continue to its logical conclusion: reluctant to admit to superstition, he nevertheless shied at the presumption in a vision of ultimate victory, whatever his part in it. Germany would win the war, of course; but it would be a conceit to plan accordingly while so much remained to be done. Allied landings in North Africa and setbacks on the Russian front, as far as the facts were known to him, were nothing worse than the normal checks on progress to be expected in war, and would be reversed in due course, but even so it would be tempting fate to assume his own survival through to the concluding moves in the struggle. It was enough to attend to immediate needs and priorities; they would lead in their time to the destiny that was Germany's due.

Meanwhile, he faced an unpleasant task in the shape of the necessary inquiry into the failure of the lookouts to spot the Catalina that had strafed them alongside the *British Prowess*. He had already questioned *Matrosen* Trockels and Arndt, during a lull between actions, warning them that they would be presented with written transcripts of their statements for perusal and signature before the return to base, after which the matter would pass into the hands of the base commandant. It was certain that because men had been killed in the Catalina's attack a serious view would be taken of their conduct, for which Altmann would himself have to answer.

"The commanding officer is responsible for every act of his officers and men—you know that!" He had made no attempt to soften a harsh tone since it would have to survive mitigation in the form of his own statement commending the pair for their otherwise exemplary records. Their lapse had been attributable to a misunderstanding, which was properly Altmann's fault. "Even so, your job was to keep an alert watch for the enemy until ordered to stand down."

Yes, they said; they knew it, but had thought that at the stage reached by the refuelling operation, amid the general upheaval, their duty was at an end but had crossed to the blind side to check. They hadn't abandoned their post, but shifted position to make contact with someone in charge, at the precise wrong moment.

"I'd rather you didn't treat me like a new recruit, Trockels! Do me the favour of returning my respect for your and Arndt's experience—you should have known better than to turn your backs on your duty together. The first officer didn't put a couple of babes in arms in such a vital position of trust—he thought he was dealing with seamen!"

Trockels apologised and Arndt looked shamefaced, while Altmann felt angry at the irrevocable fact of their failure. It had left him with no alternative to standard procedure bar a reluctant decision to emphasise the delinquents' better points in his report, at risk of his own condemnation. He could have thrown the book at them, but with the patrol some way from its end he had to consider the effect on morale of an ulcerating point of fancied injustice among the men; it possessed all the septic potential for open recalcitrance. Unthinkable. Discipline was all very well, but it had to be adjusted to suit the circumstances, and the u-boat's peculiar state of cramped confinement demanded particular process. The book as issued would not serve; it required judicious amendment. As ever on disciplinary occasions, Prien and his unbending adherence to prescription as well as principle came to mind, and while Altmann harboured no desire for popularity among his subordinates their respect was important to him, gained not by virtue of some sort of sentimental concern for his men's sensitivities but for his impartial, nicely-moderated application of justice. It was a point on which Altmann often found himself dwelling, and it defined, in principle, the width of the road he was resolved to follow. It was all too easy to veer off it to one side—Prien's—or the other, and here Altmann was grimly amused at recollection of Prien's contemporary, Joachim Schepke. Schepke had been popular with his crews, in Altmann's view too much so, opening the way to sentimentality and moral corruption. Which, in their turn, were manifested in the kind of disciplinary slackness that might well have lain behind Schepke's violent end. The logical conclusion was that survival lay on the narrow ill-defined path mid-way between the two, and while displaying the confidence of certainty Altmann picked his way along it with care.

Announcing his decision to present his own statement in mitigation of the men's failure, he felt he had compromised his principles, but comforted himself with the assurance that it was in the interests of the boat's continued wellbeing. He made it clear that the inevitable inquiry would still in all probability be the formal prelude to a court-martial, "—in which case all I can promise you is that I'll call attention to all the factors in your favour—and mine! It's better than you deserve. You can thank your general good conduct including the reports from your previous commanding officer for whatever chance you've got of avoiding severe punishment. Don't let things slip between now and our return to base. I'll be watching you."

They were duly chastened, and relieved, but Altmann continued in a mood of self-recrimination, castigating himself for the kind of weakness he deplored in others. On top of that, he gained added discomfort from his deduction that the sequence of events leading to the present situation had its beginnings in his decision to top up his bunkers from the tanker instead of doing what he should have done in the first place, simply sinking her. The cause of the gun's crew's deaths was traceable, step by step, back from the Catalina's strafing run, through the laxity of the two lookouts, to his boat's wholly indefensible—in both senses—presence alongside the enemy tanker, which brought it squarely to his own unsupported—even disputed, by implication on Benedict's part—decision. The subsequent destruction of the Catalina might count in his defence, as might his impressive record of tonnage sunk, which, arguably, would not have reached the figure it had without the additional time bought by the extra fuel oil—and, inarguably, by the lost lives; whatever the nature of any court-martial's judgment, and whatever the significance of the two seamen's involvement, he would have his own conscience to face. In some disturbance of mind, he realised that the phantoms to which he'd felt he was becoming reconciled, if not inured, had been joined by others, from which they had taken on fresh substance. And although the reasons for their presence as two distinct groups were disparate in circumstance, they shared common cause in the motivation that had brought them into being: with some alarm Altmann recognised his own conceit, and its power to override his imagined self-discipline and principles. The revelation soured the flavour of the satisfaction he had drawn from the patrol's success as an aggressive operation in furtherance of the *Führer*'s grand design. As for further embellishment of his Knight's Cross . . .

Christmas Day found them about mid-way between St Helena and Ascension Island, the occasion marked by a special dinner centred about the second rescued sheep and a tree constructed from a mop-handle, welding-rods and dyed lavatory-paper. Ensconced in his grotto, otherwise the forward torpedo-compartment decked out with signal flags and the tree, which stood deferentially before the striking red, black and white of the *Reich*'s ensign, Benedict as Santa Claus presented each man with a sardonic scrutiny, a growled "Merry Christmas from the *Führer*; make the most of it!" and a packet of sweets and a book, both provided, incognito, by a figure whose shadowy presence went unsuspected by the crew but with which Altmann was all too well acquainted. It was an acquaintanceship he regarded with cautious ambivalence as a political asset. Arthur Ehrling, leading party member and former governor of Danzig, now *Gauleiter* of Posen, the former Polish city of Poznan and present capital of the German-named province of Wartheland, was the boat's self-appointed "sponsor", an *ex-officio* function he had assumed after meeting Altmann at the boat's commissioning ceremony in Kiel. Altmann had done nothing to either promote or discourage the association, choosing to adopt a non-committal approach in which duty played the leading part. What Ehrling seemed to regard as a friendship Altmann viewed in a less personal light. He said nothing to dispel the general supposition that the gifts had been provided by an ever-optimistic base chaplain rather than the *Führer* himself, but the sceptics either way were supported by hard evidence. Among them was *Maschinistensmaat* Falke.

"First I've heard of the *Führer* dishing out anything to the troops except deathless rhetoric . . . If I wasn't such a trusting innocent I'd suspect our commander of ulterior motives."

"Why him?" asked *Oberbootsmann* Steinhoff, selecting an acid drop from his packet.

"His handwriting in these books."

"Not the God-botherer's?" Steinhoff examined the yellow sweet he had picked, rejected it and fished about for another colour.

"You believe that tale as well, then . . . No, not his. Check it with the signatures in the watch logs if you like."

"I'll take your word for it . . . What sort of ulterior motives?" Steinhoff extracted a cherry-red item and popped it into his mouth.

"Oh—thanks for the work we've done; consolation-prize for helping him gather cabbages and toothpicks for his Knight's Cross. Who knows? Maybe he's just feeling lonely and wants to be liked, and too shy to ask." Falke frowned in mock censure. "Suck it. Don't crunch. Bad for your fillings."

"*Is* he disliked?"

"Reserved verdict."

"How d'you mean?"

"Depends on whether we get home in one piece or not. Or at all. Nobody'll like him if we end up feeding the sharks . . . What's he written in yours?"

"Um—*The deed is all, and not the glory.*"

Falke stared, raised his eyebrows, and said, "Hardly the motto of the *U-Bootwaffe*, but it's the way it seems to be going . . . I bet he's quoting some political windbag."

"'Goethe', he's put under it."

"Rings a bell . . . Probably some defunct party hero like Horst Wessel—only quieter, saying things like that. Let him try it on Göring!"

"I see your point . . . What's in yours?"

"Ah—hm . . . *The world's history is the world's judgment.*" Falke shrugged, turning down the corners of his mouth and raising his eyebrows. "Someone called Schiller—" thoughtfully "—went to law school before joining the navy, I hear—"

"Who—Schiller?"

"Skipper. Maybe this Schiller was a tutor or professor or something . . . History lecturer at the *Kreigsmarineschule* perhaps."

Steinhoff shrugged, crunching the last of his sweet. "All over my head, that sort of stuff."

"As the u-boat said to the e-boat . . . . What's the book, anyway?"

Steinhoff glanced at the spine. "*Selections from* Mein Kampf."

"The more digestible ones, you must hope—"

"What's yours?"

"Mine—? Er . . . *Patriotic Verse.* Stefan George, whoever *he* is."

"Skipper trying to tell you something, d'you think?"

"Tell you when I've read it."

"To yourself, please, *Maschinist.* I never did like poetry; not even the patriotic st—"

"Ssh! *Jazzmeister*'s about to conduct . . ."

Carols rendered—revealing in Schreiber a clear, wavering tenor that surprised and moved his captive audience—there followed a short speech by Altmann, who never attempted more than simple and obvious humour in his public pronouncements, and in this instance, apart from mentioning his sharing with them all their thoughts of home and loved ones, he touched on some aspects of the patrol's action, thanking them for their loyal service, without which it would have been a very different story.

"—Whatever credit comes to this boat, and to me as her commanding officer, as a result of the successful outcome of our efforts, it will be due to you. All I've done is to make the best use I can of the first-class material granted me by the C-in-C—and, let's not forget them, particularly at this time, by German mothers in all their purity, love and strength of character—so whatever might be seen as falling short of the ideal will be my own fault and responsibility. I hope you all feel that I've been worthy of your own cheerful conduct and willing devotion to duty in the cause of the Fatherland and our beloved *Führer* . . . Our navigator—whose word I must take on trust—tells me we still have some way to go, so I'll say no more for the present, you'll be glad to

184

hear, except to wish you all a safe return home: after all, if you get there, so will I! Now—we have a sheep to deal with, and Smut has succeeded in producing—from tins!—a couple of excellent Christmas puddings, so let me also wish you an appetite to suit the occasion." Lifting his mug—the only one not containing the double measure of schnapps he had provided, unsuspected and without forewarning—he cried, "*Heil* Hitler!—*Prosit!*"

Thirty-seven days from the sighting of *Dorsetshire*, after a mostly-submerged passage from landfall off Finisterre, Altmann surfaced cautiously off Cordouan and signalled the guard-boat. Shortly beforehand he had addressed his crew for the last time, dispensing his usual thanks and advice. He reminded them about security—"Someone else is *always* listening, so no matter who you're speaking to, or where, guard your tongues! Your own loose talk might kill you"—and posted a sample letter home on the control-room bulletin-board:

My Dear Erika, I am safely back at base after a successful patrol, and awaiting further orders. I am well and in good spirits. I hope you (and our child/children/name/s) are safe and well. (With your usual ending).

He had added suggestions about presents for the family, warned about the off-limits attractions of the town and other places within reach, and silenced all murmured comment with an unwelcome order confining them to barracks for the first night after arrival, the idea being, as he explained, to allow them to acclimatise themselves to normal, not to say civilised, life after so long in the boat's conditions of unrelieved barbarism. Then Lange had rounded off with a brief reminder of the hazards of over-indulgence with the natives.

"Bear in mind that it comes under the heading of self-inflicted injury, not battle-wound," he'd ended, bleakly dead-pan. "You get no medals, not even posthumously, but there are whole regiments of poxed-up boudoir heroes on the Russian front, so I'm told; the *Wehrmacht* finds it a cheaper treatment than penicillin. That's reserved for *Reischsmarschalls* and above."

Their arrival, in the small hours, passed unremarked, a dead-slow creeping—almost, thought Altmann, a skulking—upstream between river-banks shadowy in the blackout beneath a laden overcast, and a final blending with the dark mass of the concrete u-boat pen indicated by the escorting launch. It was as if the return were a furtive retreat

185

from some defeat rather than a triumphant flourish marking a notable achievement. There was in fact a flavour of discomfiture about it, Altmann reflected: a daylight return was forbidden; the enemy's air reconnaissance had become a continuous threat to surfaced progress, and airborne attacks on anything that moved for a kilometre or more upstream from the river-mouth were becoming frequent. Even at night the risk was present, evidently an indicator of the enemy's increasing use of airborne radar. The celebrations that had once marked victorious returns had been transmuted into relatively brief, sombre formalities during a safe interval following the boat's berthing in the pen. Certainly no welcoming committee would be roused from its beds in the middle of the night.

His last act of the patrol after tying up in the pen was a final entry in the log:

20th January, 1943. Arrival Bordeaux . . .

0305 Secured starboard side alongside Berth 1, Pen 4.

All machinery shut down, shore power connected. Deck, bridge & bulkhead w/t hatches at harbour condition Green. Boat at sea berth/berth 137 days 13hrs 20 mins.

Patrol distance ex-Pt Hand 24,408 miles.

Vessels sunk: 14. Total approx 58,000gt.

Aircraft destroyed: 1 (Catalina recce/bomber)

Casualties: per MO's log.

There was a running debate about passage distance—sea-miles or kilometres? Altmann was satisfied with the logical argument that since navigation was unavoidably based on the sea-mile and the boat's log registered speed in knots, the choice of unit for distance run was obvious. And he nursed a sneaking regard for the fathom as a proper seamanlike measure of depth; the metre was a bloodless creature, of the land, and—to be blunt—a French intruder. Idly, he wondered what Germany—or the German states—had used before Napoleon's edicts.

The first news was from the base commandant, *Fregattenkapitän* von Lohmeyer, who alone of all the base staff had been on the jetty to welcome them, standing watchfully apart from the bleary-eyed mooring-party and sundry technical people whose various specialities demanded their immediate presence. Hamburg had been heavily bombed in daylight raids, and it appeared that Lübeck had been included in the target area, whether deliberately or by error on the part of the Americans von Lohmeyer could not say. But Altmann's parents were among the missing, with recovery operations proceeding slowly in difficult conditions.

VIII

OTHER boats also had "sponsors"—like Ehrling usually self-appointed, figures of more or less note in the Party hierarchy whose politically-profitable enthusiasms were served by keeping their locales and circles informed of the boats' progress, as far as it was made known to them by Headquarters. Self-aggrandisement apart, the idea was to present the German public with a focus for a need it was supposed to have for national heroes. An established custom from the Great War, it applied, mostly through Dr Goebbels's Ministry of Propaganda and Public Enlightenment, most conspicuously to the obvious exploits of the *Luftwaffe*, the glitter of which had dulled somewhat with the *Führer*'s ignominious abandonment—tacitly recognised through the thin pretence of deferment—of his loudly-advertised plan for the invasion of England. Air aces continued to appear, but in theatres lacking the implications and immediacy of the battle for control of British skies; theatres which, in fact, were distinctly depressing in their general lack of dramatic progress—indeed, by 1943, theatres which savoured of military embarrassment for the *Wermacht*.

They included the North Atlantic, but the u-boat's continuing importance as the sole standard-bearer of the *Reich*'s naval presence in international waters beyond north-west Europe ensured the validity of its continued claim to some degree of glamour. Bar one or two who had been promoted to command of desks, the first cohort of "aces"—the distinction reserved exclusively for the boats' commanders—of this war had passed, into either history or prison camps. Others had risen to take their places but to a less extravagant level as the Allies' equipment, weaponry and tactics improved: it was not as easy, Altmann reflected, to be an ace in these more fraught times; that is, if the criteria remained the same; but today a ship sunk could well be seen as the equivalent of, say, two of similar tonnage two or three years before, gauged by the effort required and the level of hazard involved. In some parts of the ocean the equivalent could well be three or even four; in some parts, in certain conditions, there was no calculable equivalent:

the only outcome would be the boat's loss for no kills. Black spots were becoming not merely more numerous but also alarmingly more extensive, and aces short-lived where not still-born. In fact, Altmann felt, the term was taking on a patina of age, reflecting the lineaments of antiquity out of place in the hectic *danse macabre* of present conditions. He felt he had come on the scene unprepared, had built up his record too slowly, and was adding to his total against the mounting pressure of circumstance. Each additional ton from now on would be logged in return for a disproportionate quota of personal effort and determination; each successive ton would drain off an increasing measure of mental, moral and physical stamina, to say nothing of wear and tear on the boat and its equipment. He felt his time was running out, and that it might do so before the next patrol's planned end was an all too likely eventuality. He would have to guard against it by whatever means came to hand.

The homecoming had been less than the happy return to which every sailor looks forward regardless of the portents, which, intimated and expressed by the news bulletins Altmann had had posted for all to read, based on Schwebke's interception of German and other broadcasts as well as the periodic official notices received from C-in-C, had not been good. And their gloomiest fears had been realised. Requests for special leave on the usual rota basis had had to be refused. Instead, they had been granted on a scale of urgency gauged by the reports of Allied air attacks on the homeland, by this time giving intimations of the enemy's conclusive intentions in the systematic methods used, including a means of confusing the radar defences. Bomber squadrons operating at night with what Churchill had called "deliberate careful discrimination" were directed to the targets by marker flares placed by single aircraft, in theory more or less foolproof but in practice prone to the vagaries of weather and navigation. As a result, while, according to Goebbels, industrial output was only superficially affected, centres of population were being devastated, if to no avail in respect of the unshakable morale of the German people. One such misplaced marker had brought a number of bombs down on Lübeck at about the time Altmann had been entering Spanish territorial waters. It had not been Lübeck's first such experience; early in the previous year it had suffered the misdirected attentions of the RAF's area bombing strategy, which had laid waste parts of the inner city in addition to scattered destruction in the suburbs. None of it had prompted the departure of Altmann's parents, who had pointed to the subsequent shift of attention to other

188

cities as sufficient reason to stay put. In this they had shared a common belief.

Attending the civic memorial service in the absence of any identifiable remains, Altmann confirmed the state of public morale by his observation of the drawn faces around him, in their set expressions and the profound reproach in their direct glances, as if warning off the impertinence of facile sympathy; their reserved comment, their dignity in the face of grievous loss. There was neither false cheerfulness nor demonstrative grief, silent tears apart, but a palpable sense of outrage. The only note of discord he sensed, and that as perhaps no more than a reflection of his own perceptions and growing awareness of the general situation, lay in the precise object of the outrage, which comprised not only the obvious metal of the enemy's insolence but also something subtle, and perhaps far more morally corrosive: there was a taint in the public mood, an ugly intimation of sentiments responding to the perception of malign forces emanating not from the direction of the overt enemy but from sources in which confidence and trust had been placed, and from which salvation, justification, right and strength were expected as the lights limning the path to the promised Eden. A more cynical mind than Altmann's would have divined a new scepticism in the reception given the pronouncements, edicts and exhortations of the system through its various promoters and practitioners. His, however, perceived instead a normal expression of mingled resolution and dismay in the face of adversity, of the resentment to be expected of people in the stress of periodic assaults on their ordered patterns of life that were the normal currency of war, of which adversity was a transient feature. It would pass.

Meanwhile, he had his own share of the bitterness, and although he had not been close to his parents, whose marriage had never, as far as he'd been able to understand, held together without the assistance of his father's sense of duty and his mother's strong Lutheran affinities, he felt their sudden absence from his affairs with more of a sense of loss than he would have expected. Competence had summed up his mother's fulfilment of her domestic functions, and there had never been much more than a perfunctory gesture of love in her relations with her son. A subaltern in the trenches during the previous war, his father had emerged physically intact but in a permanent state of moody pessimism heightened by Altmann's decision to abandon law for the navy. He'd never expressed an interest in his son's progress beyond a noncommittal readiness to meet the training costs. Altmann would have liked to have discovered a way to bring them into a more amicable union as the years advanced; as it was, his loss was laced with regret and a strangely inexpressible sorrow. They had deserved better, he felt; but he baulked at the suggestion of his change of career's having contributed to the situation. The passage of events had justified his decision; all his continuing with a legal career would have done would have been to add to the disparity between the three of them. He had wanted them to be proud of him, and with their achievement. He felt he would have succeeded: Ursula had proved an incalculably positive asset to his plan, but the *Führer*'s becoming embroiled in war with England had undone the promise of her patient diplomacy, by which she had brought about stirrings of affection in the couple that had made Altmann wonder, for the first time, at the effect a daughter might have had on them—a sister for him. But now . . . War had seemed to throw his father back towards whatever he had begun to escape while his mother had reasserted her detachment, which had distressed Ursula.

Altmann listened to the pastor's monotone unmoved. Words, spoken as if they had been sapped of useful power; tokens of form rather than of the emotions such an occasion might be expected to arouse, or allay. Minutes passed, then something in their tone, in the mood conveyed by the speaker's voice, focused Altmann's reluctant thoughts, and recollection of a lifetime's unhappiness beyond reach of his unaided help. And here, among these people mourning their dead, his impotence, his failure, seemed emphasised. Abruptly, he got to his feet thanking God for an aisle seat, and left. Outside, the earlier sunshine had given way to cloud, and a light breeze blew cobwebs of drizzle into his face. Its gentle chill had a disinterestedly comforting effect.

The sense of regret had not left him when, a few days later, back at Bordeaux, he attended the summary inquiry into the conduct of the two lookouts, and the presiding officer's decision to recommend their discharge from the service under reprimand did nothing to relieve it; nor did the incidental commendation of his own conduct as an example of soundly-judged initiative, substantiated by the award of oak-leaves and swords to his Knight's Cross. He felt that in some way he and the hapless pair had let each other down; and that his half-hope of their sharing some kind of attenuated censure had been naïve. The commendation as the essence of the award's intent only added to his deepening dissatisfaction with the trend of events in general and in his own case in particular. He disliked the feeling of being in less than full control of their influences on his affairs, contrasting the situation with that prevailing at sea.

Notwithstanding his perceptions of the public mood in Germany, however, Altmann was conscious of a sense of distrust when he received an invitation to visit Posen in an official capacity as Ehrling's guest of honour. The boat's sponsor had also professed himself an admirer of its commander, whom he had already declared to be an ace, remarking fulsomely upon his exploits, alleged and actual, in after-dinner addresses and other public assignations. He was apt to lean heavily on the descriptive, based more on over-egged, or over-schnapped, rather than informed, imagination, from which he siphoned off a certain amount of reflected glory, insofar as it was illuminated by the glow of politically-fuelled *bonhomie* among his audiences. Having governed Danzig with some distinction, not all of his own making, his ambition at the time of Altmann's visit was nothing less than to govern the whole of Poland, duly swept clean of undesirable elements of its pre-war population—"All gentleness towards Poles must be avoided," as he had succinctly put it, adding for good measure that "loathing for the Poles" was to be sown in every German heart. In his commanding view, God had helped Germany to conquer the Polish nation, "—which must now be destroyed . . . In a decade the fields of Poland will be heavy with stacked wheat and rye, raised and harvested by Germans, but not a Pole will remain." An ardent advocate of the policy of *Lebensraum*, he lost no opportunity to give his beliefs strident voice.

While in general agreement with him on the point, Altmann felt an indefinable distaste for his express conception of it, in particular an objection to the idea of gratuitous brutality; whatever manifestations of it he had witnessed or perpetrated in the course of duty, he was satisfied that it had not been merely a result of personal inclination, of an urge towards personal aggrandisement. This ignored, of course, the aspiration common to all u-boat commanders to log, and receive official acknowledgment of, the highest possible score of sinkings. But even for that excusable exercise of personal vanity there had been a valid reason, keeping it within the bounds of necessity. With, he was unable to avoid admitting, one exception; for which his reasoning at the time had since, layer by layer, worn thin, and no matter how he had tried to reface it, to prevent its erosion by the inexorable progress of time and its accompanying perspective, the stark, impermeable and impartial

191

substrate of moral permanence had been laid bare, an inescapable accusation of personal transgression that in its calculated violation of every tenet of humanity, exacerbated by its cloak of contrived necessity, had been an enormity with which he was beginning to realise he could not live as a whole man. His alternatives were either the oblivion of a hero's death, as it would be seen, or the day-by-day fostering of a pretence, a self-delusion that would never succeed in its aim: among ordinary men he would be unable to stand upright, unable to share the common experience without reserve, unable to declare himself among co-equals; always aware of an accompanying accuser ever on the margin of disclosure. His view of the motives and standards of others would never be without a reflection of his own indefensible position, and war alone could never be his refuge.

As for Ehrling, he felt he could at least suspect the man's support of his boat—and its commander—as more political expedient than patriotically-inspired personal sentiment. If a reason in the form of a flesh-and-blood manifestation were needed for his, Altmann's, baulking at the prospect of Party membership, as distinct from its support at a remove, Ehrling provided it. But, with a bitter sense of the implacable tenacity of his own culpability, he was aware that he was bound to accept an ersatz friendship which in different circumstances he would have felt fully justified in despising. He could not contemn where his own credentials would not stand examination on the same terms, and he shied at the idea of actual physical extermination of the Polish—or any other—nation claiming a geographical identity. Surely Ehrling spoke, at least in part, figuratively: the Poles as a subject nation would, for all practical purposes, be destroyed, though as people—as individual subjects of the greater *Reich*—they would remain. Surely.

More from a sense of duty, if not also foreboding, than with any pleasure, he entrained for Posen in the company of Schreiber, Hildegras and, selected from a group of unconvincing volunteers, ten petty officers and ratings, among them Helmut Steinhoff, and Klaus Falke, whose family had so far remained physically unscathed by the war. After a week's leave visiting them he had returned to Bordeaux, preferring the distractions of the port to the stifling incomprehension of family attentions as a means of releasing the unbearable tensions of the patrol. He found Ehrling an interesting combination of the authoritarianism he distrusted and the bombast he grudgingly admired, chiefly for its success in the presence of surrounding mediocrity—which, he was beginning to feel, summed up the greater part of the *Reich*'s ruling tiers. But he could not disguise the irony in his tone when he pronounced Ehrling "Personally a very nice man, Helmut."

"Yes? Even if he does hate the Poles, eh? After all, a man must be allowed to hate, as he must be allowed to love. But I pity the bastard."

"What for—being a pleasant fellow, or a bastard?"

"The Poles will kill him before he kills them. A simple balance of numbers."

"Bet he doesn't lose any sleep over it."

"Bet away. He hasn't the imagination. I predict a particularly grisly end."

"As long as we're not around when it happens—"

As for Altmann, conscience apart he was uncomfortable with what amounted to an enforced association—enforced by his sense of duty, albeit misplaced in this case, he felt, and his increasingly prominent position as a figure of war; an association Ehrling chose to interpret as friendship, cemented, as he saw it, by the favours within his considerable power to bestow, and bestowed in such a way—typically in the floodlit arena of public display—that a refusal would be not merely unthinkable but seriously damaging to the reluctant recipient's professional and social, let alone political, standing. In this Altmann was aware that his predicament was an inherent condition of the *Wermacht*, particularly the less Party-motivated element of it: the necessity of intimacy with the beast that was neither suspectly aloof nor close enough to be consumed by it. As an instance, his association with Ehrling was a delicate balancing act with no safety-net, and it disturbed him to realise that he had allowed the balance to tilt too far towards the subsumed: by accepting gifts and favours from the man he had compromised his political autonomy. The thought added an unwelcome increment to the unsettled state of his mind, exacerbated by the reception he and his companions received on arrival at Posen. It was also unsettled by the explanation Ehrling gave in answer to Hildegras's seemingly ingenuous inquiry about the occupants of a train outside Lissa. It had been halted in a siding to allow the other to pass, so was close enough to be of interest, and they had passed at reduced speed.

"Cattle wagons," said Hildegras. "You know—covered trucks with narrow openings along the sides high up, criss-crossed with barbed wire." He fixed Ehrling with a gaze of wide-eyed frankness he had discovered to be useful in ticklish situations, such as when making a conclusive move against Falke at chess; or holding the rapt attention of a girl in the King Kong or other off-limits rendezvous when down to his last five reichsmarks. Now he regarded the well-rounded features of a man to whom he had taken an instant dislike, eliciting from them a smile of condescending affability that failed to reach the small flinty eyes. Hildegras was aware of the suspicion they betrayed, but stood his ground, bland and artless. "There were people in them, actually. It was dusk—almost night, but there were floodlights—and there were hands, at the wire, and a few faces. Couldn't hear anything, of course. Too much noise—the crowd with me, wheels clanking and all that, but it looked like they were—calling—something as we passed. I just wondered, *Herr Gauleiter*—would you know what they were doing—where they were going?" He left the words hanging in a momentary silence, meeting the flinty scrutiny with candid inquiry, implying expectation of a wholly defensible answer. He sipped his drink, aware of other eyes on him as the surrounding murmur of conversation picked up its dropped stitches and continued in a lower key. Lemonade. Hildegras did not drink alcohol, and his experience at the hands of Neptune's police hadn't altered his view of it, not even as a preferable alternative to sea-water. Ingenuous expression apart, he valued a clear head at all times. Like this one. He felt a tiny fizz of apprehension, relishing its sharp-edged play upon his nerves. But he was genuine in his inquiry. He had seen similar trains before, and was curious, and vaguely suspicious. He felt Ehrling had the answer, and smiled disarmingly at the fat official.

Ehrling's gaze narrowed as he cleared his throat. "Ha—hmm . . . Yes—those trains. Well, the *Reich* is in need of work—"

"Excuse me, *Herr Gauleiter*—my midshipman is neglecting his duty." Altmann's hand gripped Hildegras's shoulder as he intercepted the exchange. "Forgive my interrupting, but some business concerning my boat—a matter of urgency—" He turned to Hildegras, now flushed and plainly discomfited. "You'd better see to that matter of the repair indent, Rudolf—you should have been in touch with the yard about it before lunch. They're waiting. The phone—my room at the hotel. Take the car—I've told the driver."

Altmann's words made no sense, but on Ehrling seemed to have the effect he aimed at, as also on the perceptive Hildegras, who stiffened, chin up, clicked his heels and nodded before excusing himself to march purposefully from the room. Quite an accomplished act, thought Altmann grudgingly. The little rogue would have to be watched. To Ehrling he apologised again, and noticed the fleeting shadow of irritation behind the eyes—whether at Hildegras's inquiry or the interruption he could not guess.

"He's apt to be somewhat—indiscreet—at times, *Herr Gauleiter.* I'll tell him all he needs to know about the labour situation."

Ehrling took a breath and puffed out his cheeks, swallowed a mouthful of champagne, and nodded, lips pursed. "Ah—just so, my dear Altmann. It's a vital element of the national effort, of course—mobility of labour. Easier to move the workers to the work than the other way round—as you understand all too well in the *U-Bootwaffe*, eh?" And he guffawed, wiping his eyes with a crumpled handkerchief. Altmann nodded and smiled. "But much as we'd all like to see it, it can't be done in first-class carriages; they're properly attended during the journey."

Altmann nodded again, tight-lipped. "Of course . . . Tell me, *Herr Gauleiter*—when do you expect to take your place as the country's director?"

Later, he upbraided Hildegras for his indiscretion, but congratulated him on his quick response to the bogus order. "It saved your hide, you know—the alternative would have meant an official reprimand from me—a kick up the backside, and transfer to something more in your line—"

"Not the surface ships, *Kapitän*, surely?"

Altmann was in no mood for humour. "*B-Dienst*, possibly," he said sourly, and the midshipman's eyes widened. "But Army Group North would be more likely, my boy! We may be sea-pickled u-boat men but we're also naval officers. Try to behave according to the conventions of civilised society; among other things it forbids the embarrassment of your host—which, in this instance, is a risky form of amusement. Ehrling's a Party official, an officer of the *Reich* government, and although a civilian he's a man of considerable influence in military matters. Rub him—and others like him—up the wrong way and you could find yourself in a sticky corner. You might be *U-Bootwaffe* ace material, but it won't make much impression on ruffled official feathers. Especially in your present primitively insignificant rank!" As he spoke Altmann acknowledged the truth of the words, albeit uttered partly for effect. Ehrling disconcerted could be dangerous from the standpoint of a junior officer of the *U-Bootwaffe*, even under the tutelage of an acknowledged veteran. But Hildegras was not satisfied; he stood before his commanding officer in an attitude of respectful expectancy which in another branch of the service might have been taken for calculated impertinence, tempered as it was by the baby-faced frankness that was his burden as well as his grace.

Altmann stared at him, feeling faintly baffled, then cleared his throat and went on. "The train was carrying labourers to one of the camps set up in these parts . . . As *Herr* Ehrling would have told you, efficient industrial production demands a flexible and mobile labour force. At the same time it reduces unemployment—people unable to find work at home find it elsewhere, and the transport is provided—"

"Cattle-wagons sewn up with barbed wire, *Kapitän*?"

Sharply, Altmann replied, "It's adequate—the journey isn't lengthy. There are attendants." He wished Hildegras wasn't so coercive in his affectation of naïvety: the fraud was infuriatingly irresistible. "That's as much as I can tell you—and as much as you need know! I won't go as far as ordering you to avoid touching on administrative matters in conversation with civilian officials, Rudolf—use your discretion, what there is of it. It could do with some practice, especially after a long patrol!"

Hildegras took the hint, ponderous as it was. He stiffened, clicked his heels, nodded solemnly, and concurred, adding, "Only one thing more, *Kapitän* . . . I saw a similar train—once, when I was at Mürwik—the *Mutterhaus*—but children were being herded into it—like cattle. I've never had an answer to that—well, I mean, I've never asked—?"

Altmann's hesitation was fractional, but he knew it had not escaped Hildegras's notice. Aware of his own discomfort at this revelation, he snapped, "Evacuees, Hildegras. You'll see more of it as the bombing gets worse . . . Now talk of something else—and to someone else. And control your impulses!"

Hildegras did as bidden, but the episode refused to slip into the indistinct whirl of impressions that marked Altmann's recollection of the visit, and its peculiarly acescent flavour lingered long afterwards, revived at odd moments by any chance incident having some enigmatic quality able to trigger the domino-train of memory. Almost invariably it led also to the schooner and its phantoms, a connection Altmann recognised as inevitable and unbreakable. He wished he had held more firmly to his principles over the invitation to Posen—after all, the long train journey would have provided a perfectly acceptable reason for refusal, more so in view of the effects of a lengthy war patrol on everyone. He cursed his weakness whenever he cast an involuntary mind's-eye back over the affair. And he, too, wondered about the trains, and the labour-camps for which their cargoes were bound. Hildegras's inquiry might have been his own, if he had had the younger man's courage—or lack of discretion.

They had been greeted by the full panoply of local National Socialist fiefdom headed by the Göring-like figure of Ehrling himself, and paraded like returning victors in open Mercedes roadsters through the less than thronged streets to the Hotel Ostland—"One of the best in the *Reich, Kapitän,*" confided a studiedly arch Schreiber, who, like the others, found a bottle of schnapps on the table beside his bed, together with an embossed card inviting him to the home of a prominent burger and his family as their house-guest. They were toured and toasted and partied and invited to sign the visitors' book at the *Rathaus*, where they were photographed being greeted by the mayor, a native of Regensburg and a local Party stalwart. And so it went on. At the end of it all there was general agreement that the visit had been a great success, enjoyed by everyone as a restorative interlude in the business of war. Everyone, that is, except the indigenous local populace, conspicuous by their sparse distribution among the largely uniformed onlookers, and in their lacklustre expression of acclaim. No amount of bluster on Ehrling's part could conceal or disguise the fact, which Altmann noted with a puzzlement he did not wholly connect with a natural ignorance of naval matters in a landlocked community.

The Hildegras diversion apart, he felt a certain relief at the visit's freedom from incident, but irritation at the effect he believed it had had on discipline: home leave and rest-periods in the camps provided for the u-boat crews were all well and good, but even a few days as a group under the informal and uncomprehending influence of politically-charged public display aimed at glamorising their demanding and acutely unglamorous toil in the service of the Fatherland were enough to weaken the fabric of mutual responsibility on which the boat's survival depended. He determined to take steps to re-establish it as a priority in the preparations for the next patrol. His parents' fate weighed more heavily in the intent he felt towards the enemy than anything that had passed during the visit to Posen, but he wondered about, and feared, the effect on his men's morale of Ehrling's injudicious declarations anent the native population. His aim in command had always been to convince his subordinates of the

Reich's moral integrity, and while the Jewish question was debatable the status of nationals in the occupied territories—the French, for example, and the Dutch, Danes, Norwegians, Belgians; and the Poles by the same token—should surely be on a common footing, given due validity by the ruling power. Ehrling's talk of destruction was mere grandiloquence. Like many otherwise obscure people elevated to civic positions, particularly when through political as distinct from personal merit, he allowed himself to be carried away by his own posturing, a small man given sudden prominence in the functions of a system, and Altmann formed an uncomfortable impression of an endemic weakness in the National Socialist grand strategy.

But first he had a few days at his disposal, and thankfully signed the base leave book. The journey to Rauenthal took the best part of eighteen hours. The derailment of a freight train caused by what a railway official described as "subversive activity" delayed his train outside Strasburg, and the line had been bombed just north of Ludwigshafen, creating another frustrating delay ended only by an unsatisfactory transfer to the Frankfurt line from Mannheim and another delay in Frankfurt owing to repair-works to yet further air-raid damage. Then there had been difficulties finding road transport from Wiesbaden to Rauenthal. He reached home in the small hours feeling that Germany was losing her grip on the situation, a feeling that led to a sense of detachment in the comparison with his own experience of war in the relative order of the *U-Bootwaffe*. Almost as if, he reflected, there were two separate and distinct conflicts, with mutually differing goals, differing attitudes, differing approaches. The idea of a shared object, shared trials, shared outlook, seemed unrealistic, like the overdone, orchestrated and somehow hollow accolade of the Posen visit. His mood during the fortnight spent in the unaccustomed intimacy of his family—three daughters and Ursula, an almost overwhelming weight of feminine attention which, while in others a novel and seductive contrast with the boat's uncompromising demands, was in some respects uncannily similar in the claustrophobic sensation it produced. He surprised himself with the realisation that he felt a need for open air and a distant horizon so similar to the effect of the boat at depth that it could be coped with in the same way: self-discipline, which in its turn produced an appearance of asceticism, even coldness. That it effectively concealed his worry about the safety of his family was evident in Ursula's manner. From the joyful warmth of welcome it shifted to an inquiring uncertainty which Altmann, to his added perplexity at his own reactions, felt unable to assuage. He took the only course that seemed open to him by sidestepping it, calling attention instead to the continuing problem of her parents' stubborn refusal to join her in a safer habitation, at least until the tide of war changed.

"Will it?"

"What—change?" Altmann affected surprise. "But of course, my sweet. As all tides—and wars—do. Attack, counter-attack, and again, attack, but always the advantage—the initiative—lies with the attacker, who must win in the end—"

"As Germany did under the Kaiser?"

"That war was never lost." Altmann felt impatient. He had no wish to discuss war strategy with his wife; had hoped to forget it for a few days. But of course it was unavoidable; it was the very reason for his being in this place with his family, and trying to prevent its tainting what should be a pleasurable—a precious—interlude. "Armistice isn't surrender; or even an ending. This war is the settlement of the question, but it means a supreme effort on everyone's part, and sacrifice. Which, in the age of the aeroplane, means ordinary men and women as part of the enemy's target. At least promise me that if you can't get them to stay here with you, you won't spend time with them—and not even in the bomb-shelters! Your father seems to think the house is protected by some kind of divine armour, like his *Seydlitz* or whatever her name was." Conscious of the anger in his tone Altmann gestured contritely. "I'm sorry, my sweet—forgive me. I'm not angry at you, or your father, though he ought to have more care for his own. But your safety is something that worries me constantly when I can do nothing, say nothing, on patrol. Now, for a few days, I can. So I try to make you see—not just my point of view, but your own danger—and the girls'. You must promise me, before I go back—hm?"

"How can I, my love? I love them. If they were hurt, injured—and I not able to help, safe here—"

"Yes—! Safe here! Doesn't it occur to you that the reason for my fighting the war is your safety? If you were killed—you and the girls—what would be left?"

"The Fatherland!" Ursula's eyes flashed. "That's your reason, or so you've said from the beginning. The Fatherland, and the *Führer*! And your—your *Lion*! Uncle Karl!" The scorn in her voice was not lost on Altmann, who felt a stirring of indignation. He suppressed it with a deep breath as Ursula continued, "Is that your real family, Gunnar—your leader and your uncle?—and the Fatherland—the *Führer*-land! Surely *they* are the things you fight for—? We—me and the girls—are incidentals. Necessary, for the future of the Fatherland, but incidental as individuals, replaceable if the need arises—"

Altmann took her by the shoulders in a grip that made her wince, and shook her. "Stop it! You're wrong—you couldn't be more wrong!" But looking into the blue depths of her eyes he was swept by remorse, and relaxed his grip; she had the power to break his heart, not by malice but by her bewilderment, her incomprehension, as fathomless as the sunshot depths of tropical waters, as ineffable, as reproachful. Would his actions affront them as they had the sea? How could he explain—but why need he? It was enough that he had his duty to perform, in a cause he had espoused from his first awareness of it. But it did not weigh in the balance against his feelings for Ursula, for his irreplaceable daughters, for the life he had hoped to make for them together—the life he was fighting for. The Fatherland was only its demesne, its security, its trustee: as he fought for the Fatherland so he fought for its leader, for its leader's appointed lieutenants; but ultimately for its wards, for the families that made up its living fabric, gave it its validity; and for one of those families in particular, obviously and properly his own, as other men—his officers and crew, for example—fought for theirs. And they would win. In the end, they would win, to bring a new order and a better way to the world. That, after and above all, had been the *Führer*'s promise. It was a promise Altmann believed—as he had demonstrated, and still did. Without it—this belief—his conduct of that part of the war over which he had control would have been a charade; and a charade in peculiarly bad taste.

He took a breath, slowly shook his head, and held her gaze as if clinging to a life-preserver. If he were to lose her—her alone—all would be lost; all that had given his motives and actions meaning from the outset. Rudderless at first, as he had come to realise, the encounter with Ursula, so vividly recallable, had given his loyalties substance and direction, set them in perspective; in her absence chaos would reign over wilderness. No Fatherland, no *Führer*—no Uncle Karl—could supplant her. They could exist only by courtesy of her presence as a living, tangible, intrinsic part of himself. At thought of her destruction he could have groaned aloud. Instead, releasing her, he said, "Forgive me. I'm sorry. But I mustn't lose you—"

Which, he thought, was the truest thing in his universe. He must not lose her—her above all others, even the girls: and he thought of his daughters, who had, in effect, denied him the son he had hoped for, but in the most charming and blameless way. He experienced a physical pain at thought of their coming to harm, not only as his own flesh and blood, as repositories of a tenderness that continually and unfailingly surprised him with its intensity in their presence, but also in their embodiment of an innocence, a trusting guilelessness, that had the power to wipe from his mind all the assimilated bitterness of war's impartial bane, to lift his spirit above the dark troughs of doubt and misgiving about his appointed charge, his allegiance to the cause. By sharing and encouraging their childish delights he could forget, momentarily, the things on which he depended as his family's provider. Somehow, he had failed to give them their due in his anticipation of a life—a working life, at least—of service to the Fatherland: it had not seemed possible, in the early days, that he would encounter a baleful presence among the scenes of heroic action in the tradition of proud self-abnegation he had adopted as his own.

But there was another grain of sand in the gears of his affairs, and though its discordant effect seemed not to be progressive it was persistent, a quality against which he had begun to feel powerless: it seemed to be leading him inexorably along a road to despair. Lange's pills had had no counter-effect, since he had not taken them, instead electing to regard them as a reminder that he possessed inner resources which should have been his bulwark against moral susceptibility: having given them due consideration beforehand his decisions and actions were above reproof, not only in their tactical and strategic sense—in their expression of his professional competence—but also morally, according to the tenets of the Party in their practical application of its—the *Führer*'s—declared ideals. Yet there was doubt, a grain of it, diamond-hard and immovably lodged, the cause of a nerve-racking, growing weariness of spirit that was almost physical. And lately it had assumed a dual character: beside it, like the diffuse shadow cast by a clouded sun, had appeared a sense of dread. In the ever-pressing demands of the boat's operation he had been able, when not off-guard in fitful sleep, to disregard it, to dismiss it as a natural but fanciful extension of the overt impression: it was inevitable that weariness of mind would expose it to hallucinatory impressions, more so in the experience of war that made necessary a sublimation of normally insupportable horror. Wounds were sustained not only by the flesh but also, and more profoundly, by the spirit, the mind, the very essence of the man as a sentient being, and Altmann had begun to doubt that, like the body, there was any natural tendency to healing. At best there would be abiding disfigurement, disablement; and, in place of emollient, embitterment and regret in a corrosive blend.

On the second evening at home, bowing to popular demand, he read the girls a bedtime story. Helene, the middle one, a dark-eyed matronly soul whose enthusiasm for the Grimms' more disturbing tales provided her with a pretext for reassuring and comforting the uncomprehending youngest, little Kläre, was evidently herself thrilled into almost inarticulate fright by the giants, dwarves, witches and other apparitions conjured into the room by the brothers' vivid powers. From the shadows created by the dimmed bedside lamp emerged the old crone planning to feast on Hansel and Gretel; enraged Rumpelstiltskin committing gory suicide; and since Margarete, at seven the eldest, a serene, flaxen-haired Dresden-ware reproduction of her mother, insisted that her father read one tale for each member of his audience, Altmann read on, intrigued to find himself drawn into the fantastic world of folklore he had not visited since his own childhood. Its byways and highways, at first childishly amusing, very quickly revealed familiar stretches and turns, scenes that echoed with remembered figures and their predicaments, and amusement changed to interest in a hitherto unsuspected level of imagery and allegory.

When he had finished he realised that he had joined the saucer-eyed Helene among a whirligig of hobgoblins against which she resolutely shielded a semi-comatose Kläre, hugging her infant sister in the knitted shawl she had wrapped round the diminutive form as a preparation for the experience. Undisturbed, dimpled chin in hand, Margarete smiled at all three with an air of abstraction: all was well with her world, already freeing itself of infancy's credulities, and a few evenings later she expressed impatience with tales of spinning-wheels and frog princes, asking instead for something original, meaning not read from a book.

"Tell us a story of your own, Father." She fixed him with a candid blue that emulated her mother's, against which he had no defence, and already her speech, measured and low-pitched, possessed a timbre of calm confidence that made him fear for her vulnerability to a world seemingly bent on destroying virtue, imposing penalties on such indiscretions as truthfulness and frankness. It was clear that the *Führer*'s steadfast adherence to the ideals he had declared to the world were bringing on his head—and on the country he had lifted out of its former position of unjust subjugation to forces that had gained by default rather than by their own superior moral and military attributes—yet further malefactions by the old enemies, who now invoked a claim to exclusive Godliness and right in their determination to crush a national claim to self-determination and a proper place of respect among legitimate sovereign states. One had to face unremitting struggle in the interests of one's integrity. Honesty and truth alone could not prevail; an element of guile would have to be employed, which required a skill that could be learned where it was not inherent.

But, in his eldest daughter's hands, at least for the present, honesty and truth prevailed, and casting about in some desperation among the meagre creations of his literal and practical imagination he settled doubtfully for a rendering of the story of Siegfried. German mythology appealed to a spirit of heroism he felt would find a sympathetic impulse in Margarete's perceptions, while the horrific spectacle, intentions and final destruction of Fafner would satisfy Helene's craving for blood-chilling entrancement without need for his expanding on the story's symbolism, of which he was himself in some uncertainty after initial conviction. Little Kläre would, of course, drift off into her own shawl-bound milky *Traumerie*, as habitually placid as a Raphaelite cherub. It had been Ursula's fervent prayer after Helene's stormy overture to childhood that her next would be a contrasting relief, and Kläre seemed to have come as a pointed answer: here you are, just this once, it seemed to say: be thankful for a child whole in mind and body, whether hell-raiser or inchoate saint. But Kläre had come as a multiple blessing, seemingly the catalyst that calmed the fractious Helene by finding in the elder girl a motherly instinct expressed in a selfless concern for the little one's wellbeing. Ursula had been content; Altmann, looking on at intervals, struck with a sense of mystified awe at the depth of emotion the three girls together stirred in him, as now. It was as much as he could do to recount Siegfried's battle with the dragon in a steady voice as he surveyed the group settled about him in the bedroom's softly-lit encompassing warmth, an illusion of invulnerable security that, quite suddenly, was shattered by a sound so discordant, so misplaced in that setting that it assumed a note of lunacy more true to its nature than the entirely normal role it played in the periodic alarms of a battle in which only by a transcendent effort of allusion could Siegfried and Fafner be granted places. The desynchronised rumble of multi-engined heavy aircraft thrummed in the still air of the room as what seemed to be a large assembly of them passed over—whether towards or away from some place in Germany Altmann could not make out; but he suspected towards; and he suspected, obviously enough, heavy bombers—Lancasters, Halifaxes: their Merlin engines had a distinctive accent, their power delivered on a more refined note than that of the Jumo diesel—which was in any case lately employed in numbers over far-distant territories at the opposite station of the compass. The *Luftwaffe*'s massed raids on England were history.

The rumbling and vibration eased decibel by decibel, and Margarete startled Altmann out of a semi-reverie with the observation that Helene neglected her dolls. "Look, Father—she likes her doll to be real." She giggled, and gently chided, "She's getting bigger already, silly—you won't be able to play mother with her much longer—will she, Father?"

And looking at his daughters, one in another's arms snuffling in half-waking awareness, Altmann found himself for an unavoidable instant back on the bridge of *Nothung*, peering over the bulwark at the pale blob swirling astern in the wash, a glimpse lost in the night that might have been of a doll, or a child. Whatever it was, it hadn't been a trick of light, or imagination. Rogge's reporting it dismissed that idea. And whether child or doll, it signified a child, somewhere, at some point, among the people in the boats.

That night he woke from phantasm to Ursula's shaking him, alarm in her words, asking what he had been shouting at, to stop, it was all right—"You're with me—!"

He was drenched in sweat, which was strange because the nightmare's invariable location was cold, as cold as the North Atlantic could be, penetrating like a fungus to the very marrow, reaching for the seat of life itself, as it would have done among the boats' occupants, sooner or later, assisting death in its agonising work over hours on end, perhaps days. And he in his boat unable to prevent it, unable to offer refuge, salvation, succour—apart from water and a few tins of milk; but also mercy, of a kind: mercy as no God would have attempted. Only man in his imperfection, his flawed conceptions of right and wrong, his warped priorities, his incapacity for moral constancy, his tendency to self-justification, could offer mercy of that kind: a terrible mercy that would bestow on its dispenser as irreversible a mark as that on its recipients.

The question remained—obvious, accusing, indelible. And his motives had been misinterpreted—by Rogge, by Schreiber, by Benedict, by others: Falke, for example. Even Dönitz. After all, they had been Jews, most of the people in the boats. They had refused God, refuted His claim as the Messiah, the Saviour. Somewhere in all this lay an element of justice; grim, stern, ineluctable—

"You were shouting—"

"Shouting? What about?"

"A doll."

"A doll—?"

"Yes—and calling—asking—about children. In a boat. Something like that." She put her arms round him and held him tight, her voice low, adding, "And you were weeping."

"Weeping?"

"Yes . . . Something bad, isn't it?" She smoothed the damp hair away from his brow. "It's not the first time—you know that? Do you want to tell me?"

He lay silent in her arms, staring up into the darkness, watching the scene fade, the images melt, slip from his mind, feeling the sweat chill on his neck and chest, thankful that she could not see his face. He blinked, drew a breath, swallowed a thickness in his throat, and said no, there was nothing to tell; just stories he'd heard; things that happened to people, to his comrades-in-arms. It was just the war. It would pass. He turned his head and kissed her, and found that she, too, had been weeping.

And later, when he repeated his urgent words, that he must not lose her, the finger she laid on his cheek seared the skin, and he winced in his turn. "Nor I you, my darling," she murmured, and brushed his lips with hers, a momentary sensation, like the flutter of a bird's wing. "Yet you leave me for—for that other love of yours, so dangerous. I die each time you go—don't you see?—and each time you return, almost as if you were a ghost, nothing more real than my hope against all reason! Even now—" she moved against him and put her arms round him, gently, softly, as if testing the substance of his body "—I hardly dare believe in your survival of all that's happened."

205

He studied her face, noticed the fine lines that had appeared, so subtly, so casually and delicately, so tellingly, and said, "I could ask for your promise—even forbid you—and trust your word. But I won't. I can't. You must be what you are, my love. But to me as much as—more than—to your parents. D'you see? I can't say more, except that I love you past telling. It's what brings me back. Not the Fatherland; that's the thing that sends me out."

"Yes," she said. "I know . . . How soon?"

Five days later he was back at Bordeaux accompanying Benedict and Schreiber checking the base engineer's work in the boat, and supervising the other officers and men on the planned re-tautening of discipline. His recommendation of Eberle for promotion was acknowledged in stiffly formal terms but also notice of a decision's deferral to the end of the coming patrol. He was thankful for his not having mentioned his intention to the man. Meanwhile the tautening process included the route-marches into the French countryside he described as recreational walks; good, he believed, for the team spirit essential to the boat's harmonious operation. They possessed an additional *frisson* of tension in the necessity for armed escorts—helmeted, belted and ammunitioned *Matrosen* scouting ahead and bringing up the rear, toting machine-pistols to go with stern glances to right and left alert to the chance of ambush by the local *maquis*, who had taken to wayside skirmishes by way of supplementing sabotage of the u-boat base, the indiscriminate reprisals for which had stirred up high feelings. U-boat crews were under orders to remain in groups of at least four when on liberty in town, and to avoid certain popular haunts. Recreational walks were a calculated risk.

"It's what's called a sense of humour in the *U-Bootwaffe*." Schreiber winced as Lange swabbed the shredded blister on his heel with iodine. "*Ouch,* dammit!—Without it, we lose the war. With it, we lose it with a grin and a merry word—"

"No need for a merry word yet, then, *Einswo*," said Lange. "Not if our skipper and his boat have anything to do with it." He pressed a square of sticking-plaster over the discoloured lesion. "There you are—good for a few more kilometres."

Ten days after that they were at sea, heading for Finisterre and the Cape.

IX

MINUTES before casting off a van had skidded to a halt on the jetty as an armed *Matrose* leapt from the running-board. On the bridge, Altmann had watched curiously as escort and driver hauled a heavy box from the rear to stagger with it through the assembled onlookers to the boat, where the driver, a petty officer, announced a special delivery—comforts for the crew. Opened later, the box contained magazines, books and gramophone records; on a floridly-engraved gilt-edged card, compliments from *Reichsmeister* Arthur Ehrling.

Altmann viewed the gift with mixed feelings—gratitude for its fitting nature, irritation at the tightening of the unwanted bond it represented, unease at the increased strength of association with a figure for whom he entertained only an equivocal regard. He hesitated to give them form and dimension, but there were distinctive salients in Ehrling's administrative landscape that Altmann sensed would set the man apart from the ideals he had attributed to the Party that would lead Germany to the ultimate justification of victory. He recognised unnameable misgivings which, for the present, he would have to set aside: time enough in the coming weeks to examine and, perhaps, dismiss them as mere chimera. Ehrling and others like him were, after all, doing their best for the Fatherland. In the circumstances gifts of almost any kind would be welcome; at worst they helped to bolster morale by signifying in some part of the system's organisation an awareness of the boat and her men as more than a military unit, more than an automatic instrument of national aspiration. And, as Altmann had already demonstrated, books provided the material for inventive morale-stiffening going beyond their mere reading. It was just that the irony of their source was tinged with an indefinable bitterness, and it made Altmann wary of a future gathering about itself a hitherto unsuspected aura of menace quite distinct from the overt threats posed by the enemy. He would not have defined his vague misgivings as foreboding, but they fell not far short of it.

The crowd on the jetty had been a smaller and less effusive gathering than its equivalent of twelve months earlier: a handful of base officers, yard officials, and casual loiterers from among the general daily work-force, together with the mooring party, careless of the symbolism of its function.

It was remarked on by Schreiber, standing beside Altmann surveying the proceedings. As the last wire had splashed into the water and Altmann ordered slow astern, he murmured, "Funny, isn't it—" nodding at the opening gap between ballast-tank and jetty wall "—only a metre or so but it's as good as five thousand miles. We might as well be off Cape Agulhas already, apart from being able to make ourselves heard still. Not that anyone's listening." He eyed the figures dispersing in twos and threes to leave the flotilla commandant and his aide, standing together watching in silence, hands clasped at their backs, leather-coated against the damp breeze whipping down from the overcast with its threat of rain. "*Kapitän* von Lohmeyer's his usual cheerful self—a picture of optimism to encourage us during the darker moments ahead . . . That 'Good luck, *Kapitän*' of his was more like the last rites." Schreiber glanced sideways at his commander, gauging the effect of his words; it was difficult to know whether or not you'd struck the right note with him lately. Too long at base with all the desk-jockeys calling the shots; too long at home, also, in a renewal that could have a demoralising effect; if they made it across the Bay the man would settle down. He switched his glance upwards to the cloud-base, half-cocking an ear, and smiled grimly to himself at his automatic responses. The gap widened. The patrol had begun.

Altmann had watched intently as the boat edged out into the river and the last of the flood. Without turning he said, "He's never been the same since those Italian boats were based here—unnerved him, especially that stunt towing the lifeboat to Casablanca. Six hundred miles, all on the surface!"

"Ah." Schreiber pursed his lips and nodded, relieved. He'd gauged the mood accurately enough. "Of course. Well—you can hardly blame him. Wouldn't be surprised if that Graziani fellow in the desert drove Rommel to a secret bottle . . . Still, they were a happy lot while they lasted. Chivalrous. Quite refreshing. Now they're back in the Med they'll probably offer Montgomery and Patton a lift after they've pulled Rommel out of the soup . . . Our flotilla chief takes life too seriously. Maybe a glass of chianti now and again instead of the cognac they reckon he soaks up by the stein—"

"Mm." Bent over the gyro repeater to check a bearing, Altmann had been irritated by the implications of Schreiber's words, flippant though they were; but at that moment, preoccupied with the handling of the boat, he'd felt no inclination to indulge an instinctive objection to criticism of the *Wermacht*; instead he muttered abstractedly, "Well, you can let it be known that we shan't be towing any boats anywhere over the next few months, *Einswo*. Our duty's to sink ships—and let their people see to their salvation themselves. We're not running an international rescue service."

No indeed, thought Schreiber, contemplating Altmann's back. Towing boatloads of survivors has never been your stock-in-trade, old chap: it's diamonds to the oak leaves and cutlery or bust this time, and hopefully those eels will all do their duty; I need a good report if I'm to see command before this shambles of a *Reich* comes apart at the seams, and good reports don't come from bad-tempered *Korvettenkapitänen* . . . Catching Altmann's mood, he had reflected on events—the army at a dead stop on the eastern front, first—at the outset—thrown back from Moscow, now badly mauled into surrender at Stalingrad and in the north making a balls-up of the Leningrad siege, obvious to the dimmest eyes through the tatty screen of Goebbels's fictional war-news; Rommel being squeezed out of North Africa by Allied advances from east and west; the French fleet—what was left of it—at Toulon scuttled by its crews when the *Wermacht* had gone into Vichy France, and even an attack on shipping here in the river at Bassens by a handful of madmen in canoes—mostly a failure, but little thanks to the *Wermacht* and the flotilla of destroyers dozing the war away at their buoys strung across the estuary entrance. And Uncle Karl himself, now in Berlin after abandoning ship at Lorient following the St Nazaire raid to set up again in Paris—and Raeder handing in his cards after the farcical performance of *Hipper* and *Lutzow* with a gaggle of destroyers against some convoy in the Norwegian Sea. They'd behaved like a lot of old maids. The surface fleet's performance to date had made it almost embarrassing to be seen in the uniform of the *Kriegsmarine*. The service's only redeeming feature seemed to be the *U-Bootwaffe*, holding its own, and quite well, all things considered, *and* notwithstanding the hysterical exaggerations of the propaganda department. Whatever the German public thought of it, Goebbels's claim that sixteen million tons of Allied shipping had gone to the bottom in 1942 had been too large a mouthful for the service to swallow, but even trimmed to digestible proportions it was still an impressive performance. But for how much longer could it be kept up?—already reports had indicated a decline in sinkings among the North Atlantic convoys in some of the war's most desperate battles, a decline not fully explained by appalling weather, said to be the worst for fifty years. Would the struggle continue long enough to give him a chance at promotion and a Knight's Cross? Maybe, but—first things first, like this patrol, and a skipper out to hit the jackpot. Schreiber sucked his teeth.

It was an unwelcome evocation of early days at the Dänholm training-camp: the Bay under moment-to-moment Allied air surveillance as the gauntlet all boats had to run at the beginning and end of each patrol had become, in the service's vernacular, the Valley of Death. It rode in on the wings of the RAF Liberators and Hudsons brought to the fray since the turn of the year, variously to accompany and replace the bumbling Sunderlands and aging Wellingtons, an air presence not only more numerous but also, now without any remaining doubt, equipped with radar operating on a frequency too short for German apparatus to detect. Modified to its limit, Metox had proved itself an instrument of false security, and there was talk of its imminent, well-overdue, retirement, to the relief of the u-boats' crews: as far as they were concerned its dangerous unwieldiness had long outweighed its usefulness, and others besides Altmann had anticipated its official disuse.

As a result the Bay crossing, extended to nerve-testing length if submerged, was more self-evidently a suicide-run on the surface. The boat's commander took his chances either way, and Altmann's most acute appreciation of the situation was of the numbers who had fallen victim to the enemy's new tactics over the last few weeks. He had decided to run surfaced by day and submerged by night: by day a sharp lookout—and lookouts had never been sharper, in their heightened sense of mortal danger—could warn of the hunter's approach in time to seek the comparative safety of depth; by night no sighting could be expected of a blacked-out aircraft before it was upon them. And even by day, with cloud cover the risk of sudden ambush precluded periods of more than tens of minutes on the surface. With the boat at full speed on its diesels the lookouts were robbed of the most vital indication of an aircraft's approach, the sound of its engines: the rumble of the diesel exhausts mingled with the crash and hiss of the breaking wash together with wind-noise set up an effective sound-curtain, and the unseen aircraft almost overhead before being heard. And there was no question of fighting it out, despite Dönitz's emphatic advice: featuring prominently on a lengthening record of casualties were stark examples of the boat's vulnerability to attack by heavily-gunned aircraft carrying conclusive loads of bombs or depth-charges. Notwithstanding the new 37mm flak-gun and the additional anti-aircraft armament—in this case a twin-barrel replacement for the 20mm gun—with which Dönitz had had boats fitted, for all practical purposes they were defenceless, as Altmann had long before concluded in respect of almost any well-armed attacker. He saw the u-boat's only virtues as a warship lying in its capacity for stealth and its ability to inflict a lethal—when it worked—waterborne blow upon a waterborne target. It was, in fact, a highly-specialised and therefore very limited weapon of war, in its present configuration rapidly becoming obsolete. Brooding on the point, he was aware of a sense of finality about this latest patrol—that if it did not turn out to be his rendezvous with destiny it would certainly signal some kind of ending, as of the viability of this type of boat—even of the u-boat itself—against an enemy whose means of defence, recently and most ominously including a number of purpose-built escort carriers to bolster the handful of converted merchantmen that had proved distressingly effective despite their limitations, were already outpacing the *U-Bootwaffe*'s methods and tactics. In some respects the convoy system had come to represent not a target but a lure, relieving its defences of the poorly-rewarded task of hunting. All the escorts and their support groups had to do was await the attacker's approach, given ample warning by their various detection devices, operated, as they now were, with formidable skill. Altmann could not ward off a pressing gloom as he mused on the point, and sought in vain to evade it by casting his thoughts back to his final moments at the base, wondering not when but whether he would return. And, going farther back, to the nightmare's vividness, undiminished by even Ursula's attempts at preventive solace, unknowing as she was of its genesis and form. Its spectral cast had begun to take on an appearance of renascence, as if imbued with a new hope, a trust in ultimate right; but the utter futility of their nebulous position, beyond revival, mocked them as it chilled the spirit of their involuntary medium.

Finisterre slipped astern a faint irregularity on the misty horizon beneath the overcast that had remained unbroken since departure. It contributed to the atmosphere of high tension in the boat, peaking on the two occasions of surfaced progress forced upon them by the need to charge the batteries. During the second a Hudson had dropped out of the cloud-base in a shallow dive that would probably have signalled disaster if the boat had not already started an alarm dive itself, warned through a ruse Altmann had stumbled upon in passing, while reflecting on the practicalities of the invention he had heard of among other u-boat commanders at the base—of an extendable breathing-tube that would enable the boat to run submerged on its diesels. The *Schnorchel*, it was called, rather unimaginatively but aptly. Trials were rumoured to be in progress already. It wasn't the complete answer but in theory it certainly seemed to offer some kind of respite, and a more practicable one than the boat apparently being developed using fuel containing its own oxygen. It would be able to run submerged at high speed for as long as the air in the boat, not drawn upon by the self-respirating motor, remained breathable. But, for the time being, all this was mere speculation, while the problem was growing more acute by the day, and Altmann had hit upon an improvement to the ploy of surfacing in short spurts. Unable to avoid the chance of emerging square in the sights of a passing air patrol, at least its unheard approach during the surfaced run could be guarded against by the simple expedient of throttling back the diesels at intervals to give the bridge watch the use of its ears. Forward progress in a longer surfaced run would barely be affected, battery-charging improved likewise, and Altmann had suggested to a sceptical Benedict that careful calculation would probably reveal a small economy in fuel-consumption—"A sort of free-wheeling effect," as he put it, encouragingly. "Like a bicycle."

"A bicycle."

"M-hm." Altmann nodded confirmation, avoiding Benedict's curious stare. "—provided it's not going uphill. Spins along under its own weight—inertia—for a greater or lesser distance before having to be pedalled again—"

"You're an experienced cyclist, then, *Kapitän.*"

"Well—" Altmann shrugged uncomfortably. "When I was a boy, you know."

"Ah . . . When you were a boy." Benedict pursed his lips, nodding soberly.

"Yes, dammit!" Altmann flushed and shrugged again. "Just a damned illustration for the slower-witted among us—"

"Of course!" Benedict rubbed the back of his neck. "Ingenious allegory, *Herr Kapitän!* A bicycle! I like it." He cocked his head and gazed reflectively at the overhead piping. "It even makes a good story-title—How I Fought the War on a Bicycle, or, My War Service in the *Fahrradwaffe.*"

"Go to hell, Herbert—"

Benedict smiled a small sad smile. "On the way, *Herr Kapitän*—glad of your company."

But the Hudson was no joke, black or otherwise, and both Altmann and Benedict knew that if the boat's diesels hadn't been freewheeling, as the engineer solemnly described it, the plane would have stood a good chance of complete surprise. As it was, two lookouts had called it in unison before sighting it and the dive was well-advanced when the aircraft, shedding a few rags of overcast, opened fire. The rattle of its guns accompanied by water-strikes all round the conning-tower formed Altmann's last impression of the attack before dropping with a few bucketfuls of Biscay into the control-room. When the first charges had detonated the depth-gauge indicated eighty metres, still going down, and it occurred to him that for all its potency as a hunter-killer the aircraft lacked a piece of equipment that in surface units represented Nemesis. He wondered how long it would be before the enemy devised some form of airborne asdic.

Watching his chief engineer at the controls, he was conscious of a sense of unvoiceable gratitude for his luck; even for the man's doggedly sardonic outlook. Even if most—all—of Benedict's world-weary manner were genuine, Altmann knew it did not reflect his attitude towards his duty, and his ability to carry it out with unwavering, even exceptional, efficiency. As he had been the key to his own and his fellows' survival thus far, his first engineer, Altmann felt, was the boat's most important human component, and human in more ways than one. His sceptical reception of all points of view, habitually alloyed with a deprecatory humour, nicely balanced Schreiber's less finely-tuned verbal sallies. Altmann would not have called the engineer popular among the boat's people, but saw that he commanded a willing respect, infinitely more valuable. Restricted to any one of his officers in a tight corner, he would have chosen Benedict for company; but as the thought occurred to him he hoped he would never have to make the choice—a constraint upon fate he knew to be his prerogative, insofar as his own competence was concerned.

The sense of premonition clouding his view of the forthcoming patrol stemmed more from anticipation of unabated descents into phantasm than of any likely attentions by the enemy. In some respects the mental demands of engagement with the steel and explosive of a tangible antagonist offered escape, but even this as an extreme solution possessed a distinct element of calamity, not in its possible outcome as much as in its prime purpose: to be rid of his abiding curse he would be prepared to enlist the active but wholly unsuspecting support of his compatriots; prepared not merely to throw them into hazard but to sacrifice them on the altar of his own redemption. As the prospect loomed dimly at the outer reaches of his cogitation he turned from it, appalled, but aware, with a sense of heightened anguish, that he was steering an unsteady course in the wake of Odysseus rather than in the triumphal footsteps of Siegfried: ahead lay the Cape with beyond it the Indian Ocean's opportunities, but somewhere, either along the way there or back, or while on station, lay the narrows policed by a Scylla and Charybdis whose forms and tactics combined both physical and spiritual threats. And what was worse, unlike Odysseus his making a safe passage between the two would carry him not to safety and happiness and a justification of all that had passed but back into the spectral company from which, it seemed, there could never be an escape. It occurred to him that perhaps he had overstepped some indefinable but definitive line marking a terrain from which no adventurer could retrace his steps and in which neither redemption nor salvation existed, but, regardless of penitence, only a blasted prospect of damnation. And quite clearly, whether on a bicycle or at the helm of the ship, he could not expect or demand Benedict's company: he could not seek or claim extenuation, far less exculpation, by association with innocents.

So they cleared the Bay, feathers ruffled by the air attack—a few bullet-strikes about the upper parts of the conning-tower—but otherwise unscathed, and turned southward to pass out of sight of the Portuguese coast for the rendezvous with the milch-cow stationed on the Cape Verdes. In his capacity as C-in-C of the navy in Raeder's place, Dönitz had retained direct control of the u-boat arm through his erstwhile aide, Godt; and having, as Altmann shrewdly suspected, little enough to do in respect of a functionally impotent surface fleet, object of the *Führer*'s vilification, had continued as the *U-Bootwaffe*'s executive commander. At his direction, boats were now operating off the Azores and in the offshore waters of north-west Africa, hitting convoys from South America and the Caribbean and the supply groups going into the North African ports in support of the Allied land-forces pushing east in the aftermath of the invasion. And in so doing they also straddled the convoy routes to and from the Cape and ports along the West African seaboard, focused upon the assembly-point off Freetown. Altmann's sealed orders instructed him to refrain from attacking anything until passing south of the latitude of Ascension Island, and would have been the cause of frustration as he watched ships in groups and singly cross the hair-line graticule of the periscope, oblivious of his presence. Instead, he took the opportunity to reflect on his continuing work, the definitive *Command & Leadership in the U-Boat Arm*, founded on a series of papers he had produced. The day after his return to the base from home he had received a request—an order in all but name—from Godt to deliver a lecture to a convention of *Kriegsmarine* officers at Weimar. A compendium of extracts from the manuscript, it had been well-received: several senior officers had congratulated him and inquired about the book's publication.

"You might think about retiring on the proceeds, *Herr Kapitän!*" a *Kapitän-zur-See* commanding a destroyer flotilla joked. "But only after the *U-Bootwaffe* has finished the job, eh! I gather you're shortly off on patrol—?"

It had been gratifying and encouraging, as had the signal of felicitations from Dönitz, and he had returned to Bordeaux with a sense of satisfaction marred by only one blemish, not in itself of any apparent magnitude but significant in its note of discord. During the informal buffet after his talk someone had mentioned a place called Buchenwald, not far from Weimar—a few kilometres up the road. A tour of a labour camp there had been mooted, and Altmann invited to join the party. Not interested in any case, but also duty-bound to return to the boat without delay, he had declined, and towards the end of the evening overheard mention of the camp's distinction: the internment of Jews and other non-Aryans for their protection and useful employment. And an assertion by someone who claimed previous experience that tours of such places by regular officers of the *Wermacht*—even of the *Kriegsmarine*—were rigorously forbidden. Such places—and there were numbers of them—were designated high-security zones. Sightseeing tours, the authoritative voice had continued with amusing regret, were reserved for those privileged to sojourn there at the *Reich*'s pleasure and expense.

On the return train journey he had tried to sleep, but managed no more than a fitful doze in the company of the schooner's laden boats, the bedraggled figure of Lebrun—Calibourdin—and the spectacle of his first watch officer vomiting over the bridge bulwark into the wind. It was strange, he reflected, that none of the replayed scenes included details of the view overside as the boat had passed through the wreckage of its own making before departing. He remembered scanning the debris picked out by the searchlight's beam, but nothing of exactly what he had seen. For some reason it had faded, to be replaced by a formalised mental impression he was able to contemplate with formalised emotions, in effect a detachment from what he knew to have been a prospect of indescribable pathos—as indescribable it had become within the limits of his powers of recollection. Perhaps, in some kind of morally-protective mechanism, his mind had set up a psychological block. It allowed him to know what had occurred, know the outcome, know its elements, but protected him from visually-explicit recollection. Yet it haunted him, and assured him of an ultimate reckoning regardless of the points of justification, as he saw them, upon which he could call. And it disturbed his sleep. That alone as an inescapable feature of the prospective patrol was a matter for dread: weariness, of both body and mind, was an occupational norm, and the practised u-boat man kept it to a bearable level with a capacity for instant transition either way between waking and sleep regardless of conditions. Two or three undisturbed hours at a stretch was as much as he could expect; a few minutes could be put to good effect. But not so in his particular case. The weariness would compound itself, the moments of release from unrelenting vigil, never longer than an hour at a time for the commander, contaminated by the recurring scene: although it had been possible to escape it for brief periods when on leave or ashore on other business, when surrounded by the evocative reality of the boat's fabric, assailed by the boat's odours, sounds and movement, its intense presence would be like a persistent beggar's; a beggar, moreover, not content with mere largesse but intent on his quarry's entire substance.

Returning with an effort to present concerns, Altmann mentally braced himself for a conflict he would have to resolve single-handed, conducted in an adjacent universe unsuspected by his companions and at continual risk of exposure, a mischance the nature of which he could neither anticipate nor take measures to guard against, only act to divert as it burst upon him, relying on nothing better than instinctive reflex. The practised deliberation of attack and defence in encounters with the enemy would be a welcome diversion, hoped for with greater fervency as such than as the means of military recognition it was convenient to allow everyone to think he sought as the ultimate, public confirmation of a professionally-distinguished wartime record. In some ways, he reflected, his success in that particular respect would add an element of mockery to the unremitting investment of his conscience by the seemingly growing company of phantoms. It gave him no comfort to reflect upon the fact that the supplementary elements—the indistinct forms coalescing from the outer darkness into numberless ranks bringing up the rear of the encircling force—were not of his direct making, but of rumour and hearsay in reference to the actions of unknown and unidentifiable individuals or organisations, the closest to which, in his experience, was the ambiguous figure of Ehrling. About whom, Altmann decided, the less he discovered the better. It seemed that National Socialism was at hazard from forces it had not, in its idealised form, either proposed or envisaged; its aims and principles appeared to have been subjected to manipulation amounting to a taint, and that this taint had brushed, momentarily, his own affairs was a prospect he viewed with increasing discomfort. He feared, above all, its effect on his ability to perform his duty to the Fatherland and his *Führer* with the willingness and conviction he felt to be the privilege and prerogative of a soldier of the thousand-year *Reich*. He would have to face the forthcoming action with a tighter grip on his moral resources, a more acute attention to the proper conduct of his command and its attendant responsibilities. Fatherland and *Führer* apart, he owed the men around him a duty of personal integrity on which they could rely no matter what the circumstances. They must never be given a hint of the weakness he knew had the power to destroy him in a way no hunting escort or aircraft could ever contrive.

As honorary editor, recovered from his wound with a slight lameness in his left arm, Palmgren resumed publication of the news-sheet, extending coverage to war news as approved by Altmann, and the boat's domestic activities. Altmann was wary of its effect on morale and although he allowed the inclusion of items selected from Allied broadcasts it was only after careful analysis, editing—the word "censoring" did not suit, he asserted—and a lecture to the boat's company on the form, use and effect of propaganda as employed by the enemy. He backed it up by issuing its salient parts in an illustrated (by Palmgren) leaflet. He also warned against the pernicious effect of rumour.

"It means, of course, that Rommel is setting up a trap for the British and Americans somewhere around Tunis," said Schreiber. "Montgomery and Patton go bowling into it with dreams of doing one another out of a pension, our Desert Fox cuts their supply-lines while they're not looking, and with the pair of them like rats in a bag he bundles the headless chickens of the remaining soldiery back to where they came from."

"You paint a rural picture, *Einswo* . . . And where's where they came from?" Benedict frowned at the oozing orange from which he was trying to cut the mouldy parts. "The fleshpots of Cairo and Casablanca, or farther back?"

"Oh—farther back." Schreiber winked at a mildly interested Hildegras. "Out of Africa altogether to clear the way for the onward march of the *Reich*, to the oilfields of Arabia—or Persia, whichever—and, beyond, the fabulous riches of Hind."

"Hind?" Benedict offered Hildegras a shapeless piece of his reduced orange and watched closely as the midshipman munched it and swallowed, nodding approval. Benedict gave him the rest and wiped his fingers on a wad of cotton waste.

"India—Hinduism's the main religion. Thus Hind. Native name for it. Known as the brightest jewel in the British crown."

"What it is," said Benedict wonderingly, "to have an education."

"Funny taste," said Hildegras, still munching. "Sort of prickly on the tongue . . . You know, I think this orange is alcoholic."

"A great advantage, I grant you." Schreiber nodded soberly. "Unfair, some would say. But—" he shrugged self-deprecatingly "—that's life. Some are favoured, others destined for the engine-room."

"A bad end," said Lange, looking up from a flaccid copy of *Le Figaro*. "If there's a sorry sight in the fruit world, it's an alcoholic orange. Mind you don't go the same way."

"So where exactly do you fit in?" returned Benedict. "Looks like you'll have to carve yourself a niche among the favoured, if they'll have you. Engine-room's booked up."

"Pissed on an orange, doc? You're joking."

"I'm working on it, Herbert—"

"What—in a u-boat?"

"If you're not careful." Lange turned a page and frowned at something it revealed. Absently, he added, "You'd be surprised, my boy—fermentation in these conditions is rapid. Of course there's also a risk of poisoning from the mould—"

Benedict's gaze narrowed, and he slowly shook his head. "What a disappointing man you are, *Einswo* . . ." As he spoke Palmgren appeared

218

with the day's edition of the news bulletin, so he added, "Ah—news from the front . . . Read it to us, *Einswo*. A niche for you."

Schreiber scanned it briefly before glancing round at his audience. He cleared his throat, looked at his watch, announced the time, and exaggerated a Berlin accent.

Today we cross the Tropic of Cancer, marked by a few brave members of our company stripping off to display an authentic night-club tan, but it's more a token of hope than reality, because it's not yet warm enough for our commander to shed his long-johns: we should be guided by his example!

Twitching an eyebrow, Benedict turned down his mouth at the corners, and nodded round at the others. Hildegras grinned back uncertainly. Schreiber frowned and continued.

Climate apart, all hands have put in a lot of hard work clearing up the mess left by the maintenance people, and our boat begins to feel more like home again with carpeting in the officers' and PO's quarters—"

"*Quarters*?" Hildegras affected puzzlement.

"A word," said Palmgren. "Sounds better than 'spaces'. Journalistic licence."

"Oh."

"Finished?" asked Schreiber, smiling menacingly at Hildegras, who coloured and mumbled an apology. "Good . . .

All our worldly goods are stowed away and the boat's homely atmosphere of hair-oil fumes, diesel fumes, eau de water-closet and mingled fart lightened by wafts of old socks and Colibri has been restored after a lengthy period of unaccustomed fresh air during the refit. And to complete the picture of domestic bliss Maschinistenmaat *Falke has made the opening moves in the first game of the patrol's chess championships, playing against the promising novice,* Matrose Gerhard. *A list of elimination rounds has been posted in the control-room—check your place on it! All must play; only terminal illness will be accepted as an excuse not t—"*

"—and even then only with my permission!"

They swung round to see Altmann leaning on an upper bunk looking down at the assembly, and Benedict shifted his seat to make room, but Altmann shook his head. Glancing round, he said, "Chess is good for the little grey cells. So is an occasional lecture, and I think we'll try setting up a brains' trust to deal with questions from anyone about anything—I have a few other ideas, and I want suggestions. But a word of caution—no gambling! You can pass it on—I'll throw the book at anyone playing anything for money stakes." He smiled with pointed exaggeration, and they all nodded. "According to *Obersteuermann* Eberle we'll rendezvous with the milch-cow in about thirty-six hours if nothing gets in our way. After that a clear run to the line and the Cape." His gaze settled on Schreiber's attentive countenance. "We've got a couple of interlopers among the hands, *Einswo*; you and—" turning to Benedict "—you, Herbert: ready to make another appearance in your unconvincing double act?"

"What worries me," said Benedict, looking worried, "is becoming type-cast in farce. My career needs to break out into more serious stuff—"

"Stay with me, *Chef*." Schreiber leaned across the table and patted Benedict's hand. "Soon now it'll be the West End for us, then Broadway—"

"It would be," grunted the engineer. "Maybe I'll settle for the u-boat follies."

Altmann wasn't sure which way to take Benedict's brand of heavy humour—if it was humour rather than a parody of it; at times he suspected a bitterness that was regrettable and saddening. It was also disturbing, and he wondered whether he was the only one concealing a parallel existence. Worse—whether it was one he shared, unknowingly, with the engineer. Benedict had, after all, been with him at the time. He was a perceptive man, experienced, tough, and a husband and father; and he was loyal—that precious above all on active service. It was easy to take men like Benedict for granted, if you were fool enough, for although they stretched loyalty to its limits the self-denial required was not necessarily equally robust: they could crack, and it would reflect not on their failings but on those of whoever had demanded too much of a human quality—demanded more of others than they could supply. It would not do. He would have to handle the engineer with greater care from now on, beginning by not allowing his merits to go unremarked, however necessarily discreetly. Benedict would interpret overt solicitousness as undue, even mocking, attention, and would naturally resent it. With a start Altmann realised that, granted peculiar circumstances, the problem he faced with Benedict was a form of the problem commanders faced with all engineers: to gain and keep their respect and goodwill. A tight-rope had to be walked, with every sense tuned to perfect pitch.

With an inward smile of recognition Altmann saw Benedict as a normal example of the engineering fraternity, but with certain distinguishing features. They made him more valuable than the average as they made him more prone to the effects of stupidity in those with whom he had dealings or who occupied positions of influence in the broader sphere of his existence. People like Ehrling, for example; and like the flotilla engineer at Bordeaux who had run a blue pencil through Benedict's list of special stores, insisting on the standard list for a North Atlantic patrol of eight weeks until Benedict had submitted an official request for transfer to a Panzer corps—which would have been gratefully endorsed from that quarter—that Altmann had forwarded to von Lohmeyer with his own refusal to sail unless with Benedict as his chief engineer. The upshot had been the flotilla engineer's abrupt replacement with an elderly, monkey-like officer whose habitual dress of oil-stained khaki boiler-suit over old imperial navy working rig was his *laissez-passer* to any boat's nethermost intestines on impulse. His beginnings in an orphanage in Bremerhaven followed by the boiler-rooms of the Kaiser's heavy fleet units had imbued in him seemingly supernatural powers when it came to the proper equipping of a boat for sea. He was neither polite nor patient, and he made his decisions promptly and with immovable finality, and, which was a delight to Benedict, always in the boat's favour. It had been only slightly dampening to learn that he did so because he regarded the u-boat as a weapon of desperation manned by pathological suicides whose last hours should be free of anxiety in respect of their duty to the Fatherland. He never acknowledged the National Socialist salute, and visiting Party officials tended to avoid him. He had gained his rank before the elections of 1933, and held it chiefly because of the Fatherland's predicament. He dealt with boats' commanding officers with cold formality as token of his conviction that they were all Nazis, and their engineer officers with professional shrewdness. Any not measuring up to his conception of (competent) heroic suicide were at risk of transfer, to another flotilla if they were lucky, out of the service if they were not—or, as one or two averred, were. *Kapitän-zur-See(I)* Werner Barkhorn was a tartar, but he got things done, even if his methods played some part in von Lohmeyer's rumoured susceptibility to the stein.

X

THE patrol's first sinking took place late on a fine afternoon almost within sight of Ascension. To judge by the smoke she was making she was a coal-burner—of, as Altmann estimated, about six thousand gross tons. His recognition information suggested a general-cargo liner type, possibly part- or fully-refrigerated, of nineteen-twenties vintage but nothing more specific. Without an escort, making some eleven knots, she was following what seemed a patternless zig-zag, by which, as Schreiber dryly remarked, she was lengthening her voyage by at least three times its direct distance to wherever it was: in a general northerly direction, probably Freetown and a convoy to England.

Fired at periscope depth, the first two torpedoes missed. Annoyed and a little worried, Altmann announced his intention of following the target and closing the range, and dusk had drawn in by the time it was down to some five hundred metres.

"Any closer and we'll be able to jam a boathook in her prop," said Benedict, adding without enthusiasm, "This will be thrilling."

With a foot on the ladder to the conning-tower, Altmann said, "If I miss this time, Herbert, it's behind the bridge-ladder up here."

He used tubes three and four. The strikes, almost together, shook the boat, rattling fixtures and fittings, breaking crockery in the galley and blowing a couple of lights; and the port motor tripped out. At the plot Eberle dropped the dividers he was toying with and Schreiber betrayed momentary alarm in the glance he threw at the bridge hatch.

Seen in the periscope, the target burned furiously forward and aft, throwing the gathering twilight into deep contrast. Amidships, however, the bridge superstructure and accommodation was untouched, and the ship lay stopped but upright, only seeming to have settled lower in the water. A boat crowded with men pulled away from her, silhouetted against the flames.

"Up, Herbert!" With sudden decision Altmann abandoned the periscope to call down to the control-room. "Guns' crews stand by—flak and one-oh-five! Two lookouts!" To Schwebke he cast a departing "Jam anything he transmits, *Funkmaat!*" before mounting the bridge ladder.

As the last dregs of aquamarine drained out of the western sky the boat surfaced a third of a mile from the burning ship. It joined two of her boats, their occupants exclaiming and pointing at the black hull rising Leviathan-like out of the depths, shedding foam like blood in reflection of the flames. Schreiber followed Altmann with the others, who dispersed wordlessly to their stations to report readiness. After a few moments' study of the scene through his glasses: "A few men—in the water near the ship, *Kapitän.*" He indicated the nearest boat, some seventy-five metres away, oars motionless. "Shall I order them to go back for them?" He sounded as doubtful as he felt—the heat was intense, even at this distance. It must be close to incineration-point where the swimmers were struggling and waving, impossibly, at the fringe of the conflagration. Oil, but not cargo: not a coal-burner after all—perhaps a conversion, judging by the tall funnel. Watching the frantic splashing Schreiber grew aware of a consuming sense of helplessness.

Shortly before their departure Dönitz had issued a supplementary order emphasising his earlier instructions about survivors of attacks on shipping. Only key crew-members were to be picked up, and then only for questioning before being returned to their companions, unless any happened to be of particular importance, such as a senior naval or military officer. Commanders were to be in no doubt about their duty to avoid burdening themselves with prisoners, even wounded. Nor were they to approach ships' boats for the purpose of providing food or water or other forms of assistance, increasing the risk of their being identified and reported to enemy intelligence. Barring the exceptions mentioned, survivors were to be left to their fate. A rider advised some form of easily-portable temporary covering for use when approaching survivors, to be mounted or hung over any identifying mark on the conning-tower—which, commanders were reminded, was in any case tolerated only because of the alleged beneficial effect on morale. As before, however, no registration-mark of any kind was to be displayed at any time.

With these points in mind, acknowledging Palmgren's signal of readiness from the deck gun, Altmann turned to Schreiber and shook his head. No, he said; Schreiber would be sending them to their deaths; nor was he prepared to risk the chance of damaging the u-boat, possibly in an explosion.

"—They're dead men!"

As Schreiber nodded acquiescence the voice-tube buzzer sounded and Hildegras at the plot reported the jamming of a distress transmission; but the u-boat attack identifier *SSS*, the ship's name and the latitude had evaded Schwebke's key. The longitude could be fairly guessed, which meant enemy investigation at any time—especially, as Altmann had mentioned to the assembled officers, since the island was serving as a refuelling base for American aircraft, if not with much frequency. The chances were that some sort of air reconnaissance would respond to the ship's last call even if the glow of its pyre had escaped watchful eyes. Time was short.

Which demanded action without delay, and Schreiber caught his breath as Altmann stepped past him to give an order to the crew of the 20mm gun: open fire on the men in the water. Stunned, Schreiber watched as the layer—*Matrose* Knecht of Catalina fame, habitually phlegmatic, unmoved by the play of human proclivity about him beyond occasional expressions of facile or scornful amusement—acknowledged the order and calmly cocked the firing mechanism, nodding to his loader, Bartels, before squinting through the sight ring. He was an essential example of the German fighting man; unquestioning execution of orders regardless of conditions was evidence of his intrinsic reliability, stiffened by an apparent indifference to violent spectacle. As he seemed to place full confidence in the judgment of his superiors, so they quickly came to place a similar confidence in his qualities, and Altmann had noted him for promotion, but only to a certain level. Knecht and his kind provided the *Wermacht* with its crucial and justly-respected corps of non-commissioned officers, and they knew it, and entertained no higher ambitions: for them responsibility had only limited attraction. As now: Knecht felt no sense of personal accountability for what his orders required him to do, nor did he feel he should. The order was sufficient in itself, covering all aspects of moral decision on his behalf. Blank-faced, he pulled the firing-lever.

Schreiber flinched at the clamour, raising a hand to shield his eyes from the muzzle-flash. Recovering, he trained his glasses on the target area. It was a boiling cauldron of red and orange and black, and in its exploding midst he saw unnameable momentary fragments, and choked on the sour bile suddenly at the back of his throat. The hammering seemed to go on for an age before abrupt cessation, followed by diminishing echoes fleeing into the night. And through the ringing in his ears he heard another sound, thin and reedy, almost a screech—in the nearby boat a man on his feet, gesticulating, as the rest looked on, their faces catching the light from the flames; souls on the fringes of hell. He could not make out the words, only sense their expression of despairing rage, helpless bewilderment; and fear. And he found that he was crying, chill tears running into his beard, his throat contracted, his breathing broken into gasps as, appalled at his own weakness, he struggled to conceal his naked vulnerability so shamefully taken unawares. But the sadness was overwhelming, and he felt it as a great weight, an accumulation of sadnesses wrought by the years of conflict, but, as he had thought, against which his training and his natural moral resilience had armed him. Now the armour had fallen away, unlocked by some undefinable key turned by this particular combination of circumstances—not in their form, no more remarkable than any other similar evidence of war, but by their timing, their arrival at some culminating point of stress that might otherwise have been passed without consequence. But it had not been, and at a tight grip on his shoulder Schreiber looked up into a hard scrutiny with a sense of despair. Altmann's face was expressionless, and after a short silence he murmured, "It was necessary, *Einswo*. Better that way than the other", and Schreiber could not be sure that his tone had not been edged with contempt.

The tumult of emotion subsiding as abruptly as it had risen, Schreiber registered the words in a flood of realisation: stunned again, his fear of Altmann's scorn was displaced by anger. God in heaven, he thought: this man's beyond belief! How can he stand there, so unmoved by what he's done, so rational, so sure of himself—so goddamned self-righteous! But then, this was not the first such instance in his personal interpretation of warfare, and there was no reason to suppose it would be the last. Schreiber was aware of an element of ruthlessness in Altmann that sat oddly with his generally avuncular demeanour towards his officers and men—avuncular not in the jovial sense but in his sometimes overstated solicitude towards his charges, as he saw them. More among the ratings and petty officers than among the officers it was accepted at face value, but the few who regarded it with scepticism took care to express their view on a cautious note: there could be no mistaking their commander's iron determination to fulfil what he saw as his obligations to the *Reich*, and in particular to certain of its leading figures. His admiration—emulation, in some ways—of Uncle Karl as the living ideal of the u-boat officer was never a matter for speculation, and in turn it assured him of his subordinates' outward respect, whatever their private reservations. Reflecting vaguely in this vein, Schreiber nodded and heaved a deep breath and lifted his chin, holding Altmann's gaze as the tears cleared, and now feeling strangely elated, as if cleansed of some clogging malaise. Clearing his throat, he said harshly, "Yes, *Herr Kapitän* . . . I see that. There was—"

"Let's not discuss it, eh?" Altmann turned away to light a cigarette and Schreiber looked on as he ordered Palmgren to open fire on the burning hulk. The first shell struck the navigating bridge—and presumably the radio room—squarely, and debris and flame blossomed upwards and outwards. The second round blew the wheelhouse to splinters. Altmann stood motionless, staring across the water at the scene, arms spread, hands gripping the bulwark-capping, occasional wreaths of cigarette-smoke drifting off on the light breeze. Schreiber watched him, and wondered.

Ordering Palmgren to transfer his aim to the waterline, Altmann watched as the shells threw up gouts of red-flecked water alongside and the wreck first leant into a mild list, then began to go down by the stern, rolling farther onto her side as she did so. Clouds of steam joined the smoke to obscure her last, roaring gesture of defeat, the black mass of her fore-section rising to the vertical before the final plunge. Then she was gone, leaving a spreading lake of erupting water, wreckage and burning oil, the smoke dispersing on the breeze. As the disturbance subsided Altmann manoeuvred the u-boat alongside the nearer of the two boats and stood for a moment gazing down at the upturned faces before throwing away his cigarette. In English he cried, "Is your captain with you?" Irrationally, he wondered if he had used the same words that night, to the man in the boat's sternsheets who might have been the man he'd wanted. Calibourdin. The name stuck in the mind like a burr to a sock.

A figure at the tiller, distinguished by his dress as an officer, replied, saying the captain was dead. *Il est mort—you 'ave killed 'im!* Altmann blinked, stared hard at the officer. "Stayed aboard with Sparks. I'm the mate—chief officer." He was also evidently an Englishman; his words rang clear-accented across the gap. Standing beside Altmann, Schreiber said, unnecessarily, "English. Well-spoken. In such an old barge!"

Ignoring him, Altmann called back, "What ship—where from and to?"

The officer seemed to hesitate, listened as one of his companions leant across to say something, and looked up as Altmann added an impatient demand for an answer. *"Empire Formby.* Buenos Aires to Freetown!"

The name tallied with that picked up by Schwebke. "Thank you . . . What cargo?"

"Chilled beef."

"Pity," murmured Schreiber. "Smut could have done something with that. A change from mouldy sausage and old pork . . ."

But Altmann was not listening. Wrestling with mingled emotions he felt torn between strict adherence to duty and something less woodenly indifferent. He was also struggling with the pressing sense of *deja-vu*, and he cursed it angrily as the deciding factor; bitterly, he ceded the moment to sentimentality, and to something he could not define but felt acutely. He bit his lip as he hesitated, scanning the huddle of men, seeing but not seeing, momentarily unable to make the next move. *Damn!* Damn these people and their calm in the face of chaos, in the face of possible death; damn their ordinariness, their phlegmatic handling of crisis, their unshakable self-confidence, even when it was clear that they'd lost all but their pitiful self-belief. For all these men knew he could be contemplating their annihilation as he had annihilated the men in the water: there was nothing to stop him. Nothing, out here in the deserted expanse of sea and sky. Yet they sat there, hunched against the breeze, returning his scrutiny, apparently unmoved, resigned to whatever fate might now befall them because there was nothing else they could do. Powerless, they were yet as unruffled—bar the individual who had hurled his shrill fury at them for a moment—as though waiting for a train to town. These damned British! They would not see the truth until it was pushed into their faces, until they had died in their millions and taken their chosen enemies with them in equal numbers, as irrationally stubborn as so many mules. He could feel it, emanating from the little crowd in the boat like a kind of glow, and he found himself comparing it with the hopelessness he had sensed in those other boats, tossing in the rising storm, caught in the searchlight's beam. And *damn* again! Was this to be the consequence of every action he engaged in for the rest of the war? Altmann lit another cigarette, and made his decision. Sentimentality would prevail; it was a capitulation, but only in the context of a battle; the war would continue; there would be further such incidents, further opportunities for decision. He drew in a lungful of smoke, exhaled with force, leaned over the bulwark and called out, "I will leave you now . . . They will send an aircraft—a ship—from the island. You will be all right—a few hours only. I am sorry I had to sink your—"

A man lurched to his feet in the fore part of the boat. Heavily-built, rolled-up shirt-sleeves, barrel-chested, thick-accented words of fog-horn *timbre* as they broke in on Altmann's apology. Startled, Altmann stared at him, trying to adjust to the accent, intimidated by the vehemence; the venom.

"You fuckin' Nazi bastard! What the fuck's your fuckin' name, wacker? Come on—what is it—von bastard Wanker? And that fuckin' tin can of yours—I'll remember it! No fuckin' numbers, but it's marked—date, time an' fuckin' place! When—"

He broke off, angrily pushed away the restraining hand of a man on the thwart beside him, spat out some expletive, and resumed. "When this fuckin' war's over I'll be after you, la'! An' I'll fuckin' tell y'why! Y—"

His tirade was cut off again by the mate's interjection, an exhortation to shut up and sit down, which he ignored, continuing in an infuriated tone that made him ludicrous in the circumstances. Yet Altmann felt rebuked, and annoyed, more at himself than at the seaman, presently asserted by Schreiber to be a native of Liverpool. The accent was distinctive, he said, even to a German ear; the English equivalent of Cologne's near-unintelligible garglings.

"I'll tell y'why . . . Yer fuckin' airborne pals killed me mam and me missus, wacker! Dropped their fuckin' bombs on Dock Street—bastards! What did two fuckin' women ever do to you and yer shithead pals, hey? An' another thing—think about it while yer waitin' for me after the war! Yer just killed me fuckin' kid brother—over there in the ship, yer fuckin' murderin' Nazi fuckin' scum! Seventeen, 'e was, poor little fucker—dead now. If you 'adn't killed me mam already this would've done the job . . ." Impatiently, he wiped spittle from his chin, spat into the water between the u-boat and his cockleshell. "Do me a fuckin' favour—don't get y'self killed before the war ends. I'll be after yer, an' that's a promise . . . O'Halloran's the name—Danny O'Halloran. Remember it, y'jumped-up—"

"Can it, bose!" The mate's words were incisive, brooked no argument. "You've made your point."

"Yeah—shut it, Dan, yer daft bleed'n Scouser! Get us all shot!"

"The fuckin' bastard 'asn't told me 'is fuckin name, yet, Tanner! Gimme a leg up an' I'll fuckin' screw it out—"

"Bloody Fritz, yer nutter! Wot's wrong wi' yer—tired o' life or wot? Siddown, f'Chrissake'n save yer breath—we got some rowin' t'do!"

Others joined in, and the man resumed his seat, breathing heavily, but his eyes remained on the figure in the white cap on the u-boat's bridge, as if memorising the face it was too dark to see in detail. His threat was preposterous, thought Altmann; there was no possibility of its ever being carried out, even if he and its utterer survived the war, which was at least in the balance: the irony of the situation struck him, and he half-smiled to himself, but the smile was a grimace. Among the most dangerous occupations of modern warfare were those followed by himself and this O'Halloran fellow. The odds were against either's survival. Proportionately, u-boat losses and losses of merchant tonnage were roughly comparable; they had become locked in a kind of mutual death-grip that, continued for long enough, would see one or the other finally destroyed but its opponent barely extant. Or at least, that had been the trend until recently. Now, the picture seemed to be taking on a less nicely-balanced aspect, and forces had entered the arena that could be seen as potentially, and unfavourably, decisive. O'Halloran's threat might be empty, Altmann reflected, but it was somehow portentous, symbolic, a token of intent that wasn't confined to the vainglorious ranting of a man in a ship's boat.

And it was something else, too. Altmann felt a chill as O'Halloran's words echoed in his mind's ear: *Yer fuckin' airborne pals—killed me mam and me missus!* Missus? His wife, presumably; if so, a strange way of referring to her; but still . . . *dropped their bombs on Dock Street*—presumably not intentionally, but wherever it was it must have been close to the obvious target. So how far afield *did* the strays go? As far as the RAF's at Bordeaux and Lorient and La Rochelle? Around Hamburg, Dresden and the rest—around Frankfurt? Rauenthal had seemed far enough away from the city, from significant targets, to be as safe as anywhere in Germany from bombing errors, as they surely were; and wholesale destruction of civilian populations by intent was surely not in the minds of any strategist, even in this mechanised, universal form of war—was it? What about the blitzing of London? Confined to the docks as Goebbels's bulletins had stated, it was an open secret that the target area had been more widespread, indiscriminate, by tacit dispensation if not explicit decree. But either way—whether by accident or design—the dead were just as dead, just as many, just as innocent. And as his mind wandered into the shadows of the unthinkable it tripped over the exposed roots of the poisonous growths unseen in the darkness, but sensed; and it recoiled, afraid even to utter the fateful names for fear of bringing about their quietus, or worse. The very word *maimed* struck terror where *death* offered an end, peace, a not-suffering. Hence, thought Altmann, aware of an intimation of desperation, the men in the water, the use of the 20mm gun. They—the kid brother and his companions, in the water or aboard the burning ship—hadn't suffered any longer than he could help. He could not have helped the mother and wife; prevented the anguish of the man in the boat. Danny O'Halloran—another name he wouldn't forget? Even in the remembrance of the ship's name, among so many others. *Empire Formby . . . Anne-Marie de Bretagne . . .* Altmann caught his breath, drew tersely on his cigarette, glanced absently at it in reaction to its sere taste. *Damn* that ship! And his damnable susceptibility to reflection, recollection, and—what? Conscience? No, not that; his conscience was clear, as he'd satisfied himself long ago: orders were orders, and he was paid—had been commissioned as an officer, a servant of the *Reich*—to carry them out. Which, in war, meant steeling oneself to furthering the cause, setting one's own reservations, principles, interests, aside in subordination to the decisions of superiors, in whose hands the collective conscience lay. Irritated with himself, Altmann wrenched the trend of his thoughts away from the course they were apt to follow in unguarded moments, denying it to them by the conclusive expedient of defining it as the path to sentimentality. And it was easier to dismiss sentimentality than something less disingenuous; it could be exposed, dismantled, dispersed, leaving the scene clear of its entrapments and extrusions, a prospect of the real that demanded the utmost of the virtues, would test them, in certain conditions to breaking-point: fidelity, courage, moral integrity, loyalty, steadfastness; the qualities demanded of her servitors by a Germany destined to overcome the squalid, the ignoble, the effete among nations whose fraudulent claim to victory in war had exemplified the venality to which they were all in thrall, a venality which had already led them, and a prostrate Germany, to the brink of financial and social ruin—to the brink and, in some individual instances, beyond. It could not be allowed to happen again, as would be the case if truth were sidestepped in favour of sentimentality. There must be no compromise in dealing with the enemy: as Uncle Karl had made clear, it was necessary to be hard if the chosen—or unavoidable—method was war; a method in which, paradoxically in respect of one of its chief instigators, sentimentality could be allowed no part.

Nevertheless, Altmann felt shaken at the passion directed at him and, by implication, the *Reich*. For an instant it had reduced the war to a pinpoint of personal vituperation grotesque in its assumption of significance. The entire conflict between nations, stretching now across

230

the world, involving millions in a fatal confrontation the outcome of which would surely see the course of history altered beyond anyone's—even, perhaps, the *Führer's*—most extreme imaginings, had for a brief interval been reduced to an encounter between two men—one possessed of the power of life and death at a word of command, the other bereft of any practicable means of defence, let alone aggression, yet, in a way, undefeated, even holding final victory in prospect. It was ridiculous, thought Altmann. They were pawns, less than pawns, in a great game that neither of them had the power to change or affect. Their only function was to play their respective parts as events swept them towards the unforeseeable outcome in a tide of fatal moves and counter-moves governed by forces now impossible to contain or restrain. But a man in a boat had taken it upon himself to negotiate the entire hellish system in fulfilment of a threat that would finally end the greater battle, in some obscure, minutely insignificant but, for him and the one he had threatened, apocalyptic collision.

Throwing away his half-smoked cigarette Altmann gave the order to get under way, and halted, another chill running down his spine. A man's form stood black against the luminous sky, against the powdering of stars, catching the dying flicker of the oil-fires left by the sinking. Lebrun—Calibourdin—silently regarding him, his face palely featureless above the beard, the soaked clothing dripping, hair plastered in a dark skull-cap on the erect head, eyes glittering in the hollows of their sockets; blood-marbled water draining away through the perforated deck-plating—

Altmann caught his breath and blinked, frozen in mid-step, reaching out to grab the bulwark again. The flames leapt, flared, died back, and the shadow-play on the periscope standard dissolved. Letting his breath go with a gasp, Altmann shook his head. *Damn! God damn his susceptibility to this recurring illusion. God—*

"*Herr Kapitän*? You all right?"

Schreiber, watching him. He nodded, muttered affirmation, and crossed to the control-room voice-pipe. With a glance round at the encroaching darkness he ordered both engines full ahead and heard Benedict relay the order. And to the plot: "What's she steering, Eberle?"

"One nine four, *Kapitän.*"

"Make it one nine five."

"One nine five, aye."

One degree! A triviality, but he was grateful for its intimation of normality; the luxury of fine detail in a setting of crude disarray. And it satisfied his sense of order. Five was a convenient mid-point, four a nondescript. He felt the strengthening breeze of the boat's forward way cool on his face and neck, and breathed deeply. After an interval he turned to Schreiber. "Normal surfaced sea watches, *Einswo*. Stand down action stations . . . Let's get out of here."

Schreiber saluted, and turned to the voice-pipe. Altmann lit another cigarette, leant back against the periscope standard, and shut his eyes. Danny O'Halloran, ship's bosun. From Liverpool. What a difficult accent to follow. Perhaps Englishmen from other parts also had trouble with it, made worse with all that lurid language. Sailor's language, with Liverpool added, perhaps. Did they all speak like that—? Sad about the brother, but war is a sad business: necessary, but sad: just look at it. God help the Danny O'Hallorans; they didn't know their own insignificance—as against, for instance, another six thousand tons on his war total.

Further developments were marked by the boat's passing out of the South Atlantic far to the south of Cape Agulhas to enter the approaches of the Moçambique Channel, keeping well beyond sight of the South African coast. Wryly, Altmann acknowledged a feeling of familiarity, sensing almost a mood of welcome in the distinctive deep blue of the current bringing the tropical Indian Ocean to its perpetual rendezvous with the turbulent southern sea, but he was conscious of the deception, and regarded with resentment the sea-birds that gathered above the boat's wake whenever he surfaced in daylight, following in squadrons at varying altitudes, a sure long-distance indicator of the boat's presence. Accordingly, he'd had the flak guns constantly manned while on the surface; and he'd catechised the lookouts, briefly: he didn't need to detail the fatal consequences of taking an approaching aircraft for a planing gull. Report a bird rather than fail to report a Catalina, he told them.

The seas of these latitudes teemed with fish, and the birds took advantage, diving for the occasional stunned body flashing silver in the wake, undeterred by rifle-shots from the bridge that never found their mark. Altmann refused to allow the use of a machine-gun, disappointing a vengeful Falke. The petty officer had taken a direct hit while making the most of his bridge airing with a cigarette, proof against the cool breeze in a three-quarter-length leather coat won in a game back at the base. "The damned shitbags could show the Tommies a thing or two about bomb-aiming," he grumbled. "Look at that—from no closer than twenty metres!"

"Maybe it wasn't aiming at you at all."

"What are you, Schmidt—a closet shit-bag protectionist? Of course it was aiming at me—I saw it line me up in its sights, but too late." He spat on the mark left by the excrement and rubbed ineffectually at it with a rag.

"Well, look at it this way, Klaus—your coat would have been a write-off if it had been a Hudson. Like in the Bay."

"Yes—and if it had been the skipper would've had us all blasting away at it. I'll be watching for it on the way home—the bird, I mean. With the left-over machine-gun ammo."

"If there'll be any, what with the skipper's way of helping survivors . . . There's talk of some kind of massacre a couple of years back—"

Falke glanced sharply at his compeer. "There's talk about all sorts of things when a man's shaping up to be a hero of the *Reich*. This one's the ace of aces, poor bastard; just the thing for the fishwives to hone their chatter on . . . War's one-tenth slaughter and nine-tenths bullshit, and it gets all mixed up. You'll get confused if you listen to the chatter, Schmidt. Work on your game instead. Talking of which—" he glanced at his watch "—time for a quick hand, eh? Loose change."

"None of mine's loose since the last time, pal . . ." *Elektromaschinist* Schmidt took a leather pouch from his locker and examined its contents. "Ah, what the hell! I wasn't born to be rich."

"That's the way, *Putsi*—live for the moment. You never know—it might be your last!"

"Who's paying you, *Maschinist*—the Tommies? Just deal the damn cards!"

On the bridge, Schreiber watched as Hildegras took pot-shots at the birds—the gannets, terns, fulmars and sparrow-like petrels that seemed to revel in the blustery conditions. The larger ones presented deceptive targets as they planed the wind-waves, sheering with unruffled ease from a bullet's occasional close pass.

"Try to miss them, Seagrass," advised Schreiber. "You might have more luck. Close both eyes."

As the midshipman threw the officer a withering look a newcomer soared across the wake and zoomed into a climbing turn to overhaul the boat at a speed that took it past and ahead in seconds, where it rounded-to and made another approach, into wind, its enormous span of wing motionless throughout. Everyone's attention was on it as it approached, a yellow eye coldly inspecting the curious-looking sea-swept ship and the group of men on her bridge. Hildegras swung his rifle to follow the huge bird, abruptly halted by a hand clamped firmly on the barrel and Schreiber's quiet "Not that one, Seagrass. Let it go. In fact—" the rifle was gently prised from the midshipman's surprised grasp "—you shouldn't be trying to kill these creatures at all. It's bad luck, and not just for them."

Meekly, sensing something in the first officer's change of manner that might be explained at a more fitting time, Hildegras relinquished the weapon and in obedience to Schreiber's order descended to the control-room and the company of *Obersteuermann* Eberle with an official request of the navigator to take him through the last twelve hours' dead reckoning calculations. On the bridge, having watched the little drama in silence, Altmann queried Schreiber's intervention "—not that I'm criticising, *Einswo*—just curious." Which was true, but his curiosity was connected with an earlier manifestation of unsuspected sensitivity to events. The incident of the men in the water and Schreiber's emotional lapse had remained at the back of his mind, filed for possible future reference but otherwise unexamined. Now, in this apparently trivial diversion, he saw an opportunity for disinterested inquiry. At least, he told himself, disinterested in its particulars; otherwise, as he reluctantly conceded, it looked more as if he were seeking a possible indication of a trait in a contemporary that would assure him of the legitimacy of his own response to events. Not exactly an alliance under duress, as it might be seen, but a private reassurance, a means of accepting his own sentiments, his own spiritual unease, as normal, controllable, natural, and not the debilitating cancer he sometimes felt it to be: a weakness wholly unacceptable in the context of a war that would decide the nature of mankind's destiny. Feelings could not be prevented, but they might be controlled, set in perspective, understood.

Schreiber was smiling artlessly. "Superstition, *Kapitän*. You know—sea-birds; especially those—albatross. Nonsense, of course, but if anything happens . . ." He nodded significantly. "It might cause trouble. Seagrass'd be an easy scapegoat for some of the men. It would affect discipline—" He shrugged. "The big bird's an easier target than the rest. He might have hit it."

His curiosity increasing, Altmann eyed the first officer. "I didn't take you for a superstitious old shellback, *Einswo*—where've you picked up all this—this *sea lore*?" Like most of the boat's company he was himself unversed in such things: experienced u-boat man as he was, he realised his outlook was narrow, with barely a glimpse of the sea's wider prospect, and at times he had been made aware of his shortcomings, not least in his ability to carry out attacks on defenceless merchantmen in a state of mental detachment that—as he suspected—impressed onlookers as ruthlessness. Which, perhaps, it was, and a characteristic to be valued in military applications, as Uncle Karl was always taking pains to emphasise. Perhaps that was what defined it—a lack of perception stemming from a certain ignorance: what some would have called a lack of sympathy. Which brought him back to the perennial question of sentimentality and yet another of its several masques.

For a moment Schreiber was silent, lips compressed, apparently reflecting. He was not given to much serious discourse except in matters directly concerning his duties, inclined to deflect talk that tended in that direction with flippant or facetious responses. But in this instance something not normally figuring in his outfit of social exchange came into play, and after taking a breath, with a glance at Altmann before turning to gaze out over the echelons of cantering white horses, he said, "I was at sea before joining the navy and going for officer training—like you, at the *Mutterhaus* after the fancy-dress party on Dänholm. The idea was a career with the North German Lloyd, you know?"

Interested by this revelation, intrigued by its having remained for so long unmentioned, Altmann nodded. Schreiber a seafaring man apart from his *U-Bootwaffe* service! It explained something of his, Altmann's, sensing a subtle facility in his first officer that could not be defined but which invited implicit confidence where, in others, wisdom suggested at best a conditional trust. Rogge, for instance . . . And a major German shipping company, though beyond that he knew little. Merchant shipping was another world—and in present circumstances an alien one the doggedly persistent activities of which represented a threat to the Fatherland.

Schreiber proceeded. "I did eleven months as a cadet in their training-ship—*Kommodore Johnsen*. Four-mast steel barque, diesel auxiliary. Bought from Vinnen in 'thirty-six—you know that company?"

He barely paused for the inevitable shake of Altmann's head. "Owned a fleet of big sailers; got rid of most of them during the thirties and went into steam. NGL ran steamships—motor-ships, I should say—but believed in sail-training to knock their trainee officers into shape—and get rid of the weeds! They lost their training-ship—*Herzogin Cecilie*—after the war. Given to the Frogs." He glanced at Altmann. "Reparations. Chartered a couple of square-riggers until *Magdalene Vinnen* came on the market, just before I joined the company. Renamed her and put her in the grain trade from Australia; brought a cargo into Bremerhaven just before this damned war started. Rotting somewhere, I suppose, or maybe used as a storehouse . . . I applied to the navy and transferred in 'thirty-seven. The rest you know."

Altmann lit a cigarette, and they stood in silence for a minute or two, Schreiber sweeping the horizon with binoculars. At length Altmann asked what had made him go to sea in the first place. It seemed an obvious question. Everyone asked it, but, strangely, he had not felt a need to know before now. But then, conversation of this kind had not passed between them before. Time and conditions had allowed little more than attention to matters in hand.

"Well—I was in the Hitler Youth. Not by choice. They forced us into the *Jungfolk*—the *Jugend*'s junior division, you know? Us—the Boy Scouts, illegal after nineteen-thirty-three. We had to join the *Jugend* or the *Jungfolk*, according to age. I transferred to the *Jugend* when I was fourteen, in 'thirty-four . . ." Again Schreiber's glasses swept the horizon. "Old enough to know it wasn't working according to the rules—"

"Which rules were those?"

"National Socialism. You know all about that, *Kapitän*. About the ideals of the Party, the way a revived Germany will finally lead the world, free of corruption, communism, the Jewish stranglehold. That sort of thing—?"

Altmann drew on his cigarette and nodded; he could not be certain of the first officer's meaning—whether or not it hinted at sarcasm, suggested a scepticism born, perhaps, of disillusion; or perhaps simply what the words expressed, an acceptance of the declarations of the Party manifesto—the *Führer*'s pledges—at face value. As he himself had done—what else? To do otherwise was to unlock a Pandora's Box of conjecture, implication, hypothesis, and with it open up a vista of unlimited, incalculable—and alarming—possibility.

236

"And I didn't like the way discipline was handled. It amounted to bullying, among our own, which put me off the idea of fighting for Germany in the army, if it ever came to that. And I didn't care for flying."

"So you went to sea?"

"Yes . . . But not exactly gladly." Schreiber shrugged. "It seemed the best of a poor choice. I wasn't university material. Read the wrong books. Coleridge, for instance . . ." He grinned. "Gave the interview panels the wrong answers. But I'd been advised against it—against the sea—by family friends and acquaintances, and they knew—they were in it already. My father's friends."

"He was at sea?"

Schreiber nodded. "M-hm . . . But he never knew me. Killed—murdered—two months before I was born. Knifed by someone ashore in Valparaiso on his way back to the ship from the agent's office with advance money for the crew—"

"What was he doing in a place like that?"

"Working for Laeisz of Hamburg—master of a barque, running to the west coast for nitrates. Laeisz was in the trade before the war—the last war—with the best square-rigged fleet on the register . . . Did you ever hear of the Flying P's, *Kapitän*?"

Altmann smiled. "Sounds like a circus turn, *Einswo*—the Amazing Flying P's!—but no. They were—?"

"Amazing enough . . . Fast carriers, built for the trade. Big full-riggers and barques, up to five masts, commanded by the best seamen in the world. My father served under Hilgendorf. Hard man, and a wizard with a ship. He could get a five-thousand ton load going at seventeen, eighteen knots, made record runs out and back, never matched, though some of the other masters got close. My father was one of them." Schreiber paused, concentrating on a bearing with his glasses, and Altmann interposed.

"You're proud of your father?"

Still studying the horizon, Schreiber said, "In a way. But of course I never knew him. Can one be proud of a stranger? I admire him, though. And my mother loved him, hated the sea, and ships. Hated my idea of following."

"Understandable . . . But why P, exactly?"

"Oh—the ships' names. Began with P. *Preussen* was a five-master; rotting on the beach near Dover after a collision. Erikson—the Finn,

237

you know?—bought a few when Laeisz sold up a few years before the war—this war. *Pamir. Passat.* Others. After the last war he—Laeisz—lost the whole fleet—reparations again. He bought some of the best ones back and set up again. My father went back to him—for a few months. He kept them going for several years, but it wasn't like it had been and he was getting old, and the trade was dying."

"And you: you didn't have ambitions in that direction?"

"Square rig?" Schreiber lowered the glasses and caught Altmann's eye with a smile. "Worse than the army!" He shook his head. "No—if I had to go to sea it had to be in some sort of comfort—"

"Like this?"

"Ah! But this is war, *Kapitän!*" He grimaced. "Still better than the army, though."

Altmann grunted. "What about your time in the training-ship?"

"*Kommodore Johnsen?* Unavoidable. But after that—liners on regular schedules, good food, a dry bunk. And passengers—maybe a rich heiress or two!"

"One's enough, *Einswo.* You'll see. She doesn't even have to be an heiress."

"I didn't mean a wife, *Kapitän*—just an immoral woman. Or two."

"I see . . ." Altmann felt a passing flush of discomfort, but of course the first officer was joking, in his usual mock-solemn way. A good woman was the foundation of marriage, family—the cornerstone of civilised society, as a National Socialist Germany would ultimately demonstrate. He decided to change the subject. "But you joined the *Kriegsmarine*—and this arm of it! Why?"

"Well—there was talk. Among the ships' people, the officers. Even among our instructors in the *Johnsen*. They reckoned war was inevitable, by the mid-forties at the latest, and probably with England. After all, *Kapitän*, they were mixing with the British, and the Americans, among the passengers and in the ports—"

"Like Liverpool?"

"Ah!" Schreiber smiled and nodded. "Like Liverpool . . . They could see—and hear—more than people at home—more than the Party told them. Some said German merchant shipping would be laid up, impounded—blockaded, or sunk or captured by the Royal Navy. I didn't much like the idea of spending a war behind barbed wire—or feeding the fishes! So I went up for the selection board and—well, they snapped me up! Open arms—" Schreiber grimaced and shrugged in a parody of self-deprecation. "You know how it is, *Kapitän*—"

"And the *U-Bootwaffe*?"

Schreiber hesitated as if not wholly decided even yet. "The talk was about a short war—you must have heard it! Hit hard, flatten the enemy, wrap things up before anyone gets used to the idea—*Blitzkrieg*. Good policy in life, if you aren't going to get anywhere by peaceful means, or if you're threatened by some lout: don't stand about arguing; step in and hit and keep on hitting til he's down; don't give him any time to get his balance. You know?" Schreiber's eyes glinted and his teeth showed briefly in his beard. "Surface ships were too slow, too clumsy, overloaded with bull, and Raeder . . . seemed too keen on protocol. Not the kind of man to go in and make short work of a fight. And some of us thought he was frightened of the Tommies—the Royal Navy. Didn't have the balls to settle things with it! But I wasn't sure, either way, til Dönitz gave us a talk on a visit to the *Mutterhaus*. The u-boat would be the mailed fist, he said. The war-decisive weapon. The whole thing would be over before the battle-cruisers could let go their lines! So—" He shrugged.

"So . . . You'd finish the war in a few days and get back to your—immoral women, eh?"

Schreiber laughed. "That was the general idea, *Kapitän*!"

"And now?"

The first officer looked away, back out on the breaking seas, dappled and glittering with patchy sunshine beneath the broken overcast. He squinted against the passing glare, and Altmann covertly eyed the crow's-feet that cut deep white grooves into the tanned skin at the corners of his eyes; and the grey-flecked hair beneath the cap-band at the ears, and in the beard. Grey—at twenty-two! Or was it three now? Barely into long trousers, and an old man. Feeling an impulse to make some sort of contact with him—some physical contact—a fatherly hand on a shoulder—that would reassure, impart confidence, imply tacit support, understanding, beyond the trite capacity of words, Altmann resisted in alarm, and turned his own gaze outwards. The albatross focused his attention as it planed downwind past the bridge fifty metres away, a wingtip flicking the crests as if the bird were enjoying a game—and surely it derived pleasure from its effortless flight? There seemed to be a good-humoured set to its flight-pattern, even to the way it held its head, slightly cocked to cast a knowing eye at the men watching it.

Then, well downwind, it banked steeply and soared, gaining height at tens of metres a second as it came round into the wind and levelled out to cruise back towards the boat, retracing its flight-path at a leisurely pace, demonstrating its sublime harmony with its surroundings, its immeasurable superiority to the creatures below, floundering their noisy, laborious way through waters that tolerated their presence with a whimsical, schizophrenic condescension. A moment's access of rage, and they would be overwhelmed to leave the albatross unmoved, unchallenged in its mastery of its element. Watching it, Altmann felt an absurd jab of envy.

Schreiber said, "Now . . ." and his glance followed Altmann's gaze. "Well—better not to tempt fate, I think. That bird—if Seagrass had shot it—"

"Yes—what?"

"Oh—just old sailors' nonsense, as you say, *Kapitän* . . . One of the books I mentioned. Coleridge. Englishman. Have you read him?"

"Coleridge? No. But I know of him. A poet, yes? Not my normal fare, *Einswo*. Goethe, Schiller, Nietsche . . ."

With a sharp glance, Schreiber said, "Ah, yes. Goethe. And Nietsche . . . Heavy going, *Kapitän*—"

"I started reading law—Hamburg. Literary weight is relative, *Einswo*. But I'm no reader—mostly what I have to read. There's a lot of—decadent—stuff around. And not well-written serious work . . . *Mein Kampf*, for instance." He avoided Schreiber's eye. "But about Coleridge?"

Schreiber made a mental note. The great work, the foundation-stone of the *Dritte Reich*. He had read an abridged version, required reading in the *Jugend*, but found it trite and bombastic. There'd been a written test, which he'd passed with a warning lecture from his section leader, and that had been his only encounter with the *Führer*'s guiding principles, apart from their practical interpretation by the *Jugend*—and the present struggle, as people were beginning to call it. He gathered his wayward thoughts with a start. "Coleridge! Yes . . . well, he wrote a long poem, *Rime of the Ancient Mariner*—"

Alerted to a pinprick of irritation, Altmann nodded. The first officer's casual assumption of a world view could border on the priggish; it touched an otherwise dormant nerve, tempted a put-down. But Altmann felt disinclined to embarrass an officer whose general demeanour he regarded with shrewd appreciation. Let him have his conceits—and his weaknesses. He had, after all, revealed the cause of his lapse. Where a landsman would remain unmoved, or at best moved by the ever-prepared imposture of sentimentality, a seaman—Schreiber was eminently one—would react from a form of it to which he was entitled by right, and to which could be attributed a more genuine significance. He had wept at the plight of men whose race, creed, nationality—language—were immaterial to their common calling, by which they lived in a shared state of perpetual peril at the whim of the very elements with which the albatross had demonstrated its effortless affinity.

"Oh, yes—I've heard of that. Coleridge, eh?"

"So . . . Well, these sailors, on a voyage to these parts—the one telling the story, the Ancient Mariner—he kills this albatross. Shoots it with a crossbow. Bad luck for them; they all die—calms and storms—but the ancient mariner survives—rescued by a sea-pilot—only he's condemned to go on forever, telling his story to anyone who'll listen."

"You don't like telling stories—is that it?"

Schreiber grinned. "That's it, *Kapitän*! And those birds—souls of dead sailors. You've heard of that? Well—who knows? Old Hilgendorf, maybe . . . Or my father."

"You don't believe that stuff, *Einswo!*"

"Believe it?" Schreiber lifted a shoulder. "Whether we believe or not, there's no sense in putting it to the test, is there? Besides, it's a thing worth watching, that bird. We can't eat it." He nodded upwards. "Just look at him! Takes the mind off war for a few moments, anyway . . ."

Schreiber's prompting of memory touched a chord, an echo of brief student days and Goethe's early distinction as a founder of the literary movement that had striven for justice and freedom against an overbearing autocratic state. *Sturm und Drang*, he'd called it. Storm and stress. Altmann had found its counter-movement in National Socialism, and a less romantically impracticable approach to German self-determination. But the storm and stress had carried through; support for the state placed strains on its votaries equal to any of Goethe's experiences, if less poetically rendered.

Following that conversation Altmann added to his score in a decisive lead over Kretschmer's record, a comfortable assurance of the ultimate accolade in the further gilding of his Knight's Cross that could not be improved on: beyond that, professional advancement and, at last, the relative security of a shore posting, the end of partings from his wife and daughters, the end of helpless worry—for Ursula as much as for himself.

First he made for the old hunting-ground off Lourenço Marques, but after a fruitless ten days during which a Portuguese frigate made a nuisance of itself sniffing about in a way that suggested suspicions of his presence he turned for open water, not so much in hopes of finding a target as with the aim of giving the men a respite from the constant, unrequited, tension of action stations, mostly submerged, and in dangerously shoal waters. And it was out here, mid-way between the African coast and Madagascar's Cape Ste Marie, that a steel-wire fishing-net fouled the port propeller and after diving-plane. They wallowed on the surface, unable to dive, for some three hours while *Dieselmaschinistensmaat* Riemann, a navy-trained diver, sweating in a canvas diving-suit and helmet, cut away the wire with an oxy-acetylene torch while two sharks circled the boat. Off-duty men caught one on a meat-hook, giving it its quietus with a burst from a machine-gun before dragging it aboard to be cut up for a celebratory feast, but Smut produced only an inedible greasy mess after trying several methods of preparation, and the mutilated corpse was dumped. They looked on in mingled fascination and horror as its erstwhile companion, joined by two or three newcomers, attacked it in a bloody frenzy before turning on each other in a fury of spray and foam that splashed the onlookers, the deck and the conning-tower with a gory soup.

But the incident came as a particularly welcome diversion in Altmann's eyes: his concern was the never wholly absent, and sometimes urgently present, problem of morale, and shortly after departing the vicinity of Delagoa Bay a signal from headquarters upset everyone's plans: scheduled for eighteen weeks, the patrol was to be extended to twenty-six, torpedo supply permitting. They were to refuel *in situ*, at a rendezvous with the tanker *Gertrud Schüler*, which would also supply additional provisions. Keys for the Enigma coding machine, extending its function period for the necessary two months, would be supplied by another u-boat, identity and location to be advised. They were heading for a record-breaking patrol in more ways than one, and Altmann's first reaction was to do whatever he could to prevent the spread of what he saw as a likely consequence: it was vital to anticipate any despondency with whatever counter-measures could be devised. It was a point he had discussed at some length in his treatise, and he followed his own advice with a lead item in the boat's news-sheet:

We have this patch of ocean to ourselves—make the best of it. In peacetime you would be paying through the nose for the privilege! So—get out on deck at every opportunity, and keep fit. Physical jerks, hose parties, swimming alongside (when the boat is stopped, please note—even those web-footed Olympians among you!). Avoid over-eating, drink as much water as you're allowed, break up the round of watchkeeping, meals, sleep, the heads. Take an interest in the news, whether good or not so good; make use of the board games and read books that wouldn't normally interest you—you'll most likely be surprised! Listen to music and make your own—don't hide your light under a bushel. Join in the evening sing-alongs. And refine your chess!

All this requires your best efforts at self-discipline. It's a challenge of a different kind from the sort of thing you're used to, but it requires the same nerve, the same determination: the pressure is on, but it's not shown on the depth-gauge! No unit of the U-Bootwaffe has yet been on patrol for the length of time ahead of us, and, as we live like moles, like moles stick your snouts above ground whenever possible, and keep in touch with the elements that give us life. And of course, if you experience any problems speak to your divisional officer. Remember, we all depend on each other to see this patrol through to a successful conclusion.

But a word of warning! Some of you tan like berries; others just burn. No matter which, the sun in these parts is a killer. Don't lie around in it, and whenever you're in the open use the sun-cream supplied by the U-Bootwaffe. Ask the doctor.

Heil Hitler!

The rendezvous was even more remote than the middle of the Moçambique Channel, in the dying swell rolling up unhindered from the Southern Ocean some one thousand seven hundred miles east of Durban and seven hundred south of Mauritius. There was no realistic chance of an aircraft or any kind of ship appearing, and the tanker's people had seen nothing since passing off the Eddystone Rock, Tasmania's most southerly fragment, after a cautious passage from Osaka through the islands of the Western Pacific and the stormy waters of the Tasman Sea. Klüge, the tanker's master, made a joke of the name and its English Channel double, but his forced smile betrayed the stress he was under and the joke was weak. He did not expect to get back to Germany, hoped for orders to divert, even to Allied internment. It might, he said, mean scuttling the ship at sea at some pre-arranged spot, "—and

243

begging a return favour from one of your colleagues—eh, *Kapitän?*" Again the unconvincing smile. "Who knows—it might even be you on your way home!" and Altmann refrained from pointing out that it would take more than one boat to accommodate the tanker's sixty-odd souls. Emptied of her cargo of oil, her usefulness to the *Reich* would at best be in doubt. Angrily, he conceded to himself the likelihood of the tanker's falling victim to Allied attack, increasing with her nearer approach to home waters. Her chances were less than those of a u-boat's getting back to base. Altmann felt a grateful pity for a man whose predicament was, if anything, worse than his own: as a comforting thought, it had a bitter tang. The tanker had no spares for the u-boat, and the provisions sent across, Japanese in origin, were meagre and of poor quality, but included some small oranges, which were welcome. Eventually a gloomy Benedict signed for his oil, and with everyone showered, shaved and glaringly smart in freshly-laundered outfits, they slipped away with a wave in answer to a short, rather forlorn, blast on the tanker's whistle. Klüge had orders to wait for three more boats, also operating in the area. Setting a course for Mauritius, Altmann felt vaguely cheated at their non-appearance, and mildly disturbed. Soon, however, his thoughts were otherwise occupied.

Off Port Louis in broad daylight he used two torpedoes to sink a British freighter of about three thousand tons, its identity never established: well within sight of the port, the effect of the attack was like kicking a hornet's nest, deciding Altmann against surfacing to question the four men left clinging to a Carley float. A sloop pursued him for a short distance but seemingly lost the asdic contact and returned to the scene while he headed off in the wake of a larger ship which had sailed shortly before the sinking. To his surprise he caught up with her off Madagascar's Cape Est, making southward, perhaps for Tamatave, at a speed that suggested engine trouble, and explained the boat's overtaking her. But, slow as she was, and maintaining a steady heading, both torpedoes fired at her missed. The first passed into limbo unremarked, the second close enough to cause a flurry of activity on board, men crowding out of flung-open doors and pounding up and down deck ladders, while from the bridge-wing a man surveyed the surroundings through binoculars as the ship took an abrupt turn towards the coast and the theoretical protection of territorial waters. Altmann decided to let her go, noting in the log that the crew appeared to have been rudely woken by something—*like, for example, the sound of a passing torpedo*. Coming across the entry later, Palmgren was amused, and surprised at this light-hearted departure from Altmann's normally strictly-correct observations. And shortly after the attack a signal from headquarters extended the area of "free manoeuvre" to all Madagascan and Mascarene territorial waters and across to the Tanganyika coast.

"Pickings becoming thinner on the ground," observed Schreiber at lunch. "A good sign, maybe—Allies running out of tonnage, so we scour the barrel."

"Believe that and you'll believe anything," sniffed Benedict. "Those figures for February and March won't be repeated—Goebbels yaps like a hyena about inevitable victory at sea, but the fact is the—"

"They laugh," interrupted Hildegras. "Hyenas. They don't yap. Their bark sounds like a laugh." Glancing nervously round he met a silent barrage of mixed irritation and amusement, and busied himself with his soup, red-faced.

"As I was saying," resumed Benedict with heavy emphasis, "the fact is the Allies are getting their act together—and building ships like sausages."

"Like sausages?" murmured Lange, lifting an eyebrow. "Interesting, if not particularly hydrodynamic. Have we come across any of these strange vessels?"

"You know what I mean." Benedict's irritation mounted. "Production-line system it's a safe bet Uncle Karl never had in mind when he talked about war-decisive weapons."

"So where are they?" inquired Schreiber, going on to answer his own question: "Not in the Indian Ocean in any numbers . . . How about the Atlantic convoys with their radar-equipped escorts and the new escort carriers—the targets we can't get at any more? Obvious alternative to a theory of fewer ships, I grant you, *Chef* . . . Might as well face it—we're here because there's no trade for us in the old happy hunting-grounds; I mean, none that wouldn't see us on the bottom at the first shot."

"I wouldn't let the skipper hear that," murmured Lange. "Or the men. No victory gained without setbacks, you know? Like Rome, the Thousand-Year *Reich* isn't going to be built in a day, and without a struggle . . . Welcome to the struggle."

Benedict feigned reproach. "I'm surprised at you, Konrad—such cynicism!"

"Not at all, Herbert—I have absolute confidence in the *Reich* and ultimate victory. With the *Führer* in charge and the Party stalwarts handling the details, all we have to do is carry out our orders and leave the worrying to our leaders: sooner or later we'll realise our destiny."

"Ah," said Benedict. "But what destiny?" His smile conveyed a worldly sadness.

"Who knows? Better not to tempt fate guessing . . ." Turning his attention to Schreiber, Lange changed the subject. "Vitamin C—you know how lately it was discovered?"

Stripping the last of the peel from an orange Schreiber tore out a segment and munched reflectively before swallowing and shaking his head. "No idea—maybe, oh, a hundred years ago? By Captain Cook—on his explorations in the Pacific. Something like that."

"Your view of history is somewhat—um—compressed, *Einswo* . . . The cure—the prevention—of scurvy, which is why we're carrying tinned orange juice to supplement the lemons—was discovered as far back as the seventeenth century, you know—by an English naval man, Sir Richard Hawkins. By accident."

"The Tommies," grunted Benedict moodily, "have an unfair share of lucky accidents. It's a mistake to think they're better organised than the *Wermacht*."

"Maybe they'll win the war by accident—?" threw in Hildegras brightly.

"If there's a few more like you in the *U-Bootwaffe* it's more than likely," returned Benedict crushingly. "But you were saying, doc—?"

Schreiber caught the midshipman's abashed eye and winked, amused but also touched by his discomfiture. He was aware of the youngster's sense of exclusion, his eagerness to be accepted as a compatriot, if not yet an equal, among fighting men, if only for the duration of the war, as he had fatally declared. Benedict had betrayed, perhaps, his state of mind by the remark, uncharacteristically personal in its blunt impact. The strain of patrol work told in different ways, and the engineer was under strain to perhaps a greater extent than even the *Kapitän*, responsible as he was for every detail of the boat's mechanical and electrical fitness. Snapping at the midshipman's no doubt unintended sarcasm was a momentary lapse. Or so it must be hoped . . .

Lange was pursuing his theme. "—by properly-conducted experiment was another Englishman, a naval surgeon called Lind—"

246

"German expatriate by the sound of it," interjected Benedict, then waved a hand. "Sorry, Konrad—go on."

"Yes . . . Lind tried several different possible cures on a dozen volunteers—vinegar, spirits of vitriol, sea-water and so on—" he smiled at the startled looks from his listeners "—but also—" and he nodded at Schreiber's orange "—oranges and lemons. I don't think he actually killed anyone, but the two who got the fruit were completely cured in a few days."

"When was this?" asked Hildegras in a spirit of restitution.

"Um—seventeen forty-something."

"A long time ago." Benedict chased a couple of salt tablets down with a gulp of coffee and a grimace. Lange nodded approval. "But what about limes? The Americans call the Tommies Limeys because they issued the juice after so many days at sea, didn't they?"

Lange nodded. "Still do in some trades, I gather. A mistake—"

"Ah!" Benedict sat back and folded his arms conclusively. "See what I mean?"

"Limes were cheaper and easier to get than lemons and oranges during the Napoleonic wars—grown on plantations in the West Indies. So the English used them instead. But—" and he inclined his head deferentially at Benedict "—it was a bad move."

"At last! Go on."

"Limes have almost no vitamin C. Useless against scurvy."

"Couldn't have happened to a better lot." Benedict got as close to beaming as anyone had seen. "Poetic justice, in a way."

"Uh-huh . . . But the whole story's much longer." Lange drained his coffee and peered into the empty mug with distaste. "How does Smut get coffee to taste so much like burnt sawdust and old engine oil—? Anyway . . ." he looked round at the others "—time's getting on—"

"In a couple of minutes, *Herr Doktor*—" Schreiber squinted at his wristwatch. "Go."

"All right . . . Well—the English navy didn't believe Lind's findings and he died without seeing them acted on—"

"If we lose the war to these idiots," said Benedict. "We'll deserve all we'll get."

"A daily dose of lime-juice," Hildegras muttered, with a cautious glance at Benedict, who ignored him.

"Could be worse, Seagrass," Lange smiled. "Quite a pleasant drink; and it mixes well with schnapps—or gin. However . . . Your Captain

Cook, *Einswo*, went on record saying citrus fruit was no use against scurvy, even though he included oranges in his crew's diet—keeping them free of illness. Said it was the *Sauerkraut*—"

"German secret weapon, eh?" interposed Benedict. "We shouldn't have to deal with these people at all, you know. How have they survived?"

"Others making bigger mistakes," said Schreiber. "Obvious. Napoleon. The Kaiser—"

"The *Führer*?"

Schreiber smiled ingenuously. "Remains to be seen, doesn't it?"

Lange hastily pre-empted Benedict's reply. "*Sauerkraut* has some value . . . Lind's successor managed to get lemons back on the menu in the navy, but only at the commanding officer's request and expense, so scurvy continued as a hazard in ships blockading the French, keeping station for weeks on end—"

Benedict snorted. "Frogs. The weak link. I know all about Trafalgar. Went the same way with their Maginot Line. Bunch of boudoir cowboys." He brightened. "Another mistake of the British—making allies of them. They'll live to regret it—already have!"

"Mm-hm . . . That was when limes came into the picture. But they were called lemons or limes without distinction and the juice looked the same anyway. And officers and officials watered it down by way of profitable practice. Of course merchant ships were more prone to the effects during peacetime, and it wasn't until voyages got shorter with better ways of preserving food that scurvy eventually died out—but it can come back at any time. Hence our lemons and orange-juice—but no limes." Lange dabbed primly at his mouth with his napkin, folded and rolled it and slipped it into its monogrammed silver ring. The others watched in mild fascination. "So—there you have it. The story behind *Einswo*'s orange."

Schreiber offered pieces of his scurvy-preventive round before consuming them himself after general refusal. In the silence this produced Hildegras said, "What about vitamin C—you said it was only discovered recently?"

"Ah—yes. No-one knew what constituent of lemon-juice actually worked, but investigation finally isolated it in nineteen-thirty-two. Now you can get it in little capsules."

"Have you any?"

"When your teeth begin to fall out I'll let you know," said Lange, rising. "Stick to lemons and orange-juice. Seething with the stuff. As you know, I'm not a compulsive pill-pusher."

A few miles off the remote islet of Tromelin Altmann used two more torpedoes to sink the unescorted British-flag *Llanedwen*. Conditions were too rough—a strong south-easterly with seas to match—to carry out the attack on the surface, so the torpedoes were fired without warning in the last glimmer of dusk. Both struck the ship, which went down without fuss to leave a handful of survivors amid a token scatter of wreckage and oily scum. Altmann decided there was no question of surfacing. The ship was clearly identified in the register and by a name-board on the deck-housing immediately abaft the wheelhouse: before taking up his attack position he had cruised past at periscope depth, its plume of foam lost in the general pother. In the log he noted *Five men seen amongst wreckage. Unlikely to survive in heavy seas. Departed immediately.*

There was always a temptation to embellish the bald facts; and an undeniable impulse to do whatever might have been possible to improve the chances of the survivors short of taking them aboard. Both had to be resisted. Altmann's fear was of his exhibiting a softening, an easing of zeal, as the patrol proceeded and his modest lead in the tonnage competition—as it was inevitably seen by the men as well as the general public in its view of the war through the Göebbels news-grinder—ratched towards an unchallengeable record. If anything, he felt, or at least cultivated, a hardening of resolve, made easier by his perception of its natural association with the inarguable demands of duty. And, he discovered with some relief, it offered a bonus, helping, in a way, with his continuing struggle against the shadows that awaited his every respite from physical attendance to the boat's operational requirements: the rightness of duty, and its justification of his resolve, somehow eased the sense of moral uncertainty—even guilt, as he felt bound to regard it—clinging to the unwritten but indissoluble tally of events crowded into the schooner's last moments. Sleep, or at least a half-waking doze, free of the accusing wraiths, seemed to come more readily in the shelter of hardening self-discipline. Lange's secobarbital served as, if anything, a useful reminder of his proximity to the abyss. That, but no more: he could not afford to do anything that would slacken the stern demands of command, whether on himself or in their authority over his subordinates. A successful patrol notwithstanding, the bare survival of the boat and her crew depended on his unyielding resolve. As ever, sentimentality was the enemy's accomplice, where it wasn't the enemy in its own right. The fate of the men in the water formed no part of his brief. On that point conscience could make no objections.

East of the northern part of Madagascar he encountered three more targets, all unescorted—"A lesser edition of the second happy time, eh, *Kapitän*?" observed Schreiber at dinner following the third sinking and ensuing events. "At this rate our eels will run out before the Jap lard."

The ten cases of lard stowed in the bilges had constituted the largest single item among the stores from the tanker, and the cook had protested a limit to the recipes in which he could use it—pastry and fried dishes mostly, but frying was kept to a minimum in the boat's already odour—and fume-laden interior. But he kept his objections to a low customary grumble, calculating on a profitable disposal of the balance on their return to base. And, inevitably, the stuff had become the focus of the boat's humorists, by this time somewhat threadbare.

Within an hour of the third ship's destruction—the torpedoes she had taken bringing the total expenditure to fourteen—the routine nature of the patrol was seriously disrupted by the businesslike arrival of a destroyer, as Altmann took her to be in the starlight, from a hasty glance as the alarm dive began to a few brief sightings in the attack periscope; and seriously not only because the warship made a determined effort to avenge the merchantman's misfortune but also because she almost caught Altmann on the surface in a situation he had so recently vowed to avoid—not merely questioning survivors but also helping swimmers into the boats and ordering Lange to do what he could for the injured and wounded. Then, in his fury at his own weakness he risked the boat by attempting to turn an escape into another attack. Two bow shots and one from the stern either failed on contact or missed their mark, and the ensuing nine hours were as nerve-racking as any similar episode in the Atlantic's theatre of operations, towards the closing stages of which Altmann sensed a growing mood of resentment among his companions—not so much in tone of voice, in manner, in response to orders, in the glances cast in his direction, as in a change of humour, almost imperceptible, and a heavier, pregnant quality to the apprehensive silences that accompanied the destroyer's all-too-audible approaches heralding mayhem. Whoever commanded the warship displayed a skill matched by his tenacity, and apart from burst valve-flange gaskets and the inevitable leakage of chlorine gas from the batteries, with the usual scatter of minor breakages and failures of equipment and fittings, Benedict diagnosed a punctured main ballast tank after a steep uncontrolled dive took the boat to a depth that tested Altmann's self-possession and outward equanimity to their limits, as he reckoned. It was a supreme test of the theory that one man's behaviour could determine the moral—even the mental—resilience of the ruck: they drew on what appeared to be his confidence as the thirsty on a spring, and the tension it produced had the effect of tightening his own hold on a restive simulacrum of composure. Just beneath its barely-rippled surface lay a suspected sump of despair; even of panic. Once exposed, under its internal pressure it would explode among them with a fatal effect unequalled by the mere physical impact of the charges' explosions. In the control-room, with a convulsive grip upon a convenient pipe-flange, Altmann felt he was literally holding his boat and her company together as a viable fighting unit; or, more viscerally, as a seaworthy vessel distinct from a tangle of wreckage taking its cargo of human remains into the depths. The metaphor was more than a figure of speech: the cool hardness of the metal, with a sharp edge painful under the thumb of his left hand, gave him the hold on his nerves without which he felt certain he would have been lost. As the boat shuddered under each salvo, he tightened his grip, and eventually felt the blood flowing. He heard Benedict's hoarse "Two hundred and ten metres, *Kapitän*—holding!" with relief that was absurdly out of place: the cracking sounds from the boat's straining fabric were intimations of catastrophe. Even so, with the accompanying cessation of the depth-charging—had the dive given the hunter the slip?—he could release his hand-hold. Blood dripped.

"All right. Keep her at that, Herbert—let's see if he's still with us." As he spoke, Altmann realised that although on an even keel the boat was listing to port. Benedict's answer to his inquiry numbed his senses for a moment: the port ballast-tank wasn't holding air. And of course the compressed-air supply was limited.

"Can you take her up?"

"I don't know, *Kapitän*—certainly not unless I can give her some headway—use the planes. At least half speed." He coughed and cleared his throat. The gas was becoming a problem.

"Right...*Einswo*—the *Pillenwerfer*! Work up to half-speed, Herbert. Keep her at this depth for the time being if you can. *Steuermann*—what's the heading?"

"Two-seven-eight, *Kapitan*."

"Very well—port easy to one-eight-oh."

"Port easy to one-eight-oh, aye."

"*Funkmaat*—have you got a bearing on her?"

"Faint, *Kapitän*—getting fainter, still going away. Bearing three-four-two, moving left, almost steady."

The destroyer's propeller-noise had faded after the last attack run. Soon they would hear her returning, but first they listened for the asdic's blind tapping. Nothing. Time passed. The only sounds were the hull's continuing protests, and the hum of the electric motors. And, if you listened carefully, a subdued hiss. Altmann heard it with apprehension. The compressed-air supply was bleeding away, would eventually exhaust itself; then—oblivion. But until that moment the leak would be laying a trail of bubbles. The question was—would the destroyer spot it? Perhaps the oil, gas and debris ejected from the boat would fool her, distract her from the bubble-trail; perhaps it was lost in the choppy sea's own effervescence. Otherwise, it would signal their end, either way: his only alternative was to surface—if he could—and either surrender or fight it out, with the outcome a foregone conclusion. And all, he reflected bitterly, because he had weakened, flouted his own principles; because he had succumbed to the temptation of sentimentality, allowed his ego to prevail over duty to his boat, to her men, to the cause. Like a raw tyro he had paused to help the enemy, to gratify his self-regard by a futile act of chivalry that would be adjudged a crime by any court-martial—and court-martial there surely would be if he survived the loss of his boat; even if he were to get her home, damaged as she would be. At the very least an inquiry. And Uncle Karl was less inclined to view acts of chivalry in a tolerant light as the war's progress took Germany farther along a road that seemed to lead away from the intended destination. That, at least, was a fact they were all taking pains to edge round.

But there was another facet to the turn of events: sentimentality and ego were plausible forces behind his actions, and, he felt, entirely authentic; but the chivalric element rang hollow in its response to a need brought about by his actions in the first place: no attack, no distressed survivors to be succoured. The tragedy of the situation was only thinly veiled by its absurdity, and there was no profit to be had from pretending otherwise. The only truthful expedient was to comply with Dönitz's advice and instructions, and leave the rest to his, Dönitz's, conscience. It was war. The whole idea was to crush the enemy, and the most merciful way of doing so was surely to execute it with despatch, to act without compunction and with complete personal detachment. Anything else—anything less ruthless—would be nothing better than an exercise in vanity and a prolongation of the agony with increased risk of falling victim oneself. Which, Altmann conceded, was so in his case, the vanity lying in the belief that in such behaviour as he had just displayed he could somehow redeem himself; absolve himself from the debt incurred by his fatal part in the lives of the schooner's crew and passengers. That by it he would gain easier means of relief from the phantoms' remorseless recurrence; from the dread he was beginning to realise defined his view of them, now transferring itself to an even more appalling scenario. And as he dreaded it, so he refused to contemplate it, dismissing it—but unsuccessfully—as mere hypothesis, as a natural anxiety common to them all in their thoughts of home. And in present circumstances he had more pressing worries which, he reflected, were an effective form of respite.

Schwebke broke in on his cogitations with the announcement that he had lost the destroyer altogether; her propeller-noise had dwindled to silence shortly after the bearing indicator had drifted off its mark. And Schreiber reported a total of forty-seven explosions, possibly signifying exhaustion of the warship's supply. Nor were there indications of any other arrivals, which gave her abrupt, solitary presence a flavour of the surreal. What had she been doing, apparently alone in the area? Altmann could conclude only that she must have been either searching after his sinking of the Llanedwen, perhaps called in by a signal from her or one of the next three targets, or en route to somewhere such as the Allied beach-heads in the island's north, or merely an unlucky whim of chance—particularly so in its outcome, which now forced him into a decision to surface, perhaps under the noses of a waiting reception-committee, as mysterious in its presence as the warship. Planing up from the depths as the compressed air leaked away, the boat reached periscope depth still at half-speed, when Altmann was able to glance round briefly at an empty ocean before giving the order. Surfacing with an initial list to port of several degrees, the boat slowly righted herself as the compressor took over from the bottles to maintain the necessary supply of air to the punctured tank. More concerned with anatomical damage Lange noticed the blood and applied a dressing to a gashed thumb.

The structural damage was immediately evident, at first to Altmann's alarm but very quickly to his relief. At least the location was visible and accessible, a ragged hole in the outer casing exposing a split in the plating of the tank itself, seemingly the result of a blow from a depth-charge splinter. It could, observed Benedict with a sucking of teeth, have been worse—"But not much. How the hell we'll patch it with the air escaping at pressure like that I'll be damned if I know."

"Hardly damned, Herbert," retorted Altmann, patting the engineer's shoulder in a show of good humour that betokened a relief he was quickly beginning to see as misplaced: small though it was, a matter of about twenty-five centimetres, the split effectively robbed the boat of its single defining distinction—had for all practical purposes laid it at the feet of its enemies. He added, less elatedly, "If you do know, it'll mean your salvation. And mine." He studied Benedict's red-rimmed eyes, their whites crazed with fine traceries of blood-vessels. The eyes of a drunk, he reflected absently; but caused by a sober attention to duty that was its own burden, notwithstanding the burden of trust placed in his competence by every man aboard. "Seriously, Herbert—d'you think it *can* be patched?"

Benedict sniffed and rubbed his eyes wearily. "It'll have to be, *Kapitän*, won't it? If we were Americans, as our first officer seems to wish, we could try a wad of chewing-gum, but since we're just sausage-eating Germans it'll have to be a welded patch, or a straight welded seal—but neither can be done while the air's escaping like that. Must be ninety tons of pressure behind it, give or take a few kilos. And before you ask—we haven't the equipment to weld under water." He blew out his cheeks and shook his head, sweeping back a stray lock of greying hair. "What a damned pig!" He caught Altmann's eye. "You could ask for ideas—fifty heads are better than two. Even this fifty."

To Benedict's thinly-veiled pleasure the idea that agreed with his own as the only course that seemed open to them came from the theoretician, Henning, and Altmann's response was to act on it without delay. Apart from the chance of the enemy's stumbling upon them, weather conditions were as good as they had been for some time, and the boat could be hove-to comfortably enough for the work to be performed in the minimum possible time: an attempt to seal the split by direct welding. The alternative, a patch, would have entailed the cutting-away of the surrounding outer casing: not an unduly difficult task but time-consuming apart from the time needed to shape and secure the patch in place. That, in turn, would have meant removal of a motor-room footplate, the only suitable metal available, creating a hazard whenever rapid movement was necessary. A welded seal was the obvious first choice. And the air-pressure could be dealt with, as Henning explained. It could be eased, he said, by flooding the tank as for a dive. The fully-open vents would release the air at such a rate that whatever continued to escape via the split would not be at enough pressure to prevent its sealing by torch-welding. An initial quick seal, or even part-seal, would enable the tank to be blown again and the process repeated as necessary to complete the job. The whole operation would occupy no more than twenty minutes—"Barely that, in fact," he ended earnestly. "I'm allowing for interruptions."

"Like the boat diving in the usual way, of course," said Schreiber, and pursed his lips. "That's what happens when we flood the tanks, you know. We go down."

Henning frowned. "That's why Riemann'll wear a lifejacket. In case the boat goes down before he finishes. Also, for the same reason, he doesn't wear a lifeline." *Dieselmaschinistensmaat* Riemann had volunteered his services before the request had been made, and was ready for action. He would have to work fast.

"You work to fine tolerances, Peter." Schreiber nodded soberly. "Still—only to be expected in a born engineer . . . I'm impressed!"

But Schreiber's mockery lacked malice, and he grinned at Henning's exasperated "No, no, no! He'll be quite safe. If the boat goes under it won't be for long, and he stays afloat until it surfaces again—in the same place; and each time the split will be smaller, and anyway I don't expect the job—the first weld—to take more than a few seconds, as I said. If we have to dive it will be only once at the most." He held up a hand as Schreiber opened his mouth to reply. "And before you think up any more objections, the air-pressure isn't that great anyway." He nodded meaningly at Benedict. "You mentioned ninety tons, *Chef*—a round figure, of course, but it's spread over the tank's whole area; pressure at any sta—"

"Ah," said Benedict. "Of course—now you point it out to me! What it is to have a scientific mind, eh?"

Henning flushed. "Sorry, *Chef*—it's just that the problem isn't quite as bad as we think. I mean, the air-pressure at the split is only a sample of the area total, isn't it? Enough to be troublesome, but not to prevent any welding at all."

Looking on, Altmann broke in. "Perfectly clear, *Zweit*. And good. Now—all we have to do is find out whether the star of the show's prepared to take a swim."

"Especially if a shark turns up," threw in Hildegras, and coloured as all eyes turned on him. He spread his hands palm-up and shrugged. "Just a thought. Maybe someone should stand by with a gun also ready to swim."

"Well done, Seagrass," said Altmann admiringly. "What mother wouldn't be proud of you? Take my Luger, but be careful where you point it. And don't drop it; it's the only one I've got."

"Just one other thing." Attention returned to Henning as Hildegras heaved a sigh of mingled relief and apprehension. "The gas-bottles. They'll have to be on deck."

"*Einswo*'ll see them properly secured," said Altmann. "No need to get them below."

Henning almost clicked his heels where he sat. Stiffening, he nodded. "Understood, *Kapitän!*" Over Altmann's shoulder Schreiber caught his eye and solemnly touched his brow in a mock salute. Henning looked away, tight-lipped, and Schreiber pointed to the need of some kind of platform from which Riemann could work. "A bosun's chair or a staging," he explained, and to Altmann's lifted eyebrow added artlessly, "Your bunk-board's the only suitable piece of wood we have, *Herr Kapitän.*"

Riemann worked fast, watched by Altmann, Schreiber and Hildegras on the bridge, accompanied by four lookouts resolutely scanning their respective sectors. The boat lay stopped, rolling in the low swell, the slight seas breaking over the starboard side-tank and deck-plating falling back to leave the port side largely free of water. The split took the weld for two-thirds of its length before a slight widening prevented the liquid metal from spanning the gap. At that point, at a signal from Riemann, the dive-vents were opened and the bridge cleared apart from the Luger-toting Hildegras. As spray thrown up from the vents enveloped him Riemann worked on, hunched over the blue-white glare of the welding-torch until the rising tide lapped round him and he scrambled up to the deck, where Hildegras stood grim-faced, Luger in hand and lifejacket inflated. Pushing up his dark goggles Riemann grinned and nodded at the gun. "Safety-catch on, I hope, *Fahnrich*—I don't want another hole to weld up today. Especially if it's in my arse."

The boat slipped away beneath their feet and they trod water amidst the whirlpools, upwellings, broken water and drifting spray of its descent, Hildegras anxiously glaring round in dread of a triangular fin's approach. The water was pleasantly cool, the late afternoon sun struck warmly down, and their lifejackets supported them comfortably enough as they awaited the boat's return, spluttering in the lop breaking over them, dashing the water out of their eyes and suddenly feeling, superimposed on an immense loneliness, the implicit malevolence of the ocean, reduced to a few square metres around them with momentary glimpses of a greater expanse as they rose on the passing crests. Never before had it been so forcibly borne in upon Hildegras that in this wilderness man, in his naked state, was profoundly out of place, faced a challenge he could not possibly meet, was reduced to utter insignificance, diminished both physically and spiritually to an extent no landsman could imagine, let alone experience. In fact, he thought, the ocean's mood was not as defined, not as limited, as malevolence; its sheer, impenetrable indifference to his presence was as terrifying as it was humiliating: he was not even held in contempt, and he awaited the boat's return to the surface with nervous anticipation, grateful for Riemann's apparent nonchalance.

"How about a little farm after the war, *Fahnrich*?" A wave struck him in the face and he coughed and snorted and spat, cursing, before continuing. "Few pigs, a cow or two—nothing but hayfields all round—mud and shit under your nice dry boots—dinner on the table—a wife in your bed every night—the same wife, I mean, true as—" He gasped as another wave slopped over his head. "Who'd sell a farm and go to sea, eh?"

But instead of the resurfacing conning-tower and the solid press of the deck underfoot they were startled by the sudden appearance of the sky periscope a few metres away, rearing up like some Vernian contrivance, rotating until its armoured-glass gaze fell on them with an impersonal malice that, for a moment, alarmed Hildegras, blinking on the prickle of salt water. He gasped and swore. "Shit! That'll be *Einswo* for sure. He acts like a damned schoolboy!" Raising the Luger he aimed at the eye, which ignored him to swing round the horizon's full circle before withdrawing as abruptly as it had appeared, like a conjuring-trick. But it was real enough. As Riemann remarked, to Hildegras's further unease, whoever was at the eyepiece wanted to be sure the coast was clear before coming up. "If he's seen something we can't, you can kiss goodbye to your farm, *Fahnrich*!"

"They wouldn't leave us?"

"You got that in writing?"

"Shit!"

Later, after Riemann had completed the repair with apparent success, and no further need for a dive, Altmann called Hildegras aside. Detecting suppressed anger, the midshipman braced himself, casting his mind's-eye back over his recent activities without encountering any obvious disciplinary enormity. Altmann wasted no time in preliminaries, producing the Luger and the remark that in different circumstances the midshipman's handling of the weapon would have brought him before a court-martial. Paling, Hildegras stared at the gun in Altmann's hand as if at a snake, and cursed himself.

Altmann kept his voice low, studying the midshipman's downy-bearded pink-cheeked features with the narrow steadiness he'd found had the power to unnerve in certain situations. Hildegras was no exception, but he took his eyes off the gun to meet Altmann's with a firm set to his jaw that earned him a discount on the price his commander had had in mind. There was no insolence in the midshipman's manner; but neither was there any hint of servility or ingratiation, and Altmann was relieved to see that while it was necessary to invoke explicit discipline from time to time, as in this instance the midshipman invariably accepted it in a spirit of stoic contrition that spoke emphatically of a self-assurance that would profit from redeemable error rather than attempt its justification. Hildegras never made the same mistake twice, and those around him, both his superiors and his subordinates, noted as much, and credited him accordingly. Altmann's private conclusion was that the *Kriegsmarine* would lose a good officer, either later in his wartime career or in his planned post-war departure; his declared resolve to return to civilian life and the study of architecture remained adamant. Nevertheless, here he was, in need of a few words of summary correction, and Altmann likewise braced himself. His anger was less with the stupidity of Hildegras's action than with the fact of his having so far forgotten his responsible position as to make this embarrassing interview necessary; and that it was equally necessary that his anger should not colour the way he chose to deal with it. Damn the little idiot!

Saying nothing, he proffered the Luger, its butt towards the midshipman, who hesitated before grasping it and making a show of inspecting the safety-catch. Looking up he met the agate gaze with a blue frankness that momentarily baulked Altmann's rasped, "Get a firm grip on it, *Fahnrich*. Finger on the trigger . . . Now, the muzzle to your right ear."

"*Kapitän?*" The blue gaze betrayed disbelief, and switched to the gun as if to make sure of its reality. Returning to Altmann's narrow scrutiny it blinked. "My ear? Is it loaded?"

"Oh, yes. Untouched since you had it." Altmann motioned with a hand to confirm the instruction. "Come along, *Fahnrich*—no time to waste!"

"But—*Kapitän*—it might—I mean, aiming a gun unless you mean to kill or wound—" His voice tailed off, and the pink cheeks flushed. Altmann studied him for a moment, then relented.

"Exactly, *Fahnrich*—safety-catch or not, eh?"

Subdued, Hildegras dropped his gaze and took a deep breath. "I'm sorry, *Kapitän*—stupid of me. Not thinking."

"And you didn't have the safety-catch on, either, you know. It was still off when you gave the gun back to the first officer! What were you thinking of—the wild west? War at sea not exciting enough for you?" Not very original, thought Altmann; simile and metaphor had never been among his accomplishments; but it would do. It seemed to strike the necessary balance between severity and risible pomposity.

Glumly, Hildegras assured Altmann that the wild west had been nowhere near his thoughts at the time. Sharks—

"Yes—sharks! Not the wild west—sharks. And not your own boat's periscope, eh?"

"It was a—an impulse, *Kapitän*. Reaction—it surprised me. I was on edge. But I'm sorry. A stupid thing to do. It won't happen again—" As he uttered the assurance its absurdity struck him and he fell silent, tight-lipped. Altmann suppressed an impulse towards sympathy and grunted. He hoped not.

"—and I hope you take a lesson from it. There won't be another. This isn't the training-school, Hildegras—it's the real thing. Schooldays are over! And that being so—" Altmann laid a hand on the stained canvas-covered log beside him "—I should make an entry in this, which will be the basis for a disciplinary hearing when we get home. You know this?"

"Yes, *Kapitän.*" Hildegras straightened his shoulders and fixed his gaze on a point directly before him. "I know the regulation."

"However—in the circumstances I need to think about it. Meanwhile, *Fahnrich*, you can give your brain a chance to do its job and let me have an essay on the subject—entitle it, say, *The Safe Handling of Small Arms*. No more than two thousand words. Let me have it this time tomorrow. By then I'll have decided what to do about the log entry."

To cover his dismay Hildegras resorted to formality, snapping to attention with "Yes, *Herr Kapitän!*" Then, about to turn away at a nod from Altmann, a thought occurred which emerged as a question before he could control it. "Um—one other thing, *Kapitän*, if I—?"

"Yes?"

"The periscope check before resurfacing. Was it—I mean—would you have left us if you'd seen a ship—an enemy warship?"

Altmann's gaze narrowed. Hildegras returned it with the artlessness that could, apparently unconsciously, be as much his salvation as the trigger of his own ruin. Such a guileless fellow! It would either carry him to distinction or sink him before he'd found his feet. Altmann smiled thinly. "Ask yourself, *Fahnrich.* What would you have done?"

Shocked, Hildegras blinked, licked his lips, and after a moment's hesitation said, "I'm not sure, *Kapitän* . . . Maybe—maybe the same."

"And submit a citation—posthumous!—of the men's bravery!" Altmann felt he was overdoing the ruthlessness, though of course the action was correct. He softened the effect of his words by adding, "You'll see things more clearly when you get command yourself, Hildegras—but let's hope you don't find yourself in a similar position, eh? Now—" he gave the log a concluding thump "—you've duties to attend to—and that essay!"

As the midshipman departed Altmann wondered which of them was more relieved at the interview's outcome. His final decision had been as spur-of-the-moment as Hildegras's startling misuse of the Luger. Which, Altmann was amused to realise, had been the first time he had looked into the business-end of a gun. At least, a gun in the hands of a man at a range close enough to see the whites of his eyes. The periscope's magnification had had a remarkable effect, even out of focus. And the interview had had its usual effect—an irritating dissipation of his anger. Perhaps, after all, the boy's planned post-war exit would be the wiser course, at least from his own point of view. An ability to disarm one's superiors wasn't by any means a guarantee of professional advancement.

Not, at any rate, in the navy. Periodic indulgence of the spleen was a privilege of rank not to be routinely thwarted without penalty, and what might find an excuse in wartime would not be allowed to pass in peacetime's obsession with petty protocols, not to mention jealousies. Altmann wondered what further reflections would be prompted by the essay; it would not be a predictable regurgitation of the training manual's contents. If anything, it would probably confirm him in his decision to submit citations on the conduct of both men. They must have known at the outset, at least in their innermost hearts, that they had put their lives in a balance weighted against them; the fact that they would have been equally at hazard if no-one had agreed to do the work—orders apart—was beside the point. Their bravery deserved recognition. Hildegras's lapse had merely afforded him an opportunity to take a fresh grip on general discipline. There was no question of an inquiry, still less of a court-martial; of which, he thought ruefully, the damned little schemer must be fully aware. That misleading baby-blue gaze. However . . .

All-but-becalmed, the crowded Arab dhow was crossing from Reunion to Tamatave, or so her sombre-featured master averred in support of a few grubby papers. At first regarding the quaint vessel with mild curiosity, Altmann was suddenly assailed by a rush of *deja-vu*, the more dismaying for the contrast in sea and weather conditions and the time of day with the storm-threatening darkness of the Atlantic night. Reflected in the glassy calm ruffled in patches by the play of random draughts, the dhow's exotic rig stood against the sky's yellow glare like a pair of sharks' dorsal fins, dark in silhouette, a negative image of the glimmer of white that had betrayed the schooner's presence in the surrounding gloom, and Altmann experienced a *frisson* of foreboding that moved him to impatience. The insistence of the dhow's master on a seeming form of courtesy added to his sense of the surreal, even the supernatural, leading him to the fringes of anger he controlled only with an effort It wasn't helped by Schreiber's affectation of *insouciance*.

Amongst the mixed cargo of dates, salt, rice, cooking stones, tinned milk, dried fish and other items of domestic consumption was a consignment of sugar-cane. The master presented Altmann with a large bundle in the interests of international goodwill, presumably under the impression—thanks to Schreiber's and Lange's best English and a white ensign produced from a selection of foreign flags supplied to boats as a vague provision against possible contingencies—that the boat was British. Schreiber's guess that the banner-like red flag, bearing Arabic characters in white, hanging languidly from the dhow's mizen peak, denoted a sheikhdom was confirmed by the master's assertion that his ship was registered at the British-protected port of Kuwait. Accordingly, at Schreiber's tactful suggestion—"Very good syntax, *Kapitän*, but the accent . . . Just a touch too—um—*pronounced*, you know?"—Altmann's part was confined to an enigmatic presence on the bridge, bareheaded and white-shirted, his act consisting of an ambiguous wave in acknowledgment of the gift while regretting his decision to inject a trace of confusion into whatever the Allied authorities knew, or thought they knew, about u-boat activity in the region rather than another sinking of negligible tonnage. The dhow was hardly worth the expenditure of ammunition, and besides, its destruction might introduce complications into any post-war rapport between an oil-dependent *Reich* and Arab governments, even under German colonial aegis. Apart from the Iranian fields, Altmann knew of the oil discoveries in areas extending along the southern rim of the Persian Gulf. Nor could he seek refuge from his conscience in the presence of Jews—far from it, though he was aware of the Arab's semitic extraction: he was also aware of the age-old enmity between Muslim and Jew which might prove to be of practical use to a post-war *Reich*. Taken all round, he concluded, the quicker he completed his business with the dhow the better, and he was conscious of a wave of relief as he turned from the ghosting vessel to make off at full speed into a declining sun.

The small freighter he overtook in the starlight came as something of a surprise. Also southbound, she seemed unconcerned about the chance of attack, keeping a steady course at a steady seven knots trailing a darker banner across the night sky. Remaining on the surface, Altmann gave the attack to Schreiber. Of the two torpedoes fired, the first passed beneath the target and inexplicably exploded about half a kilometre ahead of her in a spectacular column of pink—and yellow-tinted water and foam. The ship's reaction was to sound her steam-whistle, an asthmatic bleat of protest, as she took a sharp turn to port that disconcerted Schreiber by threatening collision. He followed his hasty release of the second torpedo with an order to turn away, and the boat's head had barely begun to swing when the torpedo struck directly under the target's stern only some three hundred metres away. The explosive thud followed by a short-lived flickering eruption signalled the ship's loss of motive power and she began settling by the stern almost before her forward way had fallen off. The steam-whistle's bleating was succeeded by a boiler blow-off as accompaniment to the crew's abandonment of their ship in the threatening dazzle of the u-boat's searchlight. Two boats got clear before the still-roaring victim rolled on her side and went down stern-first to leave them bobbing in the disturbed water in a sudden silence that made Altmann glance round the horizon almost guiltily, as if the din might have aroused the curiosity of some idling warship. Schreiber's orders to helm and engines broke in on his abstraction, and the first officer asked what to do about the boats. "This one's full of blacks," he added in a tone of mild interest. "Look at those teeth!"

As the boat drifted past close along the port side Altmann called down to the little party of what looked like Africans, their flashing eyes and teeth almost comically prominent against the dark shape of their boat and the sea about it as they returned his scrutiny, shielding their eyes from the play of torch-beams. No, no officers with them, said one in resonant accents that carried effortlessly across the gap. They were all in the second boat. White officers, maybe three; he thought a fourth had gone missing, maybe a fifth.

The second boat contained several more Africans besides three white men. One, at the tiller, said he was the master, his white companions the mate and second engineer.

"And the others, captain?" Altmann was suddenly conscious of his accent, remembering, irritably, Schreiber's remark at the meeting with the dhow. He couldn't sound *that* bad, surely? Apparently not, because the man calling himself the master answered: two. The radio operator had disappeared in the confusion. He did not know where he had got to, and no, he had not been on watch. Perhaps he was swimming somewhere nearby. The chief engineer had last been seen in the engine-room; probably gone down with the ship.

"—Don't you give anyone a bloody warning, captain?" he ended, and the clipped, flat accents Altmann detected were tinged with anger. "My ship wasn't armed, man! Five minutes would've been enough, for Christ's sake! You've lost me two men, apart from Sparks and the chief. I'd've stopped if you'd given me a bloody chance!"

Staring back, Altmann heard the angry words with a pang of discomfort, and sudden recollection of *Empire Formby*'s boat. And Danny—Danny who was it? O-something. Noted in his private journal;

some incomprehensible name. *Yer just killed me fuckin' kid brother, yer fuckin' murderin' Nazi fuckin' scum!* And then *Le capitaine—dead! You 'ear? You 'ave killed 'im!*

Damn! Altmann did not realise he had sworn aloud until Schreiber, standing beside him, turned and said, "*Kapitän?*"

Catching his breath Altmann shook his head. "Nothing—nothing..." He called back to the boat, "What ship, captain? And cargo?"

Appearing to shake his head—impatiently, in frustration: Altmann couldn't tell—the master called back, "*Blesbok.* South African. Reunion to Durban. Copra and rum."

"Your gross tonnage?"

"Three thousand eight hundred."

In the short ensuing silence the master sat, his eyes on the man on the u-boat's bridge, seeming to await the next move, resigned, perhaps, to some further outrage. The boat heaved and rolled in the slight sea, and her occupants swayed in time with the movement, three of the faces pale in the starlight. For a moment undecided what his next move should be, Altmann finally shook himself free of the thrall into which the exchange had plunged him and asked if anyone was hurt.

"Apart from the dead ones, a few bruises—nothing worse, no thanks to you, man!"

Still the impotent anger in the flat accents, and Altmann felt a vague sense of self-recrimination, faintly astonished by it and then, abruptly, angry himself. What was this man trying to do—make him feel as if he had committed a crime? He talked as if he were the victim of a road accident, blaming the other for slipshod driving; or a botched street-robbery. It was ridiculous! These exchanges with the enemy were an absurd concession to a conceit that had no place in the theatre of war: Germany had issued due warning of her intentions. Shipping that continued its daily occasions regardless had only itself to blame for the consequences, and he owed these people nothing outside the rules of engagement—which, had they been followed to the letter, would have obviated this fruitless confrontation. He would have been within his rights to have hit the ship with another eel before departing unannounced. All he needed for recording purposes were the position of the sinking, the type of vessel, and her tonnage, estimated if necessary. Anything in addition was mere decoration. Mere sentimentality, once again. Altmann took a breath. All right—conceit. And in it he found, as if discovering something unpleasant under a stone, a weakness he recognised as his own; a kind of distorted satisfaction in getting out of the situation more than was absolutely necessary, something to satisfy a kind of vanity, by which he could lay claim to some form of humanity in an otherwise barbaric act; by which he could demonstrate, to his officers and crew as much as to the senior officers concerned, the qualities that would show him in a humane light where they would otherwise be invisible in the shadow of—what? Efficiency? Duty? But whatever it was, it was a point of war. There was no personal animosity towards the enemy when met face to face like this—and by the same token, no obligation. His conceit was a sham: in war both humanity and barbarity were superfluous, concepts which could apply only in conditions of general peace. War being in itself a barbaric process his actions in its execution could not be distinguished as such; equally, humanity could not be claimed. His duty was to sink shipping. It was as simple as that. Why complicate the matter? But at the back of his mind he knew the answer, knew it in the shape of the overloaded boats in the Atlantic night, the man standing up to call upon God to bless him—in irony, had it been? Or in genuine sentiment? Irony, surely! And perhaps with better effect than he had intended, whoever he was—or had been. Dead now; a casualty of war: nothing else. He, Altmann, had done nothing more than to prosecute the war in which he was playing a legitimate part, and for which, as it had turned out, he had been properly recognised by a grateful Fatherland. He was not to be blamed for his actions. Not always commended, perhaps, but never *blamed* . . .

Suddenly weary of the whole thing he decided to make an end, and leant over the rail again. "You know where you are—yes? The coast is only about ten miles to the west. Perhaps you will find your radio man here somewhere . . ." He broke off and glanced at Schreiber, looking on in silence. The first officer shrugged and gestured non-committally. Turning back, Altmann finished with "Good luck, captain!" then, after a brief examination of the surrounding night he bent over the control-room voice-pipe. "Group up—half ahead both engines . . . Steady as she goes, the helm. Stand down action stations. Second watch-officer to the bridge." With the acknowledgment from below came something from the darkness overside, an echo of someone's cry, and to his query Schreiber replied, "The ship's captain—he says good luck to us also, *Kapitän*—"

"A good loser, eh, *Einswo?*"

"—and he hopes we'll need it."

Altmann caught Schreiber's eye. "And a humorist . . . Well—we'll see. It'll be a bad day when we have to count on luck for our survival, eh?"

Schreiber chuckled. "Let's hope better than just survival, *Kapitän*."

Altmann grunted, then remembered. "You know something about cargoes, *Einswo*—what's *copra*?"

"Ah!" Schreiber hesitated. "Dried coconut, I believe—"

"What—the stuff used in cakes and sweets?" Altmann's words betrayed astonishment: a ship-load of something usually to be found in a little packet in the pantry struck him as a gross departure from normality. "Is that man trying to be funny?"

"No, *Kapitän*—it's quite a common cargo from these parts. Only the best is for cakes. The usual kind is low-grade, used for making soap, I think. Oil, anyway. And cattle-feed."

"Soap!" Altmann nodded sagely. "Ah—I see. More valuable than usual in wartime—especially in u-boats, eh?"

"If we only had the water to go with it, *Kapitän*!"

Altmann studied his first officer's dimly-discernible features for a moment, then patted his shoulder. "Not much longer, now, *Einswo*—whatever the schedule, the eels we have left will only allow us a couple more targets. No point in hanging about afterwards—hot baths and as much soap as you like a month or so from now."

Shaken gently awake by a solemn-faced Palmgren presenting a message-pad, Altmann peered blearily at the carefully-drafted capitals. Palmgren's neatness was unshakable. It took a few moments for the message to register, and when it did he felt a flush of relief, as if a weight had been lifted from his mind, as if he had reached the end of a long and bitter journey the destination of which had never been certain, but was now before him, all but within reach. He sat up and read the message again, and the surge of relief suddenly drained away. Anti-climax; nothing had changed; the patrol continued; his responsibilities remained as before. There were five torpedoes left, and a rendezvous to make with the u-boat at this moment somewhere in these waters, on her way to the unmarked spot in the distant seas that were the new battleground. The war continued, unaffected by his momentary elation, its demands as before.

"Congratulations, *Herr Kapitän*," Palmgren hissed, beaming.

Altmann stared at him and nodded. "Thanks, *Zweiter* . . . I'd better make an announcement."

Over the p.a. he read out the decoded first part of the message. Terse and to the point, it evoked general elation. It was not, he said, so much he who was being honoured by the highest military award the *Dritte Reich* had to offer, and the first so honoured in the *Kriegsmarine*—and certainly in the *U-Bootwaffe* (cheering throughout the boat)—but his officers and men, who were now also on their way to distinction as the crew which had carried out the longest patrol on record, in any submarine service at any time since the craft's first appearance on the high seas (more cheering). He thanked them all for their resolute, cheerful execution of their various duties, their high standard of discipline and professional conduct, and for being exceptional shipmates, of both himself and each other in an honourable tradition; all this in conditions that would have tested lesser men beyond their breaking-point. And wishing them further success during the remainder of the patrol, followed by a safe arrival home, "—which, of course, is in your hands—", he paused before concluding with a *Heil Hitler* that sent an almost visible stiffening of backs through the boat, as Altmann felt. And he also felt something else, something that lay beneath the outward mantle of grim satisfaction like a patch of corrosion beneath a coat of paint, something that seemed to be feeding on itself, expanding and penetrating and degrading, and threatening to destroy the fabric of integrity, of justification and professional confirmation he had been at such pains to construct; not merely in his own interests but also in those of the people among whom he had found a like frame of mind and spirit, a common aspiration, a shared goal—and, among the closest of them, a mutual regard and honourable obligation. It was crystallised in a trust tempered and hardened by war's peculiar conditions, rendered proof against all the forces that bear on any material, but in this case only to further prove its resilience. Except against one thing—this hidden debility, this creeping rot, which would, in the end, destroy the entire fabric, break through the outer mantle, expose to view the shameful reality, the moment's weakness—of pride, hubris, zeal, arrogance, call it what you will—that had sown the germ of corrosion. That it might have been similarly sown among the others with him that night was beside the point, and not at all certain, for the responsibility had been his, and the authority, by which his conscience stood for all. The others were proof against the corrosion in their adherence to duty; in their submission to the orders and judgment of superiors. The blame, if there was any, was not theirs to shoulder, though the honour—as in the present situation, Altmann reflected with a vague sense of grievance—was theirs to share, and justly so. And now this: an accolade, and with it a general expression of approval, among men who, made aware of the concealed corruption, would be justified in withdrawing their regard, even in feeling his shame as their own, and damning him accordingly. Feeling the prickle of sweat at his temples, and the benevolent regard of all within view in the cramped confines of the control-room, he gathered himself with an effort and announced an issue of schnapps to all hands. He acknowledged their congratulations with self-effacing rebuttal, and drank their healths in orange-juice. If anyone on board was left with his own teeth in an outbreak of scurvy, he said, it would be him: abstinence had its rewards (general laughter). What he did not mention, mainly because it meant nothing to anyone but himself, was that the message's second part, restricted to the commander's sole attention, to be deciphered in person, conveyed the C-in-C's rescindment of the reprimand imposed for his earlier command's sinking at the berth. It came as a relief of more intense, and mixed, emotional impact than he would have expected, and it took several minutes for him to be certain of full control of his outward composure before emerging from his closet.

"That's it, then!" Falke threw back the contents of his mug, mark of the commander's award of the whole menu—Knight's Cross with cabbage-leaves, knives & forks and—the crowning glory—diamonds. "Nothing else left to go for."

"So?" responded Siebert. "What's he supposed to do—retire?"

"In effect, yes." Falke peered into his empty mug and sucked his teeth. "No more medals, and *Korvettenkapitänen* aren't usually left in command of u-boats for long."

"He could start again."

"Start again? What—get himself demoted?"

"No, no! I mean the medals. Like the British. You get a—a *bar* to things like the Distinguished Service Medal—"

"Cross. Officers get crosses, not medals. Medals are for the peasantry, you know. Different sort of gallantry; bargain-basement stuff."

Siebert stared at Falke and glanced round at Schmidt and Hille with a shrug. "At least they get something . . . But what I mean is, he could just start totting up another tonnage score for a second helping. The first Knight's Cross and bar—"

"Clasp. They call it a clasp. When you get it a second time . . . Some of them start collections."

"The sort we don't want running this show," said Hille. "These keen types can be a bit trying."

"Rather sail with one than bump into one," said Falke. "And it's the man, not the medal."

"Why don't you tell him that?" said Siebert. "I can't help thinking he thinks it's the medal. He'll probably wear it in bed."

"Come on, Ernst," said Schmidt, punching his shoulder. "He's not that bad, for an officer. I can think of one or two who'd give you plenty of reason for moaning. Your problem's the climate. Heat's getting to you, that's all."

Falke concurred. "You're too hard on him, *Putsi!* He's kept us afloat—more or less—so far, not bad when you look at the figures. We don't get the diamonds, but here we are still, with a tot of schnapps—good stuff, too; obviously brought along in hopes if not deadly intent—and a fair chance of getting home." He smiled lopsidedly at his listeners. "He'll bust a gut to get back in one piece, just to lay hands on the actual glassware. Be thankful for a man's vanity, Ernst my lad. It'll keep *your* hide intact!"

The rendezvous with the other boat turned out to be a fraught affair and another cause of irritation. Altmann hated bungled plans and the usual consequence of added peril. Without the code keys he'd have been deaf and mute, ending the patrol in the dark with the likelihood of a blunder for lack of up-to-date information. The signal from Headquarters gave a position for the meeting with a Lorient-based boat commanded by *Kapitänleutnant* Öhlschläger, a name unfamiliar to him. Most of them were unfamiliar now: as at the *Mutterhaus*, it was difficult to remember the names of the lesser beings who followed, in contrast to those who had gone before, of whom even the undistinguished could be recalled without much effort. And in present conditions the chances of getting to know, or know of, the newcomers were slimmer than they had been. They came and went with a frequency unremarked bar entries in flotilla records.

Arrived at the rendezvous, Altmann found himself alone at the appointed time, but a reluctant decision to call up Öhlschläger was anticipated by a signal requesting another rendezvous farther west. He had been delayed by a chase and sinking off the Cape. He cast himself in a more favourable light in Altmann's eyes by suggesting the new position as a bearing and range from the original, rather than the grid-coded latitude and longitude, by which, if overheard and deciphered, an enemy attack could have been mounted. Eight hours later they met, in boisterous seas and a long, deep swell that made transfer of the precious items an anxious proceeding, but accomplished without incident. After exchanging the usual greetings and courtesies, Öhlschläger departed to the north and east while Altmann set a course into the Moçambique Channel with the intention of combing the African coast as far north as Mombasa. If he got that far without first expending his remaining torpedoes he would have to turn back and begin the homeward passage: apart from the dwindling and deteriorating provisions, fuel dictated the limit of the patrol, and there were no more replenishment tankers at hand. Nor was he inclined to attempt another *British Prowess* escapade, downed Catalina notwithstanding.

Not three hours after the rendezvous Schwebke picked up a signal from Öhlschläger: under attack by aircraft, damaged and unable to submerge, and giving his grid position which, Altmann noted with irritation, negated the man's previous precaution by risking the enemy's making a direct reference to the boat's known position as a key to the grid code. But it didn't explain the aircraft's presence in the first place. And it was too far away for him to be able to do anything constructive, if that were a viable definition. Instead, he listened to successive signals repeating the first—Öhlschläger seemed to be under attack by more than one plane, using bombs. Altmann stopped the engines and the thin bleeps of the Morse were the only sounds in the boat as all hands paused to listen. After the signal's third repeat the wireless joined the general silence, which Altmann cut short with orders to resume the passage. He wondered what tonnage Öhlschläger had logged to date; perhaps enough to balance his boat's, though of course the figures were not directly equivalent: the point of balance lay well along the beam towards the target. Possibly—as in the North Atlantic—it no longer even existed. It was a nice calculation Altmann preferred not to attempt, at least for the present: enough, he felt, that he had managed, so far, to achieve some degree of balance on his own account, even to the extent of keeping it tilted in his favour.

Off the Portuguese port of Beira an unescorted freighter of about five thousand tons turned north at just less than eight knots to follow an erratic course weaving to and fro across the territorial line. Submerged and falling back in the remaining daylight hours Altmann surfaced after sunset and caught up with her some four hours later, a dark shape against the skyline showing no lights, which settled the point, and he fired the remaining stern torpedo. It missed, but exploded only metres beyond, throwing the ship into a panic. To the amazement of everyone on the boat's bridge she made a heeling turn to port and headed straight for the beach through heavy surf which, he decided, obviated the need for further action. Instead, they watched as the freighter became ever less distinct against the coastline, visible chiefly by her propeller-wash, until, viewed through the range-finding glasses, she appeared to have stopped among breakers a short way off the beach. Schreiber voiced the obvious conclusion, everyone agreed, and Altmann ordered the resumption of their northward course after rejecting the idea of a gun action in neutral waters. He puzzled for some time over the form of log entry to cover the event, ending it with the baldly truthful comment *Unable to confirm vessel's loss*. Someone might decide that salvage was worthwhile and practicable—in which case, he mused, the fortune of war might bring her into his sights for a more successful second shot. The encounter left him with four torpedoes.

The strident tones of the p.a. cut in on Schreiber's impromptu jazz-club session. He swore as Hildegras, scrambling to his feet, bumped the gramophone and the needle zipped ruinously across Paul Whiteman's *Rhapsody in Blue*. The midshipman's horrified apology was drowned in a repeat of the call from Palmgren, keeping the bridge-watch.

"*Attention! Attention! Captain to the bridge! Captain to the bridge! Enemy units in sight! Enemy units in sight!*"

"*Zweiter*—stuck in a groove," grunted Benedict, rising to allow Altmann a clear passage to the control-room. "Or is he just concerned for the hard of hearing?"

In the boat the temperature stood at a just-bearable forty-five degrees, higher in the engine-room, where the watch had been reduced to two men in one-hour stretches. Already two *Dieselmaschinisten*—Siebert and Müller—and an *Elektromaschinist*—one Fink—had succumbed, passing out on the footplates, Fink injuring himself during an accompanying convulsion that moved Altmann to lecture the boat's company on aspects of discipline affecting their health. Far from being a matter for sympathy, he had told them, heat exhaustion could be logged as self-inflicted injury apart from its causing others extra work. "We're supplied with salt tablets, to be taken at every meal

271

without fail. That's an order, not a suggestion. They're more important than water, believe it or not, and if anyone else follows these smart fellows in their irresponsible attitude towards their own survival I'll ensure they get their wish with a transfer to the eastern front. And while they're waiting the doctor will make sure they take their tablets. Think of your shipmates even if you don't value your own lives!" He had congratulated himself on keeping the irritation he'd felt out of his tone. Some of the men behaved like children, a damned liability. He did not like punishing them, but he would carry out his duty with the impartial rigour he knew could not be relaxed; and the more trying the conditions the more vital it was to the boat's survival, let alone the patrol's success—which, he reminded himself, could not be taken for granted even at this stage: two hundred and sixty-odd thousand tons of enemy shipping to his name so far, and with four torpedoes remaining he stood some chance—firing-pistols permitting—of adding perhaps another twenty thousand to a total that would eclipse Kretschmer's record. It would confirm the diamonds beyond question, and the extra pay that came with them—plus likely promotion. It would also assure him of the toe-hold ashore hinted at by von Lohmeyer, which would assuage Ursula's anxiety, and his own about her and the girls. It might even, by removing him from the malignantly-evocative surroundings of the boat, especially of its bridge, have some effect on the phantoms. That, above all, would be relief of an order reducing diamonds and promotion to mere baubles.

Altmann's thoughts spooled through these frames as he waited at the foot of the ladder for the descent of the men who had been taking their turn in the fresh air on deck, then mounted to the midday sunlight. From a sky of pale-blue porcelain it glinted on the vista of indigo levees rolling from one horizon to the other, the channel's undress tropical outfit, windless apart from the ten-knot breeze of the boat's forward way. His shirt cooled as the sweat evaporated—blessed benison!—and he gulped at the salt-laden air as Palmgren pointed ahead and a few degrees to starboard, handing him the bridge binoculars. Two mastheads, he said. One big ship, or two smaller ones in company. No smoke.

Picking them out in the magnified field of view Altmann congratulated the watch on their vigilance. The masts were barely hairline cracks at the sky's rim; but—"You said *enemy* units, *Zweiter*. How can you tell?"

"What else would they be around here, *Kapitän*? They can't be a supply-ship or an auxiliary, and the last warship was the *Scheer*—us apart—"

"M-hm . . . What about our little yellow friends, though?"

Palmgren looked stunned, then snapped his fingers and sucked his teeth. "Japs! Of course—it never occurred to me, *Herr Kapitän!*"

Altmann smiled briefly. "Just a thought. Hardly likely, or we'd have had a signal. As it is, you're probably right—and merchant, not naval." Someone up here had hawk's eyes, he thought; then, catching his breath with a rush of apprehension, he handed back the glasses and snapped, "Action stations, *Zweiter*—alarm dive! Jump to it!" Hawk's eyes, maybe, but that ship or ships over there might have better: radar! In these conditions it would pick him up as clearly as a pyramid in the desert: *damn!* His own fault for chancing a while on the surface for the sake of bodily comfort as much as the battery-state. Slipping down the ladder in a tepid cascade after Palmgren and his lookouts he ordered periscope depth but found the viewpoint too low to see anything.

"We'll keep on this course, *Einswo*. Have the tubes ready. I'll attack anything above, say, five thousand tons. Give it another thirty minutes, and we'll see." To Benedict he said, "Stay at this depth, Herbert—I'll have a peep every few minutes."

Acknowledging the order, Schreiber passed the word on, and turned back at a tap on the shoulder. *"Herr Kapitän?"*

Altmann held the first officer's gaze with a quizzical look. "We've time to kill, *Einswo*—how about a little—what d'you call it?—*mood music*, eh?"

Schreiber hesitated before switching on a grin and nodding. "Have you a preference, *Kapitän*—big band, quartet, sextet—?"

Altmann punched Schreiber's shoulder. "Is it so long, *maestro*? Keep your cacophonies for the Yanks when they need cheering up! In the bottom drawer of my locker—anything of the *Ring*, eh?—Not too obvious. No Valkyries." He paused, hesitating as a thought struck him, then he said, "No—not the *Ring*. Dig out the *Flying Dutchman*. Haven't played it for a while, have we?"

Concealing his surprise, Schreiber shook his head. "No, *Kapitän* . . . Not since early last patrol."

"So—now's the moment! Let's have some company in our quest!"

Company? thought Schreiber. I hope not. Not that sort, anyway. We've enough on our hands without chasing a ghost about the ocean. Or being chased by one.

"No Valkyries?" queried Falke of anyone within hearing. "What's this—boar-hunting in the Black Forest? Still Wagner, I suppose—"

"For the benefit of the philistines among us," said Hille, nodding ambiguously at Falke, "Wagner—yes. We've heard it before, a while back; last patrol. *The Flying Dutchman*." Hille's father was a piano-tuner and failed concert pianist who had given piano lessons before the war.

"So now we sail under false colours—and an overture! To exactly what, I wonder?"

"Last sinking before packing up for home, I hope." Siebert sounded more hopeless than hopeful. Running with sweat, his face was coarse-complexioned, blotchy-red where others were tanned, and bore two painful-looking wens. "It's not asking for much—just to see a thermometer below boiling-point again!"

"Four eels left, *Putsi* . . ." Falke patted Siebert's shoulder consolingly. "Can't take them back with us. Not with a war on." Turning to Hille he went on, "Why this instead of Siegfried?—a Dutchman! Something we should know, *Musik-Meister*?"

Hille considered for a moment, brows knitted, then gave his listeners a brief resumé of Van der Decken's story. "—and so he's doomed to sail the waters off the Cape forever unless he can earn redemption through the purity of a woman's love." He paused. "For the patriots among us, if Wagner doesn't hit the right chord there's a German version of the story. Skipper name of von Falkenberg."

"So why did Wagner choose a damned Dutchman?"

"You'll have to ask him when you meet," said Hille dryly. "Falkenberg's patch is the North Sea. His ship's got no helm, and he spends his time playing dice with the devil."

Siebert said, "More in your line than the Dutchman, Klaus—"

"For his soul," added Hille. "Obviously cleaned out of cash. Ever played for souls, anyone?"

Falk worked a little finger vigorously round in his right ear, inspected it, and sniffed. "We're all doing that, right now. Been doing it since nineteen-thirty-nine. Who needs dice when we get depth-charges?" He grinned. "I might run a book on them."

They greeted this in silence apart from the evocative strains of woodwind and percussion, glancing uncertainly round at one another,

274

and Falke added, "Sometimes I wonder about our commander's motives, you know. What it is making him tick—apart from duty to the Fatherland, of course. Can't fault him there—"

"Glory?" suggested Hille. "He's heading for the all-time tonnage record, if he hasn't already got it."

"You're a cynical little fellow on the quiet, Hille," said Falke with primitive irony. "But right enough. A woman's love's a bit of a sop compared to investment by the *Führer* as a hero of the *Reich*. And what woman, anyway?—he's already faithfully married, as he's let us all know in intimate detail. Unless he's overdoing the haloed husband to cover something more interesting—hanging a tail on some Frog tart, maybe—"

"Tart or Joan of Arc," said Siebert feelingly. "Who'd care if she could get him out of this before something nasty happens? What I'd give for a couple of weeks off Iceland!"

"Stuff that!" returned Falke warmly. "Without me, *Putsi*—that's a convenient memory you got there—"

"Investiture," said Hille, catching Falke's eye. "Anyway, she's not French. Norwegian."

Falke stared at him. "There is one?—You know her?"

"No—I mean in the opera. Van der Decken's redemption. It has to be the love of a Norwegian girl he knows. Forget the name, but he's allowed ashore every seven years to work on her."

"So . . ." Falke drew a breath and blew out his cheeks. "Dunno which I prefer, in the circumstances—maybe the Dutchman. Better odds. But I sense some serious psychological quirk in our commander. First he's killing some damn dragon, now he's looking for redemption—if we're lucky. Frankly, playing dice with the devil would fit this set-up better. Temperature's about right, for a start." He removed the strip of flannel hanging round his neck and mopped his brow, then wrung it out at arm's length. A few drops of sweat fell to the deck. "Look at that. Best part of a litre a day . . . Yes, *Korvettenkapitän* Altmann will bear watching."

"A nutter," muttered Siebert, rubbing red-rimmed eyes. "That's all we need."

"We're all nutters." Falke shrugged. "Certifiable nutters—what else in a service like the *U-Bootwaffe*? I mean, you can't call this way of fighting a war *sane*! But—" he sighed "—with his taste in music and choice of times to listen to it you'd have to suspect the skipper of something more than simple insanity. Look at his eyes—he never

275

sleeps! Nerves shot, maybe—music holds it all together at times of stress, like during an attack."

"So let's hope nothing busts the gramophone," said Hille.

XI

ARRIVAL alongside in a light drizzle beneath a post-dawn overcast was a sombre business in surroundings disfigured by war, buildings on both sides of the river huddled together as if ashamed of their disorderly state and apprehensive of the portents of daylight. Rows of windows revealing only the lightening clouds beyond had the appearance of cataracted eyes looking down upon the few inhabitants picking their way through the debris of the streets and quaysides at this early hour. Contemplating the scene, Altmann concluded that whether it was the US Eighth Air Force by day or the Tommies by night the enemy seemed to conduct his bombing half asleep; it was a dismaying prospect, and a pointer to the direction the war was taking. Closer at hand, beneath frowning brows of bomb- and shell-scored concrete, the pens, precisely-formed caves, extended a geometric welcome as the boat's mooring-parties heaved her onto the fenders of the outer jetty, brought to a berth for the first time in seven months. Altmann's tonnage total apart, the patrol's two hundred and nineteen days set a new record in the submarine's story, let alone that of the *U-Bootwaffe*; but the return was something of an anti-climax and, as Palmgren remarked, not a little disappointing, circumstances notwithstanding.

Amidst the general activity on the jetty a group stood apart looking on, two of its members in the uniform of senior naval officers, the third a small intense-looking man in a tan-coloured boiler-suit topped with the tarnished scrambled-egg of a senior officer's cap: Barkhorn. Behind them were parked a staff-car and an ambulance. There was no band, no cheering; there were no smiling girls, no flowers.

Breaking the silence of early morning with a clatter the brow dropped into place as a murmur of voices drifted aft from the forward torpedo hatch, where Schreiber's inert form was being manhandled from below strapped into a stretcher. His head and eyes were bandaged. He was still in coma. First to board was Barkhorn, who hauled himself onto the bridge in his monkey-like fashion to shake Altmann's hand and grunt a welcome and an expression of general sympathy before dropping through the hatch in search of Benedict. On his heels over the brow hurried four medical orderlies to take over from the boat's stretcher-party. Altmann waved them forward, and watched as they carried Schreiber to the ambulance attended by a hen-like Lange, whose prognosis offered little hope of the first officer's post-war resumption of his pursuit of immoral women passengers; or of much else. Then, with a nod to Palmgren, he descended from the bridge and followed. On the quayside he was greeted by the two leather-coated officers, von Lohmeyer accompanied by a *Kapitän zur See*, a man of medium height and build with a face that suggested fewer years than its cold expression sought to convey. Returning Altmann's salute von Lohmeyer introduced him: Max Reinhard, *Führer der U-Boot* for the western area, second only to Dönitz himself, bar Godt in his broader rôle. Both men shook Altmann's hand, von Lohmeyer momentarily disconcerting him with a tight-lipped smile hinting at suppressed disquiet, while his companion, far from displaying any evidence of sympathetic interest, was cool in a way that seemed to acknowledge the shared experience of operational command with some distaste. It was as if, thought Altmann, he were affronted by the sea-weary state of the officer before him; as if the crumpled, mouldy uniform, the amateurishly-trimmed beard and over-long hair, and—the breeze being in the direction it was—the undeniable bodily stink that was the u-boat's sardonic gift, had been deliberately staged to contrast with and in some way mock the senior man's immaculate turn-out.

One of those, thought Altmann, disappointed; he'd heard of Reinhard, of course: a gold-plated desk-jockey whose war had been transferred from the Atlantic to paper seas by skilful selection of friends. He had held brief command, barely long enough to loose off a handful of torpedoes as his qualification for promotion and the desk job. Perhaps, mused Altmann drily, to remove him from the vicinity of other boats as a hazard. He had been unable to understand Reinhard's function from the time he had first heard of it. His posting was superfluous: Dönitz and Godt between them attended to all the *U-Bootwaffe*'s practical requirements. Yes, one of those. The selection process turned one up every so often; they survived by some supernatural means to be moved into a corner from where they could do as little harm as possible to their own side, and this one was no exception. He could not be shuffled off into some obscure dead-end, did not commit convenient enormities of the kind that offered a pretext for professional extinction, was proof against higher-ranking disapproval. Despite himself, Altmann regarded the senior man with curiosity, and even the unimaginative von Lohmeyer seemed to be aware of the embarrassing quality of the meeting. Altmann was amused by that.

"Welcome home, Altmann—and congratulations!" Reinhard's words sounded forced. They rattled like stones in a rusty tin; perhaps, thought Altmann, meant to convey authority and decision. He nodded.

"Thank you, *Herr Kapitän*—" He glanced at the ambulance, into which the orderlies were loading their burden in silence. As Lange followed it inside they closed the doors noiselessly and drove off with a whine of worn gears. Good luck, *Einswo*, he thought; let's hope they can do something better for you than a white stick. An immoral heiress would be the answer, but your chances in that direction are less than slim. Perhaps a—but perhaps it will be enough just to keep your life, for whatever it'll be worth . . .

Reinhard went on, "But a nasty business, the plane surprising you like that."

Altmann did not miss the edge of censure in the tone. As if he'd been lax in allowing himself to be jumped.

"Yes, *Herr Kapitän*—but it could have been worse. The flak-tug saw it off. My guns wouldn't have been enough. Those Liberators can take a lot of punishment. His aim wasn't good, but another run would probably have settled things. As it is . . ."

Altmann turned to cast a narrow gaze over what could be seen of the boat above quay-level. The deck-casing and bridge wore the rusty-green cloak of extended sea-time, a cloak bearing the tell-tale marks of battle in splashes of bright metal, and in places the dark rents of heavy machine-gun strikes. The 20mm flak gun hung awry on its mounting. The partly-raised attack-periscope, to which ran the hoists of little white pennants denoting the patrol's kills, appeared slightly out of the vertical above a slash of gleaming metal and slight buckle in the housing at shoulder-height. A heavy machine-gun or cannon round had jammed it firmly in position. And in his mind's eye Altmann could see more: the smashed gauges and light-fittings in the boat's compartments; the starboard propeller-shaft, discoloured where it had run hot in the vicinity of the stern-gland and intermediate bearings, bent by a near-miss. Like a clap of thunder the Liberator had leaped on them out of the clouded darkness shortly after their meeting with the flak-tug off the estuary at Point Hand. Neither Metox nor its ineffective substitute, had either been used, could have detected the approach of a radar-equipped enemy, and it was clear, more so in poor weather conditions, that these night-flying aircraft were. Also using a floodlight switched on at the last moment, the Liberator had made two runs over the boat and her escort, dropping a total of four depth-charges or bombs before making off, either out of bombs or in trouble. There had been no question of diving in the shallow estuarine waters, leaving Altmann no option but to fight it out in company with the tug, which might have scored conclusive hits on the aircraft before it could complete its attack. Sundry cuts and bruises among the others apart, Schreiber, on the bridge, had been hit by splinters from the .50 bullet-strikes on the bulwarks as Knecht had been flung to the deck by several hits on the flak-gun, sustaining a few cuts and a broken arm. Efficiently attended to by Lange, who later remarked on the strange fact that no-one had taken a direct hit, he had insisted on staying aboard to accompany the others in any ceremony that might precede the crew's dispersal on leave and harbour duties.

And there was the ensign. It hung in anonymous folds stirring uneasily in the light breeze and it was not immediately apparent, on the short ensign-staff, that it was at half-hoist. It seemed to Altmann an inadequate mark of general sentiment among the boat's crew at Hildegras's abrupt and—somehow, despite the circumstances—shocking death. It had been the only death of the patrol, and that it had taken the most hopeful and youthful of the boat's company, apart from his general popularity among both officers and men, had been the cause of a unanimous feeling of indignation—not at its direct source but at the casually random vindictiveness of fate; at its disinterested, irreversible decision. And its timing, displaying a capacity for irony that humiliated as it angered. Some had even expressed a willingness to have taken his place, though *Maschinistensmaat* Falke's reaction to such extremes had been scepticism at their timing.

"I'm next, Schmidt, *mon brave*—now's your chance. Just smarten up a bit and you can have the one with my name on it absolutely free of charge. You've got until we cross the Bay, by my calculations."

"What—til the next gutful from a feathered shit-bag?" Which betrayed Schmidt's fear: reference to Falke's little accident off the Cape was an attempt to disregard the less amusing implication of his offer—that anything with his name on it in any sort of action would also have everyone else's, since his station was the diesel motor-room. There would be no question of trading fates.

But Falke had come through without a scratch, and anyway, Schmidt had refused his offer, grumbling that people like the *Maschinistensmaat* were incapable of a properly serious view of any of life's injustices. Falke had agreed. To take any of it seriously, he said, led only to tears. It had not been designed for the serious approach.

"What about this damned war?"

"A joke, *Putsi*. A bad one, I grant you, but a joke."

"You're crazy."

"Now there you got a point, but on its own it's not enough to cut me out from the crowd."

The masts to which Palmgren had called Altmann's attention had been those of a single ship, a merchantman of nine thousand tons and a target Altmann could not afford to pass up. Moreover, she had been unescorted, relying instead on her speed, some sixteen knots by his calculations. And he'd had to make up his mind without delay: she would get away from him if he were obliged to spend much time at depth, even allowing for her occasional course alterations evidently following a nominal zig-zag. She was the British refrigerated liner *Clan Finlay*, a relatively new addition to the company's fleet at barely four and half years old. And she had been armed, with machine-guns on the bridge-wings and a single four-inch naval gun on the poop. Along with the gun had been a brave crew—foolish, in Altmann's view, but brave, and a waste, in the same way as Hildegras's end had been a waste. In his anger at the turn of events Altmann had felt that after the war the enemy's naval people should be held to account for arming these manifestly unwarlike ships, whether for self-defence or not: their non-combatant status was compromised and lives hazarded by their almost invariable—at least under the red ensign—penchant for taking on a better-armed assailant, with the inevitable result. They were the one type of armed surface-unit with which a surfaced u-boat could cross swords on more or less equal terms—even on advantageous terms, with her torpedoes—though not wholly risk-free. The defensively-armed merchantman should be the prime evidence of a war crime on the part of her own side. To give her warning, as to an unarmed target, was to take an unwarranted risk, notwithstanding the balance of force. She left the u-boat no choice but to attack from a threatened position, whether surfaced or submerged; which meant, inevitably, without warning. And Altmann had decided accordingly. She had been, after all, probably his last target and he had cautioned himself against carelessness in the savour of the moment. Faced with the reality of an approaching target he felt the reliability of all four remaining torpedoes slip deeper into doubt; there was sure to be at least one dud. So the likelihood of another target, save the high-risk kind reserved for the gun, was remote, and in any case after this one his remaining fuel would not allow further time on the hunt; he would have to turn for home. If he were left with an eel—two at best—he might get an opportunity to use it *en route*. Meanwhile, here was a near-certain kill, and a substantial final increment to his tonnage account.

In the absence of listening escorts he'd felt safe in ordering the broadcast of a piece of Wagner, and a work he'd been keeping for some suitable moment: his successive periscope orders as the target's range closed broke in on Van der Decken's orchestrated agonies, which in turn had disturbed his mental deliberations. Disconcerted, he could not put his finger on it, but something about the title had tempered the thrill of the soaring cadences with a twinge of dread, and he had surprised himself at the fluster with which he'd suppressed the play on words that suggested itself on an apparent impulse: from Schreiber he'd learned of the seaman's whimsy of stretching "Dutchman" to cover Germans. And with it a momentary appearance—actually less of an appearance than a presence, right there with him in the control-room—of the phantoms. For an instant he'd wavered, moved to consider warning the approaching ship, and he'd held to his decision only with a conscious effort. Every damn time, some shadow of that mid-Atlantic scene intruded, not visible, but palpable in a way he could not define, touching some normally passive sense with enough substance to distract his attention—demand it, fleetingly—as if exacting a toll, some kind of tribute to a restless quirk of memory that lay just beneath the surface of awareness, an irritant for which there was no unguent, no balm, save the pressing absorption of action.

Turning to run ahead of the merchantman had reduced the rate of approach and given him time to determine the base course, roughly north-east, presumably to round the northern tip of Madagascar for some destination to the eastward; India, perhaps, or an island like Mauritius or the Seychelles group, unless to the island itself in support of the Allied occupation. And he'd calculated the extended time as sufficient to put him in an attacking position at twilight, with his target in silhouette while he remained undetected to the darkening east. Undetected, that is, by eye; but as far as he could make out this merchantman, modern as she might be, was not fitted with radar. And it seemed that, as yet, few, if any, were: not such a small mercy.

He had fired the first torpedo at eight minutes past seven, zone time, at a range of eight hundred metres, followed by a second at the instant the first had struck, throwing up a yellow-flecked geyser abreast of the aftermost cargo-hatch. The second had struck farther forward than expected, at the break of the forecastle, presumably because the ship had slowed at the first strike. Stopping dead within three lengths, she had settled slowly by the stern. Lights had flickered about the midships accommodation, and boats had been launched with notable despatch. When Schwebke reported a distress signal Altmann, coldly furious, had ordered Palmgren and his gun-crew to open fire on the bridge, and the signalling had ceased at the first hit. Angered more by the stupidity of the gesture than by the chance of its giving away his position, Altmann had manoeuvred towards the boats to question, reprimand and warn the ship's master, with no intention of acting against him or his companions. In doing so he had closed the range to the burning ship to some six hundred metres, noting that she was settling fast, when the gun on her poop, already licked by the flames, had opened fire, stunning everyone on the boat's bridge and deck. Before Palmgren could bring his gun to bear two shells had burst nearby, one falling short and the second in mid-air after howling close overhead shortly following Altmann's order to fire the third torpedo. A dud, it had vanished into the night as Palmgren found the range and added to the inferno which had begun spreading to the sea's surface around the ship's stern. After its two rounds the ship's gun had fallen silent, and as the flames had engulfed it and the poop Palmgren ceased fire. By this time the scene was brilliantly illuminated, the ship's boats standing off in a group, pinkly etched against the gathering night beneath the black cloud rising among the stars, mopping them up like a dirty rag. As Altmann reached a hurried decision to save his last torpedo, Schreiber, moving about at the after end of the bridge, had exclaimed in alarm, calling to Altmann. Slumped at the opening to the flak-gun platform was a body, and the dark stains on the shirt and upturned face were blood, distinct from the shadows cast by the fire. It flowed viscously, blackly, ominously, and Altmann saw that the still form was Hildegras's. Scrambling onto the bridge a minute later Lange had pronounced him dead. Shell splinters, he said. One had severed an artery, another gone through the chest cavity. Evidently the second shell's air-burst, but Altmann had blamed

282

himself for giving the midshipman permission to quit his station at the plot after the third torpedo had been fired, acceding to his request to observe procedures on the bridge. He had barely arrived when the shell burst, its fragments catching him in an exposed position. It was the kind of timing that gave fate its reputation and low social standing.

But, Hildegras's death apart, Altmann's most lingering memory of that night, standing in relief from the fresco of impressions, was of Schreiber, by his side as he had exchanged words with the officer claiming to be the ship's first mate—"Master's stayed aboard, cap'n"—and driven to further anger by the pointless gesture. "*Damn* these stupid people! Do they *want* to die?" A staying hand had caught his arm, uncharacteristically and at some personal risk, and Schreiber had said urgently, "*Kapitän*—don't do it! Once in a war is enough! God will forgive a mistake, but not a second time, even in anger—!"

By which Altmann had been reminded, with a shock of dispelled self-delusion, that others beside himself were still in the company of phantoms; but not, quite certainly, of a shared sense of something he could not bring himself to regard as guilt. Whatever it was, its peculiar attentions were clearly reserved for him. Others—Schreiber, for instance—had seemingly reached some sort of accommodation with their demons; or had erected an effective redoubt.

More by way of relieving his fury—fused as it had been with something less definable and far less admissible in a return of the sense of an accusing presence—than as a necessary measure, Altmann had sent the fourth and last torpedo into the dying ship, and she had gone down within seconds, taking her master and her gun's crew—or their incinerated remains—with her. And presumably, in a chance parallel with the end of the *British Prowess* not far from this location, also those of the wireless operator and his equipment. Abstractedly, Altmann wondered whether he, too, had been drunk at the time: an occupational hazard, perhaps.

As he'd later reflected, *Clan Finlay* had been the most expensive kill of the patrol—in certain respects of the boat's whole commission to date, in fact. Next day, in a heat-hazed ocean as serene as an ornamental lake except for the startling explosion into flight of a shoal of flying-fish, Hildegras had been buried with as much propriety as Altmann had been able to allow while on the alert for searching aircraft or surface units. And from the midshipman's effects he had recovered the essay on the safe handling of small arms: impressed with

Hildegras's obviously painstaking work, he had an idea it would find a place somewhere among the training manuals produced by people less practically qualified than its terminally-experienced author.

Turning back to meet Reinhard's gaze Altmann caught a faintly inquiring expression—almost a look of curious sympathy—that flitted across the square-jawed face, gone as Altmann, surprised and vaguely disturbed, realised its nature. But the officer switched on a smile that just avoided a grimace as he nodded. "As it is, *Kapitän*, you've lived to tell the tale—and a tale Germany will be glad to hear. Of course the *Führer* will make the presentation in person—a few days' time—but meanwhile the Commander-in-Chief wishes to hear what you have to say. He sends his apologies for not being here to meet you—press of duty, of course—but *Kapitän* von Lohmeyer here will take you to his quarters immediately. The admiral's on his way from Paris by car; should be here—" Reinhard glanced at his watch "—in about half an hour." He cleared his throat. "And you're to have your officers and crew mustered at two this afternoon for the decoration ceremony, which will include the boat, exceptionally. Iron Cross First Class. A distinction. But her men have done well. Germany'll be proud of them; they're to be rewarded accordingly."

Von Lohmeyer nodded at Altmann in confirmation, and perhaps, puzzlingly, as a mark of encouragement, adding nothing to Reinhard's words. There was something aloof about the flotilla commandant, Altmann decided. An awkwardness, or unease, of manner. He was no Straubhals; had not the feel for men you'd expect in a u-boat officer. But he obviously made an effort, clumsily and without warmth. Perhaps he was shy; perhaps he nursed a grudge; perhaps he had personal troubles. Who could tell? War made strange selections, played incomprehensible tricks, picked and chose according to its own arbitrary, inconsistent practice, played its own choice of tune regardless of its patrons, who early lost their authority. Presumably von Lohmeyer was a good man in a position of heavy responsibility. Either that or he was endowed with the right professional connections. He was known to be a prominent Party member. It helped.

Drawing himself up Altmann acknowledged Reinhard's instruction—his order, in effect—with a curt nod. But after a pause he said, "I—my wife—" After the boat and her men, his chief concern was for Ursula and the girls. "I'd like to speak to her." The boat was safe, for the time being; in her commander's temporary absence Palmgren and Benedict between them could handle whatever further movements would be required, primarily, of course, her shift into the shelter of the pen.

And there had been mail. Uncle Karl's emphasis on morale included an efficient mail service, regarded, as he had made clear, as of prime importance, equal to that of plentiful food of good quality and leave as generous and regular as could be managed. In return he expected every last breath of effort from his crews, and, at least as far as Altmann had been aware so far, he had got it. There had been no flinching, no suggestion of backsliding, of seeking an easier path, plausible alternatives, excusing of failure. The *U-Bootwaffe* demanded all its acolytes had to give and more; and in return it furnished them with whatever recompense lay within its brief. It was, above all, an honourable service with a tradition of conspicuous bravery, and despite the obvious hazards—indeed, the actual casualties, proportionately higher than any other service except, perhaps, the armies on the eastern front—enjoyed a regard among Germany's sea-minded patriots that seemed to assure it of a continued supply of raw material, if not, in more recent times, invariably of ideal quality. Very few sought alternative postings, and Altmann was indisputably among the confirmed; but after a seven-month patrol in virtual isolation he was entitled, he felt, to ask for a concession. Even in face of higher authority's requirement. Uncle Karl could wait a few minutes. In the circumstances Altmann felt confident of impunity.

Again he thought he caught the fleeting look of something, some softening, in Reinhard's eyes, but the impression evaporated as it occurred, and the officer's reply confirmed the doubt. Not possible, he was afraid; the trunk lines were under repair after damage sustained in an air-raid the previous day. Reconnection was scheduled for ten that morning, not before. After that, of course, the service would be at Altmann's disposal. He inquired about the mail: they had received it, he trusted?

Together with several official communications and, somewhat unwelcome, an effusive declaration of congratulation from Ehrling (how, Altmann wondered, had *he* got to know of the patrol's activities?), there had been six letters from Ursula, one a month, the last dated three weeks before and sent in the wake of the others with no knowledge about her husband's movements beyond periodic official confirmation of his continued existence, not wholly to be believed. Her certain anguish in dependence on silence was well-concealed by the neat blue script, and her news was of family—their family—and her parents, still foolishly, or valiantly, sticking to their beleaguered fortress, already breached by the peripheral effects of turmoil; several near-misses had reduced the habitable part of the house to the ground floor and basement, from where her father conducted his affairs as defiantly as ever, turning out for duty with the local defence volunteers. At home the girls were well, and safe, and making good progress at school; and behaving with gratifying eagerness to please, becoming quite the demure young women who would surely break hearts one day, even as they showed a ready aptitude for domestic organisation and industry. He would be delighted with their progress, she knew; and they were so proud of their sailor father, and contained their impatience to see him again with such touching dignity, only occasionally allowed to slip. And of course she missed him; and longed for his return, and prayed for his safety. She lived only for his touch . . .

Altmann had had time only to glance at them; slipping them into his desk-drawer he had carried on with his immediate duties with a flush of renewed vigour, breathing purer air, seeing with a clearer eye, braced with a sharper awareness of the camaraderie among his men, enjoying their own revived spirits as they went about their various tasks, joking with them, sharing their boyish excitement—for in many respects, including years, they were still barely more than boys—at the prospect of home leave, even their philosophical resignation at the prospect of an inspection parade and presentation. And their apprehension, those who came from the cities that were among the enemy's chief bombing targets; they were to go on immediate leave, or as soon as transport could be arranged. The accumulated exhaustion of the months of unbroken sea duty seemed, at least while his attention was still required in the heightened activity of arrival, to have been swept aside to leave him with a feeling of light-headed elation mingled with a strange sense of detachment. He was experiencing a state of artificial vigour generated by nervous rather than normal bodily energy.

The sensation was heightened by the effect on his physical equilibrium of solid ground beneath his feet. He seemed to be walking on a partly-inflated air-mattress, which caused him some embarrassment: stumbling as he stepped from the brow to the quay, he cursed to himself at what he thought were the knowing stares of the onlookers. But it passed, swiftly overtaken by a feeling of deep contentment at the knowledge of Ursula's continued love for him, of her generosity of heart and spirit and the undimming wonder of her having accepted him for husband. At a time when most couples had slipped into comfortable familiarity—or, as happened, disastrous schism—he felt that Ursula shared his undiminished delight in their bond, which had, if anything, become firmer and more durable as the years had passed—and perhaps, as he suspected, because a large proportion had passed each of them separately from the other. The reunions had rekindled their passion, which had the power to blot out the spectres that accompanied him on each successive patrol. He realised she was a refuge not only from the oppressive weight of operational responsibility but also from sensations and sentiments over which he had no independent control, and which pressed in upon his perceptions with malign arrogance, threatening as they implored: their anguished, appalling intrusions could not follow him into the conscious light and warmth of Ursula's unfailing, confident support. And it was support of him not only as her husband and the father of her children, but also—except, shortly before his last departure, for her understandable lapse, from which she had almost immediately turned back—as a soldier of the German renaissance, a faithful servant of the great *Reich* that would ultimately triumph over the forces of a morally- and racially-degenerate world-threatening alliance. Above all, she understood the crucial part played by the woman in the moulding and consummation of a virile, confident and pre-eminent nation, having its moral base firmly set in the principles of the mentally and bodily healthy—and racially pure—family. At least, that was the impression she gave, convincingly; and he had never deliberately sought to test it.

The meeting hardly ranked as an interview. Dönitz's manner was informal to the point of friendliness, and his first words were to invite Altmann to be seated, indicating a comfortable armchair as von Lohmeyer excused himself having, he said, pressing matters to attend to. Still in his sea rig, Altmann felt scruffy and out of order, but Dönitz exhibited a warmth and charm that was as unexpected as it was rare, obviously seeking to put his subordinate at ease, presumably in recognition of the success of his patrol and to substantiate approval of his conduct, which, he confided, was to be fittingly rewarded with a suitable shore posting and further promotion. Altmann was to take command of the Twenty-Second U-Flotilla at Memel. An officers' training unit. Striving to conceal his disappointment, he listened with less than enthusiasm to Dönitz's sales pitch as, remaining on his feet, the admiral paced slowly to and fro. It seemed to be a way of relieving an inexpressible tension.

"You may not think it equal to an operational posting, Altmann, but believe me, it's among the most vital to the success of the u-boat effort." The fine-drawn features were taut with sincerity, and despite himself Altmann felt a compelling sympathy, prepared at least to grant the admiral a fair hearing. He was shocked at the change that had come over the man since their last meeting. "In the *U-Bootwaffe* the average commander's life-expectancy, as I'm sure you know, is about four months at the moment, and it's no secret—these young fellows know it, Altmann, yet they still come forward. The least I can do is to present them with a commanding officer who'll inspire them—as you've inspired your own men during your operational service, let me say! I need a man who can assure them that their sacrifice and devotion to duty won't be taken for granted—wasted! Frankly, Altmann, the only man—the ideal man!—for the post is you. I haven't had to make a choice."

Altmann held the candid blue gaze, and felt his disappointment ebb. Apart from the fact that this was an order and not, despite its tone, a request, he decided to agree with Dönitz's view, not as transparent flattery but as a pragmatic assessment. There was nothing to be gained by seeking to avoid the posting: protesting his unfitness for it would not necessarily lead to a more acceptable alternative; quite possibly it would dash his hopes altogether by implying contempt for a generous decision. After all, there was no sound reason to suppose that because previous appointments to the post had been the last step upwards in careers of limited distinction it would be the same in his case. Dönitz's famous reticence might well be concealing further plans, and he had hinted as much. Altmann's best course would be to accept with good grace—it would at least assure Ursula of his comparative safety—and stand prepared for further developments. Uncle Karl was not given to throwing unused potential onto the scrapheap, and Altmann felt confident of his reserve of competence and professional ability which, perhaps, the posting would enable him to demonstrate. Moreover, his making something of a name for himself with his papers on leadership, to be followed, soon he hoped, by his definitive full-length work on the subject, lay in the same general direction. So he heard Dönitz's concluding—conclusive—words with the beginnings of anticipation:

the admiral was aware that the move would deprive front-line operations of a first-class senior officer, but was in no doubt that the training post would make far better use of his talents, to the great benefit of the service and the *Reich*.

As for the imminent official recognition of his accomplishments to date, the *Führer* would himself invest him with the diamonds to the oak leaves and swords of his Knight's Cross. Confirming Reinhard's assertion, Dönitz expected notification of a date within the next ten days or so, but meanwhile he would take pleasure in announcing the award that afternoon at the official welcoming ceremony.

All of which Altmann found gratifying, allowing it to disperse the darker residues of his cogitations over the last year or so, and, within the last half-hour, sudden misgivings about Dönitz's apparent dismissal of the tacitly-acknowledged disposal of *Anne-Marie de Bretagne* and her people. But, praise apart, he reassured himself on the point, recalling the general perception among u-boat commanders, substantiated by the implications of several tactical orders, not least among them Dönitz's standing order number one-five-four, that the fate of survivors was viewed ambiguously by high command, even unstated approval of their incidental—in a manner of speaking—elimination: whereas new tonnage could be produced with relative ease, the trained manpower its operation required was less readily created. Accordingly, of equal, if not greater, strategic value to the u-boat's mission than the loss of the ship was the loss of her crew, and Altmann had touched on the point in his analysis of war leadership.

Yet, here in this room, face to face with the Commander-in-Chief himself, a trace of unease had arisen at the progress of events since his arrival that morning, and he eyed Dönitz's erect figure conscious of a stirring of apprehension. He noted the pallor, the fining of the face's contours, the thinning hair above a seemingly broader, deeper brow, the startling loss of weight—his shirt collar was a good size too large, and the immaculate uniform seemed to hang slackly where it should have displayed its trueness of cut. Only his bearing, as upright as ever, contrasted with while diminishing the overall effect of the changes in his appearance, evidently brought about by the strain of conducting a sea-war—on which Germany's military success showed tendencies to increasing dependence—with such a limited array of weapons, practically the *U-Bootwaffe*'s range of types alone. For all his confidence in the *Reich*'s ultimate victory Altmann felt bound to admit that the news was not good, even filtered through the Goebbels sieve. Events in the north and east were being played out in the feverish light of impending disaster, no less so to the south, where the Italians had dumbfounded German High Command by unconditional surrender to the Allies. The breach had been sealed by the *Wermacht* but against Allied pressure that could only increase. It seemed that the *Führer*'s policy of personal supervision of Germany's land forces after their mismanagement by his senior commanders was meeting with less than glorious success in actions and campaigns that seemed to get bogged down in confusions of ways and means, a stubborn and ever better-equipped and prepared enemy notwithstanding. Uncle Karl and the navy were conspicuously excepted, if not ignored, while the much-vaunted *Luftwaffe*, mounting no substantial defence against the Allied bombing campaign, seemed to have slipped into a rôle shrouded in shamefaced mystery and the small print of Göring's sulky disgrace. Yet it was clear that Dönitz was under some stress; and not only in a general sense, thought Altmann. Nor, at this distance of time, could it be the event mentioned by von Lohmeyer on their way here from the quayside: Altmann had been saddened to learn of Uncle Karl's loss.

"You know he had two sons, of course," von Lohmeyer had said. "If he seems more—preoccupied—than usual, it's because the younger, Peter, was lost, presumed killed, with his boat shortly after you sailed in May. Second officer, U-954. Last heard from somewhere off Cape Farewell in contact with a convoy. *Kapitänleutnant* Odo Loewe in command . . . Did you know him?"

No; Altmann had not known him. Nor Dönitz's son, whose death was another of fate's incomprehensible caprices, perversely reassuring in their expression of contempt for men's conceits: they made beggars of kings and princes of felons, defrauded the righteous and rewarded the knave. And all with a rich sense of irony: Altmann reflected on the certainty that while Uncle Karl had been dealt such a wounding blow, his standing among naval men—or at least the *U-Bootwaffe*'s—would have risen in proportion, perhaps sufficiently to cancel the decline it had suffered as he had retreated from the front line to Berlin via Paris in face of the Atlantic war's increasingly problematical progress. His personal loss weakened the argument that he had sought to insulate himself from the consequences of his decisions, which did his reputation as a military leader no harm at all, if at a level closer to sentimentality than to professional long-headedness. And its professional element had come under closer scrutiny in recent months: it seemed that since Altmann's departure the *U-Bootwaffe*'s fortunes had suffered an alarming reverse in the North Atlantic, with a mounting loss-rate that made ugly arithmetic even uglier when set against a sharp diminution in the monthly figure of tonnage sunk. There was more than mere irony in this, surely? Was, in fact, some all-powerful hand playing a decisive part in this cataclysmic convulsion of mankind? Schreiber's God, for instance? Or, conversely, some opposing evil genius having, as God did not, a certain sense of humour—black humour, to be visited on the feeble creatures whose collective wit had not breadth enough to recognise and avoid the onrushing juggernaut of self-destruction?

Veering away from an unfamiliar line of thought, Altmann was conscious of a sympathy for the man which, he felt, should be cautiously deployed. He also felt sure there was something more immediate on Dönitz's mind, something connected with his, Altmann's, precipitate removal from the boat when it seemed, even now, that a delay of a couple of hours to allow him time to at least make himself presentable, apart from attempting to get through to Ursula, whose assurance of his safety was his present concern and anxiety, would have been a reasonable concession. He felt that, for some arcane reason, he had been waylaid; and certainly not for the comparatively trifling purpose of congratulating him on his conduct of the patrol, as distinct from the formality of the operational report, yet to be presented. Watching Dönitz as the admiral's panegyric appeared to run out of momentum, and bringing reasoned argument to bear on his misgivings, Altmann's awareness of tension grew sharper, and he sensed a mood of hardening resolve in the other man culminating in his abruptly halting to look down with an unsmiling expression, stern but devoid of severity. The steady gaze seemed to have shed its customary iciness, and the words their characteristic incisive intonation; but the decision remained, like the edge on a scalpel as Uncle Karl made the cut that would either save or take away the life of his patient. And it was made without the anaesthetic that would have cushioned the shock.

Altmann's first reaction was a flush of chill nausea followed by a numbness that spread like an infusion of hemlock through his veins, his muscles, his nerves, deadening his mind, robbing him of the power of movement and speech as he struggled to assimilate the meaning of the admiral's words, to fit it into a frame of reality. Remaining seated he stared up at Dönitz in perplexity, unblinking, chewing his lower lip, gripping the chair-arms without pressure, as if listening to an outline of tactics, details of some official activity in which he would be involved, the recounting of an instructive episode: anything but the crushing impact of the tidings that were obviously the overriding reason for this unceremonious encounter. His first rational sensation as his faculties righted themselves with the sluggishness of a swamped boat was irritation at von Lohmeyer's and Reinhard's duplicity in lying to him, as they surely had, about the telephone lines. Then the shock set in.

He was not aware of the glint of compassion in the admiral's eye, and to conceal it Dönitz, concluding with a murmured "I'm deeply sorry, Altmann", turned and crossed to the window, where he stood contemplating the grey morning, hands clasped at his back.

Altmann sat on, unmoving, gazing blankly at the gilt-framed battle-scene on the opposite wall; wind-torn seas blending with ragged overcast and a spray-swept u-boat lining up on a warship's indistinct form. Obviously the Great War. Maybe Weddigen's action against the English battle-cruisers. Which were they?—*Hogue*, *Cressy* and another he couldn't bring to mind at the moment: *Hawke*? *Aboukir*? The Tommies certainly picked some resounding names—but they had legitimate claim to a world-class choice, didn't they?—and old Müller would have ticked him off for slacking . . . Well, Weddigen had done things in style at any rate; no homecomings to a struggling Germany, no skulking in concrete bunkers; no awkward sympathy for irretrievable loss. Instead, a brief hour of glory, the recognition of a grateful *Kaiserreich*, and a warrior's death to seal the pact. And the way it was done in those days—a good clean fight, hand to hand, almost. No asdic, no radar, no likely air attack. Altogether a simpler business: you aimed your boat at the target, like a peashooter. No worries about duds, just your aim, your own steadiness of eye and hand: hit the mark and—bang! Or miss, and oblivion under the onrushing forefoot. It was a good painting, thought Altmann: captured the atmosphere; the artist must have put in some sea-time. Then he thought, God—dear God! and for an instant was back on the bridge with Schreiber's hand on his arm, looking down in anger on *Clan Finlay*'s boats. *God will forgive a mistake . . .*

She'd been gone nearly two weeks as he'd read her letters; letters wrought by a dead hand that in the words, for that single, unsuspecting first glance, had exercised its departed power to touch his deepest emotions; then—now—lost forever, swept into eternity. But for that instant she had been with him again, and he with her, her confidant, her longed-for companion, her ever-to-return Jason; her love and lover and the father of her girls, their sailor hero and storyteller, defender and champion. But they, too—swept into the void, wraiths drifting back through the galleries of recollection, already merging into the dying echoes and twilight glimmerings of memory. And as he patted his pockets in search of his cigarettes, remembering after a moment that he'd left them in the control-room, despairingly glancing round in hopes of an abandoned packet, his abstractions switched away from the anguish, only to confront the hard-set familiars of his waking dread . . . *Le capitaine—il est mort! Dead! You 'ear? You 'ave killed 'im!* And the man on his feet in the boat. *God will bless you, captain!* The irony—no, mockery, surely?—was obvious, artless; even simplistic, now he came to think of it. How could he have thought otherwise?

A chance in a million. Hit by anti-aircraft fire the bomber had come down before reaching Frankfurt. A full bomb-load. It had missed the centre of Rauenthal, crashed among houses on the southern fringe wreaking complete devastation. In the houses they would have known nothing, felt nothing, heard nothing. And there had been almost nothing left; only fragments, assailant and victim inseparably mingled, to commit to the collective grave. Dönitz had attended the funeral service on Altmann's, and the *U-Bootwaffe*'s, behalf. He had even made a point of making the acquaintance of Ursula's parents after ensuring their provision for travel from Frankfurt. Irony again! That they had—so far—survived in the face of greater day-to-day danger than that of their dead daughter and grandchildren was, Altmann mused, a cruelly perverse whim of fate, doubly so in face of his own survival.

And God?—where did He come into this—into not merely his survival but his survival as a hero of the *Reich*, to be decorated and honoured and moved to a place of relative safety leading, most probably, to yet greater things? How was it that this God—the God mentioned by Schreiber, the God in whom his parents had professed a belief as the final Arbiter between good and evil, the Font of justice and mercy and love—how was it that this God had taken their innocent lives and left his guilty one to what was yet to be gained from an earthly existence? Reflecting further, Altmann felt bound to conclude that if, in fact, justice was yet to prevail, then it would be by way of facing him with yet greater trials, yet more brutality, an approach to death that would exact full payment for his actions. And, he was surprised to realise, it had already begun: it was not a question of his being spared, but of his being taxed through the loss of his loves—and his friendships; of all whose presence in his life had made it worthwhile, given it point at a level far deeper than that reserved for the cause, for the Fatherland and the future of its people. One by one, and in an unsuspecting group, they had been taken from him: first Liebeherr, crushed in the wreck of his boat; then immaculate Greischen, caught out in the ultimate indignity of impotent defence; then his parents, whose imperfections had in the end been the cause of his deeper understanding; and now Ursula and his daughters, innocent of everything but trust in him as their support and provider. He had belonged to them—and they to him, friends and loved ones both. Now, there was nothing. Nothing that mattered as they had. The nearest to them was the boat and her crew, and even there he had suffered loss, most tellingly young Hildegras, and the wholly reliable Schreiber, the eminently seamanlike *Einswo* who would be difficult to replace. That was where he belonged—with the boat and crew, all he had left. Yet even that was not to be, it seemed. Instead, a wider platform of service to the cause, and a training flotilla where, to complete the irony, he would survive to look back on a war most would count a success. And suddenly Altmann knew what the term meant: Pyrrhic. His would be a Pyrrhic victory—always assuming it would be a victory at all, for events were developing along doubtful lines. The seeds of victory had been sown, but on whose land? Where, precisely—in God's name!—was Germany's war taking her? Where were the wonder weapons so long promised? Without them—including a more efficient design of u-boat—how was the *Wermacht* to halt, let alone defeat, the gathering forces of not only the Tommies and their colonial accomplices but also, now, the Americans, the Russians and the increasingly recalcitrant French? Even the vacillatory Italians, unreliable allies as they had proved to be. He glanced at the figure of the man at the window, and wondered, noticing—perhaps an illusion created by the trend of his thoughts—a droop to the shoulders that hadn't been there before. A droop, and a roundness, as under the burden of a great responsibility, and a greater knowledge, as, for example, of the real state of affairs.

But he was thankful for Dönitz's extraordinary devotion to the wellbeing of his particular arm of the *Wermacht*. He was good like that; always thought of his men. Did whatever he could for them. He'd made the *U-Bootwaffe*, more or less single-handed; it was his baby, his ward and charge. Altmann wondered whether or not he did the same sort of thing for the surface-ship people, now that his responsibilities also embraced that sphere of naval operations. Such as it was. It was common knowledge that his sentiments in that direction had never been warm; but on the other hand his devotion to duty was as unwavering as it was formidable and extensive: he would not allow personal prejudice to affect its necessary impartiality.

Altmann felt it was a pity he'd been brought up in a tradition that had such Spartan ideas of manliness. Taught from the cradle that men don't weep, in the end you couldn't; at least, while conscious. Certainly not for yourself; there could never be a case for self-pity. But for others? Not for Dönitz, whose personal loss must surely have been expected, or prepared for, in his professional strategy. He had just mentioned the u-boat commander's life-expectancy, which applied similarly to officers and men—if anything better in his case, at his bridge station during surface actions, more exposed but free to jump clear of a doomed boat. Its span had shortened as the war had progressed, but the present figure was not much lower than it had been six months before, at the beginning of the *U-Bootwaffe*'s sudden reversal. Perhaps Dönitz had wept; his son had been no more than a couple of years older than Hildegras; but his tears would have been for a life wasted, not for the continuing life's impoverishment. For his part, however, Altmann could not weep; only acknowledge inexpressible compassion. As, it seemed, Dönitz felt for him.

Yet he felt he could have wept: for Ursula and the girls, who had trusted him; for young Hildegras, who would still have been alive if he'd refused the boy permission to leave his post; for Schreiber, who would recover, perhaps, but to a world of unrelieved blankness and dependence on others. But, whatever it might bring by way of relief—and he doubted its likelihood—it would be an empty gesture; mere sentimentality, a sign of weakness, of no merit, no value, no possible practical avail. Weakness apart, it would serve no purpose, no end; if anything, it would add only to the sense of futility to which the waste of life threatened to expose the national struggle. Yes, he could have wept; but only if he had been able to disregard the motives and ideals that had been his guide and bulwark from the beginning.

So of course he could not, concluding that, taken all round, his situation wasn't worth tears; not when he was merely paying a price, settling an account. The bill was fair; there was no question of his being overcharged. It was excessive, but he had enough—or had to find enough—emotional and moral capital to cover it. If, in fact, that was the sum of it; if there were no further charges, no incidental costs, yet to be demanded. Apart, that is, from the pain. The pain was intense, exquisite, exploratory, creeping around in his guts like a worm, probing upwards and outwards, into his heart, his mind, his very bones. He wondered; at his ability to bear it without some kind of assuagement, and for how long: the pain, and the loneliness which, he was astonished to realise, had taken the opportunity to claim his recognition, and, insolently, his intimate acquaintance.

PART 3
THE SURVIVOR

I

MUKERJEE looked uncomfortable and mopped his brow with a grubby handkerchief. The overhead fan did nothing to cool the air in the room; instead it stirred it into a languid central vortex leaving stagnant pools in the corners gathering and exuding heat. Now, late morning had assumed its full day-dress of oppressive humidity in a blinding white light that sapped the colour from everything exposed to it. It struck into the room past the partly-open window-shutters to lay bars of polished steel across the bare floor-boards, contrasting with the dimness meant to induce a lower temperature but which added to the oppressive atmosphere. Mombasa in mid-March was a sweltering niche in the coast past which the cooling remains of the northerly monsoon drifted uncaring; the room—Mukerjee's office—was a niche in a row of crumbling apartments of Arab design lining an alley off Fort Jesus Road, along which no breeze of any kind troubled to pass. Mukerjee exchanged the handkerchief for a glass of fruit squash, sipped, and eyed his companion with a melancholic air.

"It is not matter of choice, captain," he murmured, "but one of necessity, which I most greatly regret. If it were simply personal choice there would be no question of your dismissal or resignation. But—" he shrugged and contrived to look even more sorrowful "—it is matter of politics, and my own survival in business. The country is in hands of majority native administration, as you know, and making laws concerning commercial interests. I must change my employment policy or take nose-dive. Government is wanting employers to take Africans instead of other peoples, and first to go must be foreign nationals. Later, I know, even British subjects—Kenyan citizens, Asians and British together—will be given marching orders, and I need time to make arrangements for my family if I am having to sell up." He sipped from his glass and patted his lips with the handkerchief. "Two years, three maybe, I must keep the show on the road, and it means I must change my people for African Kenyans. All I can do is try to keep loyal servants as long as possible, but I must begin by ending employment of foreign nationals." He put his head on one side and raised his hands palm-up. "As a Dutch national, captain, I am most keenly regretful, but I must be replacing you a.s.a.p."

Seated in a cane chair clear of the bars of light, the object of his regret shook a cigarette from a pack and lit it before answering. He was well on in middle-age, thinning fair hair receding from the temples but curling behind the ears and on the neck, square-shouldered and slightly paunchy, with smallish blue-green eyes; in stronger light a three-day stubble more grey-shot red than fair tended to accentuate the face's tan while it concealed the lesser creases. In pale contrast a scar ran across the left cheekbone, prominent enough to be visible in the subdued light; as was the stony gleam of the eyes, focused steadily on the Indian's face. They always caused Mukerjee an inexpressible feeling of discomfort, though why he could not say: the master of his ship was an enigmatic fellow, but had never been other than a model of loyalty and efficiency; a man of few words and minimum, but effective, action. Having to ask for his resignation was not only an embarrassment but also a severe blow. He had relieved Mukerjee of almost all the worry of the import/export side of his business, acted as his agent on the coast and farther afield, contributed to his business not merely the services of a competent ship's master but also a moral element that gave it a cachet setting it apart from the other Asian enterprises of which the country's retail commerce was largely comprised; to Mukerjee's certain knowledge the man neither womanised nor drank to excess, and their association had been more of a partnership than that of employer and employee. Mukerjee had at one time entertained the possibility of offering him a holding. Now, however—Africanisation was the watchword in a Kenya on the brink of independence, and, as he had said, he needed time to arrange for his own salvation. This was the first of the moves in that direction, and probably the most upsetting. No African could replace Captain Kees van Haaften as master of the *Ndovu*—Swahili for "elephant", a name that had displaced the original *Johan Burger*, as Panama's ensign had replaced the Dutch tricolour at the gaff; the man had, after all, once been her owner, and knew her as no other man would ever do. It was a most tragic business, but—

"So you'll keep McDade?"

Van Haaften's accent was slight, savoured more of the clipped colonial inflection than Dutch, and a smoker's hoarseness overlaid the incisive tone of voice.

Still endeavouring to look regretful, Mukerjee half-shook, half-nodded his head in the Indian's peculiarly ambivalent gesture, saying, "Oh, yes . . . If he will stay. He is not presenting same difficulty, and I wish him to stay as long as possible. I cannot afford to lose both captain and chief engineer—not at same time, you understand."

"Sure—who wouldn't?" Van Haaften blew a stream of smoke fanwards to accompany his dry rejoinder, and picked a shred of tobacco from his tongue. "So what happens to me—am I supposed to sign off right now?"

"Oh, my dear God, no!" Mukerjee allowed agitation to raise his tone and widen his eyes. "I would not be so dishonourable, captain! No, no—you must stay at least to hand the ship over to your replacement as going concern, yes?"

"If you say so, Mr Mukerjee."

Mukerjee nodded vigorously and his jowls shook. Weight was becoming a force to reckon with over the last couple of years. He said, "But of course! When you leave I will be wanting your assurance that the man in your place is ideal choice!"

"No second-best, eh?"

With an uneasy chuckle Mukerjee raised a hand as if to stop further comment. "Every choice must be second-best, captain—after your good self."

Van Haaften did not reply, but sat smoking contemplatively while Mukerjee studied him, lips compressed. Finally the Indian said, "You know, captain—this is situation only brought forward by circumstances—" He sipped noisily. "I have had a problem, thinking of how I'm to tell you that after next special survey I will not be able to keep the ship running." He waved a restraining hand as van Haaften opened his mouth to speak. "Please—excuse me—but hear me first.

I'm thinking—perhaps—it will be making you feel a little bit better, no?"

Sitting back, van Haaften blew smoke through his nose. His expression was unreadable. "Go ahead, Mr Mukerjee. It's your party."

Clearing his throat, Mukerjee licked his lips then launched into an explanation of the situation, which was roughly what van Haaften already understood. Most of it was his concern in any case, as that part of the business for which Mukerjee had made him responsible from the day he had accepted the Indian's offer of purchase. It had followed seven years of voyage chartering during which he had struggled against maintenance and running costs with a losing hand, chiefly owing to a lack of operating capital. Owner of a chain of general stores and transport interests throughout the colony, Mukerjee had been well-served by van Haaften and had decided to take on the ship and her master as an economical alternative to increasing charter rates, not least by virtue of the earning capacity of otherwise spare cargo space. He had not interfered with the ship's management, leaving van Haaften as free a hand as he had had when her owner: the ship carried Mukerjee's merchandise, earned revenue by the carriage of others' goods, and in the Dutchman's hands had given no cause for worry. Until now, when two developments had reached a critical pitch almost in step with one another: independence, with its statutory upheaval, and the problem of the ship's growing maintenance costs. She was becoming more of a liability than an asset, and as Mukerjee had said, it was more than probable that she would not get through her next special survey without soaking up capital he was not prepared to lose—for lost it would be. His plans did not envisage continued residence in an independent Kenya where, he calculated, his business interests would be seriously compromised by political measures that would deprive him of trusted employees; even of his rightful assets. But for the present he was playing for time, and its extent would depend on his paying at least nominal service to the new employment regulations. He could keep the ship running until the date of survey, at which point he would be in a position to conclude the disposal of his business interests preparatory to departure for either India or UK—most likely the latter, where he reckoned to be able to set up with prospects of a comfortable living.

"So you see, captain, we would soon be talking of this matter in any case."

"Yes." Van Haaften stubbed out his cigarette and rose to fill a glass from the jug of fruit juice. The ice tinkled loudly in the comparative silence of the room; street noises penetrated the shutters, muffled by them and diminishing as the sun approached the zenith. The bazaar's early morning hubbub was subsiding towards afternoon somnolence. Van Haaften returned to his chair. "So what d'you want me to do—apart from resigning? I can't make you an offer for the ship. She'd cost me as much as she'd cost you. I haven't the money."

Mukerjee's head gyrated again and he sighed. "Yes—it is inescapable fact of life, captain. She is old, and even Mr McDade will not be able to keep his engine running til doomsday, isn't it?"

Van Haaften smiled, a tired twitch of the thin lips, and lit another cigarette. Mukerjee refused the proffered packet and took a Burma cheroot from a box on his desk. They smoked in silence for some minutes, the air growing heavy with the mingled aromas of the tobaccos and, invisible and odourless, their parallel patterns of thought. Finally van Haaften caught Mukerjee's eye and lifted an eyebrow.

"Yes," said the Indian. "I will explain. And if you have better idea, please to explain yourself, no?" Van Haaften nodded, saying nothing, and he continued. "You will be joined on next voyage by the new captain—he is native Kenyan, trained in British company with British certificate, all above-board and hunky-dory. As you know, the voyage is to Durban and back calling with inducement at ports *en route*. When you are getting back I will make proper request for your resignation—or accept on your own initiative, as you wish—and our ways will take different directions, very sadly. But—" he held up a hand to forestall van Haaften's interruption "—*but*, my dear captain, it will also be necessary to make businesslike ending! The name of my family is at stake, you know? I do not want peoples to be going round saying Kuljit Mukerjee is a thoroughly bad egg and a snake in grass! In England—if I go there—I start with clean slate and reputation to make as upright citizen and businessman, not at risk of old acquaintance and victim of double-dealing coming there also and denouncing me like a reprobate! So—when you leave me I will be paying you bonus for long service, and twelve month salary as on day of resignation. It will give you time to find half-decent job somewhere else . . . Perhaps you will return to your home country, no?"

The other blew smoke at the fan and watched it whisked to shreds as the downdraught caught it. "Perhaps," he said. "I haven't given it any thought."

Mukerjee rocked his head again in understanding. It was a matter that would require careful consideration; as had his own similar predicament. He did not pursue the point.

Van Haaften emerged from the alley into Fort Jesus Road squinting in the glare, half-gasping at the cocktail of heat, noise and odours that assailed his senses as he turned to make his way through the throng towards Kilindini Road. He would walk back to the ship. There was no hurry. He felt the sweat break out afresh at his neck and back, his loose cotton shirt stick in the usual places, and he decided it was an occasion demanding some kind of ceremony or ritual—the end of the game. It was inevitable, of course, but its timing had come as an unpleasant advance of an uncalculated conclusion. He had avoided the need for some kind of forward plan—indeed, he had decided there was none. There had been, he'd believed, nothing left to plan for. The decision to bind himself to the ship's fate had been made long ago—made for him by circumstances. There had been no question of survival beyond it, though he had not expected the moment to come upon him at such a time, nor with such abruptness: the end of the game he had expected to continue indefinitely—or, at least, for as long as he lasted. Now that it *had* come, however, he wondered whether or not he had been too precipitate in his decision; whether, in fact, the situation would be amenable to thought, would perhaps reveal another way. But to where? Beyond the ship he had seen only a blank, not even a wilderness. He had set out with her not to gain some safe haven but to keep moving, always moving on, his gaze fixed ahead on an ever-receding horizon, from landfall to landfall, one destination leading to the next in an endless train that had kept him a stranger to his surroundings, aloof from them, uninvolved except on a footing of transient business: the cargoes he'd picked up had dictated his movements, and port by port, sea by sea, he had followed his leads unquestioning, laying a hand on the helm only when the chance arose of the offered cargo taking him back on his track. Those cargoes he'd refused. He was not going that way; he declined to give reasons. So sometimes the ship had run in ballast, earning nothing but taking from him as much as she did when fat with lading.

Walking along, breasting a tidal stream of humanity, he felt himself a stranger again in a place that, years before, and despite his intent, had taken on the features of comfortable familiarity. The medley of faces and dress flowed around him trailing all the emanations of crowded humanity, brushing by then opening gaps to expose the cracked paving throwing the sun back in muted tones and gusts of musty heat, and he remembered, and experienced again, the way he'd felt on his early visits: out of step, out of place, conspicuous and clumsy and uneasy, under pressure from the inarticulate urge to complete his business and depart; but the cargoes on offer, increasingly by Mukerjee, could not be refused, had obliged him to return, voyage after voyage, and the passage of time and the habits of familiarity had, by increments, drawn him to the idea and the substance of the place, so that after a while, despite himself, he had come to feel at ease amongst its cosmopolitan population, its raffish, swaggering, open-minded, open-handed perspectives, its chaotic admixture of architecture and period and posture, and its uncritical acceptance of contributions to its heaving, racketing ferment of commercial and social intercourse, and after a while the idea of a home port had gained a purchase on his plan of no-plan. There it had lodged like a wind-blown seed, to germinate, root and sprout, rise and throw out leaves to the light and air, and produce a small, hard and tart fruit that, carefully and properly handled, could taste sweet enough; but always with a threat of corruption, the possibility of toxic canker, a flavour of the decay, the putrefaction, the dissipation away from which his aimless odyssey had been intended to carry him. His realisation, by slow accumulation, of a sense of place had been tempered with caution, drawn upon when, realising the parlous state of his finances faced with the mounting cost of maintaining an aging ship to insurable standard and running her with at least a half-able crew, Mukerjee's voyage charters had led to his offer to buy the vessel. Van Haaften's acceptance had cemented the home-port attachment and a further increment of confirmation in his uncontested, uninvestigated place amidst the town's commercial affairs, so that his present situation, this sudden re-estrangement, produced the illusion of a reversal of time rather than the commencement of another epoch and a resumption of the odyssey. For there could be no resumption; not without the ship, and not in another: he hadn't the capital to equip himself anew, and he would not—could not—work for another owner. It was an unpleasant prospect, and he decided to look in at Pavlides's as a place of respite from the assault on his senses and perceptions triggered by Mukerjee's words; a place where he could collect his wits, try to think, or to sift through and evaluate the thoughts that had already claimed his attention. He needed a drink.

Sergos Pavlides ran the Paradise Bar on Kilindini Road. Outwardly, it looked and functioned much like the other establishments of its kind along the road and in connected streets—The Rainbow, the Sunshine Day & Night, the Anchor, the New Bristol, the Star, the Casablanca, the wildly inapposite Nazareth and other such places drawing their clientele from the unattached tourist trade and—the greater part—from the shipping that kept up an ever-renewed presence as the town's *raison d'être*, lucrative in several respects, official and unofficial. At varying levels, Sergos Pavlides partook of both, discreetly and to unknown financial advantage: as he put it, succinctly enough, it kept him in clean shirts. Which they were. He also shaved every day and took frequent baths. He smelled of cologne, but only at close range, and beneath the overlay of tobacco-smoke. In that way he was a clean man.

The Paradise Bar itself traded in undoctored drink, safe food, juke-box music and dance, however interpreted, and girls, in whom Pavlides took a nominal financial interest as the provider of a *lieu de rencontre*, reserving the right, sometimes exercised, to refuse admission to, or throw out, undesirables including any the worse for drink or who took anything but a soft-drink on the premises. For any other distinctive peccancy he took no responsibility. Among his customers there were no limits apart from a standard of behaviour governed by his mood of the moment, generally equable but prone to sudden lapses supplemented by a well-publicised facility in unceremonious weight-lifting. He was rumoured to be capable of throwing a two-hundred-pound Scawegian—for example—bodily across the pavement into the path of passing traffic; but no-one had actually witnessed such a thing, and no-one evinced a desire to do so, whether as onlooker or chief participant. Pavlides himself, mountainous, pale and sweating—despite the air-conditioning—under the neon strips of the bar that fronted his establishment, which included what he called a restaurant, unsmiling and piggy-eyed, gave out his careful measures of comment in a voice that had been pegged out and dried to a creaking *vibrato basso* in the smoke of the Turkish cigarettes he favoured. They alternated with a perpetually-charged saucer of minced peppered raw steak, from which he took pinches every so often, like a man taking snuff. His jowls moved continuously on either side of a small red purse of a mouth.

On the official side, or as near to it as he got, he conducted a business—assumed for obvious reasons to be as financially viable as the bar—as a kind of shipping agent and cargo broker, supplying such items as crew—even officers, variously defined—tally clerks, supercargoes, surveyors and any other mercantile functionary that might be required, as well as arranging shipment of any cargo in either direction by any means. This included, by rumour of a similar quality to that of the flying Scawegian, live bodies to the monsoon-borne Arab dhow-masters who frequented the old port, and with whom most of his shipping business was conducted. Since the retreat of the greater part of the Royal Navy's presence to points west of Suez the shade of Wilberforce, which had lurked in the offing like a pious Marley, had dissolved to leave a conscience-free Pavlides—if, in fact, he was—to make what could be made from the inter-tribal disturbances up-country via the agency of unidentifiable entrepreneurs. As that of a man of parts, Pavlides's story was a success except for one thing: he could not return to his native Greece, mostly owing to the exercise of some of his parts while in successive command of several ships owned by his countrymen, whose business interests, not all set out in the manifests, had been compromised accordingly. Another rumour burdened Pavlides with a wife and children in some place like the Piraeus, to whom he sent money in default of his physical presence. Van Haaften had met him by informal appointment arranged through a stevedore's clerk on his first visit to the port; it had been through the Greek's shrewd offices that the business relationship with Mukerjee had been instituted. As the social focus for all his coastal and farther-distant voyaging since then, the Paradise Bar was the obvious place in which to consider a situation that seemed to hold nothing in prospect better than a road to nowhere; the road he had been following from the start, drawing him on, as it had turned out, to this final dissolution, leaving him gazing into the void.

At just after noon the place was quiet, its air-conditioning sealing it off from the street in a sub-arctic cocoon that chilled the sweat in van Haaften's shirt and made him shudder gratefully. The Wurlitzer was silent and a few men sat drinking at the tables in a blue-skeined murmur of conversation. Two girls perched on stools at the bar were chattering like a pair of pied babblers in a thorn-tree. They turned as the barman—tall, stringy, in continual movement that seemed to blur his outline, sunglasses of the sort that suggested he navigated his surroundings by memory, sound and touch, white t-shirt with the logo *Blue for You* emblazoned across the pectoral area, gum-chewing, polishing a glass—hailed van Haaften and banged a bottle on the counter.

"Hi, cap—early today!—usual fix?" and the girls stared boldly, smiling.

Seyyid was half-Arab, half-Kikuyu, slick and bumptious and capable. He was also honest, working, as he was, under detailed, sincerely-meant and entirely-credible threat of a broken neck in the event of delinquency. He liked the job, and life, too much to take the chance, or at least to overtax his luck. As van Haaften nodded a greeting he produced a small glass, gave it a vigorous massage with the cloth, squinted through it at the overhead strip-light and slammed it down next to the bottle. Then with a jerk of his head towards the girls as discreetly suggestive as a horse-dealer's pitch he loped out of sight. Van Haaften ignored the girls. After a few moments Pavlides came through, chewing gently, genie-like in a waft of Turkish smoke. He wore slippers indoors.

He returned van Haaften's greeting. "Been expecting you, some time today." He nodded at the bottle. "That's on the house. I have one with you." He half-filled a tumbler from a bottle of *retsina* and raised it, fixing the other with a button eye, small and bright and hard. "You wanna eat?"

Van Haaften shook his head, took out his cigarettes and lit one, sucking in the smoke and holding it before letting it jet out through his nostrils. "You know?"

"Yeah. I'm sorry, hey, Kees? Not good." Pavlides cleared his throat, popped a little ball of raw minced steak into his mouth from a cache under the counter. He chewed silently for a moment before asking, "What you gonna do—?" and answering van Haaften's shrug with, "You wan' I look for something, ha?"

The gin tasted clean and good on van Haaften's tongue, and he held it there until the chill went off it, then swallowed, and felt the fumes rise in his throat and on upwards towards the fulcrum of his thoughts. Other than the Sea Breezes Hotel and the Netherlands consulate the Paradise Bar was the only place in town that kept the real *genever*. Pavlides shipped it from Holland direct. Only passing Dutchmen drank it, if they thought to ask for it; most drank lager. It was van Haaften's drink. Bar an occasional Tusker he never touched anything else, and never drank too much at a time, in public. He wondered how much of it Pavlides would sell after he'd left. Savouring its lingering tang he shook his head. "No thanks, Serg. Not yet, anyway. Maybe I'll think of something."

"Okay. Maybe." Pavlides washed the steak down with a mouthful from his glass and leaned forward, gripping the edge of the bar-top. Pitching his voice an octave lower than normal he grated, "Man here wanna talk to you. Ask for you by name." The button eyes held van Haaften's. "I tell him nothing, ha?" He inclined his head fractionally to accompany a shift of the eyes to one side, over van Haaften's shoulder. "You don' wanna talk, I say you don' come today." He straightened, and resumed his normal tone. "Okay. Eat later. When you like, but before two o'clock—cook's afternoon off."

Van Haaften did not turn to look. He took another mouthful of gin, held it, swallowed and drew breath, taking the fumes down with it. In response to the lift of an eyebrow, Pavlides murmured, "Table next to the juke-box. Young guy with glasses. Yank, I think."

Refilling his glass, van Haaften picked it up and turned. The man sat alone toying with his beer, apparently lost in thought: thin, and narrow-shouldered, dark, crew-cut, wearing a gaily-patterned open-necked cotton shirt and a stainless-steel watch that looked too heavy for a slender wrist. Van Haaften caught his eye as he crossed to the table. Standing over the man, he said, "I'm told you want to speak to me."

Rising, the man stood half a head taller, lanky and stooping, reminding van Haaften of a stork, and took a breath. "Captain van Haaften?" and at the confirming nod he added, "Can you spare me a few minutes?" He indicated a chair. "I think you can give me some information, if you'd be kind enough."

They sat regarding one another. The young man was clean-shaven, smooth-complexioned, tanned. His thinness was a mark of health rather than insufficiency. He exuded what van Haaften took to be all-American youth, but of the tennis-court rather than the football-field. College somewhere, he supposed. And self-possessed. His glance was direct, pleasant, guileless behind rimless glasses of a minimum thickness. The eyebrows were level and marked, the brow above clear. The hands that rested loosely about the beer-glass were large but slim-fingered, graceful, like a woman's. Van Haaften wondered what a man like this could want from him. He said, "Well—what can I tell you, Mr—?"

The man smiled. The mouth was wide, the mobile lips finely-chiselled with an eye to balance and precision; and to a capacity for humour.

307

Its words came in attractive form, measured, modulated, the accent unpronounced, almost English. "Forgive me. My name's Cohen. Jake Cohen. From Boston—Boston Massachusetts."

"Mr Cohen . . ." van Haaften waited, keeping his expression blank, but he noted: Jew. An American, but a Jew. The Jake would be short for Jacob.

Taking a draught from his glass, Cohen licked the strip of froth from his upper lip. He said, "I'm looking for someone, captain—been looking for some time—"

"Yes?"

"—and the trail's brought me to Mombasa. I made a few local inquiries, heard of this place and Mr Pavlides, and your ship—the *Ndovu*—right?" He pronounced it *Nadovu*.

Van Haaften nodded wordlessly and sipped his drink.

"You're well-known round here—like Mr Pavlides. And Mukerjee."

"Your—information—is right."

"I met the padre at the Missions to Seamen, down the road here."

"Ah—" Van Haaften allowed a smile to pluck at a corner of his mouth. "Of course. A mine of local knowledge."

"I guess so . . ." Eying van Haaften, Cohen took another pull at his glass. "Not bad beer, at this temperature. In this climate. But I don't drink much." He smiled. "Weak head."

Van Haaften drained his glass and regretted the absent bottle. Contenting himself with his cigarette he said through the smoke, "So who are you looking for, Mr Cohen—someone I know, you think?"

For a short interval Cohen was silent, but he kept his gaze on the other's face, his lips compressed and a slight furrow between his eyebrows, as if gauging his moment. Finally he said, "Well—yes, I think so. I think you know him quite well, from way back . . . Guy named Altmann. Gunnar Altmann. A German."

Afterwards van Haaften wondered whether or not his reaction had been noticed. He felt an age pass before he took in a deep lungful of smoke and blew it in a thin stream up into the glare of the strip-light. Daylight never gained unfettered, or uncontested, entrance to the Paradise Bar. He allowed the mushrooming smoke to draw his gaze from the American's, watching it while he gathered his thoughts. How strange that name sounded.

He turned his eyes back to Cohen's, tightened his lips, turned down the corners of his mouth, shaking his head. "Altmann . . . Not offhand." He took in another lungful of smoke and let it go in a pensive cloud. As it cleared he said, "What about him?" and marvelled at the lack of interest his tone of voice expressed. He felt himself at a remove, as, say, in the company of the two men at a nearby table, but looking on, hearing the exchange, noting the interplay of look and gesture, curious about its nature, to see where it would lead.

Cohen sat back and blew out his cheeks as if facing a disconcerting prospect, like a competent climber faced with a testing scarp, not unexpected but never before attempted. He paused, seeming to consider, took a pull at his glass, then: "He was a u-boat commander—world war two. What they called an ace. Sank over two hundred and seventy thousand tons of Allied shipping."

Van Haaften picked a shred of tobacco from his tongue. "Maybe I should have heard of him, then." And he felt a prickling at his neck, as if someone—something—had entered the room, taken up a position at a discreet distance, not yet prepared to claim familiar acquaintance, but awaiting a suitable moment.

"I guess so—you were around at the time. Germany made no secret of her successes . . ." Cohen swirled the last of his beer round in the glass, and drank it off. "He was a hero of the *Reich*. Knight's Cross with all the bits and pieces, only one in the *U-Bootwaffe*—"

The figure van Haaften could not see stirred at the last word, which seemed to echo in the air, like the tones of a bell in a far-off valley.

"—and a *Kapitän-zur-See* by the age of thirty-three, youngest-ever commandant of the *Kriegsmarineschule* in Flensburg. Some going, in a small and shrinking navy! In the *U-Bootwaffe* it was more than that."

"More?"

"Sure. It was surviving. That was enough on its own. He survived. Not many did—not when they got into the thick of it, like he did. The road to the Knight's Cross usually ended before it got there."

"You've been doing your homework."

Cohen inclined his head, acknowledging a compliment.

"Did it uncover anything else about this fellow—this naval prodigy?"

Frowning, Cohen appeared to reflect, then said yes, it had uncovered quite a lot, some of no significance, but of Altmann's naval career plenty. For example, that his path to the naval college's commandant's

309

desk had taken him first to command of a training flotilla at Memel, before transfer to the college as an instructor in submarine warfare which had gained him promotion to *Fregattenkapitän* and, ultimately, *Kapitän zur See*. He had become the *Kriegsmarine*'s authority on the subject, apparently, particularly in the associated field of leadership and command. "—Impressive record, between one thing and another, wouldn't you say?"

Van Haaften took a last lungful from his cigarette and stubbed it out in the tin ashtray. Pavlides didn't supply anything heavier; in glass, for example: too versatile a material for its simple purpose. "And so this—Altmann—interests you because of his career as a hero of the Third *Reich*—and alive when the usual condition of such figures was—is—dead?" To the sardonic tone of his words van Haaften added a sceptical note with "Alive at the time, anyway." He was not prepared to admit anything to this strange young man, whatever his purpose in coming here. Some kind of historical research, he supposed; for a post-graduate degree at one of America's innumerable obscure universities. He would become an expert on the subject of Altmann, Gunnar, ace u-boat commander and hero of the Third *Reich*, who would be good for a comfortable living and well-upholstered retirement. But Altmann was dead. A headstone bore witness to the fact, there were written records somewhere. If van Haaften had known, or met, him it was long ago and unremembered. Nor, as far as he knew, was there any testimony of such an occurrence.

Apparently about to say something, Cohen hesitated, looked ruefully at his empty glass, and seemed to have reached a point of irresolution, some kind of bifurcation with no clear pointer to his destination. Abruptly, van Haaften sensed a tension in the air, and experienced a strange interconnection between himself and the American, taut, finely-drawn, at the limit of its tensile strength, exerting what pull its elasticity had against the critical balance of centrifugal force that, overcoming the restraint, would send the transilient points spinning away from each other into the endless reaches of human estrangement. A single word would bring it about, the imbalance that would break the connection, never to be regained; as a single word would add another strand to the thread, bind the points together in a permanent union sharing a common fate. Van Haaften felt a tickle at the nape of his neck as a bead of sweat traced a downward path into the absorbent band of his loose collar, and he reached round to rub at it. The tension slackened.

Cohen spoke. He paced his words with care. "Altmann sank something over fifty ships. One of them was a sailing-ship; French schooner, running without lights. Her captain took a chance doing that. Altmann was within his rights, as far as the German rules of engagement went. The Frenchman was wrong. He took a stupid chance, but he took it with some reason."

"What was that?" Van Haaften ignored another tickle at his neck, but the chill that ran down his spine struck like a cramp, and he caught his breath in a cough as his thoughts whirled. Cohen seemed unaware.

"The schooner was carrying passengers. In the normal way that should have meant showing lights and a chance of being allowed past by any German warship."

"So?" The cramp passed, left a feeling of debility; van Haaften concentrated on Cohen's words with an effort.

"But the passengers weren't ordinary ones." Cohen rubbed his forehead for a moment, his gaze lowered. The breath he took before continuing seemed to accompany a mental squaring of the narrow shoulders; a mustering of resolve, perhaps against some emotional pressure, or just tiredness. He might only recently have stepped off an aircraft, for example. He looked up, half-smiling. "They were refugees. Making a run for it, from the Nazi *Reich* that had made life impossible for them in Europe, as for so many."

"I see."

"Do you?" Cohen's smile assumed a new firmness. If it expressed amusement of any kind, it was with a bitter twist. "Perhaps not everything. So I'll tell you. These refugees were Jews—German Jews. They gave all they had left to the Frenchman to pay for their passage, which was a chancy one, across the Atlantic to the freedom they hoped for on the other side. Can you imagine their desperation?—the sea in a small ship, under sail, terrified them. The sea at the time—as a theatre of war—was worse . . . Yet the alternative was worse even than that. Infinitely worse. Unimaginably worse to most people—at that time. But not now, hm? Anyone can imagine it now, can't they?"

Van Haaften cleared his throat, and nodded. "Perhaps you are right." He kept his eyes on the American, but was aware of the movement of the figure behind him; perhaps a step or two, closer, to be able to hear more clearly. He resisted an urge to turn; there would be no point. There

311

was nothing there—nothing that would not retreat, diminish, vanish when faced with his knowledge of its cause and its substance—

"Sure I am! And being able to imagine such things is a measure of how we've slipped down the scale of civilisation. The slip before it was probably being able to imagine the previously unimaginable state of humanity in the trenches of Flanders. And before that—oh—" he shrugged "—who knows? Boer War. Gettysburg. The Crimea. Mutiny in India. Little Big Horn. French Revolution. The *Conquistadores*. Carthage. Thermopylae. Troy. All the way back."

"To what?"

"Dawn of civilisation, I guess. The dawn of something, anyway, but if it was civilisation give me barbarism every time. I'll go for the barbaric bit. Maybe we dumped it thinking we'd found something better, but it might be just a little more bearable than civilisation, even if only in admitting its failings."

Cohen had been leaning forward, hands gripping the edge of the table, almost belligerent in his vehemence, but at the silence which greeted his last words he seemed to wake to something; glancing away from the blue-green stone of van Haaften's stare he sat up and asked tiredly, "What d'you say, Captain van Haaften?"

"Say?" Van Haaften shook his head and wondered what was to be said. How was he to answer the passion in this young man's words? Apart from agreement with the sentiments expressed he could think of nothing to add, only wonder how much more the man knew about Gunnar Altmann's career. There was nothing he could say, only invite further disclosure, and perhaps—what? Dread it? Fear it? He felt confused. He said, "I think maybe barbarism—barbarity—would be a mistake, as a choice—"

"Yeah?" Cohen chuckled. "Turn our backs on the noble savage and stick to our cookie civilisation?"

"What choice do we have?" None, he thought. None, apart from eternity, or the abyss. Neither appealed, whatever civilisation's faults. We were stuck with it; maybe in time it would work better, rid itself of the canker and the rot and the repeated abominations excused as inhumanity when it was humanity itself at fault; sick, but perhaps curable; maybe it could survive its illnesses to emerge into something better than barbarism, better than the civilisation it had forged in the heat of its own passions.

"We already made it," said Cohen flatly. "Now it's a question of what we make of it, and so far it's working out to be a hash. A heap of shit—excuse me. People forget; or if they remember they think they know better than the ones before them, and they don't learn from them, and they make the same mistakes, only bigger. It'd get to be boring, if it didn't kill us first." He picked up his empty glass, studied it absently for a moment, then said, "There's something more you've got to know. About this guy Altmann." He got to his feet. "But I could do with another beer. You?"

"I'll get them." Van Haaften turned, half-expecting to see what he knew wasn't there, but saw only the bar and Seyyid in animated verbal engagement with the babblers. At his nod the barman leaped about among the bottles and glasses and with a flourish reconstituted himself at the table, where he set out a fresh Tusker for the American and the bottle of *genever*, with a clean glass. "All on the house today, cap." His affected drawl was evidently meant as a mark of recognition of the American as the focal point of some unclear occasion. "You eat'n'? I tell cook. He got afternoon off later."

Van Haaften lifted a hand in demurral, and Seyyid nodded blindly in conspiratorial assent. "Okay, cap—when you ready!" He vanished to rematerialise behind the bar in resumed communion with the girls. Quiet at this hour, in the evening the place would be heaving, the air-conditioning locked in a losing battle with the heat and humidity exuded by close-packed, excited flesh fuelled by alcohol and the suggestive or blatant sentiments of the juke-box's disembodied cast. In a time of famine the Paradise Bar would be among the last in town to stay solvent. Its clientele was faithful and evangelistic and spanned the world's seaboards, and, as the tourist trade developed, had begun to spread into their hinterlands.

There was, indeed, more about Altmann, and the American turned to it through a digression. "Does the name Eck mean anything to you?" he asked. "*Kapitänleutnant* Heinz Eck?"

Van Haaften filled his glass, took a mouthful and held it long enough for the gin to bite, then swallowed, relishing the astringent rush of the after-taste. He shook his head. No. He might, as a merchant marine man, have heard of Eck; but it wasn't by any means a matter of common knowledge. Better not to have heard, as Altmann surely had.

"He commanded the same type of boat as Altmann's second—and last." Cohen dipped a fingertip into his beer and licked off the result.

"But only sank two ships with it. One of them was a Greek freighter, the ss *Peleus*. Eck and his men machine-gunned the survivors in the water. Used hand-grenades, too . . ." He caught the other's eye. "Real civilised, huh?"

Wordlessly, van Haaften held Cohen's gaze, lips compressed. Cohen went on. Eck, he said, had some time later been captured when forced to beach his boat following an air attack. After the war he and some of his men had been tried as war criminals, found guilty and shot.

"He was the only u-boat commander to be tried on a criminal indictment. Germany—Dönitz—denied any other instances of the kind. Said he would have tried Eck himself if things had turned out differently." Cohen smiled. "But he never got the chance. And we've only got his word. Who knows, hm?"

With a shrug, van Haaften said, "Always the winners decide. Germany lost. We can't know what would have happened if she'd won."

"Right." Cohen took a long draught from his glass. "But it was bad luck for Eck."

Van Haaften looked sharply at the American. "Of course! But in which way do you mean?"

"Well—there were witnesses, apart from his own men. The men in the water—"

"He killed them, you say."

"No. I didn't say that," returned Cohen. "He machine-gunned them and threw hand-grenades in among them . . . But three survived, and a passing ship picked them up. Another merchantman, a Portuguese. The survivors told the story, and identified the boat. When Eck was captured the boat—his—was right there behind him on the beach. Cinch, huh?"

"How did the survivors identify it? I think they didn't show their numbers."

"By Eck's personal motif—I don't know what it was, but it was enough. They did that, the boats' commanders—or most of them. They liked to identify themselves, so the welcoming crowds would know who they were cheering when they got back from patrol. They painted little cartoon figures on the conning-tower, or some kind of symbol, or a coat of arms. Easy to see . . . Case of pride before a fall—and some fall!"

Coldly, van Haaften said, "Why tell me all this? I don't see the connection with Altmann, unless it's something to do with the same type of boat."

Sitting back, Cohen eyed him sombrely. Seconds passed, then the American took a deep breath and lifted the curtain on a scene that had been gathering dust for twenty-two years.

"The connection's a kind of similarity," he said. "Maybe the only instance of it in the war, though it didn't carry through to the ending. The endings couldn't've been more different." He paused, as if expecting comment, but at van Haaften's silence he continued, carefully, as if picking his way across a swift stream on stones. "So far as I could discover the schooner's sinking wasn't fully-reported at the end of the patrol, which isn't surprising. Altmann played safe, though there was doubt about what exactly German High Command had in mind when it issued its directives about attacks on Allied merchant ships. He only reported the sinking of the schooner in the usual way. No mention of passengers, or murder—in cold blood, just like Eck did the Greeks. That's the connection. Obvious enough."

Sitting motionless, van Haaften controlled a gasp with difficulty, frowning and repeating Cohen's words to himself with a feeling of dull bafflement. Murder? A word. War changed its meaning, surely? But no—apparently not. Not in Eck's case, so not in Altmann's. But . . .

"How do you know this? If it wasn't reported, how could you find out such a thing?—if it happened. What proof have you?"

Cohen was watching van Haaften with an expression that seemed to mingle regret with curiosity; a look almost of sympathy. A hint of something like sadness played round the chiselled lips, and he took a draught from his glass as if to time his reply, holding the beer briefly before swallowing. He said, "I'm the proof, Captain van Haaften."

"*You?*" The other was startled. "How are you the proof?"

"Well—like it happened with Eck, there were survivors of Altmann's attack. Just two. An old man and a child . . ." The sad smile returned, the look of near-sympathy. "I was the child."

Van Haaften experienced momentary disorientation, as a man shot in process of some everyday activity. There was no pain, just an impact that winded him and knocked him to his knees, his mind clawing back from a slough of bewilderment that rapidly turned to alarm at the realisation of what had happened, the more devastating for its rational tone, its calm delivery, as in a pleasant drawing-room conversation, while all about whirled the phantasmagoria of unleashed chaos.

A shadow fell across the table: Pavlides looming over them exhaling Turkish smoke. He looked from one to the other. "You gonna eat, eat

315

now, or you spoil the cook's afternoon off. Talk in the restaurant, ha? I close it. Nobody else come."

II

THE cook's afternoon off wasn't shortened by preparation of a late lunch, a club sandwich prescribed in detail by the American, accompanied by the balance of his beer. Van Haaften stuck to his *genever*, omitting the cigarette until Cohen had finished. Food held no appeal, and the gin buffered the effect of the American's story, to which he listened with a sense of inevitability.

"I can't remember anything about that night myself," said Cohen. "Nothing at all. Like most people, I guess, my earliest memories date around age four or five, and they're not clear; hard to describe the impressions they've left." He licked a blob of mayonnaise off a finger and munched in silence for a few seconds before continuing. "So I can only tell you what the old man told me when I was old enough to understand—or no, not understand, only remember what he said. He died when I was eight, but he left me some notes. I kept them, of course, and added my own."

"Have you got them now?"

"Sure—but not here. No need—I read them and referred to them so often I can almost recite them *verbatim*, so they're locked in a safe. I know where they are, in case I need to check a detail or something." He smiled. "You can't be sure you'll get through to tomorrow in the same shape as today."

"I suppose not . . . And the safe?"

"Apartment in Boston." Cohen chewed thoughtfully. Then, after a draught from his glass: "So what I'm going to tell you is mostly what the old guy told me, and what's in the notes in the safe. I've never questioned the truth of it, and what I discovered later fitted the story. So . . ."

Cutting without warning through the night to throw everything on deck into dazzle and black shadow, the searchlight's beam sent a shock-wave through everyone on board, wherever they happened to be—on deck or below. And those below came scrambling into the open, into the glare and the flying splinters and blast of gunfire. The fourth shell, striking the bulwark on the port side amidships, killed the master's wife, who had just hustled several passengers back below while ordering

316

the deckhands to get the boats ready. The sixth, demolishing the poop deckhouse, also damaged the port boat, but not badly enough to prevent its use—in the circumstances; in normal conditions it would have been a write-off. By the time it got away fire had broken out in several places while shells were hitting farther forward. The starboard boat escaped relatively intact, a few planks started in violent contact with the ship's side but shielded from the gun by the hull until the firing stopped, save for a single round which passed overhead. From the searchlight's initial sundering of the night to the last eruption of bubbles from the sinking wreck some thirty minutes had passed, leaving the boats alone on the sea with the killer, which came among them dispensing food and drink and basic medical supplies, for which the old man assured the commander of God's blessing, evidently without the irony being noticed. He had been a jeweller and silversmith of Hamburg; his business had been destroyed and his wife beaten to death on the night of November 9th, 1938—the Nazi party's *Kristallnacht*. After it he had led the life of a fugitive, avoiding the drafts to the labour camps thanks to the kindness of friends, not all of them Jews. Through them he had obtained the papers that enabled him to get as far as St Malo.

Aboard the schooner he befriended Cohen's mother and her ten-month-old child: the husband had been arrested and sent to somewhere in Poland and their home ransacked. Friends had helped her to cross Germany into France and further contacts put her in touch with Calibourdin and his wife. The voyage was planned as an escape for all. Calibourdin was under suspicion of spying and in daily expectation of arrest with his wife, and had no confidence in Britain's winning the war. America was the only safe destination, and his only chance of getting there was to keep out of sight of all other shipping. At night he had run without lights.

When the u-boat returned to open fire on the boats the man grabbed the infant from the dying mother and rolled overboard on the farther side. He had left no description of that action, told the boy Cohen nothing, apart from the fact of its occurrence. After it the u-boat remained for a short interval, playing its searchlight over the scene before disappearing into the rising gale. The man expected to die with the child in his arms but soon after the u-boat's departure he collided with a one of the two floats the schooner had carried in addition to her boats. A dead man—one of the deckhands—was secured to it by a length of rope, which the old man succeeded in detaching, and he spent the next three hours clinging to the float while the whimpering child had subsided into an ominous silence, wrapped in the man's coat but constantly swept by the seas. Again the man expected death, but was determined it would take the child first, comforted to the end as far as possible. Cold would be the agency. Most died of cold; drowning was less precipitate with its mercies.

The third hour brought first light, and—unbelievably and wholly improbably—a ship. Her grey bulk loomed out of the driving spray, plunging into, through and over the seas in explosions of spume and green water, swept for almost her full length to emerge streaming and rearing before the next headlong plunge, seemingly intent on emulating the u-boats that were her normal adversary. She was a destroyer, and travelling at speed, alone, bound on a mission that would change the course of the war, and she was past the float and its half-dead burden before a lookout saw them and for a split second debated with himself whether it was worth reporting a piece of war litter. He saw it almost every day, had grown inured to the evidence of a convoy's passing during the destroyer's spells of service as a unit of an escort support-group; but not on this occasion. On this occasion there were no convoys for hundreds of miles; their routes lay far off, and a u-boat could evade the hunters in this monochrome desolation with comparative ease. But here was a glimpse of the kind of thing it habitually left lying around, the foulness of its passing. A second glimpse, and a movement, a trick of the half-light perhaps, a lurch of the float: the huddled figure seemed to raise an arm, barely above the shoulder before dropping it. Grabbing his handset the lookout spoke tersely to the bridge.

The ship's people were startled to discover not one but two bodies, one of them a small bundle they thought at first to be nothing of value, the survivor's possessions, barely worth the effort of recovery. By the time the pair were nested in the sick-bay among many hot-water bottles, the ship was back on her pell-mell course and the doctor remembering the adage about one hand for the ship and one for himself as he administered a sedative to the elderly chap and wondered whether the sprog would be able to take solid food when he woke. There was time to make sure: at first blue with cold and shivering alarmingly, barely conscious, he was now pinkly warm and sleeping, as the MO put it, like a bug in a rug; infants were tougher than people thought; the survival instinct was strong from birth. He saw them ashore to an ambulance within half an hour of the destroyer's arrival at her destination, the US Navy base at Boston.

"All roads led to Boston, eh?" van Haaften murmured.

"Convenient, I guess—nearest US port to Europe, of any size."

"It was a chance in a million. This—Altmann—would never have expected a warship to appear just at that spot at that time, even if he was worried about being discovered."

"I guess not . . . So—sure, in a way, me being here, in this spot, at this time, is a chance in a million." Cohen gestured with his glass, and drained it. He sat back, eyeing his companion as if mildly amused at the joke. "In several million, even, huh?"

The Dutchman topped up his glass and toyed with it pensively, then sipped, swallowed, and sucked his teeth. "But chances have causes . . . What was a destroyer doing tearing across the North Atlantic on her own like that?—obviously not looking for u-boats. And how is it that I've never heard of this extraordinary voyage—was nothing reported in the papers about the rescue of such remarkable survivors by a warship—were no questions asked?"

"To your last point—no. Not publicly, anyway, and I can't say whether anywhere else. The whole thing was top secret, so even if the ship had run into the lost continent of Atlantis nothing would have been said, far less made public as news. The navy needn't have said anything about where the two had been found, or how, and the old guy made up his mind to say nothing except to the boy, when the time was right. And maybe he was warned against spilling any beans. They could've made things hot for him, and he knew all about that kind of thing."

Van Haaften nodded. "Yes—I see. But that doesn't explain—the destroyer passing that way like that: making a fast crossing alone, and all the secrecy—?"

"Oh—I had to do a little homework on that, too. I'm not a technical man, but maybe you'll know what I'm talking about. I didn't find out until a few years ago—a problem with radar—producing enough power in a short wavelength to give it the range and accuracy needed. And to enable smaller units to do the job—portable ones light enough to fit in airplanes, for example. There was a kind of race between Germany and the Allies to develop a system that could work at ultra-short wavelengths. Centimetres instead of metres. Right?"

"Correct. It was necessary to find a way of generating powerful high frequencies in a small component. Ordinary radio valves could produce the frequencies but not with the power required."

"That's what I discovered. The British developed a prototype that could do the job, but they felt it was unsafe to take it any further in England—risk of some agent getting to know about it, or even getting his hands on it. And always the possibility of a British defeat. So it was sent to the States for further development in safer surroundings. They called it the—the *magnetron*, right?"

"You are correct," said van Haaften. "A lump of copper with holes in it."

Cohen's eyebrows went up. "Is that so? No big deal, then."

"A very big deal," retorted van Haaften. "The tolerances are very critical. The holes must be perfect, machined to exact size . . . And the electronic principles involved. A complete break with conventional processes, undeveloped in Germany, and it lost her the war at sea."

"So I gathered—but exactly how?"

"The u-boat needed to operate on the surface at times—on passage, when attacking, when having to make high speed following a convoy. When radar moved from land bases out into the ocean, aboard ship and—decisively—in the air, it was the finish. The boat could be detected by asdic—sonar—when dived, and by radar when surfaced. No place to hide. The *schnorchel*—the breathing-tube that allowed long periods submerged—came too late, and it couldn't protect the boat from sonar." Van Haaften shrugged. "Once accurate and powerful radar could be carried by escorts and air patrols, the u-boat's day was over, and the chance of starving England into surrender was lost." He smiled, but there was a tired look in his eyes, and Cohen noticed it.

"You seem to know a lot about it for a merchant marine man—?"

Van Haaften returned Cohen's gaze with a frank stare and a dismissive shrug. "The training deals with history as well as technicalities, you know—learning how to use radar means also knowing something about where it came from. And, believe it or not, I read for my own amusement—and enlightenment. The—*merchant marine*—man is not just a truck-driver!"

Cohen coloured slightly and looked uncomfortable. "I'm sorry, captain—landsman's ignorance, I guess—"

"You were going to tell me this destroyer was carrying the magnetron prototype to the States, yes? And of course Germany had to be kept in—in the dark, as they say."

Cohen nodded. "You got it."

"So your elderly friend was in a dangerous position."

"He sure was. Even though he had no intention of saying anything to anyone there was always the chance of someone getting to him—like a Nazi agent. And he was a Kraut, after all, Jew or not. So they interned him for the rest of the war—to stop him fouling up one way or the other. Not that he knew anything about the radar business. Just the fact of the destroyer's voyage, which he didn't even think was unusual. But it would've been enough for the Krauts to smell a rat, or make a guess." Cohen toyed with his glass, frowning. "As it turned out he died without telling anyone about it—except me. They—the authorities—told him where to find me when they let him out. He gave them the idea we were related."

"I see." Van Haaften studied his drink in silence for an interval, then murmured, "Wrong target . . . The chance of a lifetime, missed by a few hours."

"How's that again?"

"Altmann—sinking a schooner full of Jews when he might have been the one to set the Allies' radar project back far enough to give the *Reich*'s people time to catch up—even get ahead."

"Well—we can thank God for that!" Cohen ran his fingers through his brush-cut and blew out his cheeks, as if marvelling at a narrow escape. Which he was. "I guess you could say all those people didn't die for nothing, then."

Van Haaften's brow creased and he bit his lip, and said that was one way of looking at it. But it was not to be thought of as a mitigating factor in Altmann's favour: that would be taking too much for granted. For all practical purposes the magnetron might as well have been a thousand miles away. Ships crossed each others' tracks every day in their scores without seeing so much as a masthead on the horizon. The likelihood of a meeting between particular ships by chance was hypothetical to the point of fantasy. If he had missed the schooner his chances of stumbling upon the destroyer would have been no better, and no worse. There was no connection, only what someone had called the fortune of war. As for the megnetron—it was replaceable, and the destroyer's loss wouldn't have held up the radar project for more than a couple of weeks . . .

"So—you made it to America, by courtesy of the Royal Navy!"

"I sure did—and the old man's. He was ill for some time afterward. Pneumonia. Nearly died, which would've blanked off everything earlier than the destroyer for me. But after I recovered I was passed to a Jewish orphans' organisation which got me adopted by a Boston couple. The old guy contacted them after the war—"

Van Haaften broke in, asking the old man's name. Just "the old guy" was a little uninformative.

"Oh, sure . . . Solomon Fraenkel. Sol. He was sixty-eight then. Died before he made seventy-six—"

"But not before he told you about the sinking, hm?"

Cohen nodded. "Say—can we get coffee in this place?"

Seyyid answered van Haaften's call and, approving the coffee, Cohen continued his story. There was not much more to tell—or, as he explained, nothing beyond the stage to which he was prepared to go with van Haaften, who sat in silence, smoking, sipping his *genever*, allowing no particular expression to cross his features, his eyes registering polite attention, squinting at times in the drifting smoke while the sun slanted through the west-facing windows.

Fraenkel had told the boy what he had not divulged to others, such as the destroyer's captain and the American authorities, to whom he'd given the impression that he and the child, alone among a handful of passengers, had survived an attack of no particular unorthodoxy by an unidentified u-boat. To the boy he related the salient details of the schooner's curtailed voyage, of the u-boat's part in it, and showed him the notes he had made, telling him they would be his when he was older, when he would be able to decide what, if anything, was to be done: Fraenkel did not believe that officialdom would trouble to investigate the matter to any depth, if at all. The loss of a few unnamed Jewish refugees with their French abettors in an obscure incident of no particular distinction was of negligible political significance at the time, less so in a post-war world preoccupied with cares of a more generally apocalyptic nature; would in any case be no more than a tiny augmentation of what had already been discovered on a staggering scale, involving figures whose depravity satisfied the most ghoulishly sentimental of avengers. He had never believed that anyone in authority would pursue the u-boat's commander beyond the reach of routine inquiry with its perfunctory and unsatisfactory conclusion. As for the truth—well, as in other instances, only unauthorised investigation—unauthorised except by a legitimate personal interest—would stand a chance of success. The settling of scores had been some people's lifetime occupation, the more relentlessly prosecuted if the motive were not mere vengeance but also justice. And that, old Fraenkel decided, would be up to his youthful compatriot, and the God to whose will he was bound to accede.

And he told the boy his real name, for he had been given the name of the couple who adopted him, and their chosen first name—Jacob. His real name had been Gluckmann; Aaron Gluckmann, which was all Fraenkel knew. Mrs Gluckmann had never told him where she was from, or what her husband had been. She had not wanted to talk about things she had lost forever, nor had she felt it wise to disclose to one another personal details that might yet have been turned against them. The Cohens were kind, brought Jacob up in the Jewish faith and tradition, and treated him as the natural son they were unable to have; they also made Fraenkel welcome as a visitor and supposed distant relative, and through his business connections Cohen had found him employment in his—Fraenkel's—own craft; and he and his wife saw eventually to the old man's funeral arrangements. Cohen was a broker of non-ferrous metals, and well off. Life with him and his wife had been happy, and the boy had attended good schools and, in due course, Columbia University, where he had majored in company law. He planned to set up on his own account one day; meanwhile, he had a job waiting with a Boston firm, which had been generous in deferring its commencement pending the conclusion, successful or otherwise, of his pursuit of the past, its exact nature undisclosed.

"Taken all round, I've been lucky," said Cohen, pouring a third cup of coffee. He took it without milk or sugar.

"Luckier than most of your people in Germany in those days."

Cohen nodded. "Another reason to thank God."

Van Haaften studied the healthy, regular features before him; the brown eyes were clear, untroubled, intelligent, the high brow unlined, the wide mouth tending more to an upward than a downward curve, the complexion bearing the vibrant bloom of skin that revelled equally in sunshine and rain, wind and calm, Boston December and Mombasa March, turning each to advantage in conveying a general impression of physical and mental balance: good nature, an easy self-confidence that spoke of a benign background and an assured place in the scheme of things as he saw them. Jacob—Jake—Cohen was the kind of young American expecting, and expected to attain to, a successful professional and social career in a country that allowed its citizens—well, most of them, but certainly the Jewish element and especially the comfortably-off—almost unconditional freedom of enterprise and initiative, the rewards of which it left largely uneroded by taxes. For all its political sensitivities and delusions, life in post-war America embraced a curiously innocent approach to personal and national wellbeing, based on a deceptively simple constitution symbolised by the flag, the icon towards which the people looked for confirmation of their assumptions of national ascendancy on the world stage, war in Korea notwithstanding. Justice, flawed to a greater or lesser extent, was defined with all the clarity and simplicity of a strong man's creed. Similar, in certain respects, reflected van Haaften, to the way it had been when he was Cohen's age. Similar, and so very different. John F. Kennedy's charisma swayed millions. So had the *Fuhrer*'s, even across national boundaries. There the similarity ended. Between him—van Haaften—and the American lay the essence of the difference. It would not be changed by anything either of them could arrange or act upon.

Musing in this vein, van Haaften found himself regarding Cohen with the stirrings of contempt—not personal, but in general, at first; the contempt of an older generation for a younger, of one that had lived through, and suffered, tribulations the other knew of only in theory, if at all, and for which it cared little or nothing, pursuing its ideals and conceits with a certainty and self-confidence that had not—yet—been tested to destruction and beyond. The American's easy manner, guileless good nature, pleasant demeanour and air of moral probity stemmed from a soft-living outlook in which all good things come inevitably to hand as of right, as though God-given and deserved, a due reward for virtue gained by application and diligence in the best of all possible worlds. There was an air about Cohen that brought van Haaften to mind of the present decadence of the western powers, and an irritation that what had been fought for with such bitterness and pain had finally got into such lax hands, hands which through their own self-indulgence were losing the prize to the gathering forces of anarchy and disorder. Cohen represented a generation in sore need of toughening up, deprivation, challenge and hazard, things with which it would have to contend for survival, and from it gain a proper appreciation of life's values, which were not to be dispensed with unconditional liberality among the baser elements, where they would be corrupted, disgraced, diminished and finally eliminated. It had been like that with the Jewish problem; while others laboured under the yoke of reparations in a Germany brought to resentful penury by the punitive measures of treaties signed under duress, the Jews had prospered, not only in Germany but also in the rest of depression-hit Europe, Holland included; and taken advantage, as they would again, and were already doing: look at this Cohen, for example. He could afford to be easy-going, pleasant, confident—afford to call civilisation a heap of shit, when he could stand clear of the ordure and stink of its decay and pass lofty judgment—even look forward to a career in which such a standpoint would be materially profitable. Strange, thought van Haaften, that he had chosen law—though of course Jews had been and were prominent in the profession among others.

A thought occurred to him. How had Cohen discovered the name of the u-boat's commander?

"Oh—yeah. Vital detail." Cohen drained his cup and replaced it carefully. "Old Sol did a drawing in his notes. The logo—the symbol—painted on the conning-tower. Just like the Greek survivors in Eck's case he caught sight of it as the boat came up to pass over the food and water. He told me they gave them sausage. Pork! And Germans aren't supposed to have a sense of humour!" Cohen shook his head and grinned. "Been interesting to see how long they'd've held out if they hadn't been—well—" He shrugged and his mouth tightened. "Academic point . . . Anyway, the searchlight's scatter and someone's torch lit up this design on the conning-tower for a few seconds, and he stood up in the boat to see better. When he told Altmann he'd get God's blessing. Kinda distraction."

"And this—design?"

"Yes . . . chivalric, you'd call it, maybe—no, not chivalric!" He laughed in self-deprecation. "Wrong word . . . Heraldic, that's it. Kinda thing you'd see on someone's coat of arms, I guess. A short sword gripped two-handed with its point down. About to give the *coup de grace*, obviously. Some kind of legendary or mythical connection, maybe—German folklore, something like that. I'm not familiar with that kind of thing, apart from fairy tales—Grimm's, you know?"

Expressionless, van Haaften nodded. "Yes. That kind of thing."

"A mark of conceit, as I said, and enough to hang a man. Kind of a calling-card. Makes the detective's job a cinch." Cohen smiled, but in his eyes van Haaften saw curiosity, and a hardening of their brown softness. "If there'd been no mark—no logo—my chances of discovering whose boat it was would've been roughly nil. Thank God for vanity, huh?"

Taking a breath van Haaften forced a smile. "As you say—thank God . . . But how do you get from the *Kriegsmarineschule* to Mombasa?"

"Good question! Especially if you've been told the man you're looking for was shot dead by accident and buried with full military honours in the last Nazi funeral of the war—or a couple of days after it ended, anyway."

"Who did you hear that from?"

"Several people. And organisations. It's not official secrets stuff. Newspaper reports, army records at the British Ministry of Defence, *Bundesmarine* records, ex-*U-Bootwaffe* service associations in Germany . . . People have been helpful rather than obstructive. Officially, Altmann's dead. There's a headstone to prove it."

Van Haaften snorted. "Yet you say he's here somewhere—and that I know where!"

Cohen's smile turned down into a grimace, and he chewed his lower lip for a moment. Picking up his coffee-spoon he toyed with it, frowning, then looked up and nodded, taking a breath. "I guess so, captain." He sat back and dropped the spoon with a clatter into the saucer, then blew out his cheeks, removed his glasses and rubbed his face with both hands, dragging the flesh below his eyes down in red-rimmed arcs. Dropping his hands finally, he repeated, "I guess so", and slowly replaced his glasses to fix van Haaften with a watery regard in which speculation seemed to emphasise the American commonplace.

Van Haaften wondered whether to protest at the patent irrationality of Cohen's position or ridicule it as an irrelevance; instead he conceded the point to satisfy a curiosity he decided was indefensibly morbid; but morbid or not, it insisted on acknowledgment, and satisfaction. After all, if Altmann were alive, it would be interesting to know how the American had obtained his information.

"So what do you know that all these—these *sources*—have missed? How have you got hold of such information?—I assume you haven't dug up the coffin to find they buried a few rocks for a joke!" Van Haaften ended with a scornful snort and examined the remaining contents of his glass before draining it off.

Cohen watched, lips compressed in an expression of enigmatic dispassion. Then, as van Haaften's gaze met his he said, "There was no need."

"What do you mean?"

"Just that. I knew what was in it—not rocks. And not Altmann."

"A resurrection?" Van Haaften almost sneered, but Cohen did not appear to notice. Nor did he pursue the point. Instead, he veered off in a new direction with a question: had van Haaften heard of a man called Wiesenthal "—Simon Wiesenthal?"

After a moment's pause in which Cohen regarded him inquiringly, van Haaften cleared his throat and said, "The Nazi-hunter?", startling himself with the strangely acrid taste of the words. He had not uttered the key word for as long as he could remember. It would have savoured of blasphemy. Now he sought to sponge off the traces of its passing with an innocuous "Of course—I could hardly have missed the Eichmann affair . . . Are you telling me Altmann was—"

"No." Cohen shook his head and raised a hand. "His people—Wiesenthal's—knew nothing about the schooner. But they have information about lots of Nazis and Nazi sympathisers, most of it picked up along the way as the big shots were being investigated and tracked. I contacted him, asked him if he could confirm Altmann's death, or give me any kind of information about him—as a Party member or supporter, which is what the funeral obviously meant."

"And?"

Cohen did not answer immediately. Instead, he took the lid off the percolator and peered in, sucked his teeth in disappointment, and sat back to return van Haaften's gaze. His smile conveyed regret. He said, "And no more, captain. For Altmann's ears only." He bit his lower lip.

Van Haaften stared at him, nonplussed. Finally he said, "How will you manage that—telepathy? Or maybe a session with a medium—witch-doctors are the people to see in this country."

"Oh, no." Cohen's tone was light, as casual as if remarking on the weather. "Face to face. I'll tell him in person."

Squeezing the bridge of his nose to give himself time to think, van Haaften finally broke the ensuing silence with another question. It was genuine, and expressed something so fundamental to the American's argument that he was surprised at its not having occurred to him before. It occurred now accompanied by a sensation of cautious relief. He said, "As far as I can make out, you're the only one—apart from this Altmann—who knows of the incident, yes?"

Cohen studied van Haaften's face in silence for a short interval, then nodded, pursing his lips and lifting his eyebrows, as if querying the reason for such an obvious statement. Was it not the whole purport of his story? "Sure," he said. "As far as I know, anyway. There's always a chance that someone'll come forward—maybe one of the u-boat's men—if they get to hear about my search, but—" He shrugged. "I'm not having it put up in lights on Broadway."

"And the only evidence you have—beside yourself—is the collection of notes left to you by Fraenkel?"

"Right again."

"I see . . . So, tell me, Mr Cohen—as a lawyer: with only your word and a few notes which refer to a boat once commanded by a—distinguished, shall I say?—officer of the *U-Bootwaffe*, whose personal motif was common knowledge and easily ascertained by inquiry—as you have said—what proof is there that your story is true and not a fabrication, even if the sailing and subsequent disappearance of the schooner—without a passenger-list—is documented? Your living person is not in itself proof, as you must realise. Nor even Fraenkel's, late departed. You have proved nothing beyond your own continued existence, and at best, if you are able to obtain official confirmation of it, your rescue by the British destroyer. You are nothing more significant than another survivor of the war at sea. That alone is not enough to bring a prosecution, and I think Wiesenthal's organisation requires evidence of the kind needed for legal process, not so? Or are you telling me it engages in assassination?"

Taking a breath, Cohen released it in a silent whistle as he ran a hand through his crew-cut, and the brown eyes met van Haaften's frankly. "That's about the size of it, captain. I mean, about the legal angle. Only Altmann would know my story's true, and it's not enough, as my word against his—unless he confesses!—to indict him. And I don't know whether assassination's a Wiesenthal specialty or not. I didn't ask. He isn't with me on this, beyond what he helped me find out about Altmann's career."

"So where is it all leading, Mr Cohen?"

"Oh—well, as I've said—to a meeting." Cohen shrugged. "I hope. You see, Captain van Haaften, my business with Altmann doesn't require proof—apart from my own existence." He shrugged, taking a breath again. "That's all there is to it."

Van Haaften's gesture expressed something of his perplexity. "So what exactly is your business, Mr Cohen?"

"Sorry, captain. As I've said—for Altmann's ears only." Cohen glanced at his watch. "Time's flying—nearly a quarter after three already." His glasses flashed a reflection of the windows at van Haaften, momentarily giving him the look of a blind man. He pushed his chair back. "Got a few things to do—can the barman give me my check—?"

"Leave it—I'll see to it . . ." As Cohen got to his feet van Haaften remained where he was, and looked up at the American. "Altmann—?"

Cohen said, "Tonight. I'll meet him tonight. You'll tell him, captain, won't you? I'll be at the Leven steps, up at the Old Harbour, at—what'll be a good time? Midnight?" He coughed apologetically, took off his glasses and pulled out a handkerchief to polish the lenses. Blinking at van Haaften, he added, "Are you staying, or—?"

Van Haaften smiled, squinting up at him. "I have some business with Pavlides." He paused, studying the other's face intently for a few seconds, and Cohen returned an inquiring look. "Be careful on those steps, Mr Cohen. They're old and badly worn, and the lighting round there's not good. The only interest anyone will take if you have an accident will be in the contents of your pockets."

Cohen grinned. "What they'll find in a Jew's pockets'll spoil their whole day!" He settled his glasses in position and stuffed the handkerchief away. Turning for the door to the bar, he paused. "Forgive me asking, captain," he said, the levity dropped. "But that's quite a distinctive scar you've got there—some kind of accident?"

Van Haaften's glance was sharp. "A fight. When I was at school. Why do you wish to know?"

Cohen looked embarrassed, and shrugged. "Oh—no particular reason. I'm sorry, captain—shouldn't have asked." He laughed uncomfortably. "Curiosity, I guess . . . Well, so long, sir. Thanks for lunch. It's a pity I won't get a chance to repay you."

For some time after the American had gone van Haaften sat on, smoking, and watching the patches of sunlight from the windows make their slow way across the dingy room to the farther wall. He drank no more of the *genever*, but after a while called Seyyid and ordered fresh coffee.

III

ALTMANN—already the Dutchman's name had resumed the ersatz flavour of its first adoption—kept the Luger in working order, periodically stripping and oiling it and checking the clip of bullets. Apart from its obvious function it was also something of a memorial—to a time, a way of life—and death—and, immanently, a particular man, for the last time it had been aimed at anything with whatever intent it had been by the midshipman Hildegras at the boat's periscope.

So long ago: twenty years. The boy would have been thirty-eight now. A successful architect, perhaps, known for his elegant buildings, his graceful conurbations; or perhaps measuring success in respectable obscurity providing in modest comfort for a wife, children . . . As things had turned out, however, not so much as a headstone marked his short foray into the foothills of life. As a substitute, the Luger lacked distinction, notwithstanding its symbolism as an arbiter of fate.

He worked the breech action to be sure it was clear and picked up the clip, pausing to examine it, counting the rounds, remarking to himself the fact that they had been issued with the weapon on his first taking up a command. He never left the clip in place, always made sure the chamber was empty whenever he had finished handling it. The safety-catch alone wasn't enough of a safeguard; there had been accidents, some of them regrettable. The gun had never been fired, in anger or idleness, and he amused himself with the thought that for all he knew the thing didn't work. He was less amused by the thought that if it did a man's death would confirm it, and very shortly. The joke was that his own death would confirm its malfunction. He smiled, but too late to catch the fleeting humour. For the first time in his life he was about to kill a man, an individual, more than a component of an enemy unit: a fellow human-being, an identifiable, unique personality whose existence had been revealed in more than two dimensions, whose destruction would rob the world of something of value, however insignificant in its affairs. He was about to reduce a man to a piece of refuse, an agent of decay and corruption, while watching the life ebb at a distance of mere centimetres—within reach, but beyond recovery. Strange, he thought, that he should be so disturbed at the prospect of despatching a killer intent on his specific person when he had been able to contemplate the killing of many possessing no knowledge of his person, let alone an intention to kill him, with equanimity. Duty, he supposed, made the difference; and belief in the rectitude of the cause that required it. Now, in this particular instance, he could claim no such protection from himself; none, that is, apart from the simple demands of self-preservation.

It was a curious paradox, he reflected, that a man would be prepared to die for a cause but not if the cause were his own life. Well, that was obvious enough: the proposition was an absurdity. Yet, if one argued logically, and pragmatically, what better cause was there to die for than one's own life? But perhaps that was not the right way of putting it: perhaps it should be that a man would not die for his own life, but risk death—risk it in the hope—even the trust—that matters wouldn't take him that far, though robbing him of everything else; leaving him with nothing but his life, and doubt about its worth as mere existence. And when young, the certainty that matters would not go as far as death, a certainty that continued unshaken to the very last flicker of dying light; like the certainty, however irrational, that the boat would, somehow, survive the shock of detonation, the unimaginable pressure of untested depth, the inrush of water. Perhaps, he thought, Prien, Schepke and others who had followed them out of life as the war drew on—Liebeherr, Rogge, Herbert Benedict, Palmgren, Henning, Falke, elevated to *Obermaschinist* . . . Little Greischen even, in his different view of the inevitable; and Hildegras—had all been certain, up to the last instant, that they would somehow emerge intact.

Yes—and Schreiber. Discharged from the naval hospital at Kiel unfit for further service, to return to a mother widowed by the sea and deprived of a whole son by it. His attempts to offer assistance had met with polite rebuff from the mother, speaking, so she had said, for a son unable to reply in his own hand; his last letter had brought no answer and inquiry revealed the address's location in a suburb of Bremen devastated in the daylight bombing raids mounted by the Americans. He had missed the memorial service, which in any case had been only one of a ritualistic series in the absence of identifiable remains. And a memorial to what? The loss to the *U-Bootwaffe* of a prospective commander, certainly; and perhaps to the post-war North German Lloyd of a distinguished commodore, even a training-ship bearing the name. *Kommodore Schreiber.* She would have been a full-rigger, of course; followed across the Southern Ocean by some albatross or other . . . And the woman, the mother and widow: she had served the Fatherland to her last breath, her last drop of blood, but in a bitterness that had struck at him from between the lines of her concluding letter in terms that belied the formal phraseology of the neat script; almost a personal accusation that had shocked as it saddened him.

Altmann wondered, as did all his kind, all too often, what exactly had been in the minds of the about-to-be dead. Perhaps, at the last, neither hope nor despair, nor an irrational certainty of ultimate survival, but a terror so great that it anaesthetised the mind for the last moments, itself a mercy in the face of eternal extinction. And perhaps, in the last moments, age advanced at a rate exchanging years for microseconds, so that no man died young, but aged, broken, deranged, uncomprehending. It was a kind of comfort, he suggested to himself, that age—elapsed years—made no difference at the end; except that in a way the older man had the better deal, apart from having had, if not enjoyed, a longer life.

He raised the pistol and squinted along the barrel at the night sky framed in the open window of his day-room, took up the first pressure on the trigger, squeezed it against and past the resistance of the firing-spring. Click. That would be it: death of a killer, and his own survival. He slid the clip into the butt and thumped it home, then set the safety-catch and the cocking mechanism. Aiming through the window again he squeezed the trigger, felt the baulk of the first pressure then, experiencing a momentary surge of blood through his veins, squeezed harder. No movement. The trigger remained hard against the safety stop. He relaxed, sat with the gun resting on his knee. His own survival—but for what? What was left worth surviving for? He sat back, absently contemplating the stars through the window, and reviewed his present circumstances.

Age, for example. He was fifty-two. Not old; but not young either, and able to contemplate death without a quickening of the pulse; to see it more as a means of settling all debts, of tying off all loose ends, than as the curtailment of a project. What in a younger man would cause anguish, frustration, anger and a sense of injustice, to an older presented itself as a viable solution, a legitimate exculpation, an impartial, limiting culmination of all mortal vanities: a true valuation of a man's conceits, and a reduction of his pretensions to the common weal. So the question stood: what qualities—if any—possessed by whatever might remain of his life could make it worth pursuing?

A re-sat mathematics examination had opened the door to aspiration—to self-justification—even if his mark had been only a suspect three percent above a bare pass. The narrowest squeak in German naval history, Liebeherr had called it, and Altmann wondered what his friend would have said about its distinctive outcome. Short, that is, of the ignominy of defeat, last in a series of events that had, brick by brick, demolished the laboriously-constructed curtain-wall of his private citadel, forcing its abandonment as his only chance of survival.

332

Brick by brick, and in runs at a time. Most of them had been indistinguishable in comprising the wall's general structure: daily occasions, passing acquaintance, the minutiæ of normal life in its progress, both according to plan and under the random pressures and buffetings of chance. Others had been placed to enhance the appearance as well as to contribute substantially to the wall's strength in crucial sections. In his work—his chosen profession, or calling—a steady, if not conspicuously rapid, advancement through the ranks to command as the *U-Bootwaffe* had expanded, slowly enough, in response to the looming prospect of war; and the qualified triumph of his part in its eventual, inevitable, outbreak and progress, all the way through to the desk in the commandant's office at the *Mutterhaus*. He had marvelled at the fact of his occupying, officially and two succeeding occupants later, the very seat from which Vice-Admiral Niethe-Grapow had expatiated upon the dire consequences of another failure, avoided by a hair's-breadth to earn him the admiral's pointedly reserved congratulations.

But the congratulations he had volunteered at the wedding of his niece to the same mathematical sloven had been almost effusive, expressed with the hope that having such a wife as his incentive Altmann would discover a hidden facility with figures in their application to safely-managed absences from home. Which, however fulfilled, had not proved of any practical use in preventing the loss of the wall's second foundation-stone and a resulting breach. Before that catastrophic event random assaults had opened other gaps—Liebeherr's abrupt exit and the removal of a part of the wall that had protected a particularly estimable—irreplaceable—possession and privilege in his friend's bluff and unsentimental regard. Greischen's unnecessary death and another run of bricks gone, taking with them the quiet encouragement his dryly perceptive company had extended, continued in the letters he'd written at intervals dictated by events. Several more in the men who had died under his command, and Schreiber's living death with whatever it had led to after the wall's final collapse into the general ruin of the *Dritte Reich*—the dust and rubble of his further promotions and seemingly secure shore-based postings, the value of which had in any case been negated by the stricken bomber's fatal descent. It was still a matter of some bafflement that he had continued while lacking the lodestone of familial responsibility and reciprocal support, concluding that he had somehow found a way of transposing his sentiments, shifting them from a lost point of bearing to augment those he had allocated to the service and the greater cause: his dedication to the *U-Bootwaffe*'s interests and through them to the furtherance of the aims and principles of the National Socialist *Reich*. It had been possible to shut his mind to what had once existed at a personal level outside those foci of loyalty and duty, which had seemed to be enough for what remained of his aspirations, satisfied with so much less than the hoped-for returns.

And now, after scraping together the vestiges following the disgrace of the *Führer*'s suicide and exposure of the shameful internal machinery of the monstrosity created in the guise of a renascent German Fatherland, the end of a day in which even the gimcrack edifice he had constructed from the scrapings had been razed by forces he had always felt to be in waiting, their emplacement, strategy and timing beyond prescience. His tentative occupation of the base established by dint of circumstance in this far-flung haven had been summarily invalidated by the shredding of its loose fabric, tacked together as it had been by wilful self-delusion: persuading himself that he could call a halt to his flight had been evidence less of calculated risk than of folly. Which left him facing the sombre fact that whatever had gone before, and been lost, had been the sum of his allotted share of life's collation—perhaps something more than his share. Ursula, for instance. The happiness she had brought him, in such punishingly brief instalments, had been intense and precious beyond description, perhaps so much so that it had consumed—as had been their shared intention, consciously or not—what would otherwise have spanned a full allotment of years in a matter of instants, flashes of passion in a night with no end except oblivion, threatened from moment to moment.

So what was left? The money he had saved, a few thousand score of Kenyan shillings; the money with which Mukerjee had bought the ship, and would sever their business arrangement; and his identity as evidenced by the master's licence and other official documents bearing the seal of the Netherlands government variously before and during German occupation—of uncertain validity and likely to prompt closer examination and investigation if presented in support of an application for employment, or a marine mortgage: the money, a limited reserve not readily negotiable outside the country, was not enough to purchase another ship outright. And employment by whom? Shipping companies were looking for younger men, and, at any age, men with verifiable and reputable records of previous postings; Dutch companies were making particularly discerning selections, and openings were few, apart from which he could not entertain the prospect of a return to Europe, Holland in particular. Besides, his qualification as a master was out of date, lacking the supplementary competencies introduced since the war. A qualification in the operation of radar, for example: he was sourly amused at the irony in such a thing's being, once again, a block to progress, if in a different manner from its earlier manifestation. He could take a course, he supposed, at some suitably undiscriminating training venue, but even so it would be at risk of inquiry into his identity, even in the form of mere routine verification. And there were other obstructions, effectively blocking avenues that would have been open to a *bona fide* holder of a mariner's papers. As for avenues that might offer a way out regardless, did he want to follow their shadowy deviations—was he finally so bereft of self-respect that he could contemplate demeaning himself and what he could salvage of his principles for the sake of merely continued existence—of the life of a pariah, both professional and social? Or would that, as a final consequence of his career between his decision to abandon law and his impulse to make whatever could be made of a Dutchman's ill-fortune, be his means of redemption? He could see no other way, short of the nihility in which he would join those who had gone before.

Which, he reflected, might be the solution he had spent the last twenty-two years refusing to acknowledge—to the still-recurring visitations of the phantoms against which his only defence lay in the contents of the bottle he kept discreetly, as he thought, to hand. If the others aboard this ship with him knew or guessed anything they preferred to play their parts in the masquerade as long as he played his: lack of appetite at breakfast and habitual reticence which occasionally deepened into brusque moodiness was the master's prerogative and bred no resentment among them. He knew his business, which was enough: it assured them of a living. Whatever might have troubled him apart from the normally manageable demands of the ship and her people was kept to himself, and no-one felt moved to the indiscretion of inquiry, or even to express curiosity amongst the others. As the chief engineer, McDade, a pugilistic Glaswegian with an exceptional record of bad discharges and exponent of an equally exceptional and informal version of engineering practice, had observed, a man's entitlement to a life other than the enslavement which kept a shirt on his back was sacrosanct. Early on he had sensed an enigma in the Dutchman, but having himself a past at which he occasionally cast a reflective eye, usually through a softening veil of single malt which had long lost the power to affect his temperament in the way that had ensured the bad discharges, he had made it clear that discussion of the captain's ways in his hearing would incur a forthright expression of his disapproval. It would have surprised him to learn that the captain saw in him a benignly distorted shade of a man whose violent death he would gladly have helped to bring about at an early period in his seagoing career. Altmann dwelt amusedly on the fact, and the probable results of disclosure. Which, of course, could not be countenanced; and in any case the resemblance of McDade to Herbert Benedict lay only in certain professional traits and not by any stretch of sentimental imagination in physical or temperamental characteristics. Nevertheless, there were moments when Altmann felt grateful to the testy Scot for his fancied understanding of the situation, as he had felt grateful to Benedict for a better-grounded conceit, but while it eased the continuous pressure of anxiety under which he felt himself, at times, to be labouring with diminishing effect, against the spectral objects of his half-waking retrospections it could provide neither relief nor refutation. And whatever sanctuary he had found in his circumspect resort to the bottle it had steadily crumbled around him in counterpoint to the tolerance of toxic excess developed by his system. His natural aversion to self-reduction through an indulgence he had always regarded as a moral failing had been suppressed, but at the cost of his studied integrity, and a substantial part of his moodiness following a night of mental and spiritual struggle was the product of disgust at his weakness. His realisation that it had become a condition akin to an illness added to his sense of self-contempt. No McDade could release him from what he feared was a trap, but was he being offered an escape through the unheralded appearance of the American? And if so, by what means, and to what?

He stirred, reaching for his cigarettes as he put the Luger on the desk, and sat on, smoking and pondering. At one point his glance strayed to the locker in which he kept the supply of Pavlides's *genever*, but with a grunt he switched it to the clock on the bulkhead. He had had enough of the stuff at lunchtime, Seyyid's coffee notwithstanding. Perhaps more coffee. He stubbed out the cigarette and rose to press the call-button for the steward. Removing the clip from the Luger he ejected the chambered bullet and replaced it with its fellows, dropping clip and pistol into the drawer and closing it.

Later, preparing to leave the room, he slipped it with the clip into his trousers pocket. Just less than an hour to go: his watch agreed with the clock. Enough time to walk across town to the Old Harbour. He glanced round the cabin. Nothing out of place. The steward would be back for the coffee-tray shortly. He took a pace towards the doorway and paused, frowning. Then, abruptly, as if arriving at a long-debated conclusion, he turned back to the desk, replaced the pistol and clip, locked the drawer, pocketed the key, and in a swift movement crossed the cabin to emerge into the alleyway which took him past McDade's cabin. The light was on, glowing through the curtained doorway. He caught a snatch of short-wave radio static and a distorted voice, very English. Some programme on the BBC overseas service: McDade was always listening to the news from home, as he called it, though he hadn't been there since a year or two after the war. Altmann hesitated, decided against saying anything to the engineer, and made his way to the quayside and the dock gates. The policeman on duty nodded to him as he passed. He was well-known. He could have got the gun through unquestioned.

Declining the invitations of the waiting taxi-drivers he walked briskly towards town past the seamen's mission, the first landmark. He had never called there, though the padre often came aboard to chat and offer his services to the others, even to McDade, or perhaps especially to McDade, whose spiritual ambivalence extended to the proffered dram, always refused, a ritual that had become a standing joke. The unlikely friendship between the pair was founded on the padre's physical, rather than spiritual, proficiency, embracing the refereeing of the football matches he arranged between ships' companies and the boxing coaching he offered in person to all comers, extended to occasional, well-attended, matches between ships' champions, or sacrificial lambs. Chief among them were young seamen and apprentices and cadets, while McDade, occasionally present in a strictly secular capacity, provided critical comment and, occasionally, supplementary advice and instruction in the nature of what he called self-defence. It was all very well, he sniffed, to learn all that Queensberry rules stuff, but a young lad ashore visiting the places that attracted him, usually at night after a day's work, needed a few tricks up his sleeve to avoid giving his mother a nasty surprise when returning home; in some cases in order to return home at all. The tricks had been forged among the slipways and fitting-shops of Clydebank and Govan and the tenements of the

Gorbals where their purpose had been rather more utilitarian than recreational. But the boxing was the tie between two otherwise unlikely parties to a friendship McDade ineffectually disguised beneath scornful references to "Yon sass'nach Bible-puncher w' hus leadin' left!", belied by a patent respect for the impressive collection of cups marking a notable amateur career in days before, as their holder averred, he had heard the call. Most of Mombasa's shipping fraternity, both fixed and periodic, awaited in waning expectation the ultimate confrontation and, so asserted the more dramatically-inclined, conversion in the shape of a no-limits exhibition bout between dog-collar and sweat-rag, but sceptics suspected connivance at a long-running fraud and amusement in the ambiguous hints both men dropped from time to time. There would be no fight, at least of the kind that would pack out the mission with the unrepentant profane. Between that and the ever-rumoured non-event of the Paradise Bar's flying Scawegian, van Haaften's view, occasionally expressed, was that as a sailor's town Mombasa left something to be desired. Which, as McDade would point out to anyone hearing it, showed that, for a Dutchman at any rate, the skipper had a sense of humour. He had never inquired into the cause of Altmann's disfigurement, and Altmann took pains to avoid any suggestion of interest in his and the padre's shared pastime.

Walking on, he turned these reflections over like picture-cards, allowing himself the vestige of a wry smile as he added the likely footnote to his half-joking verdict on the port's nautical credentials: a headline in the *Mombasa Times* would do it, and discovery of the body of a well-known Mombasa-based ship's master in the Old Harbour would make the front page.

Passing beneath the giant tusks bridging Kilindini Road he made his way into the populous neighbourhood of bars, clubs, restaurants and cinemas that at this hour was reaching a pitch of charged excitement, the thronged pavements spilling their contents into the road among cruising taxis, wobbling bicycles, rickshaws, cars, motorcycles and scooters, an eddying, undirected, pleasure-driven, loosely-blended multitude amongst which, like pike in a mill-stream, lurked beggars, peddlers, pimps, pickpockets, hucksters, itinerant vendors and sojourning bagmen, trailing in the wakes of the sailors who regarded themselves as freemen of the port and its diversions. Conspicuous in their creased, unbuttoned shirts and drainpipes and winkle-pickers, their perspiring, determined, sun-flayed faces set between jaw-length sideburns that hung, handsomely or intimidatingly, from Brylcreemed reproductions of Elvis-inspired thatching, they tended to congregate, like rooks about favoured trees, in the approaches to the bars. As Altmann passed by doors opened to disgorge their flushed and glassy-eyed clientele on gusts of canned pop and rock music and the smoke of cigarettes and fumes of gin and beer and cheap perfume, and admit the replacements who moments before had debouched from another melting-pot farther along the road. The Paradise Bar was in full swing, its frontage bulging with the pressure, a tremor in the pavement beneath Altmann's feet. He quickened his pace as its doors swung apart to liberate a blast from the juke-box in company with a reeling group of sailors and shrieking girls, slamming shut again to cut off *The Lion Sleeps Tonight* in mid-ululation. It was the sort of night on which a flying Scawegian would not have attracted much attention, and instead Altmann looked up at the flashing lights of an aircraft making its final approach to the airport, a shadow blanking out a lane of stars in succession as it crossed low overhead, briefly overlaying the ambient din with its throttled-back drumming. Another world up there, he thought; and another out at sea, where, years ago and only a couple of hundred miles distant, he had ducked in reaction to the Catalina's last strafing-run; watched the *Clan Finlay* go down in the blaze of her own pyre; and where the remains of young Hildegras had slipped over the side on a day of flat and brooding calm. That sinking had been his last action of the war, apart from the scuffle with the Liberator that had settled Schreiber's future out of hand.

He switched his thoughts from the too-often re-run scenes back to the road, becoming aware of an undercurrent of tension that had not until recently disturbed the cycle of revelry. Among the indigenous element he noticed a higher pitch of voice, broader grins and more expansive gestures, a more febrile quality to the habitual tenor of night fever, and he returned an occasional *jambo* or *salamu* absently while noting its unaccustomed edge of affability, or affected good humour, or, distinctly, brashness bordering on impertinence; even a swagger seemingly assumed for his particular note, evidently as a white man. It was a mood he had sensed patchily in recent months, and in increasing openness, attributing it to the rapid changes being made in national government preparatory to the country's imminent independence from British colonial authority. A man of the tribe from which Mau Mau had sprung would be the head of government, with consequences providing the current subject of conjecture in every bar and club, cafe and restaurant, shop and office, across town, of which Altmann knew his present situation to be one, as so regretfully spelled out by Mukerjee—the Indian's own position yet another, quite beside financial considerations.

Passing the last of the road's sailors' dens, he glanced down a side-road towards the sports club where at one time the rule had been whites only but was now indiscriminate, open to any who aspired to the peculiarly English pastimes of cricket and tennis beneath the blazing sun on the baked earth and spiky grey tendrils pressed into service as the nearest approximation to the village green the season allowed, with the club-house's spacious verandah standing in for the pavilion. Attained through the well-meant offices of the assistant harbour-master, Altmann's membership was a privilege of which he seldom availed himself, and then only to sit apart, looking on from a cane chair attended by a fezzed and *kanzu*'d bearer, drinking a slow cold Tusker and wondering how things would have looked if the war's outcome had realised the *Führer*'s dream. Certainly it would not have included the prospect of black African rule, whatever part the Asian—Indian and Pakistani—element might have played, and the Arabs as the other political element of the scene, with their obvious and often alluded-to connections among the oil-rich sheikhdoms not far off over their sea's north-eastern rim. But now . . .

Now, of course, the British were in process of losing the last substantial components of the empire they had been guaranteed by the *Führer* in return for a free hand in Europe, and losing them through an azotic mixture of contrived guilt and lack of moral conviction alloyed with what seemed to be a post-war incompetence emanating from the remote fastnesses of political administration in London. Altmann was conscious of a despairing contempt for a people who had expended so much energy—blood, toil, tears and sweat, as Churchill had put it—in fighting off the *Wermacht*, to say nothing of the Japanese, albeit in alliance with the Americans, only to let the entire structure for which they and their forebears had bled, toiled, wept and sweated fall back into the hands of the inferior races from which it had been so expensively wrested. They—the British—had approached empire in the wrong spirit—one of benevolent despotism that had metamorphosed into the precipitate free-handedness of post-war dissolution, backing away, step by craven, dissimulating step, from colonial responsibility faced with upstart political and guerrilla-style intimidation, of which Mau Mau had been a classic example. India having achieved what it called its freedom, and the start of a perpetual conflict with its newly-wrought Mohammedan neighbour, Britain was handing over territories that, in Africa, had almost immediately begun a descent into pre-colonial chaos and post-colonial corruption which, ironically, were making even greater demands on the erstwhile ruler's resources in ways closely akin to blackmail with the communist powers implicit in the plot. One thing was certain, Altmann affirmed to himself: if the Fatherland had been the victor none of this sort of thing would have come about. But of course there, too, blood, toil, tears and sweat had been expended, only to be nullified by men who had allowed power to distort their judgment, most tellingly in the *Führer*'s decision to go to war several years before Germany was prepared. Of his many mistakes, that had been the greatest and the most strategically disastrous: from it all else had flowed, like a noxious effluent overflowing onto fertile soil with almost minimal interference from without. As Altmann had later decided, the system had suffered from serious design faults—faults of principle—which in the end would have destroyed it independently of external pressures. If only, he thought, the key figures had not been so carried away with their political success in those years when the Allies had shown themselves to be weak-willed and complacent in matters of treaty obligations—matters of duty and honour, in which they had failed, and for which they were still paying the price, victory over the *Reich* notwithstanding. They had made as much of a *hash*, as Cohen would have called it, of their success as the Party had made of the cause, obsessed as it had been with the Jewish question and the *Führer*'s impetuous drive to establish *Lebensraum*.

The Roman Catholic cathedral stood massively against the stars as he walked on into Fort Jesus Road. Here the crowd had thinned to a few loiterers and more purposeful figures, silent and anonymous in the gloom between the well-spaced street-lights; and road-traffic was reduced to a fitful trickle. Dimly-lit shutter-flanked windows, mostly above street-level, took the place of the neon and floodlight of the bars and dives, diffuse murmuring the place of carousal. The Old Town retained its shabby dignity and attachments to its past, which crept diffidently into the open with the advance of darkness, and Altmann felt some of his irritation dissipate to give place to a sense of resignation. There was no point in dwelling on the might-have-been. Today was a different world, and Dönitz no longer *Grossadmiral* and *Reichsführer*,

341

no longer The Lion, or even Uncle Karl, but the husk of a man who had served over ten years in solitary confinement as the salvor of Allied consciences, or at least a settler of their doubts, still convinced that given the fleet he had demanded from the start his *U-Bootwaffe* would have wrought Britain's defeat before the Japanese had tipped America into the stew on a decisive scale endorsed, in effect, by the *Führer*'s immediate declaration of war. That impulsive act had emphasised, among other things, the fact that Dönitz's war-decisive weapon had never been cast in the weight of steel necessary to its purpose, and salt had been rubbed into his wound by Churchill's post-war confession that far from the *Luftwaffe*'s having posed a serious threat in what became known as the Battle of Britain, it had been the u-boat alone which had brought Great Britain to within an ace, to use the word—two or three weeks—of surrender in the far less publicly-lauded but more agonisingly prolonged and brutal Battle of the Atlantic. That, thought Altmann, must have been bitter punishment for the man whose vision had been constantly belittled by a demi-god whose self-belief—or self-delusion—had convinced and motivated a generation as it led him into a mire of paranoia from which self-destruction had been the only escape—short of the success which had eluded the attempt made on his life by the von Stauffenburg clique: another piece of mismanagement in high places.

But if his *Reich* had prevailed—if the Allies had made more mistakes than the Axis—*would* a victorious Germany have made a better job of empire than the decadent British? Perhaps. She had, after all, had her empire, most of it on this same African continent, and though she had lost it, it had not been through the perseverance of native truculence as the British were losing theirs. Surely not. Under the *Reich* civilisation would have remained firmly in white—Aryan—hands, as civilisation and not the ramshackle, demoralised travesty of Cohen's hypothesis. But that had been the Party's cause: civilisation at a level above the inferior processes of lesser races, and the cause had seemed to him, Altmann, to be worth the struggle. Until, at the end, the full extent of that cause's means had been exposed to public gaze as the degradation of humanity it had become in the hands of the figures who had assumed—arrogated to themselves, seen in retrospect—the moral leadership of a nation; figures towards which Altmann had looked for his example and guide, at least in the early years. Latterly, of course, that trust had faltered, though he had attributed his misgivings largely to his personal experience of war and the losses he had suffered through it. It had not been until the last days that he had seen the truth as it had affected countless others, and the nature of his own part in it in proper perspective. That had been the most conclusive of the assaults on his citadel, tearing down a crucially-placed buttress. From it had come his acceptance of the fate of his friends, his parents, his family as due payment, if not full restitution. Full restitution entailed more, perhaps more than could be rendered from mortal resources.

Coming up with and passing the Anglican cathedral he slowed his pace at the monument to someone called Wavell. Not the Wavell who had routed those fools of Italians in Ethiopia, and later in the North African campaign rescued after his departure by Rommel, but the commander of a local defence force in the Great War. It was flanked by two naval guns, one from the cruiser *Königsberg*, the other from one of her victims, *Pegasus*, in a forgotten action ending in *Königsberg*'s destruction trapped in a backwater of the Rufiji delta, an object of target-practice for the British monitors *Severn* and *Mersey*. In the sleepy summer classroom at the *Mutterhaus* old Müller had explained the tactics, and mistakes, of that long-ago campaign by which Germany had lost her East African possession to what were in effect British commercial interests. Which, in turn, had lost them to the native races certain to reduce them to a state in which other, more ruthless, less sentimental, powers would find a purchase for commercial and political exploitation. As he walked on Altmann tasted a bitterness at Germany's ineptitude, by which not only she but also the world had lost, where something of value could have been retained and brought to fruition of universal benefit. But it was over. The European struggle for power and suzerainty had resulted only in mutual impoverishment, a reversion into petty squabbles and domestic peevishness, and, of course, the ruin of the German state, carved up between the dangerously-opposed forces—of so-called democracy with which, as a form of administration, whether of a u-boat or a nation, Altmann had never been in sympathy on principle, and the abiding tyranny of communism, which the *Führer* had sworn above all things to eradicate; yet he had allowed himself to be distracted by the Jewish question, which, as far as Altmann could see, had been just that: a distraction; but one which had morphed into obsession. Even he himself had allowed it to distract him from his duty, and his moral obligations, as a naval officer. For which, like the *Führer*, he would have to pay, and in the only acceptable currency. Justification, however argued, however tenable, had no validity.

Now he approached the massif of Fort Jesus, rising against the night sky like the pens that had sheltered the boats at Lorient and Bordeaux—of which, he mused, it was in principle a forerunner in its function of depot to the *caravelhas* that had brought the Portuguese soldier-traders round the Cape in their search for a fabled Cathay; and would it, he wondered, still be standing when the abandoned concrete redoubts of the *Führer*'s Fortress Europe had finally crumbled to dust? Would they last even as long as this ancient relic of empire had so far lasted, and still in use? Strange to think that if Germany had won her great struggle it might even now be serving the very *U-Bootwaffe* that would have played a decisive part in its change of tenancy, overlooking the harbour which would certainly have served as a base apart from, or as the alternative to, the haven it was for Arab traders in ships the design and construction of which pre-dated even the fort's. And again would they—these cranky iron-fastened dhows: *sambuks* and *booms* and *bagghalas* that drifted with the monsoon from and back to their home ports in the Yemen, the Hadramaut, Oman and the territories of the Gulf seaboard—would they remain, still plying their undocumented trade, long after all this empire-building and dismantling and metamorphosis had collapsed into the diminished chaos of forgotten history that seemed to be its destiny? He felt it more than possible; certainly more possible than the thing that now sounded absurdly fanciful—the thousand years of both the *Führer*'s *Reich* and Churchill's British Empire and Commonwealth. The greatest empire the world had known had lasted—what?—a couple of centuries or so? No time at all. And as for the *Reich* in its several versions including the ramshackle Weimar and the mishandled *Dritte*—one looked at only bare decades. And better not to look too closely at the last. Better that it were forgotten, left to rot in a backwater of history like the *Königsberg* in her Rufiji delta grave. If, that is, people like Cohen would allow it. Which, of course, they would not, for at least as long as people like himself, Altmann, remained. Of that simple precept the American—the Jew—had left him in no doubt.

Pausing under the fort's loom while he sifted through these thoughts, Altmann crossed the road to make his way along the Ndia Kuu and the last thoroughfare leading him to the meeting with what he had decided would give him the answers to all the uncertainties, all the conjectures, all the hypotheses and suppositions, that had accumulated like the sea-grass and animal fouling on a hull too long at sea. And as with a hull too long at sea, their removal was likely to take with it the strength of the plating they had penetrated and eroded and rotted, and the hull be good for nothing further than the breakers' yard, or the conclusive effects of the breakers—of both kinds—on some desolate strand.

As he strode along he looked about him with the revitalised interest of a last view, absorbing the minutest detail here, the generality there, taking note of his surroundings as the unrepeatable elements of a terminal display. It comprised glimpses into the interiors of establishments still open for business at this late hour, passing impressions of dark faces, bearded faces, wreathed in smoke, catching the yellow light in lines and clefts, glancing eyes meeting his for an instant, passing back into the limbo of no return; the murmur of conversation in snatches, a discordant strain of stringed music, the smell of wood-smoke and frying oil and ghee interlaced with the rancid vapours of the open drains lining the road, lapped at by cringing dogs that scampered off to bark meanly at the far end of unlit culvert-like alleys. Balconies overhung the pavement, some open to the night backed by the dim-lit rectangles of windows, others enclosed in the filigree of carved wooden screening, concealing their resident womenfolk. And the occasional intricately-carved wooden door, sometimes iron-studded and bound, that evoked scenes of ancient actions, a scaled-down version of the entries to Saracen castles and Mogul forts, grand beyond the unassuming commonplaces of a town's main street. Traffic was light now, most on foot, and anonymous in flowing pale *djelabas, burnouses* or rags, and an occasional beggar whined from his doorway or alley corner as Altmann passed. When one clutched at his trouser-leg he halted with a rebuke on his lips, but instead found himself emptying his pockets of small change and following it with the contents of his wallet, a few twenty-shilling notes, that left the beggar silent in stunned disbelief. Altmann turned away, repelled, suddenly recalling the old man—Fraenkel, it must have been—on his feet in the boat: *God will bless you, captain!* And as he had cried out he had taken note of Siegfried's sword, caught in the searchlight's back-scatter on the side of the conning-tower; the mark of conceit that could hang a man . . .

Altman strode on. Giving some stinking beggar his loose change because he would shortly have no use for it was hardly likely to ingratiate him with whoever or whatever Cohen and Fraenkel—and, now it occurred to him, Schreiber—thought of as God. It was rather too late in the day, and it didn't weigh anything reckonable in the balance against the payment he owed and had left too late to make, except in whatever form Cohen had decided. Which, he had concluded with rueful admission of a just measure, was obvious and inescapable. There was no question of living beyond this encounter, which had been inevitable from the moment he had found himself in the company of the phantoms who had followed him out of that night of unhinged zeal, solemnly determined to exact whatever was necessary to restitution—if one man's life could account for the loss of many.

Which, Altmann reflected, was in any case all that was left; everything else had been forfeit in one way and another. He stood now, in effect, naked before his conscience, which would sit in judgment this very night, though its decision was already made. It needed only the corroboration of the survivor in order to carry out the sentence, which would bring the matter to its long-postponed conclusion. At his trend of thought Altmann felt again the sense of impending absolution that had touched him in the Paradise Bar on hearing Cohen's explanation of events he had until then thought would live with him for a full span of life. But in carrying out his self-imposed mission Cohen would relieve Altmann of the burden for at least the last few minutes of his time: in taking Altmann's confession he would confirm the justice of his cause in his acknowledgment of the German officer's moral failure.

Crossing a last road junction Altmann quickened his pace towards an alley leading off to the right, and swung into it tight-lipped, sensing a mounting tension that carried him back to the almost-forgotten sensation that preceded the moments immediately before the attack. They were the last in which the nerves were allowed free play; ended, the mind cut the connections with fear, uncertainty, conjecture, to leave only calculation, judgment, decision and concluding motor responses culminating in the torpedo's release and the ensuing hiatus before the shivering, sweating detoxification of a missed attempt, or the flood of relief and the exaltation of spirit that exploded in the mind and blood in direct response to the strike; and the calm that followed as the adrenalin drained away; the sense of absolution, release, consummation . . .

Emerging into the deserted open space between a white-limed house and the low battlemented wall edging the drop to the jetty below he glanced at his watch: two minutes to midnight. The timing was precise, exact, satisfying. He looked round, out over the harbour and its clusters of smoky riding-lights marking the anchored and moored dhows and sundry small-craft, up at the deeps of the night sky strewn with stars like glass-dust and splinters, reflected in the lightly-ruffled water in multiples of their innumerable millions, and breathed in the night smells of the port and the surrounding terrain, earth and sea and humanity combined in a distinctive but undistinguishable compound making up a small part of life's experience, more acutely perceived as it marked its concluding moments. The steps to the jetty descended from a bay let into the outer edge of the open space, and Altmann hesitated briefly before taking the first of them. His footfalls rang against the wall rising on his right, replaced when he reached the bottom with the lapping sound, strangely and incongruously soothing, of water against stone. He looked round, and after an initial flush of bafflement at his apparently solitary presence he stiffened as a figure detached itself from the shadows beneath the battlemented wall. Tall, thin, glasses reflecting the harbour's lights in minute flashes, slow-paced, Cohen came towards him. "Captain van Haaften?"

Altmann took out his cigarettes and fumbled one free of the packet. "No," he said, deciding against a search for his lighter, which might have been misinterpreted: everything spoiled by a thoughtless move. His lips twisted. That would be about as things had been from the start; a series of misinterpreted moves. He must try to get this last one right. Cohen had halted. "No," he repeated. "*Kapitän-zur-See* Gunnar Altmann, late *Kommandant* of the *Kriegsmarineschule-Mürwik*, and commander in the *U-Bootwaffe* of the Third *Reich*. As you know."

IV

OTHER than the stars and the moored shipping the only light came wanly from a lamp-standard on the jetty where a flight of weed-grown steps led the unwary into deep water. Set back from the edge a palm log provided seating, unoccupied at this time of night, and Cohen gestured towards it. They sat side by side looking out over the water, Altmann, lighting his cigarette, surmising that Cohen was in no hurry to conclude his business. In which case, he decided, he would try to get some answers to the obvious questions, beginning with the follow-up to the American's polite admission of a fact that had been obvious from the beginning. He had even indicated as much with his inquiry about the scar on Altmann's cheek, the single distinguishing mark that would have settled any doubt in the mind of a knowledgeable pursuer. Cohen had known it from the outset, so the question had to be asked: how? How had he found his way from a few notes and the information gleaned from the official sources he had mentioned to this final meeting-place where all the ragged edges and loose ends of failure would be trimmed to a neat, square edge leaving no unpaid debts, no ungranted concessions, no lingering regrets, no guilt, no remorse: where an end could be made of a matter that had gone wrong from the start to leave the only—for all practical purposes—surviving participant free to follow his own destiny, rid of the last and most malignant connection with a past from which nothing of positive value was retrievable. Cohen's eyes were on the future, of which he needed a clear view; the removal of this last obstruction was not only an imperative but also a point of honour. If revenge came into it, it was discountable; there was no need. The cause was just, and Cohen's intentions were the true and morally proper response to the injustice of the cause Altmann had espoused. It was, Altmann realised, the absolution he had sought for the last twenty-two years. The consequences of the chance downing of a bomber had not been enough to relieve him of the phantoms; payment had been made to the full extent of his resources, but it had fallen short. Now, this American—this Jew, and not a phantom but a tangible component of the scene burnt permanently into his recollection—had come to face him with the account, and with it the means of payment. It was right that he should accept, and it was his release. But the question had to be answered: how?

Cohen was sitting hunched forward, elbows on knees, hands hanging, gazing out over the harbour. At Altmann's question he stirred, sighed and sat up, scratching his scalp and blowing out his cheeks. "How?" Turned towards Altmann the glasses flashed reflected lights at him to accompany the flicker of a smile. "Yeah—you had to ask. Okay; I'll tell you. You're entitled to know, and no-one else is interested anyway." He took off his glasses and polished them in silence for a minute or so, then took Altmann back to that dark night on the path from the *Sporthalle* where Gottlieb had challenged him twice before firing the shot that had killed him. Or was supposed to have done.

But of course it hadn't, as Cohen explained. It had missed because that was part of the plan, which was to get Altmann out of Germany under cover while the nation—what remained of it—mourned a hero, an officer and, as far as was known, a gentleman-knight whose record stood as an example of honourable devotion to duty untainted by any suggestion of misconduct when all around was evidence of misconduct on a scale of depravity almost beyond comprehension. Altmann had stood as a figure of German integrity intrinsic, as it was supposed to have been, to a service as ruthlessly warlike and aggressive as any military force in the nation's history—ruthless but always fair and even-handed. It had given no quarter and asked none, had acted at all times according to the rules—hadn't it? If there were doubts men like Altmann could stand in refutation of them.

"Except, of course, for one thing," said Cohen, and Altmann drew on his cigarette, remaining silent. "It's the only explanation: somehow, Dönitz must have learned the truth about your tangle with the schooner, and didn't want the story getting out, especially to any still sympathetic to the Nazi regime or the Party or whatever. Eck hadn't been hauled out of chokey at the time, so his story wasn't yet known, but one was enough: Dönitz was fighting for what he thought might have been retained of the *Reich* with the Allies' agreement and couldn't afford to have one of his own officers—his star turn!—shown to be a war criminal like the low-life smoked into the open by the Allied advance through the concentration camps. Am I right?"

"Yes." Altmann took in a deep draught of smoke and nodded. "Yes. Dönitz knew. I had to tell him, at the time of my promotion to *Kapitän zur See* and command of the *Kriegsmarineschule*."

"Oh—so you told him . . . What'd he say?"

"Nothing much. He knew already. Or guessed. If I'd said nothing he'd have had to bring it up anyway. As you say, he was worried about the risk of the Allies finding out: he'd have had to ask me—he had to know it was true and not just his intuition. He said he'd known it, or felt it, when I reported after that patrol. If Germany had won the war nothing would have been said, but as it was . . ." Altmann shrugged. "It's just as well. I don't know if the Allies made inquiries or not, but after the Eck business they may have done, and maybe found out about the schooner . . ." He drew on his cigarette and sat silent for an interval, Cohen eyeing him curiously. Then he went on, "So you're right about all that, Mr Cohen." He turned to the American and studied the shadowed face for a moment. "But how did you find out? Have you spoken to Dönitz?"

"No. I told you—I got in touch with Wiesenthal. It's a longish story, but what it comes down to is that after the war, as I said, his people ran checks on all the Nazis and sympathisers they could get information

349

about, and your name came up in neon, for the obvious reasons but not for anything to do with the schooner. They never have known about that. But they found out that you were spirited out of Germany."

"Yes?"

"Your sentry—Gottlieb. The prime witness. They traced him to his home in a place called—something like Cloppenburg—not important. Found him dying—cancer, tuberculosis, something like that. Only twenty-one, poor bastard . . . He spilled the beans. End of the road for him anyway, so the warning he'd had from Dönitz's people about talking didn't matter, even assuming anyone was left to do anything about it. Told Wiesenthal's man he'd been party to the whole thing, lying about the shooting, which he was coached in beforehand. Aim high, that was the order. Two challenges, then shoot, and aim high. The others would do the rest, and take him through the subsequent interrogation. Then he was paid off and told he'd be making a mistake if he thought he had anything to offer the papers. Lived the rest of his life—all three years of it—worried sick about being followed and bumped off, until towards the end. Swore he'd told no-one, and went over his story, all the details. So Wiesenthal knew something had been going on, and sniffed around some more. Official papers, not secret, in government departments. Found your death certificate, properly filled out and signed, and traced the medic responsible. This time an old guy, in a slum in Bremen, forgotten by the world, living on handouts, soup kitchens, abortions, anything. Nazi Party member, shady war record, easily screwed. His mistake was denouncing some of his comrades to the Allies, so no free ticket to Buenos Aires for him, and scared of his own shadow. He admitted the body they buried wasn't yours . . ." Cohen's teeth gleamed. "How about that?"

"Very clever, whoever found him—"

"Wiesenthal's got contacts all over. You'd be surprised. We Jews are in everything. Artisans, academics, engineers, brain-surgeons, jewellers, musicians, auto dealers, industrialists, physicists, bee-keepers, stand-up comedians—" Cohen coughed apologetically "—civil servants, booksellers, tailors, lawyers . . . Some of them—quite a lot, actually—survivors of the death camps, you know? Vested interest in finding the people they owed—owe—so much to. Like Eichmann, among lesser suppurations." Cohen paused, sniffed, and gazed up at the sky. "Never see them like that at home," he said. "The stars. Seems like we're right in among them here. Closer to them near the equator, I guess."

"So what was this—doctor's—story?"

"Amazing . . . He told them the body of an officer—an *Oberleutnant zur See* killed in some kind of disturbance during the last days before the British got control of north-west Germany—was buried in your place, and you were given his papers. His name was—uh—"

"*Oberleutnant* Dieter Kühn," said Altmann flatly, and blew smoke at the stars. That name; another ghost stirred, but it was only his own reflection. "A *U-Bootwaffe* officer. No known family at that stage of the war. Got command a week before it ended but never took it to sea. Unlucky fellow."

"Seems so—"

"What about him?—you're doing well so far!"

"Thank Wiesenthal—he was happy to tell me all he knew. Or so he said." Cohen shrugged self-deprecatingly and Altmann felt a grudging liking for him. There was nothing of the triumphalist about him. Nor was his self-confidence evident in cockiness or bombast or contumely, but rather in a modest manner and a pleasantly understated assumption of mutual regard in his obviously innate courtesy, the entire disposition decently cloaking an implicit determination not to be deflected from his intent. Beneath the slightly ennervated air pulsed a vigour that would drive him to the conclusion, satisfactory or otherwise, of whatever task he undertook. Ruefully, Altmann decided that he would make a successful, even a formidable, lawyer: the self-effacing manner was a blind, a dangerous deception. Dangerous, that is, for whoever failed to see through it in any confrontation. It was calculated to sabotage his adversary's prudence, seduce his indiscretion, and liking the man, Altmann was also wary of him. Which, in the circumstances, was something of a wasted sentiment: why be wary of one's confessor, one's judge, one's executioner? Before him, the point of concealment was negated, void. Absolution required total candour; the time for evasion, for sophistry, was past, and for that also Altmann liked the man: what else could he feel towards someone about to relieve him of the burden of years? Briefly, the perverse humour of the situation struck him, but, controlling an impulse to smile, he paid closer attention.

But, the American continued, although the switch of identities was noted, because Wiesenthal had no knowledge of the schooner's significance nothing more had been done apart from filing the information against the possibility of future need—something, for example, must have prompted moves to get Altmann out of Germany.

Then, as it happened, Kühn's name had come up again in intelligence received from the Jewish underground organisation in Holland. For the purpose of concluding unfinished business it remained in being for several years after the German surrender and return of an elected government, responsible for, among other things, the killing of a Dutch Nazi Party member who had been instrumental in the arrest and deportation of a number of Jews during the occupation. The man had been a sea captain, owner-master of a short-sea trader, the *Johan Burger*. Although interest had been primarily in her master, reporting to Wiesenthal on the man's elimination in the docks at Rotterdam mention was made of the ship's mate, a German named Dieter Kühn, about whom nothing was known except that he had been with the Dutchman from soon after the occupation's end, making coastal voyages on government contracts. The Dutchman's name had been van Haaften.

"Which was where the trail went cold," ended Cohen. "All Wiesenthal could tell me was that Kühn—you—were last heard of in that report as the ship's first mate. No reason for following your onward movements had come up: whatever prompted your removal from the scene had no evident connection with Jewish interests."

Altmann finished his cigarette and flicked the end into the water. He reflected on the chances of life: where he had escaped the attentions of the Allies, which had been the aim of the exercise, then, quite fortuitously, the Wiesenthal organisation's net, his path had failed to take him clear of the improbable chance of a survivor's deciding to find out what had become of him—of the improbable chance of a survivor, let alone two, which in turn had depended on the near-impossible chance of the destroyer's unique voyage bringing her upon a speck on a stormy ocean seen by a lookout at the last moment. If one betted, even in the teeth of the overwhelming odds, on such a train of events one's money would surely be lost if the entire span of human history were combed. But it had happened, and here he was, listening to a tale that would end right here on a palm log overlooking Mombasa's Old Harbour. Well, it was the best he could hope for, all things considered: there was nothing else left. No future, no prospects, and the tormenting company of phantoms right through to his last breath in some as yet unknown and unguessable hole in an unguessable state of bodily and mental dissolution. Not even Pavlides would be able to offer him anything of a viable alternative: he had passed beyond reach of the Greek's powers of appointment and placement. But not of the survivor's.

Altmann's musing was interrupted by the slap of sandals and the murmur of conversation as two Arabs in flowing, extravagantly-sashed *burnouses* beneath short waistcoat-jackets and imposing draperies of headware held in place by *aghals* of a regal elaboration, descended the steps to make their unhurried way to the landing, passing behind the two men on the log with flashing glances.

"*Salaam!*"

"*Salaam alek-um!*"

"*Salaam!*"

A boat was approaching, a dim light detached from the assembly of riding-lights and closing with the jetty, in charge of a dark man in ragged *burnous* and turban who *salaamed* as the two stepped aboard. Altmann and Cohen watched as the boat set off in a wide turn back to where it had come from.

"Good timing," observed Cohen. "You speak the lingo?"

"It's called discipline," replied Altmann dryly. "If they said they'll be at the steps expecting the boat at a certain time, that's the law. If they have to wait, it will be the last time—with that boatman, one of their sailors: he'll be finished." He smiled. "And no—I don't speak the . . . lingo. A little Swahili. *Salaam* is universal. Just a politeness. Life is too short to learn Arabic."

Cohen stared at him for a moment. "I guess so. What with the script and all . . . What were they—those two?"

"*Nakhodas*—dhow-masters—probably." Altmann smiled. "Men of substance in these parts."

Cohen nodded in slow acknowledgment. "You wouldn't lose them in a crowd."

"If you found them in one. They don't mix with the lower orders." Altmann lit another cigarette. His tongue felt like leather. "You were telling me—the trail went cold?"

Peering at his watch, Cohen rubbed his scalp vigorously. "Nearly a half-hour . . . Yes, that's right. Cold as far as Wiesenthal was concerned, and he dropped it there; asked me to let him know if I came across anything further, you know?"

"And have you?"

"No. My baby, this one. At least, for the moment . . ."

"I see . . . So?"

So, continued Cohen, he had begun his own investigation, with the ship's name and the name of her mate to go on. It hadn't been as difficult as he'd imagined, since port records were open to inspection to *bona fide* inquirers. In some instances money had had to be applied, and Cohen had been prepared for that. Even so, the first check had been a surprise: he'd found that the mate's name had changed and that the master's name was—still—van Haaften; the dead man, according to Wiesenthal's contact. He'd continued the chase, now curious to know the explanation: either Kühn had gone and Wiesenthal's informant had been lying for whatever the reason, or the wrong man had been bumped off, unless something else had happened to Altmann's identity. In any case, he had to follow the ship's movements, on a trail that was years old. It was just as well, remarked Cohen, that harbour authorities seemed to keep logs and registers dating back to the Flood. The *Johan Burger* had left her spoor wherever she went, and her voyaging had taken her ever farther from her native shores, clearing port with the next duly noted, and Cohen had followed. From Rotterdam to Mombasa had taken him a month or so over a year, in and out of both small and major ports, south to Lisbon and the Canaries, northward and westward to the Azores, east to Gibraltar and on into the Mediterranean—ports in Morocco, Tunisia, Libya, Spain, France, Sicily, Italy, north into the Adriatic, back south to Alexandria, north again to Greece, into and out of the Black Sea and eventually to Port Said, through the canal into the Red Sea, north into the Gulf of Aqaba and south to Jeddah, west and south to Port Sudan, across to Aden and along the coast to Masira, Muscat and across to Karachi, then south and west to the Seychelles before the onward passage to Zanzibar and a short hop from there to Mombasa. From which great port, Cohen had noted, the voyages had been to the Seychelles, Mauritius, Bombay and Karachi, with occasional sallies south as far as Durban, but always returning, so that the impression he'd gained was of a bird of passage circling before settling to a perch, presumably some kind of steady or lucrative trade worth exploiting for as long as it lasted. Then, quite unexpectedly, with no prior indication, the ship had disappeared, here in Mombasa.

"I thought that was it: blank wall! Nothing—absolutely nothing—to go on. I almost dropped it there. I was getting tired, too. I didn't want to get into discussions with the harbour people, so I hadn't said anything, just that I wanted to see what shipping was using the port. And the *Johan Burger* had vanished! I wised up by chance. She'd cleared inwards but not outwards, and no such name on the berths, so if she had, it hadn't been logged. So—I had to ask, and the assistant harbour-master told me—change of name and port of registry! Now she was the *Ndovu*, Panamanian flag. Real smart, I thought. And I also thought, not smart enough. If this guy Altmann had scented me—not likely, but he may have just been taking precautions against anyone interested—he'd have to do better than change his ship's name; and if it *was* him he hadn't changed his alias—van Haaften. If it wasn't, I'd wasted a whole lot of my step-father's money!" The journey, profitable or otherwise for the ship, had cost Cohen—or his stepfather—thousands. "He told me it's non-returnable. Just as well, I guess."

"I suppose so . . . Does he know what it's all about?"

"He's never asked, but I guess he's got a pretty good idea. For a stepfather—even a father—he understands things—in general terms if not in detail." After a brief pause Cohen went on, "Anyway, that's a resumé of my private mission. Except for one last thing."

"Which is?"

"I heard talk—when I called on the padre at the seamen's mission. Some men off the ships there—couple of yours, I reckon. Sitting around drinking beer—looks like Jesus lets the wine stunt run to Tusker round here. Or the padre does, anyway . . ." Cohen smiled. "The talk. About Mukerjee and all this Africanisation after—and before—independence. The guess is he's putting a black—a native Kenyan—in your place, which got me wondering what sort of a deal you're working here. I thought the ship was owned by van Haaften himself." Cohen was studying Altmann's face. "Do me a favour, *Kapitän*—fill in the blanks?"

Altmann took a breath and blew out his cheeks. Why not? There was nothing to lose, and it would give him a little more time, perhaps to think more rationally, perhaps to see another way through this surreal situation. But to what? He drew on his wasting cigarette and felt in need of a drink—"I mean," added Cohen, "from the time you dodged the burial party. If you don't mind. That is—if you do—well . . ." He shrugged. "I guess you'd have your reasons."

Altmann threw Cohen a sidelong glance. "No—you're right. No reason to keep the filling to myself, in the circumstances. So . . ." He sucked in another draught of smoke and let it go slowly, watched it drift away on the almost motionless air, thin out and shred in the lamplight. Like all his plans and hopes, he thought; from the moment Dönitz had handed him the letter that had never reached Liebeherr, the great enterprise had begun to split at the seams—his, the *Führer*'s, Uncle

Karl's, the *Reich*'s; and here he was, confessing all—or about to—to a man whose survival would finally rush in like a high wind to sweep the remnants of his illusions into the oblivion to which fate had consigned them at the outset. Why not tell this American all? As the sole survivor of that night's horror, and the patient tracker of his quarry, he deserved at least that much in repayment; and he was, after all, about to render him, Altmann, the absolution his soul craved, now above all else, since all else had turned to dust. Another pull on his cigarette, and he threw the stub into the water, watching its red parabola all the way down into inaudible extinction. Then he turned to Cohen.

"Have you heard of Odessa, Mr Cohen? Not the port. An organisation."

"Odessa?" Cohen shook his head. "No. Can't say I have."

"Mm. Something Wiesenthal must know of . . ." Altmann shrugged. "All right. First, then—it's a word made up of initial letters: *Organisation der Ehemaligen SS-Angehörigen—*"

"How's that?—my German isn't—"

Raising a hand Altmann smiled thinly. "Organisation of Former SS Members. It—"

"Don't tell me you—"

"No!" Altmann's tone was sharp. "No connection . . . But the—arrangements—expanded to cover any Party member or supporter with reasons for getting out of a defeated Germany. I don't know more than that, but I should think it played more than a secondary rôle in the escape of people like Eichmann to South America and other hiding-places."

"And you?"

"It was not fully developed when I found myself a fugitive in my own country, but its foundation had been laid in the closing months of the war by SS officers, who made arrangements for certain of their compatriots—people likely to be of interest to the Allies—to join the French Foreign Legion—"

"The *French*—?"

"So I heard. The Legion needed volunteers and no questions asked. But I never was an army man; too much shouting and stamping—" Involuntarily, Altmann touched the scar on his cheek, and Cohen noticed, but said nothing, and Altmann was silent for a short interval. *It'd pass muster as a sabre-slash, Maggot . . . quite a distinction for a naval officer . . .* The future had looked promising then, and losing a fight merely part of the exhilaration; he hadn't lost them all, but win

356

or lose it was the last that counted: you were only as good as your last fight . . .

"So how—?"

With a grunt Altmann returned to the present. "By the end of the war, as I say, it had expanded to handle anyone loyal to the cause with reason for avoiding the authorities—anyone in or sympathetic to the Party, for instance."

"Like you."

"Like me. My credentials were unquestionable, underwritten by the *Reichsführer*."

"The *who*—?"

"Dönitz." Whatever Altmann's eyes expressed was concealed by shadow, but his tone conveyed something of his bitterness, and Cohen refrained from comment. Altmann lit another cigarette and the silence crept slowly on. Finally he sighed, continuing, "A hero of the *Reich* . . . And by then there were other ways out of Germany than through the Legion's recruiting office. Without going into details . . . I made it clear I didn't wish to start ranching or whatever was on offer in South America, so I was passed down the line to Rotterdam and put in touch with van Haaften. I was also provided with papers as a first mate in the German merchant marine, which enabled me to sign on with him, as Kühn."

After that, Altmann explained, he had sailed with the Dutchman on coastal voyages, some under Dutch government contract carrying construction materials and foodstuffs, while he learned the business of a merchant vessel. It looked as if he might have found a way of making a living in his permanent identity as Dieter Kühn, which, on balance, was as hopeful an outcome as any other and better than most; until one night alongside in Rotterdam after a short drydocking and refit, alone on board with van Haaften before preparing to sign on a new crew. Taking a stroll ashore before turning in, during van Haaften's absence on one of his periodic sojourns among his circle of female acquaintance, Altmann had discovered his body in the alley between two storage sheds. Pinned to it by the knife that had been buried to the hilt in his chest, presumably after its use to cut his throat from ear to ear, was a triangular scrap of yellow cloth, replica of the mark forced upon Jews as one of the preliminaries to their disappearance among the death camps. On it had been inked the words *Israel Avenges the Innocents. Deut. 19:21.* "—the work of your Jewish resistance people, hm?"

357

Cohen rubbed his neck, sucked a breath through his teeth and sighed. "I guess so . . . What did you do?"

"I got out, of course!" Altmann drew tersely on his cigarette. "It would have been dangerous to make a run for it in Europe, or try to get back in touch with the people who had got me out of Germany, so I took the obvious way, and used the ship. After all, her owner was dead. She was an orphan. I couldn't become her stepfather by claiming a change of owner, but I could change my own identity and take the place of her father—van Haaften's papers were in the safe. All I had to do was change a couple of photographs and practise the signature. So I became Kees van Haaften, and got to hell out of that place as soon as I had crew and officers signed on."

"Didn't any officials ask questions?—people in places like shipping offices and harbour-masters' offices and ship-chandlers must have known the guy."

Altmann smiled again, without amusement, and shook his head. Cohen should understand that Europe in those chaotic times of readjustment to national administrations after occupation, as in Holland, was a place of confusion and haste, and changes of faces. People who might have known van Haaften by sight had either moved on or were harassed and impatient, besides which the master of an obscure trading vessel wasn't a particularly significant figure in the general whirl of local commercial and political affairs. Petty officials and flunkeys casting careless glances at papers that displayed no obvious sign of fraudulence weren't looking for ex-*U-Bootwaffe* officers or even for ships' first mates masquerading as their masters. In any case, it was worth taking a better than even chance, and the chance had proved safe. Altmann had cleared Rotterdam in ballast for Lisbon, with the stores he had and a crew of runners and a handful of officers only too glad of a berth that didn't delve too deeply into their records.

"What about van Haaften himself—the body? Didn't anyone—the police—investigate, start asking questions—look for you and the ship?"

"I dumped it. Easily done—the ship was on a river berth. The ebb took it away, out to sea. I heard nothing more, and if it was found it was probably past identifying, and probably only one of many at that time. The war's taken its time giving up its dead—and creating them." Altmann's glance at Cohen was sharp. "The killing wasn't switched off with the surrender, you know."

Cohen returned a quizzical look. "As you've explained," he said.

"And I stripped it—the body—of identifying papers. A wallet in the jacket. And his watch. His name was engraved on the back—" Altmann suddenly unstrapped his wristwatch and handed it to Cohen.

Holding it to the light, Cohen studied it in silence. Handing it back, he said, "Kinda—morbid—isn't it?"

"Yes. But it's also part of my insurance—you follow?"

"Oh, sure. Nice detail." Cohen paused, then said, "Another detail, maybe not important: what about Kühn? How'd you cover for his disappearance? One or the other—him or van Haaften—had gone, and the ship's papers—the register or whatever—must have shown him as the first mate."

Altmann shrugged. "It was not a problem. Everyone signed off before drydock in the normal way. When van Haaften was killed the next voyage's articles had not been opened. We were the only men on board, but officially neither was, until the next voyage began. Like any officer—any man—Kühn was free to go, and as far as the records show, he had gone, no-one knew where, nor did they care. Why should they? The new mate—a Lithuanian—took his place, and he signed off in Lisbon, replaced by a Spaniard wanting to get home to the Canaries. That's the way it's done in merchant ships, and it was the way I did it for the rest of the time, except for McDade—"

"Your chief engineer?—according to the crew lists I've seen."

"Correct. From Scotland."

"What's so special about him?"

"Several things." Altmann's lips twitched. "He can hold his drink—very important; comes of long practice. And he keeps machinery running against all the laws of mechanics—even more important. The ship is old. Spares are hard to find, and expensive . . ."

"So he's a paragon—is that special?"

"Oh, yes . . . But, as you might have noticed, he's been with me from the time I picked up a cargo of cotton and rice at Alexandria. He was on the beach—left behind by his ship after a few days in the guts, as you might say, of the *kasbah*, and sacked, as his owner's agent informed him. Not that he minded: he has no wish to return to England—or Scotland. His reason is interesting: twice torpedoed on North Atlantic convoys, and on both occasions having his pay stopped from the day his ships went down. Even I thought that was unduly harsh, you know. And who knows—maybe I was responsible! He says he's had enough of the country and its merchant navy. What he will do when Mukerjee pays him off I don't know . . ."

"Does he know—I mean, about your war service?"

"No. He thinks I'm who I say I am. He hates Germans, especially Germans who served in the *U-Bootwaffe*. If he discovered the truth I think he would kill me. It's a unique situation, don't you think?"

"Kinda risky . . . How d'you sleep?"

"Badly."

"I guess so . . . If for no other reason, huh?"

Altmann's gaze narrowed, and he nodded. "Anyway, other officers and crew changed as I went along, signing voyage articles, until I found myself working more or less regularly out of this place. It seemed safe enough. No-one showed any unusual interest in me, and I was put in touch with Sergos—Pavlides; lucky for me, he took a liking to me, asks no questions, passes trade my way, helps me find crew—" Altmann smiled "—at a fair rate . . . And he put me in touch with Mukerjee. Mukerjee took over when I was bust and let me carry on as before. By then I had a more or less regular crew of locals—Kipsigi, Kikuyu; Arabs in the engine-room—and officers who stay for a while before moving on. The first mate is South African—almost a Dutchman himself! He's been with me for nearly five years, takes a month or so off every year to visit relatives somewhere near Durban . . . Usually the captain has to be a national of the owner's country of—of *domicile*—his registered office—but the rest of the crew can be a complete—what is it called?—*pot-mess*. From anywhere, as long as they are qualified according to the regulations of the country where the ship is registered. It was the Netherlands, of course, and the Dutch consul here wasn't out to make difficulties; but when Mukerjee bought the ship it was switched to Panama . . . It's not like a warship."

"Not like a u-boat, huh?"

Altmann turned the idea over as he strapped the watch back on to sit smoking pensively while Cohen watched him, silent and patient. No. It had not been like a u-boat. It had not induced the comradeship, the close-knit intimacy of interdependence under unrelenting threat, the sense of honourable service to the Fatherland and the cause; nor the mutual regard between men whose respective functions demanded of them, and mostly got, the utmost they had to offer in skill, loyalty, courage, humour—and, though it was not something any would have admitted in so many words—a love for each other that cut deep, to

360

the heart and guts, when others of their kin were lost. It was not a sentimental, nor a perversion of sexual, love, but a brotherly attachment born of shared experience, a shared nurture and a shared intent and responsibility and pride, which placed all not of the brotherhood firmly outside the pale of understanding. At least, thought Altmann, that was the way he had looked upon it, and back at it, and preferred to see it: that there had been flaws, cracks, jarring discord, and a final descent into desperation and failure were matters he had acknowledged with sorrow and anger, and bitterness at the fact that even in his own case the record had been seriously marred, and had demanded restitution, more than merely an admission of personal deficiency; a moral lapse driven by some infernal combination of circumstances among which was the shame of the boat's sinking alongside, and his reprimand from Uncle Karl, whom he had looked upon with a proud respect he could express only in a resolute adherence to duty and a justification of the trust placed in him as a commander intensified by a determination to atone for his momentary but momentous fall from grace. It had not been through his direct omission, but as the commanding officer responsibility for all the actions—the errors and omissions as well as the virtues—of his subordinates lay at his door. Whatever punishment was meted out to the individuals directly at fault, to him was imputed the ultimate blame: the crew's conduct and efficiency were matters for which he bore full liability: when they did well, he earned approval; when they erred, his was the castigation, and to the extent of his influence on their actions, through his own personal attributes as well as the disciplinary system his rank represented, his professional standing lay in his own hands. But in his action against the schooner he had overstepped the undefined limit, payment for which could not be through another reprimand, nor even an actual punishment, in service terms: demotion, even cashiering—even relegation to the punishment battalions that had underlain the disciplinary code—for bringing the service into disrepute had not been open to him. And, as it seemed, the payment so far had not been enough . . . No, he thought: serving the ship as he had done for so long now had not been like service to the *U-Bootwaffe*. The two were worlds apart, and his place in one of them was—had been, from his present terminal viewpoint—nothing better than a fraud, and a cowardly one at that. But it was, at last, about to end, and in a way that would settle his outstanding account. The only way, in fact. The events of that fateful night had been a failure on his part that could not

361

be ascribed to the normal demands of duty, nor the responsibility for it shifted back up the line of command. It had been his decision, for which he should have been called upon to answer, and would have been if he had had the courage to declare it as a major point in his patrol report. By his failing in that duty he had, in effect, made Dönitz himself complicit, open to accusation and censure for not acting upon a matter of which he had obviously been aware: its concealment had been successful, as a mutually-agreed pretence, only because he had chosen to refrain from specific inquiry.

Taking a last draw on his cigarette, Altmann threw the stub after the others. "No, Mr Cohen. Not like a u-boat."

Cohen did not answer, and in the ensuing silence Altmann sensed a train of thought in the American running parallel with his own, and that it was approaching the same point of determination at the same pace. The exchange between them had possessed an air of unreality in its apparent affability, as if two old friends had been comparing notes which, concluded, would bring them to another parting, on terms of mutual regard and with expressions of mutual well-wishing and the hope of another meeting, by fortunate chance, at some future time. But it was as much of a pretence as the exchange with Dönitz in the grand salon at Kerneval, both parties to it complicit in a plot to extend the agreeable element of life beyond its natural limit, and on this occasion it had reached the full stretch of even that artificial span. There was no further means of concealment, from the truth or from each other's explicit cognisance of it, and no avoiding the decision that had now to be made and acted upon. Glancing at Cohen, who was leaning forward again, shoulders hunched, elbows on knees, gazing out at the constellation of riding-lights, Altmann became aware of a tension that had been building under cover of the genial tone of the conversation, and that it would not be dispelled by any further contrivance. It was time. There was nothing further to be said that would serve any purpose other than pointless deferral of a certainty. It needed only the final, recognisable signal for its execution. Which, thought Altmann, was a fine word, exact and fitting. He said, "So, Mr Cohen—you have the picture. I have nothing more to tell you." And he thought: how trivial such an ending sounds, how commonplace. The occasion called for something more sonorous, more evocative, more indicative of the gravity of the matter that had brought them both to this conclusive rendezvous, standing as they were in the shadow of the principle to which all men turned, in a last reckoning, for their vindication—or absolution. It was not to avenge the innocent that Cohen had sought him out, but to exact justice as he saw it: his moment had come.

V

COHEN sat up and stretched, removed his glasses to rub at his eyes before replacing them and turning his gaze upon his companion. Altmann could make out a sombre expression in place of the deceptive blandness, and waited, suddenly assailed by doubt; he was aware of a sensation of misjudgment, the same thrill of mingled anguish and anger that came of the realisation that he had miscalculated a target's movements. Cohen had somehow taken up another course when it had seemed his last opportunity had passed. He took a breath and said, "So now the last move, Captain Altmann, and a clean break with all that crap."

Baffled, Altmann asked him what he meant.

"Well . . . Here I am, the survivor of your night to remember: maybe the only one in the know apart from Dönitz and whoever of your old crew got through the war—and I guess *they* won't be looking for you." The glasses flashed, concealing whatever the eyes might have conveyed. The voice, still even and temperate, had taken on a hard edge it had so far lacked. "I'm your Jiminy Cricket, captain—when you thought you'd got away with it."

"Jiminy—?"

"Conscience—folk tale, Italian. *Pinocchio* . . ." He sat back. "Forget it—we haven't come here to tell each other fairy tales."

The word fell like a stone into the pool of Altmann's thoughts. *Pinocchio!* Of course: the boy-puppet made by the lonely old craftsman Gepetto; and little Helene's delight at the prospect of someone's nose growing longer each time he told a lie, warning the uncomprehending youngest in her maternal way; and as the scenes at bedtime floated back to him across the pool from one of its forgotten backwaters Altmann suppressed a gasp of dismay; the chill that enfolded his heart had been so long absent that its return had an almost physical effect, as a short jab under the ribs from a rallying opponent. Feeling his grip on the conversation slipping, he said sharply, "So what *have* we come here for, Mr Cohen?"

Apparently noticing nothing of the harsh edge to Altmann's tone, Cohen chuckled, but it was a sardonic comment, emphasised the words that followed. They were there, he said, to complete the record. To give the erstwhile *Kapitänleutnant* Gunnar Altmann of the Third *Reich*'s U-Boat Arm the chance to finish the job he'd started "—if you've still got the nerve, that is!" And he got to his feet and stood, hands at his sides, looking down at Altmann, the wan light touching a lop-sided smile. Now, his posture completely lacking in menace, wholly open to assault, a manifestation of submission to whatever might befall, but without fear, without entreaty and without any suggestion of defensive insolence, he stood motionless, a tall, narrow-shouldered figure flatly cast in a suspended play of shadow and penumbral light. The effect was ephemeral, like a shadow-play in mist, but not quite: the image possessed a greater substance, a dimension not apparent without closer scrutiny. In so passively provoking mortality Cohen gave ultimate expression to the natural honesty, the inherent artlessness, that had moved Altmann to be equally frank—and equally fatalistic, though with the difference that where the American had everything to live for, he, Altmann, had nothing: of the two he stood to lose the least by his demise. More than that: he stood to gain, by a final release from torment. Yet here was the American apparently not armed, not prepared for what had seemed the obvious purpose of his journey, but instead presenting himself for elimination as the only remaining threat to Altmann's continued masquerade. If he, Altmann, had the nerve to carry it out. Face to face.

Bemused, and suddenly aware of the sweat on his brow and soaking his shirt, Altmann said, "I think you have misread the signs, Mr Cohen . . . As I have!" He lit another cigarette, noting that only one remained, and the slight tremor of his hands. Natural reaction, he thought: if matters had turned out as he'd expected he would now be among the phantoms of his nightly expiation and waking dread. Instead, the one-sided confrontations would continue, and he reflected on the fact that a tremor of the hand, however slight, was something rare in his experience, and seldom a result of obvious physical danger: he had seen men shaking with the uncontrollable effects of violent action or sustained high tension, even while they denied the terror—or, as had happened, been destroyed by it—and had been fervently thankful for his own resilience under such assaults on his susceptibilities. His first awareness of it had been in the ring: expecting fright he had found instead a cool pressure to calculate his tactics and chances, which, he'd realised, had passed for courage. Now his hands trembled, seemingly of their own volition, but—surely—it was a sign of the cumulative effect of the recurring nightmare contrasting with the solid substance of Cohen and what he could have represented. And perhaps the years: he was getting older, and recent events had accelerated the process, mentally as well as physically . . .

He looked up through the dispersing smoke. "I thought you had come to kill me." The tension had evaporated, leaving him with a sense of deflation, flatness, lassitude. Even, with grotesque irony, disappointment.

"But you've got a gun?" Cohen's voice caught on a half-cough, and he cleared his throat. "You can't have come here thinking that without the means of defending yourself!"

"Why not?—haven't you?"

Cohen seemed to sag, and he let a breath go in a low hiss, shaking his head. "Of course not! What the hell—forgive me—would I do with the body? And I'd be the first one the police would look for—strange face in town seen with you the day before your death—killing—by several people who knew you. And now a couple of dhow-masters! I'd be easy to trace—follow—with my airline bookings and all. I haven't come here *incognito*, captain. I didn't need to, did I? And by the same token I'd be missed if anything happened to me. You may be able to keep your pal Pavlides quiet but I guess the padre at the mission would be a horse of another colour, huh? Still—as I said, I came to give you the chance of finishing the job." He resumed his seat. "But—apart from the practical difficulties, which are no guarantee, after all—I reckoned on both of us walking away—"

"Because I haven't the nerve—the guts?"

"In a way. You see, Captain Altmann, I wanted to know. It's been bugging me since I was old enough to understand what happened that night—what happened in that war—and I had to meet you—see you, face to face, in the flesh—see what sort of a man could do what you did. Well, I got my answer, in a couple of hours' talk with you, right there in the Paradise Bar." He grinned, and Altmann marvelled at his apparent equanimity; almost serenity, wildly out of place. "Hell of a name for it, huh?"

"And what was the answer, Mr Cohen?"

"Oh—" Cohen took out a handkerchief and mopped his neck "—that you're a normal sort of guy. Not a born killer; just doing what most other men would do, only you did it better . . . I guess killing isn't your—your *métier*."

Altmann grunted, and curious to hear more, said, "In spite of all the evidence? Not just the schooner, you know—you yourself mentioned my record: two hundred and seventy thousand tons, more than fifty ships. Two hundred and seventy-three thousand, and fifty-two, to be exact! Do you think I managed all that without killing anyone else? My job—my duty to the Fatherland—was killing; killing ships, and men! And my success was marked with citations, and a medal, the highest military honour the *Führer*—the *Reich*—could bestow. And early promotion—" Altmann broke off, aware of a return of the harsh inflection, hinting at indignation, irritation at evidence of naivety—silly sentimentality—in his interlocutor: in this soft-living American, this Jew—this survivor of the most insanely shameful act of his life, with which he was still living through every succeeding hour, every sleepless, spectral night, only partly-relieved by the lessening effects of alcohol—the *genever*, the only spirit of sufficient potency his stomach could bear without pain, and his head without derangement. He drank to escape, and he wondered at the fact that it hadn't—so far—turned him into an alcohol-dependent hulk, though he had come to understand that his instinctive repugnance for loss of self-control was bolstered by what seemed to be a higher than average tolerance for the stuff that would induce it. Rarely as it occurred, his ability to drink others to a standstill, or worse, was in part owing to his cautiously-gauged intake rate, in part to an apparently hard head. For which he was grateful; but it gave his spectral followers the advantage, and he would not turn to stronger remedies . . .

Then, as a thought crossed his mind, he smiled crookedly. Cohen returned a puzzled frown. "Something I said?"

Altmann rubbed his chin with a rasping sound. "Yes and no . . . This meeting, with someone I would never have expected to see, instead of with the only one who ever suggested something of the kind . . . But even him—it would have been a surprise."

"Another survivor?"

"You are very perceptive, Mr Cohen . . ."

It was a feeble stroke, and Cohen ignored it. "D'you still expect to see him—or her?"

"Him. A ship's petty officer—bosun . . . He was very angry."

"Is that so?" Cohen's eyebrows went up in exaggerated surprise. "What could you have done to upset him—?"

"I killed his brother."

"Uh-huh . . . That figures . . . It'd make just about anyone sore. Poor judgment on your part."

"Poor judgment?"

"You shouldn't have gone around introducing yourself after your knightly deeds . . . I assume it *was* a sinking—"

Altmann nodded.

"I thought one of the principles of war was to keep personalities out of it—at that level, at the time of action. It's the machines—the guns, the torpedoes, the tanks, the airplanes and ships—they're the things that do the killing. Not people. People just get killed. The idea is you keep out of sight. That way there's no hard feelings . . . Am I to understand this bosun guy sort of got talking to you?"

"He said—" Altmann paused, remembering the scene—another phantom production, but less persistent, less clearly-limned against the glare of its wartime setting; and because, despite its overt threat, it had been the kind he understood, with which he felt confident of dealing, a natural issue of war's inarticulate chances. "He said something—a threat—he would look for me after the war." Shrugging—"I think he must have been killed, or given up. He would not have had your determination, your—resources."

"Like being a Jew?"

Altmann fell silent, turning his gaze out over the harbour, allowing it to wander from riding-light to riding-light, absently wondering what each represented; what might have been passing between the ship's people; the men, the officers, the master—the Scheherazadian figure of the *nakhoda*. He felt a passing tweak of envy: those Arab dhow-masters, free of the convolutions and contrivances of western ways—the Godless ways they regarded with the amused contempt of Allah's faithful towards the infidels, who would one day be gone while they, the believers, remained to thrive in the glory of the One True God. All they worried about was the direction of Mecca half a dozen times a day, he thought sourly. Maybe there was something in this belief business after all. He turned back to Cohen. "Yes—like being a Jew. Among other things."

"Maybe—if he got that far—he was satisfied with a headstone."

"You could be right, Mr Cohen . . . But, if anyone, he was the man I would have expected."

"Sorry to disappoint you."

367

Altmann smiled. "Any disappointment has nothing to do with your presence instead of his!" A mosquito whined towards him and he watched it, a tiny shimmer of reflected light. They were few just here, the water being salt, but one was enough. He took a regular dose of paludrine, and insisted on his officers and crew doing the same; as he had insisted on the boat's crew taking their salt tablets . . . The mosquito hovered, hesitated, landed on his forearm amid the sun-bleached hair, prepared to thrust into the subcutaneous reservoir. Altmann struck swiftly, with a sharp smack, flattening the soft, intricate tissues into a smear. He rubbed the remains out of existence, switching his attention back to the other. "In spite of your reasoning you were taking a chance, Mr Cohen. Some would have said a foolish one." He blew smoke forcibly upwards and spat out a shred of tobacco. "If I may say so, *your* judgment is less than prudent . . ." Then, after a pause, he asked, "Do you gamble—I mean, for amusement, for—kicks?"

No, said Cohen; he never gambled. And—if it was what was in Altmann's mind—neither was that evening's meeting a gamble. It was the outcome of careful thought and deduction, and the fulfilment of a promise he had made long ago, to an old man, and to himself, and to the schooner's dead, Jew and Gentile alike. He could no more have refused or avoided it if he had been certain of its bringing about his own death. He had not been certain that Altmann would not come armed in some way, would not have come with intent. It would have been a logical thing to do in some respects. But he had relied on one thing, something he had learned in theory, as an axiom, a result of his studies at Columbia. It applied in all areas of human activity, political and commercial and social, whether organised or anarchic, tyrannical or revolutionary, and the evidence for it was set out for all to see in official records, legal treatises and case history, military records, political records, commercial records, literature, folklore, in the rise and fall of nations and empires, groups and individuals. It was a characteristic without which no man would be whole, no man able to regard himself as master of his instincts, as a creature risen above the brute, with which he would share common ground barring an ability to recognise and overcome the vein of malice imbued in him as in no other creature on earth. His ability to defeat it was the measure of his humanity, and it was axiomatic that as a moral individual acting on his own perceptions and understanding, that ability was more likely to succeed than if he were acting as part of a group, part of a corporate body, part of a nation, part of an empire—a *Reich.* The temptation—the pressure—to behave according to the intentions and actions of the group was likely to override his personal, individual tendencies and convictions, particularly if his membership of the group were voluntary; even more particularly if it were keenly so, in which circumstances the division between the nature of his personal motives and that of the group's would be that much less marked. And the group was more likely than the individual to descend to the level of the brute. It had no sentient substance, was subject neither to conscience nor to its absence: the group had no mind, yet it subsumed the thinking of its members, substituted its morality—or amorality—for their sense of individual accountability, released them from their respective consciences without making itself responsible for a collective equivalent: it had not the power to do so, irrespective of the legalities involved. Accordingly, the actions of its members were conscience-free, amoral, without any kind of ethical reference apart from the falsely-assumed one of the group, essentially opposed to that of the individual. As part of a group he would behave differently—in the group's name—from the way he would when alone and alone answerable to his conscience. What Cohen had learned was that, short of some mental or psychological deficiency or disorder, whether permanent or the temporary result of some provocation or influence, a man will not of his own free will kill a fellow human being. It was not a matter of nerve or guts, but of rational, moral conduct, by which the ordinary man was ruled and against which he would not normally act.

"You see, captain, when you attacked that schooner you were acting according to orders, which was fair enough; then when you discovered that she was carrying passengers, and those passengers were Jews, you chose to see those orders as licence to go further—further than you would have done without them!"

"What makes you think that?"

Cohen stared, and gestured, lifting a shoulder. "Well . . . As I've explained. You were an officer in a front-line fighting service of a country ruled by people who by then made it clear that certain groups—racial, political, social—were to be taken out of the picture as a matter of policy. And Jews were at the top of the list. Of course the details weren't common knowledge, not at that time, but people like you must have known or at least guessed what was happening to Jews as a section of the general public—and you were a Party member, for God's sake!—excuse me."

"No!" Altmann protested, and felt the familiar frustration, the helpless impotence, at the old, standard argument; and a wrong assumption. He took in a lungful of smoke and held it before saying, "No, Mr Cohen—I was not a Party member!"

Cohen snorted delicately. "You know something, captain?—Nazi Germany seems to have been governed by a political party that got into power with no members and no votes, unless, of course, all the people who did join and vote for it were dead by the end of the war except for the few national heroes, leaders of the *Reich*, who were, perhaps wrongly—who knows?—executed after the Nuremburg trials, along with your compatriot Eck. How was that, d'you reckon? Selective weapons or something? Did the bombs dropped by the Eighth Air Force and the RAF sniff out the Nazis as they fell and leave the rest without a scratch? Did the GI's have recognition training so they killed only Nazis among your soldiers and left the good Germans to surrender honourably? Did the convoy escorts sink only the boats commanded and crewed by Nazis and let the others carry on with their—their *mercy* missions? Was your admiral—Dönitz—a saint or something? What happened, hm?"

Ignoring the taunt, Altmann said, "I was not a Party member, but I voted for it; I agreed with its principles, and still do—"

"You *still do*—?"

Altmann stiffened. "Yes. It offered Germany the only way out of the humility she suffered under the treaty—the Treaty of Versailles, after the Great War. She could not go on under such an outrage, with people made destitute—starving—by inflation and no work for them—except for Jews! They took care of their own, even as Germans. It could not go on. The National Socialist Party with the *Führer* at its head offered hope, and restoration of our national self-respect—our pride!"

Silence fell. Altmann felt cold, and regretful of his frankness, and he eyed Cohen curiously. The American seemed to be at a loss, his gaze averted, his mouth a thin line. After an interval he sniffed, and rubbed gently at his forehead before looking up. Altmann could feel only admiration for the calm tone of his next words.

"Your pride, huh?" Cohen sighed. "—In a couple of boatloads of smashed bodies, what was left of a few defenceless refugees from your National Socialist show-piece? In the few thousand half-dead and dying survivors of the system by which others in their millions had been worked to death, turned into fertiliser and glue and lamp-shades, used as guinea-pigs for what was called medical research, and their remains incinerated in specially-designed furnaces—even thrown naked into pits of quicklime like so much condemned meat!—all for the greater glory of the Thousand-Year *Reich*?" Cohen paused to breathe audibly, evidently moved by his own words and striving to retain his calm. Then he continued, self-control evident in a note of strain. "Your *pride*?—in your squalid bit-part in the filthiest extrusion of bestiality the human race has ever succeeded in producing, for the love of Mike!" He shook his head, staring unblinkingly at Altmann. "I try not to use profanities, captain, but, so help me God—shee-ut!" He rubbed agitatedly at the back of his neck and sucked his teeth.

"That was not the way it was meant to be!" Altmann felt his anger rising, and took a breath. So easy for this man, this youth, with no experience—no remembered experience—of material hardship, no experience of armed conflict or even training in it, to pass judgment; so easy for someone like him, a graduate in but not a practitioner of law—to condemn from the elevated redoubt of rational argument and moral assumption. He seemed to take it as a foreordained truth that his own conduct in circumstances of that kind would be free of such aberration, yet he had just voiced a theory implying that the ethics of an individual's actions were subsumed by a wider consensus. That where the state could be indicted the individual was exempt, unequipped to act independently, according to his own conscience, his own claim upon morality. Angrily, and reluctantly, against his earlier assessment, Altmann felt bound to conclude that besides an outwardly ingenuous demeanour this American college-boy possessed a sense of self-righteousness that would forever deny him the insight he would need to gain distinction in his calling—if that was how it could be described. He would learn from experience, but wherever it failed to take him his perception would always be deficient. It would be difficult, if not impossible, to gain his understanding of any matter in which he had played no active part. But . . .

"The *Führer* was betrayed by the men he trusted; they went too far in their ways of carrying out his policies, and they failed in their duty as servants of the *Reich*, and as soldiers, so that he was driven to the limits of his wits—the limits of his sanity!—having to take over where they failed, taking so many reins in his own hands, unable to rely on his appointed chiefs. In the end it was too much for him; his judgment became warped—"

"*Warped?*—you can say that again, captain! That maniac gave the word a whole new meaning!"

"All right—I'm not trying to defend him on that count. But it was the incompetence of his subordinates that drove him to behave as he did, and not the power he had as a leader. He discovered he was leading donkeys when he thought they were lions, and it broke him—"

"Even your boss—your Lion—Dönitz? Was he a donkey?"

"No! The only one who did not let the *Führer* down—though it could be said that the *Führer* let him down: u-boat production never had the priority it needed and deserved, and yet the *U-Bootwaffe* was the only arm of the *Wermacht* that served the cause faithfully to the end, and did what was expected of it—more!" Altmann broke off, feeling hot with the effort of expatiation in the face of scepticism. And he realised, despairingly, that he was not succeeding. Dully, he said, "We fought an honourable war," and was shocked to feel a tightening in his throat. He swallowed, and added, "We did our duty. In war you do what you have to do. There is no purpose in making moral judgments when morality itself has been excluded from the proceedings—by both sides! War is not a moral act! It is a means to an end, and the only way to fight is with everything you can bring to bear, so that the war is ended as quickly as possible. That is what Germany attempted to do, and what I joined the *U-Bootwaffe* to do. It is not my fault that the plans were in error, that people in high places did not justify the trust placed in them. I tried to do what was expected of me, nothing less—and nothing more!"

"Like killing the survivors of your gallant effort—that wasn't your fault?"

"*Lieb Gott!*" Raw frustration exploded in his words, and taking a last, impatient draw on his cigarette Altmann hurled the stub into the harbour. "They would have died anyway—and in terrible agony! The weather was bad and getting worse; there was no chance of a rescue, and I could not take them on board. Even if I could—where would they go then? Back to the country they had just escaped!"

"Very considerate of you. Looks like I owe you after all—"

"*You did not have to make the decision!*" The ensuing silence was sulphurous, as after a thunderclap, and Cohen sat stiffly, expressionless, while Altmann shook the last cigarette from the packet and dropped it. As he bent to retrieve it Cohen said evenly, "You made a bad one, captain. That's all I can say."

372

Altmann lit the cigarette and pocketed the lighter, his thoughts in turmoil, his anger turned in upon himself at his outburst. He must remain calm, as he had done time after time in the face of extreme stress; now of all times, he must not allow himself to be provoked. What was done was done. He could not answer for the actions of a lost cause, and he would not demean himself before a man who could never understand the pressures that governed decisions in war, for all his lofty theorising. And he must not reveal his own misgivings; his own knowledge of failure and acknowledgment of error. He must retain at least an outward simulacrum of self-respect; had to retain what traces of pride were left him. He drew deeply on the cigarette and spoke through the exhaled smoke. "What do you want me to do, Mr Cohen—beg your forgiveness?"

Cohen regarded him sombrely for an interval before saying, "A moment ago you called on Him, captain . . ." He shrugged. "I guess without any particular intent. So tell me something—do you believe in God?"

Altmann hesitated, throwing Cohen a narrow glance. Then he shook his head. No. How could a merciful God, as people called Him, have allowed the war—the agony of humanity in all wars, the agony of his own people above all, and in that last war above all—to happen? His parents had believed, but they were dead. Killed. Their God hadn't granted them any special favours.

"Which God was that?"

"They were Lutheran. Not notably devout, but regular churchgoers; honest people, worked hard . . . Not political."

"And you didn't—"

"I stopped going to church when I went to law school—Hamburg. Before I joined the navy."

"You read law?"

"No. One semester, and I saw it would be a mistake. For me."

"Uh-huh." Cohen nodded and pursed his lips. Altmann watched him warily. At length the American said, "Has it ever occurred to you that things might've been different if you did believe—had believed—in God?"

Drawing on his cigarette Altmann delayed his reply, giving the point a moment's speculation. Finally he shook his head. "Perhaps . . . But there's no reason to suppose that He would have saved anyone—the storm—"

"I don't mean them—us . . . I mean you. Have you never thought He might have saved you from all this?"

"How—by letting me go on my way while He dealt with the boats? By playing with lives—mine for yours—or theirs?"

"Maybe. It's His prerogative! If you'd had faith in Him you'd have left it to Him after doing what you could." Cohen paused, struck by the point he promptly voiced. "And it needn't have been a trade in lives—look at what happened!"

Altmann frowned. "What?"

"Don't you see? Me being here—the destroyer! Wherever she found me and Fraenkel couldn't've been far from where the boats would've been if you'd let them go. There was some other wreckage about, according to Sol, enough for the destroyer's people to come to the obvious conclusion, corroborated by the old guy—and fooled by him! The scene of a sinking, but of course by then the bodies—the remains—had sunk as well. If any traces were still afloat no-one was going to pick them up for examination in those conditions; they would just have made the obvious assumption, as they did! Just think captain—" Cohen's eyes gleamed behind the lenses "—if you'd been a little less zealous in your duty to the *Reich* the whole business would've been different—your whole life afterwards would've been different. Left to God, what was a mistake would've been settled in the best possible way—in the circumstances. As it was—or is . . ." Cohen gestured. "You needn't have done anything, captain; but you could've done better than that, and sent a radio call for help. The destroyer would have picked it up, and stopped for the boats—as she would've done anyway—and not wasted time looking for you, with her special mission and all." Cohen eyed Altmann curiously. "But you didn't do that. Rather than do what you could for life you chose to go along with the fashion for death."

"It was too dangerous," said Altmann flatly. "My first duty was to my crew, my boat. Calling attention to myself was too much of a risk to take. And I don't make decisions on the possibility of fantastic coincidence."

"Not so fantastic if you believe in God, captain!" Breaking off his gaze, Cohen yawned and stretched and glanced at his watch, frowning. "Pardon me," he said; then, gathering himself, "You had an excuse for sinking the ship, sure. But none for the rest of it. My point is that if you did do what you had to do—as you explained—it would've been different if you'd had someone other than your—*Führer*—to answer to. And I don't mean Dönitz!"

With a flush of irritation, Altmann snapped, "I knew my responsibilities. That was what I answered to—"

"And that's what you're still doing, captain?" Cohen gave his words a sharper edge. "Or are you answering to something else?—because you sure are answering to something, and it isn't responsibilities you shucked off when you became Dieter Kuhn! You've made that clear enough. I said you're no killer, and that's what I believe; what you did that night was outside your normal kind of behaviour, but you still have to face the fact that you did it as a matter of choice—call it decision if you will—and it was yours, not Dönitz's, not your maniac of a *Führer*'s, whatever they may have raved on about in their flights of Party rhetoric!—and I guess you've been facing it for the last twenty-two years!" Cohen paused, peering at Altmann's shadowed features, chewing his lower lip. Then he went on, "And it's been a problem for you—maybe your biggest, even with what's happened just recently—your ship, your job, all that stuff. From where I'm standing, captain, it looks like the end of the line for you—at least, in any kind of self-respecting way. Your real identity's on a headstone, and the one you've hijacked won't stand much examination by the kind of people who could offer you a living worth anything."

"Do *you* believe in God, Mr Cohen?"

Cohen looked startled, and scratched his head. He said, "I was born a Jew, captain. It was my good fortune to be brought up a Jew, among other Jews—in America. I belong to a synagogue, and I attend regularly—when I can . . . Sure, I believe in God. Isn't it obvious?"

"It must be a comfort."

"In a way, yes . . . It's also pretty uncomfortable at times."

"How so?"

"He expects things of me—the way I behave, act, toward others, for example. He expects certain standards, and they're not always easy to achieve; and He punishes transgression—in His own way. And He forgives; he understands human weakness—after all, He made us!"

"Do *you* forgive?"

"Depends. I'm not God. A man sometimes finds it hard to forgive; sometimes too hard . . . Are you asking, captain?"

"I'm not sure—"

"Okay . . . Let's say you are, huh? Hypothetically, you're asking forgiveness for something that's been on your mind and looks like staying on it as long as you live and breathe."

"All right—let's say I'm asking for forgiveness—"

"So you can get a night's sleep, huh?"

"Yes. For that."

"Well, I've got news for you, captain . . . You're asking the wrong man!"

"How is that—you're the survivor. Do I have to ask—phantoms?"

"The ones who follow you around, you mean?"

"Yes—the ones who follow me around."

"You could try. But they're all in the mind . . . You could try, but you won't get much from them. After all, if they forgive you they'd be banishing themselves, wouldn't they? Signing their own death warrants, if you will!"

"I suppose so."

"So they won't do that—they won't forgive, even if they could . . . So why not try God?"

"But—" Altmann paused on the next word, drew on his cigarette, and went on, "But I don't believe in Him!"

"You could try, just the same. He's all you've got, when everything else has gone. I can't forgive you, captain. I haven't the power—I haven't the authority—and I'm glad that's so. Try God. You won't be the first, and I hope you won't be the last."

"And if He doesn't choose to forgive—?"

"I don't know. You're a Gentile. Maybe there's some place for you, along with Eck and the others, but of course they've already been punished. Maybe that's the way out. If it is I'm not the one to help you through it. I didn't come here to banish your phantoms—or help you escape them. I came to see how you were making out with them . . . As I say, try God."

As he spoke the slap of sandals heralded the arrival of three more Arabs at the foot of the steps from the road, and both men turned as they approached, murmuring among themselves. They were less impressively-robed than the earlier pair, seemingly of lower rank, or of smaller ships, but they were typically courteous, lacking the African's compensating impertinence, condescending where the African asserted from a sense of dispossession, a racial distinction that would not be obscured by political or social sophistry. Altmann appreciated it. He felt that Arabs would never make slaves, while the African . . .

"Salaam."

"Salaam alek-um!"

At the head of the jetty steps one of them drew a silver pipe on a chain from his *burnous* and at length, in answer to its piercing, reedy blast, a skiff appeared out of the gloom to bear them away like—

"Sons of Sindbad," observed Cohen musingly. "A magic carpet'd be no surprise."

"You are a romantic, Mr Cohen." Altmann took a last draught of smoke and threw the remains of the cigarette into the water. Feeling for the packet he remembered it had been the last, and resigned himself to minor purgatory.

"I guess so. Maybe it's why I'm here, other things granted . . . . One thing I'm not here for is to relieve you of your conscience, captain. Not in the way the judges relieved Eck of his, anyway. He's out of the shit, if I can put it like that; and it's probably the only way he would've understood. I reckon he wasn't like you—his way of fighting wasn't yours. There was no—explanation—for what he did, apart from brutality, though my point about the individual as part of a group interest probably held good. On his own, under his own uninfluenced moral code, he probably wouldn't have done what he did. But he didn't act from the same motive as you: he didn't have the excuse of the weather, and a somewhat threadbare justification for his action. I accept that, but not wholly, as I think I've made clear. So I look for something further, something more exacting—more retributive—than a bullet. And being a Jew, I turn to God, and pass the case to Him."

"You mean you aren't going to let anyone else know—Wiesenthal? The authorities—here or wherever?"

"That's right." Cohen smiled briefly. "No proof, remember? Instead I'm going to leave it to God—and what I know, now, is your conscience. Cutting all the schmaltz, captain, I want you to live for a while—however long you've got left—with what you did that night. You've lived with it for the last twenty-two years; I want to know you'll live with it for—who knows?—another twenty-two. Just like a lot of people—Jews, Gentiles, whatever—have to live with what you and your countrymen did for them in the name of some crazy idea of *Lebensraum* and racial purity. You aren't the only one living with ghosts, but unlike the others—or most of them—you live with ghosts that remind you of your failure. Maybe God's let you live this long as a just punishment. Maybe He made sure that ship's bosun lost the scent, if He let him live through the war! My God is big on an eye for an eye, captain. A tooth for a tooth: you'll have heard of that, I guess—you quoted a Bible reference, on the piece of cloth pinned to van Haaften's body. Look it up if you don't know it . . . And forgiveness comes with penance—payment of the check after the table's been cleared. If you want redemption, Captain Altmann, you won't get it from me. My purpose was to find out if you were still around, and to make sure you know you aren't the only man who knows what happened. After that . . . Well, it's out of my hands."

Altmann felt the ensuing silence heavy with presentiment, and blocked his thoughts from speculation with an effort. In casting about for an alternative, for some point of determination, he struck upon a point of only incidental interest, but interest all the same; or perhaps mere curiosity. He said, "Tell me—"

"Yes?"

"Your father—your real one—"

Cohen took a breath. "What about him?"

"Have you never tried to find him?" Altmann watched Cohen's face intently, saw a tightening of the mouth.

"Would it surprise you if I said no?"

Altmann shrugged, said nothing, waited, and after a pause Cohen went on to say he had nothing but a surname to go on. Not even a place of origin. To look for an individual with a name common to many and no other identifying feature apart from his having a son, among millions—alive and dead, and not even fully-recorded—wasn't a practicable proposition "—and I guess I've had to work with enough upsetting information without going into the details of the death-camps . . . Some things are best left as they are, captain. After all, the filial feelings I have are satisfied with my stepfather; a decent man I've grown to love and respect. Stirring up something that might have a regrettable effect on everyone concerned seems to be a risk not worth taking—wouldn't you agree?"

"You are very wise, Mr Cohen." Altmann smiled, a brief twitch of the lips, and broke a short ensuing silence with another query, hesitantly put; he was not sure of its wisdom. One final thing, he said—

"What's that?"

"Were there any other children in the boats—apart from two boys? I saw two boys."

"Oh . . . Sure. Sol listed the passengers—he named a few, not all. The rest were just numbers, making up the total of thirty-two."

"How many children?"

"Six. Two boys, me, and three others."

"How old—the three others, I mean?"

"Sol didn't know, but estimated, in his notes—between three and seven, about—"

"Girls or boys?"

"All girls. Sisters . . . Why?"

Three young girls, capitaine . . . Sisters . . . Altmann felt the cold shock burst upwards from his bowels; up through his guts, a pale, icy flush expanding into his chest cavity, pressing on his heart, chilling it and the blood in the arteries, spreading outwards again, and up into his throat, where it swelled and choked off the flow of fluid, brought drying surfaces into painful contact as he tried to swallow, and he clamped his teeth together, not trusting his power of speech. Cohen peered curiously, repeated his question, and after a pause Altmann regained control, uttered his next words as if measured by vernier and cut from a bar of iron.

"A doll . . . There was a doll. In the water—"

"A doll!" Cohen seemed to sense something of Altmann's agitation, and hesitated before asking, with remorseless pedantry, "Was that before or after your act of mercy, captain?"

"Before—after the ship had gone down." But Altmann's words conveyed as sudden a lapse into indifference, as if a channel of vitality had been shut off. He swept a hand across his brow and took a breath, letting it go in a gusty sigh. He avoided Cohen's curious scrutiny.

"I guess it gave you a kinda—jolt—knowing there were children among us."

"A jolt?" Altmann stared at the American. "I suppose you could call it that. I wondered, for a moment . . ." But what was the point in pursuing this fruitless line? The whole business was set, its component events juxtaposed immovably in the mould of time, indifferent to argument, supposition, hypothesis, like flies in amber. The doll was unimportant. He had had no need to mention it, only to connect it with its explanation, in his own mind, to his own satisfaction. It could not have been a boy's possession. The girls explained it, the three sisters . . .

"It doesn't matter," he said, and like a swimmer suffering an attack of cramp finding the shoaling bottom underfoot he turned with hopeful relief to a change of subject. "How do I know you won't speak of this—to anyone?"

"You don't, except for my word. The word of a Jew. Trust it or not, as you will. If you don't—well, I guess you'll spend your time wondering what's going to happen next, what you'll wake up to tomorrow, that kinda thing. Maybe, after all, the guy you spoke to—the one whose brother you killed." Cohen paused, and sighed, and peered again at his watch. "It's not for me to carry out whatever sentence you deserve, captain. I've done what God required of me—confirmed your identity, so the survivor of your act of mercy—me—can get on with his life knowing justice has been done, as God decides—"

"As Allah wills."

"Pardon me?"

"The Arabs—it's the way they see things. As Allah wills. It's the same God."

After a pause Cohen said, "Oh . . . Actually no. There are differences—different decisions. Check it out if you like." He sat silent for an interval, seemingly in reflection, then stirred and rose to his feet. "God's the answer to your problem, I guess. Beyond that, I can't offer any advice, except maybe the other God—"

"What other God?"

"Your Lutheran Christ . . . The guy my people had nailed to a cross. Like you, we had no choice. Or thought we didn't. But I don't want to go into that, or we'll be here all day. Maybe He's your answer, captain. You could ask Him, anyway—if you can bring yourself to."

"What do you mean?"

"Well—he was a Jew. Remember? If you've still got a problem with that . . . He got himself crucified to save people like you. But like with my God, you've got to believe first. If you don't—well." Cohen shrugged. "If it's any consolation to you, I don't claim indemnity. I'll have to face God one day, and by the time I'm your age, who knows what I'll have to answer for? Maybe I've got another war to go through, but next time as a soldier. With the world—civilisation—in the hands of men who think God's a passing superstition I reckon I've got a good chance of that. And whatever comes with it—like finding myself having to make difficult decisions, huh?"

Altmann regarded the American with renewed respect. "Yes. It's quite possible—"

"Only one difference."

"Yes?"

"I hope to God—excuse me—I haven't been suckered into doing what's best for the group—the nation, the party, whatever I'm supposed to be fighting for—if it goes against what I believe right now. I hope, if I have to face that kind of dilemma, I'll have enough guts to get it right, so I don't spend the rest of my life without a name of my own, living from day to day expecting a call from God knows who—or what!" Again he yawned, and stretched, and, seeming to tire of the subject, said it was getting late, and he had a plane to catch at ten that morning, a connecting flight to Nairobi, and home, and Altmann started at the word: home. The American—the Jew—was going home, to his people, to his friends, to his job with the firm that was holding it for him. To a career, and, certainly, to eventual marriage, children, something called happiness, perhaps, if he could close off his mind to things that would surely dispute it. Things such as the truths and delusions that men face with such unpredictable reactions. Perhaps Cohen's time of trial would come; and perhaps he, too, would fail, and fall, and have, in the end, to answer for it to God. But at least, thought Altmann, he had God, or a God. He, Altmann, was not sure there was one, between one thing and another. And he wasn't sure whether or not he deserved one.

"Time I hit the road."

He looked up. Cohen was stepping over the log, raising a hand—did it mock? salute? bestow absolution?—turning towards the steps up to the road, pausing at their foot, beginning the climb, in a low voice calling over his shoulder, "So long, captain."

Altmann did not answer.

VI

BEYOND the low-lying mass of Mafia Island lay the Rufiji delta and the wreck of the *Königsberg*; to starboard and back towards the south-east, the actions against the *British Prowess* and *Clan Finlay* had taken place. And the burial of young Hildegras. And five and a half days ago *Ndovu* had passed off the surf-swept beach north of Beira on which lay the wreck of the ship that had turned in panic from the explosion of the defective torpedo to escape what had certainly been in store for her farther along her planned course, or any course keeping her in deep water. On his first passage chartered to Mukerjee Altmann had been surprised to find her still there, not salvaged or scrapped *in situ* long since but a landmark conspicuous from seaward, marked on the chart. Inquiries had turned up her name: she was, or had been, the Egyptian-owned *Al Hafizeh*, a general-cargo carrier built in 1910; too old, Altmann had surmised, to have been worth recovering in any form. He had been amused by the fact that his official record of sinkings was short by one ship and four thousand tons, as he had amused himself debating the practicability of setting up a company to salvage the wreck, an enterprise that would, in a way, have negated such a claim; but he had never taken the idea any further. By that time her cargo, if of any value, would have been long gone. The Portuguese harbour-master at Beira had outlined what he knew of the story of the survivors' epic trek back along the coast, carrying their fever-stricken companions in makeshift litters, arriving at the port with a startling tale of a running battle with a submarine—German or Japanese—that had forced them onto the beach with gunfire and torpedoes, all of which had missed thanks to the master's cool handling of his ship. With the aim of salving the cargo an attempt to reach the wreck from seaward had been thwarted by the heavy surf, and an overland attempt abandoned in face of excessive cost.

Occasionally Altmann had reflected on the fact that here was a reminder of his war free of fatal connotations. It represented a minor failure, nothing more: the one—or one of the ones—that had got away, for which he had no cause to reproach himself, though at times he had dwelt on the way fate made its moves; on the whim of chance that decreed the success of one encounter and the failure of another, and the respective consequences—life-changing in this case, negligible in that. He realised the futility of pondering the outcome of a transposed hypothesis: the Egyptian ship had not been carrying passengers. If he had come across her instead of the schooner; if it had been the schooner within reach of neutral territorial waters, a convenient beach . . . *God will bless you, captain!* And the old man had been making sure of his sighting of the device on the conning-tower.

Seated in his day-room, Altmann poured out another measure of Pavlides's *genever*, mulling over the undimming recollections, and over the events of the days following Mukerjee's disclosure of the political and commercial situation, since when his last voyage as master of *Ndovu* had brought him to within a day and a half of handing over to the man who, at that moment, was presumably asleep in his temporary berth in the pilot's cabin: the new master, token—or symbol—of his country's imminent independence from colonial rule. Altmann raised his glass and uttered a sardonic *"Prosit!"* He grimaced at the spirit's effect: close to room temperature—a night-time eighty-plus Fahrenheit—it went down like hot sand, and he decanted the last drops from the bottle that had been on his desk for the last two hours, adding to them from a new one out of the fridge. He sipped the crisp fresh liquid aware of the accumulated effect; a certain muzziness behind the eyes, a certain dullness of feeling in the limbs. A third of a bottle of this stuff in one go was more than he was used to; the fresh bottle presented a challenge. Again he raised the glass, muttered *"Prosit!"* and downed the rest of its contents in a single swallow, which made him cough. Refilling it, he sat back fixing it with a moody eye, picking up the thread of his thoughts with some difficulty, tracing it back towards its beginnings, as he did so casting his glance to either side in an effort to discover the point at which everything had started to go wrong.

His realisation that the Treaty of Versailles imposed untenable conditions on Germany had prompted his first decisive move: a career in law had been more his father's idea than his own, a practicable alternative to the printing business which, under the change of national government generally taken to be a foregone conclusion, would present its proprietor with difficulties over and above the technical and logistical problems of normal business, exacerbated as they were by the country's financial straits. His father had warned his wife and son that he might be faced with a choice between compliance with unpalatable edict and closure, whether forced or at his own discretion. And the son had in any case shown no interest in it.

Nor in law, and it had come as a relief when his decision to try for the navy had met with no objection from his father; indeed, with the support, both moral and financial, indispensable to entry as an officer. And there, Altmann discovered, he had found his calling—both to his spirit and to his sentiments as a patriot. A resurgent Germany had been the stuff of ambition, the *Führer* its embodiment, a figure that inspired the highest ideals of nationhood and pride of race. Hitler and the Party had wrought order from waxing chaos, self-respect from humiliation, and in the navy—in its u-boat arm—Altmann knew he had found a means of expressing his loyalty to and belief in the cause, a means sufficient in itself, obviating any pressing need to join the Party. Law was for rhetoric, theory, pedantic debate; dust and deliberation; musty office and stuffy court-room; exposure of and involvement with the squalid, the sordid, the devious—the depressing—facets of human intercourse, in none of which could Altmann summon up the interest, far less sense of vocation, that success demanded. And success—prominent distinction going beyond a firm, beyond one's immediate social and professional circles—was the only possible aim, in whatever one undertook. In law he would have been a failure, of that he was in no doubt. In the navy—mathematics permitting—he knew beyond doubt he could hope for—expect—success; and he could aim for distinction, especially in such a distinctive service; especially in the event of the war for which the *Führer* had set out to prepare the country from the moment of his first appearance on a public platform; perhaps, even, from the moment he had emerged from the trenches at the signing of the armistice. The aging von Hindenburg had been an obvious and convenient front, the Weimar Republic a temporary stepping-off point and bench-mark by which the Party would be able to gauge and broadcast its progress. In those early years Altmann had discovered the exhilaration of shared enthusiasms, disciplined effort, appreciated achievement, and the means of realising ideals that required of him physical and mental stamina of a quality and quantum that took him to, and extended, the limits of his resources, and on it all he had prospered. But only up to a point.

The first check had been the premature—as had been widely agreed—start of the war; a time when the *U-Bootwaffe* had not yet reached the strength in number of operational units declared to be necessary by a Dönitz lacking the executive authority he craved, and needed. The friction between him and his immediate superior, Raeder, had been the second check. The arm of the navy in which lay the key to victory over an island enemy had been hobbled, if not crippled, from the outset by its deliberate subordination to the overestimated needs of the surface fleet, which in turn had been overshadowed by the perceived urgency, not to say novelty and glamour, of those of Göring's all-conquering—RAF and USAAF excepted—*Luftwaffe*, while the *Führer*'s heart and faith clearly lay with the *Heer* and its capacity for high-speed *Sturm* tactics. For all the symbolism it might have possessed when lying alongside in view of the passing throng (treated to superficial views of it in tightly-regulated displays and demonstrations in the run-up to hostilities) the u-boat lacked appeal in the eyes of the *Wermacht*'s high command, working, as it did, out of sight if not wholly of mind, by stealth rather than by dash and spectacle.

And its invisibility had been further assured by the concealment of its operations from public—including media—scrutiny. It had been chiefly through orchestrated official publicity—the work of Goebbels's propaganda machine—that the u-boat had become a focus of patriotic sentiment, particularly in the embarrassing wake of the air battles that had bloodied Göring's nose without realising his loudly-voiced guarantees. And, in the end, even the u-boat had failed to live up to popular, if not official, expectations, though not for want of valour and skill among its exponents—at least, not until towards the end. Its failure, Altmann was convinced, had lain in its lack of numbers in the beginning, above which it never rose, enabling the enemy to retain enough of an advantage to allow the development of counter-measures that decided the contest: as with the land forces, the whole strategy had depended on initial hitting-power, deficient, as it turned out, by the narrowest of margins. And as with the land forces, once the enemy had gained enough time to consolidate and recover from a failed or delayed or over-prolonged underweight initial onslaught the outcome was inevitable. If Dönitz had been given the operational strength for which he had asked—if the *Führer* had been less precipitate in his decisions to open hostilities on several fronts—the *U-Bootwaffe*'s success against the Allies' ocean supply-routes would have been assured, and with it every chance of ultimate victory. As it was . . .

"If." Altmann snorted, and held up the glass and squinted through the straw-tinted liquid at the lamp on his desk, grunted *"Prosit!"* and threw it back. Blinking away a sudden watering of his vision he lit a cigarette and sat silent in a ruminative cloud.

Things had gone wrong for Germany at the outset. Carried away by his own charisma and the mass hysteria it produced in the people, the *Führer* had been moved by vanity to act without proper thought, eventually without regard for advice, and his Party lieutenants with him, eager for personal power at any price; between them they had variously extirpated and squandered the scientific and military resources that, properly husbanded and deployed, would have borne the Fatherland through to its rightful, dominant, place on the world stage. And they had dissipated the regard they had gained from the people and the soldiers to whom extravagant promises had been made about a triumphant future at the head of the racial pecking order, instead leading them into the bloodbath of a fight to the finish against an enemy faced with no option but outright victory. And, confronted with irreversible ruin and certain execution, the *Führer* had clearly determined to take the collapsing fabric of his brainchild, his heart's fixation and life's vindication, his Thousand-Year *Reich*, with him; in which aim, for all practical purposes, he had succeeded. Now, Germany stood divided east from west between her occupying enemies, her people in the west materially prosperous but spiritually dislocated, looking back—those that could face it—in anger and shame on their unique blemish as a nation with Churchill's final pronouncement still ringing in their ears—or in the ears of any who had listened, and taken note: . . . *for as long as men desire peace, they should ensure above all that Germany is never reunited . . .* Or words to that effect. And in the east, under the heel of the communism the *Führer* had sworn to wipe out at a stroke, who knew? The only indicator of the living conditions was the occasional desperate attempt, occasionally successful, at escape to the west by ordinary people driven to put their lives in the balance rather than continue in the situation in which the war's end had left them. And only last year the sometime capital itself, a state within a state, had been divided similarly by a three-metre-high wall overlooked by machine-gun posts and patrolled by dogs and armed soldiery, none of which was in place for the purpose of preventing crossings from west to east. Instead of Poland, after Czechoslovakia Russia should have been the objective, as many had believed. It might even have gained the approval, moral if not active, of the western democracies; England would certainly not have stood in the *Führer*'s way as she had over Poland. But, supported by the Allies, Russia tardily attacked had proved to be the *Führer*'s undoing . . .

Altmann blew smoke at the lamp and refilled the glass, raised it and exclaimed, "To a reunited Germany, Churchill *old chap—prosit!*" But not, he added to himself as the cold *genever* cleared his throat of nicotine, to another damned *Führer*. One had been enough, supported by the incompetents, the psychopaths and megalomaniacs, who had misdirected and corrupted the affairs of state for their own dark ends. Their wretched machinations had cast a national ideal of noble proportions in the likeness of depravity itself: they, if any group, had deserved the hell on earth of incarceration in places like Auschwitz, Sobibor, Mauthausen . . .

And what had become of the world since? What had Britain and her allies made of their victory—a better world? Was that country itself better off than it would have been under the Third *Reich*'s protection? Not if events since 1945 were anything to go by: the British had lost the respect of most subject nations in the way they had handled a war about which they had been warned almost from the moment the *Führer* had come to notice in the politics of depression Europe: Churchill and a handful of others had seen through the fog of complacency that had allowed Germany to flout treaty obligations, but—fortunately as it had seemed—no-one had taken notice, preferring an ostrich-like absorption with domestic and empire affairs that placed little importance on the internecine agitations of a defeated foe, apart from a gratuitously futile gesture like guaranteeing the national sovereignty of a country in which they, the British, had no substantial commercial or political interest. And that foolishly, after showing themselves to be malleable over the earlier annexation of countries of similarly negligible interest. Who could blame Hitler for thinking he was dealing with the same attitude towards his Polish adventure? And not only that, but the British had not possessed the military strength—not even in their navy—to back up their guarantee, as was subsequently proved. Their reliance upon the French to make up the deficiency was a mistake a schoolboy with a grip on modern European history could have avoided, but of course England was not ruled by schoolboys with a historical bent: she had elected to government bumbling optimists, liberal-minded gasbags more concerned for their political hides than for hard reality, and suffered accordingly. Russia apart, the *Führer* needn't have done more than wait a few more years, when, with properly-equipped and trained armed forces and a better-tuned political establishment, he could have annexed Britain as easily as all the others, for Churchill would have been more securely shackled to the political irrelevance and advancing years from which he had been snatched at the last possible moment. And to which, Altmann reminded the empty cabin, he had been returned immediately upon the resolution of hostilities, bar a brief, pathetic revival a few years later. By which time the British had lost all but a few relicts of empire and were rapidly being overwhelmed by the very people they had once ruled, fleeing from the looming or actual disorder of their newly- or imminently-independent countries to the shelter of a welfare state at which the rest of the world gazed in mingled wonder and derision while itself taking advantage of it wherever possible. Altmann was satisfied beyond question that nothing of that kind would have occurred after a German victory: the *Führer* had not merely guaranteed the British their empire but would have ensured its continuance, not only as a political and commercial entity but also a dominant force for world peace—on his terms; for, of course, one's own were the only terms on which peace was worth having.

And the victorious British, with their welfare state? If there had been one thing that had achieved what all the *Blitzkrieg* Germany could have brought to bear could not, it was the ruinous erosion of morale wrought by the idea of something for nothing: the neo-communist idea of rewarding the parasitic element—the idle, the incompetent, the worthless, the work-shy, the fraudulent, the inadequate—even the criminal, the flotsam and dross of society—at the expense of the competent, the enterprising, the hard-working, who, as a part of society systematically squeezed and coerced out of its rightful deserts by a sanctimoniously punitive taxation regime, were variously leaving the country to the benefit of others or succumbing to the pressure. And without such elements no state could hope to survive, let alone flourish, as a sovereign entity. As Benedict had remarked, if Germany lost the war to these idiots, she would deserve all she'd get. And she had been fighting not a nation so much as the man who'd led it: without Churchill—and the Americans he talked into supporting him, helped, of course, by the *Führer*'s maniacal declaration of war after Pearl Harbor—the British would have lost all, and richly deserved to do so. It was a bleak comfort to see the process resumed at a less headlong pace, but a comfort all the same. Perhaps Germany would triumph at the last, whenever that happened to be. There were signs that defeat had done for the Fatherland what victory might not: discovered in the people a moral tenacity, a determination to survive as a nation, to recover and rise from the ashes, a European Phoenix that would ultimately throw off the bonds of occupation to take the lead under the direction of someone free of the paranoiac obsessions that had destroyed the *Führer* almost as he rose to power, the obsessions translated into the driving force and compelling rhetoric to which a justifiably resentful people had been so tensely poised to respond. Next time, thought Altmann, things would be different.

But of course he would not be there. Saddened at this, he refilled his glass and raised it. "To a new Germany," he said, and rose to his feet to click to attention. *"Prosit!"* He hiccupped, and patted his chest, adding, "Pardon me." Under the influence of the ship's gentle roll he resumed his seat and looked morosely round the room. It was a comfortable box, sharing the deck below the navigating bridge with McDade's similar quarters. A day-room-cum-office with a small

388

sleeping-cabin off, and a shared shower and lavatory. Brass-framed windows gave views ahead and to starboard, curtained at night for the watch's benefit. It wasn't Schreiber's North German Lloyd, but fit for its purpose, which was to provide a home for the ship's master. With—apparently—no family ties, van Haaften had occupied it for some eight years before his violent exit, and another man for a couple of years before that, from the ship's launching. And he, Altmann, had been comfortable enough in it for the last seventeen. It was like an old slipper, and as mellow, with its old-fashioned brass fittings and faded floral fabrics, and mahogany furnishing and panelling glowing with the deep lights of age and good housekeeping: it had brought out the pride of possession in the stewards concerned. It was a pity he would leave it soon, reflected Altmann, refilling the glass and lighting another cigarette; it had grown on him: not the quarters normally allotted to a *Kapitän-zur-See* of the *Kriegsmarine* but a damn sight better than a Type IX u-boat commander's hutch, and rather more airy than a coffin. As the thought struck him he rose again to attention, raising his glass. "To *Oberleutnant* Dieter Kühn," he said, and paused on another hiccup. "Unsung hero of the *Dritte Reich—prosit!*" Regaining his seat he drew deeply on his cigarette and blinked at the bottle through the smoke. Only a quarter of it gone. He would have to look sharp. Time was passing. He splashed a little on the desk-top as he refilled the glass and dabbed at it with a piece of blotting-paper, noting the spreading ink-stains. "Not surprising," he observed. "Stuff would strip paint." Then, after a reflective pause, he added, "Sorry, Serg—not that bad. Mustn't get it on my hands, that's all." And he chuckled at his joke; a shame he hadn't thought of it before. He could imagine Pavlides's face. Van Haaften didn't come up with jokes very often, and the Greek's tastes ran to more obvious humour. Still . . .

An England better off under the Third *Reich*'s protection. Actually, a moot point. Affirmative if the *Reich* had been the expression of the higher ideals of the National Socialist cause, but, as things had emerged during the Allies' advance and after, most likely not. The indescribable depravity to which the death camps had borne witness had turned all that on its head, betrayed his loyalty, his belief, his moral integrity; had turned the deaths of his men, his friends, his parents, his wife and daughters, into a grotesque travesty of sacrifice. That they had died for the furtherance, in effect, of such a monstrous perversion of national determination was almost beyond bearing; and that he had thrown his own aspirations, his own sense of honour and duty, behind it, even to the extent of active contribution to the overall exercise in moral degradation, compounding the felony in his averted gaze when confronted with evidence—glaringly apparent in retrospect where it had been at least publicly discernible at the time—of the policies and methods of a governing power bent on mass organised persecution of elements of the population it had declared undesirable. On top of which, as he was latterly obliged to admit, he had sought to exonerate himself by self-deception, by attempting to disguise as a squalid distortion of mercy an act of calculated brutality. It was this single exposure of something in his nature for which he had no rational explanation that had conjured the phantoms of his subsequent anguish, the only means his conscience had of exacting payment for a gross departure from the norms of humanity. Even in war it had been a descent into the depths, a dark place of vile slimes and formless, oozing putrefactions. He had allowed the national mood of vengeful self-justification, emanating from and personified in the messianic figure of the *Führer*, to affect his judgment, to corrupt the instinct for moral discrimination that distinguished the civilised from the savage, the man from the beast. But was the *Führer* to blame? Had he, Gunnar Altmann, apparent civilised individual, not had enough moral integrity to draw a line at some point, some limit of personal involvement? The fact was, he told himself, he had *known*. How in the name of sanity had he allowed himself to be persuaded otherwise? Reason had given place to excuse, and the excuse had failed from the outset, from the moment the MG34s had ceased their work and his order to turn away and resume the passage had been repeated in the hollow tones of the bridge voice-pipe.

And before that—?

Here, Maggot—rinse your tonsils in this. Special import.

Rot-gut from that damned Jew—?

No. Sadly, the firm is just out of business, courtesy of the Röhmish hordes, so I hear. What you have there, little Maggot . . .

"The Röhmish hordes, for the love of God!" Altmann drained the glass and coughed, recovering by a noisy clearing of his throat. Drawing on his cigarette he filled the glass again, muttering, "You too, Liebeherr, you poor swine—but *you're* all right, aren't you?", after a moment's reflection adding, "Don't suppose *you* were running from a damned schooner, too . . . Were you?" And, raising the glass, *"Prosit!"* A hiccup erupted as he drank, and half the glass's contents ran over his hand and splashed his shirt, a small icy shock. He swore softly, dragging out a handkerchief and dabbing.

The bottle was almost half-empty. "Try again," he said. *"Prosit!"*

Then there had been that visit to Posen as Ehrling's guests . . .

All gentleness towards Poles must be avoided . . . the Polish nation must now be destroyed . . . not a Pole will remain . . .

And Hildegras's indiscretion—a deliberate feint to draw the *Gauleiter*? Or had he been genuinely curious about something he could not have imagined in the purpose of the train outside Lissa?

Cattle-wagons sewn up with barbed wire, Kapitan?

It's adequate—the journey isn't lengthy. There are attendants . . .

. . . a similar train . . . at Mürwik . . . children . . . like cattle . . .

Evacuees, Hildegras. You'll see more of it as the bombing gets worse . . .

Yes, thought Altmann: a lot more. By the labour-camp—the Belsen, the Buchenwald—full. By the million. By the generation. Old people, the middle-aged, the young, little children; the sick and the lame; the perverts and misfits, the political undesirables; but most of all the Jews. The chosen people. The Fraenkels, the Cohens—the Wiesenthals—

"But the British—the Allies—didn't fight the war for *them!*" Altmann's protest hung in the air like a pennant, stirring in a passing revelation. "The Poles, maybe—even the French—but not for the *Jews,* damn them!" He drew sharply on his cigarette and stubbed it out, then drained off the rest of the glass's contents and shook his head. *Damn you, Cohen! Why didn't you have the guts to do something—? Just that damned smile, and shrugging off your responsibility on your damned God! You'll make a good lawyer—fine words, and let the accused hang himself on his own gallows . . . Sentence passed by Judge Conscience!*

He had known. They had all known—every German able to think and reason, able to see and hear and draw obvious conclusions had known; and they had chosen to be blind and deaf, chosen to convince themselves of the nation's noble ideals and the rightness of the *Führer's* cause. But he, Atmann, had gone further . . .

Hadn't he paid—even yet? Hadn't it been enough that he'd lost everything, from friends and shipmates to his own wife and children? And more—he'd lost even himself, and his country. He was not van Haaften, whose rotting remains had probably fed the gulls on some tide-swept estuarine bank; not Dieter Kühn, who had vanished after signing off as mate of the *Johan Burger* and whose papers had, to

Altmann's certain knowledge, in any case been destroyed. And if he was Gunnar Altmann, late commandant of the *Kriegsmarineschule*, sometime hero of the *Dritte Reich*, he lay beneath the headstone Cohen had found in the Mürwik churchyard, his presence on earth reduced to a death certificate in some obscure official file. And perhaps in the fading memories of an old man, first in the confinement of Spandau, now wherever he was passing his last days. Uncle Karl. The Lion . . .

No—resurrection was not a practicable proposition. There was no route back, no means by which the severed threads of a verifiable, sentient existence could be recovered. *Kapitän-zur-See* Gunnar Altmann was dead. And as Kees van Haaften his existence was confined to this ship: beyond it, his papers would have no validity, were not on their own sufficient evidence of his *bona fides* to get him through the most cursory of scrutinies, by a prospective employer or business partner, or a government official. The ship was—had been—the necessary clincher in any instance of inquiry: he was Kees van Haaften, master and erstwhile owner of the Panamanian trader *Ndovu*, ex-*Johan Burger*, or he was no-one.

"No-one," he said, examining the bottle's depleted contents. Nearly half-empty, and he could still read the label. Not bad, for a moderate drinker. This would be the first time he had caned more than half a bottle at a sitting; if he got that far. He had an even harder head than he'd thought. Or hard enough while he remained sitting, anyway; the cabin's movement was the ship's doing in an open seaway, nothing worse . . . And being no-one, he reasoned, he would not be missed. After all, the ship had a master—that black chap, who could sleep like a hibernating bear. He had a name—what was it again? Kidogo? Kidigo? Something like that, but a name, and papers—a British master's certificate with the ink still wet—and an identity he could verify, a country, a claim to existence as a human being and not—one assumed—a slaughterer of old men, women and children, Jews or not. "No damned excuse," he muttered. "War's over—" He filled the glass and raised it. *"Prosit!"*

With a hiccup he placed the empty glass carefully on the desk and lit another cigarette, then sat smoking for some time, hiccupping at regular intervals, occasionally frowning at a train of thought that eventually came to rest at the Leven steps, and a review of the exchange with the American—the Jew. The Jew who had come to the meeting believing he ran the risk of a violent end but trusting in something—a hunch,

392

an assessment of a man's character and the effect of circumstances, a fatalistic trust in some Being, some Essence he called God—to bring him safely through the opportunity to face a murderer with the truths he had spent half a lifetime evading, or subsuming, perhaps, in a view of his past from which he had sought to purge all guilt by self-justifying argument confirmed by his subsequent continuation of a seemingly normal life. Yet he—Cohen—had guessed that there was something more; that a man of the kind he believed Altmann to be could not have lived normally after such a cataclysmic event, an event in which he had played a central—indeed the crucial—part, chiefly because it had been of his own making. And Cohen had to do two things: one was to let the murderer know that his secret was known to at least one man in a position—and with a reason—to do something about it, the other to satisfy himself that in surviving the war Altmann had embarked on a life of torment, not only in his insecure identity as a ship's master, and one soon to be dispossessed at that, but also in his subjection to the natural retribution of conscience—with which, of course, he was cursed. Cohen knew, or had gambled—his denial notwithstanding—on the belief, that he had not been dealing with another Eichmann, another fiend in human form of the kind that had played such a pivotal part in the internal moral contortions of the *Reich*. If he had believed otherwise he would—surely—have dealt with matters differently. As, for instance, coming to the meeting equipped to bring the episode to its logical end; which, thought Altmann, would have been a mercy of a similar order to that by which he'd claimed mitigation for the fate of the schooner's people. Cohen had had the chance to absolve the killer of all further torment, as had been done in Eck's case, albeit officially.

Instead, the man had left it to higher authority—to God, no less! Which, Altmann realised with a start, and another hiccup, brought him to the reason for his deciding to go unarmed. What, exactly, had lain behind that decision—that impulse? For an interval his thoughts drifted to one side, back to the interview with Dönitz at the end of that last patrol, to that scene in von Lohmeyer's quarters when he had learned of Ursula's and the girls' deaths as the final blow of the war in his personal experience of it, and he remembered the pain—remembered, but no longer felt: the pain, and the admission of his need to express some kind of penitence, the paying of a debt—but to whom? To what? Not to those who had died at his hands—they were beyond restitution. Not to whoever survived them—wives, parents, children, whoever: Cohen excepted, they had no personal knowledge of him, could not be recompensed by anything within his power to provide or produce. What would they gain in return for their loss by his death, apart from—perhaps—a sense of requital, which would have no real value, would not ease the bitterness of heart and mind that sought such a balancing destruction of life. Then to whom—to what—did he owe this debt, and in what form? The loss of his family had been the single most soul-destroying experience of his life; an overwhelming storm of anguish that he had coped with only by shutting his mind to the fact, a brutal wrenching of mind and heart away from the scene of devastation towards an exclusive concentration upon his duties as a senior officer of the *Kriegsmarine* and, eventually, commandant of an institution that required of him the kind of paternal attention he would otherwise have devoted to . . .

Discipline had slipped in the wartime conditions that displaced the deliberate rigour of a decade before. He had had to take a firm grip from the first day, particularly among an older intake of midshipmen already looking back on active service at sea, some in u-boats. But that had fallen well within the compass of his power of command and force of personality, and he had exercised an instinct for discretion to notably beneficial effect. And the place had been haunted, of course: more phantoms, his younger self among them. But in contrast to the schooner's intense shades these had come as a kind of solace, replaying their parts in scenes to which he'd gladly given otherwise unoccupied moments; even the fight with that army gorilla, and Niethe-Grapow's gratifying, if qualified, compliment. He wondered at his youthful confidence in the promise of a triumphant national resurgence, or had he even then been choosing evasion of the truth? It had been a disconcerting experience, taking the admiral's place behind that vast desk to face the echo of the pale young man so plainly dismayed at the prospect of rejected ambition, so vastly relieved to have passed the test by however narrow a margin. And—seemingly never known to the admiral—at his friend's getting away with his plundering of the commandant's spirits locker. Liebeherr's faith in audacity had taken him farther and faster than most, but at the last it had failed him: *Idiot! You'll come a cropper one day . . .* But never imagined in that way. Perhaps, if audacity's promise had been kept, it would have been Liebeherr at last in legitimate possession of the cognac supply and he, Altmann, a name on the roll of honour: the fortune of war. And there had been other ghosts, from which no solace could be drawn. He had tried to avoid them, knowing their haunts: *I see that dog Gretchen steering for the Rhinemaidens. Come!*

That night: had the aircraft been silent in its stricken approach? Or had it been one among many, the thrumming of their engines filling the house with that menacing vibration, a trembling dread, before, with no further warning, oblivion? And surely it had been oblivion—surely? In the house. In the boats. Surely there had been no knowledge; no pain?

Quite suddenly Altmann felt tears running down into the stubble on his cheeks, and the blurring of the room about him was nothing to do with the inoffensive bottle, and he hiccupped and swore and dashed a hand across his eyes, and splashed another shot of *genever* into the glass. The now-tepid spirit burned in his throat and made him cough. His cigarette lay smouldering in the ashtray, and he stubbed it out, then reached across to the drawer in which he kept the Luger, and took it out, with the separate clip. He counted the bullets. Eight. Still the original ammunition. It would have been just his luck to have drawn the gun on Cohen and found the bullet a dud, like those damned torpedoes. But instead it had been talk, and a strange mixture of relief and renewed depression at the prospect of continued life—for Cohen; for himself. . . .

. . . they won't forgive, even if they could . . . So why not try God?

But I don't believe in Him!

You could try, just the same. He's all you've got, when everything else has gone. I can't forgive you, captain. I haven't the power, and I'm glad that's so. Try God.

And if He doesn't choose to forgive—?

I don't know. You're a Gentile. Maybe there's some place for you, along with Eck and the others, but of course they've already been punished. Maybe that's the way out. If it is I'm not the one to help you through it. I didn't come here to banish your phantoms—or help you escape them . . . Try God.

"Okay, Mr Cohen." Altmann slipped the clip into the pistol and checked the safety-catch. "I'll try God. As you say, there's nothing else . . ."

EPILOGUE
REDEMPTION

PICKING up a copy of the *Mombasa Times* Robbie McDade took his beer over to an easy chair in the lounge of the seamen's mission. Settled comfortably, he took a long appreciative draught and turned to the article on the front page, wondering what sort of a cock-up the reporter had made of the story. First glance told him it had been kept short.

DISAPPEARANCE OF SHIP'S CAPTAIN
by our Staff Reporter
The well-known Mombasa-based freighter Ndovu, *owned by local businessman Mr Kuljit Mukerjee, docked yesterday evening after a passage from Lourenço Marques interrupted by the tragic loss of her master, Captain Kees van Haaften. Captain van Haaften was a familiar figure in Mombasa maritime circles for the last thirteen years and will be missed by colleagues, associates and friends in the port as well as shipping people in other ports on the east African seaboard as far south as Durban.*

It appears that Captain van Haaften failed to answer a call to the bridge, for which he had left instruction, as the vessel was passing off the southern cape of Zanzibar early on Thursday morning, April 28th. A search of the ship drew a blank and the course was retraced for the time that had elapsed since the captain's last appearance, when he had left his customary night orders with the officer of the watch, New Zealander Mr Alan Marshall. Mr Marshall, the ship's second officer, reports having heard and seen nothing before handing over to the first

396

officer, South African Mr Rick Venter, who raised the alarm when he received no answer to his call. The sea search proved fruitless.

In whatever the manner, it seems that Captain van Haaften disappeared somewhere between the vicinity of the island of Mafia, off the Rufiji delta, and the position off Zanzibar. An inquest, which will be attended by the ship's officers and crew, is to be held on Monday 2nd May by the coroner, Mr Jeffrey Hatherley. Mombasa's police commissioner, Chief Superintendent Barry Denham, says foul play is not suspected. Mr Mukerjee has expressed his sadness and regret but reserves further comment until after the inquest.

Captain van Haaften was a Dutch national, believed to have been a native of Rotterdam. The Dutch Consulate has been informed.

This paper will carry a full report of the inquest.

———————————

Printed in Great Britain
by Amazon.co.uk, Ltd.,
Marston Gate.